The General's Women

The General's Women

A NOVEL

Susan Wittig Albert

PERSEVERO PRESS

www.PerseveroPress.com

First Edition, March 2017

This is a work of fiction. Names, characters, places, and incidents are the product of the author's imagination or, in the case
of historical persons, are used fictitiously.

Publisher's Cataloging-in-Publication data
Names: Albert, Susan Wittig, author.
Title: The General's women: A Novel / by Susan Wittig Albert.
Description: Includes bibliographical references. |
Bertram, TX: Persevero Press, 2017.
Identifiers: ISBN 978-0-9892035-8-6 (Hardcover) |
978-0-9892035-9-3 (Trade pbk.) | 978-0-9969040-2-5 (pbk.) |
978-0-9969040-0-1 (ebook) | 978-0-9969040-1-8 (ebook) |
Subjects: LCSH Eisenhower, Dwight D. (Dwight David), 1890-1969--Fiction.
| Eisenhower, Mamie Doud, 1896-1979--Fiction. | Morgan, Kay Summersby-
-Fiction. | Eisenhower, Dwight D. (Dwight David), 1890-1969--Marriage. |
World War, 1939-1945--Fiction. | BISAC FICTION / Historical | FICTION /
War & Military | FICTION / Romance / Military
Classification: LCC PS3551.L2637 G46 2017 | DDC 813.6--dc23

Leave Kay and Ike alone. She's helping him win the war.

Major General Everett S. Hughes

You didn't often see a general kissing his chauffeur.

Chicago Tribune war correspondent Jack Thompson
to Lieutenant General "Slim Jim" Gavin

We have no secrets from Kay.
Eisenhower to General George S. Patton

Table of Contents

PART ONE

LONDON AND WASHINGTON, MAY–NOVEMBER 1942

CHAPTER ONE
The Driver

London
May 24–26, 1942

K ay Summersby scowled. *The luck of the Irish.*

"Who did you get?" Nancy asked, adjusting the belt of her brown wool MTC uniform.

Kay blew out an exasperated breath. "A two-star nobody with a German name I can't even pronounce."

"Oh, poor Kay," Margaret purred. "*I* got a three-star." She flipped her sleek blonde hair. "General Hap Arnold."

"So nice for you," Kay muttered under her breath, crumpling her driver's ticket. *She* was the senior driver. She had every right to be assigned to drive the top man in the American military team that was coming to London to sort the war—finally—and get it back on the right track. But the second lieutenant in the War Office had decided that since this assignment was such a plum, the girls would draw straws. And wouldn't you know it, that was the day she got her hair done, and the hairdresser (who'd been bombed out twice) was late. So *she* was late.

"Too bad, Kay," the lieutenant had said, handing her the ticket. "A major general. He's the only one left."

The luck of the Irish. But it was appropriate—wasn't it?—for a woman who had been born Kathleen MacCarthy-Morrogh on a neglected estate on an island in County Cork and was still as poor

3

as an Irish church mouse—unlike Nancy and the other civilian women drivers in the Mechanised Transport Corps. All of them were volunteers, but they came from wealthy families and didn't mind laying out fifty quid for their smart uniforms, while Kay was still in hock to her mother for hers. The two pounds ten she got every week from the MTC barely covered her half of the flat in Kensington Close that she shared with her younger sister Evie, let alone paid the hairdresser and bought lipstick and silk stockings, a villainous eight shillings a pair on the black market.

The luck of the Irish, she thought darkly. And the drawing, as it turned out, was only the beginning.

☙

On Monday morning, Kay dragged herself out of bed at five a.m., gulped tea and toast, and parked her olive-drab Packard with the other four staff cars in front of the American Embassy at 20 Grosvenor Square. The stately square with its park of graceful trees and spring-green grass wore a slightly startled look, for the mannered and genteel buildings were sandbagged, and armed soldiers stood guard at the embassy's entrance. Kay and the other drivers were waiting to pick up the military VIPs they were supposed to ferry around London for the next week. The Americans, like the British, organized everything by rank. Her general wore just two stars, so her car was at the end of the row.

But the brass, grounded at Prestwick by an infamous Scottish peasouper, didn't show up on Monday. Or on Tuesday. No use to grumble, Kay knew. Waiting for the Americans had been the lot of the Brits since the war began back in September 1939. As the Luftwaffe's bombs blitzed London, Prime Minister Churchill went begging to President Roosevelt, desperate for help. But the isolationists over there—led by that wretched Charles Lindbergh and the pro-appeasement American ambassador, Joseph Kennedy—had dug in their heels, and Roosevelt had driven a hard bargain:

a few dozen antique destroyers in exchange for rent-free bases on British land in the Caribbean and Newfoundland.

Until Pearl Harbor, five months before. The Yanks were in, and the lot Kay and the other drivers were waiting for were meant to shoulder their share of the load. It was about time. The Prime Minister, dear old Winnie, was doing his best to placate Roosevelt, but even he was short on patience these days. He was rumored to have growled, "You can always count on the Americans to do the right thing—after they've tried everything else."

Not that Kay disliked Americans. She certainly preferred the friendly and open American men to the stuffy, hidebound British, whose notions of class—and attitudes toward the Irish—were positively petrified. And she loved one American in particular: Captain Richard Arnold, of the Special Army Observers Group. Dick, tall and dark, a wickedly handsome West Pointer with an outrageous sense of humor. Dick, whom she was eagerly waiting to marry, when they were both free, which could be as long as another year. Her husband Gordon was willing (he had his eye on a new wife), but Kay was learning that divorce in America was more difficult to get than divorce in England and just as humiliating. And of course the war slowed everything down. Patience was alien to Kay's passionate Irish nature. But war, she had learned, was as much about waiting patiently as it was about cleaning up after the bombs. The war had brought her American to England, and waiting to marry Dick was just another part of her war.

So she waited for her two-star. However, when he finally arrived—on Wednesday, at Paddington Station, three hours late—Kay's Irish luck did her in again. The fellow ignored her car, climbed into the limousine that belonged to the new U.S. Ambassador Winant, and drove off to spend the rest of the morning closeted at the embassy. There was nothing for Kay to do but drive back to Grosvenor Square, empty, and wait at the curb out front.

And wait and wait, as the other generals came out of the building and were driven off. Her breakfast toast and tea had become a distant dream and Kay was getting hungrier by the minute. Finally, in desperation, an hour past lunchtime, she risked a half-block dash to the fish-and-chips shop in North Audley Street, where she could keep an eye on the embassy—paying first, as she had learned to do in the Blitz, when meals were forever being interrupted by bombs. She was halfway through her Spam sandwich (another dubious American import) when she spotted two officers, one tall and slim, the other tall and broad-shouldered, coming out of the embassy and walking toward her Packard, the only car left.

"Oh, bugger," she muttered. Abandoning her sandwich, she grabbed her bag and dashed for the door and down the street.

"General Eisenhower?" She slapped a sloppy half-salute at tall-and-slim.

Tall-and-broad-shouldered was annoyed. "I'm Eisenhower. He's Clark."

"Summersby," she said, adding hurriedly, "Sorry to be late, sir. Waited through lunch, you see." She opened the rear door. The men got in and she slid into the driver's seat and started the car. "Where are we off to, sir?"

"Claridge's," Eisenhower said. To Clark, he added, "Don't know about you, Wayne, but after that morning, I'm ready for a drink."

"Hell, Ike," Clark said. "I'm ready for the whole damned bottle."

Kay looked in the rearview mirror and saw Eisenhower's face relax into a wide grin that some women might have called "charming." But she was not charmed. Gritting her teeth, she put the Packard in gear. She had gotten up at five in the morning for three days in a row to drive a two-star Yank two short blocks down Brook Street.

At Claridge's, she opened the rear door and the men got out. "Nine tomorrow morning," Eisenhower said. He looked at her, and she saw that his eyes were an icy blue. "Sharp," he added brusquely. "I don't like to wait."

"Yes, sir. Nine, *sharp*, sir." Under her breath, she muttered, "Don't get your knickers in a twist."

He blinked. "What did you say?"

She shut the car door. "Nothing, sir," she said. "Nine sharp sir. In the morning."

℃

That evening, Kay went round to her mother's flat in Kensington—the Warwick Court flat they'd shared had been bombed out. Evie was already there, the sleeves of her white blouse rolled up and her delicate face ruddy from stirring a pot of mutton stew on the kitchen range. It wouldn't be the best mutton, either, but what the butcher had left on offer by the time their mother, Vera (called Kul by her family and friends), got to the top of the waiting queue.

"Look what I've brought!" Kay spilled the contents of her bag on the table. "From Dick."

"Apples!" Delighted, Evie picked one up and held it to her nose. "Wonderful, Kay! I got lucky and found some Stilton—we'll have cheese and apples for dessert. What a treat!"

For three years, German submarines had prowled like jackals along the shipping lanes, torpedoing the merchant ships that brought food and supplies to the British Isles. The first casualty of the war had been petrol, which was immediately rationed. Bacon, butter, and sugar were next, followed by meat, tea, jam, biscuits, cheese, eggs, lard, milk, and canned and dried fruit. Chocolate wasn't rationed—yet—but everybody saved it for the children.

Fresh fruit wasn't rationed, either, but it cost the earth, when you were lucky enough to find it. Dick, whose work often took him back to Washington, had brought tonight's ripe, rosy Baldwin apples from America, which seemed to Kay to hover beyond the western horizon like a golden mirage of unimaginable abundance. When the war was over, she would go to America with Dick and have all the apples and strawberries and chocolate and nylons she wanted, and an automobile and the petrol to drive it anywhere. She would go to America, where the future was always just around the corner—unlike England, which clung with a willful stubbornness to its past.

Kay's mother looked up from setting the table. "Did your general finally get here?" she asked, and laughed when Kay told them about the two-block drive to Claridge's. "Well, just remember that the Americans are here to help us out of a tight corner," she said. "Do your best by the fellow. And do be on time."

Kul was Welsh, convent-schooled in France and as bright and quick and vivacious as her daughters. As a young woman (too young, she said regretfully), she had married Kay's father—a retired lieutenant colonel in the Royal Munster Fusiliers—and gone to live with him on Inish Beg, a tiny island dropped like an emerald into the sparkling estuary of the River Ilen, near the old harbor town of Skibbereen. The family had once been wealthy but their fortunes had changed for the worse, and by the time the two were married, the old manor house on Inish Beg had fallen into disrepair.

Kul went to the stove, lifted the lid of the pot, and poked a fork into a dumpling. "Hand me that bowl, Kay, and I'll dish up the dumplings. Thank God we can still get wine—Evie, there's a bottle of Beaujolais in the sideboard. Open it for us, please." She pushed back her gray-streaked hair. "Oh, I do wish our Seamus were here. Mutton stew is his favorite."

Kay handed her mother the bowl. "Sheila will be coming at the weekend, won't she?" Sheila was working in Brighton.

"Yes. Will you?"

"No," Kay said, and made a face. "I'm working—for that American general."

Kay, the eldest, had grown up at Inish Beg with her sisters Evie and Sheila and their brother, Seamus, now with the Royal Engineers. There'd been no money, growing up, but that hadn't mattered. All four were outdoor children, but Kay had been the most fearless—and the most rebellious—of the lot. Her father, an expert marksman, taught her to shoot and ride and sail. Clad in brown corduroy bloomers and knitted jumpers, she galloped her gray gelding bareback across the open fields and sailed her father's small skiff down the Ilen to the Celtic Sea and back again. Skimming on the incoming tide with the wind behind her, Kay, an imaginative child, pretended to be one of the wild Nereids, riding on the back of a dolphin. In the meadow, there was a fallen cromlech where, with a ritual of oak and mistletoe, she was an anointed Druid priestess. In the priests' tunnel under the old house, she was an unrepentant Jesuit who refused to acknowledge the heretic Protestant Anne as Queen of Ireland. And sometimes, in the garret where Nana's gowns were laid in a chest with camphor, she was Queen Anne. Making believe, in costume.

There was enough money to send Seamus to school in England, but Kay and her sisters suffered painfully under a succession of underpaid and inadequate governesses. Still, the girls were quick and curious and intelligent enough to teach themselves most of what they needed to know, including bridge and poker and chess. They read in their father's voluminous library, which was especially rich in history and mythology. They created their own secret gardens, played pranks on the few servants who were left, and delighted in riding with the hunt.

But their father, Donal, was plagued by the brooding melancholy that haunts the Irish like a black dog, and his years of military service in West Africa had taught him to prefer men and horses to women and children. Kul had at last been defeated by her husband's depressions, the dark, damp, lonely Irish winters, and managing a manor with no help. There was enough money to give the girls a debut, so on the pretext of arranging a season in London for her daughters, she took them and left. She never went back.

Kay, given a choice of a debut or six months in Europe, was quick to choose travel. She went off to visit her mother's school friends in Helsinki and Oslo, then to Brussels for a month, and after that, Paris, where she was surrounded by beaux. At seventeen, she was beautiful: tall and slender, with dark auburn hair brightened by gold glints, a mobile mouth, and gray-blue eyes set in a diamond-shaped face.

Back in London, Kul reminded her that beauty is what beauty does and that life was about *doing* something. Under the usual male entail arrangement, Inish Beg would go to Seamus and there was, of course, nothing for the girls. "Better to have a skill you can rely on than a husband you can't," Kul said practically.

Following her mother's advice, Kay enrolled in a six-month training course at the Triangle Secretarial College in South Molton Street in the West End, where she spent mornings learning how to type (not very well), take shorthand (slowly), and manage an office. Following her heart, she enrolled in afternoon classes at the Chelsea College of Art and Design, where she studied fashion. But she was lured from her studies by the offer of a small part in *The Miracle*, a play retelling the legend of a medieval nun who runs away from her convent with a handsome knight and is eventually accused of witchcraft.

Making believe suited Kay, and she found a job as an extra on a film in production at the Elstree studio, north of London. It was a low-budget quickie, but it was fun and exciting, and she began thinking about a career in the movies. She had just taken another part—a larger one this time—when she was lured away again, this time by Gordon Summersby, the son of a wealthy London publisher. They met at a glittering party in St. James Square, fell in love during the first Strauss waltz, and were engaged by the time they walked out into the misty dawn. But that hadn't lasted either—and now the war.

The girls and their mother sat down at the table and began to eat. "The stew is good, Mum," Kay said, although it wasn't, quite. Still, these days, one said what needed to be said or heard, whether it was true or not.

"Thank you," Kul said, gracefully accepting Kay's small lie. "Better for Evie's dumplings."

Evie, always the realist, wrinkled her nose. "It might be even better if we hadn't had mutton stew the last time we ate supper together."

They all chuckled at that. There was food in England—nobody

was actually starving—but one had to wait forever in queues and there wasn't much variety. Kay couldn't remember when she had last laid eyes on a salmon fillet.

Kul glanced at Kay. "What do you hear from Gordon?"

The subject of her dissolving marriage was a tender one, and Kay hesitated. "I got a letter last week. He's in India, with the Royal Artillery." She dropped the little bombshell she had been holding. "He and Nancy Thomas—Dylan Thomas's sister—are planning to get married."

"Dylan Thomas, the poet?" Evie was interested. "I didn't know he *had* a sister!"

"She's in Egypt with the Auxiliary Territorial Service," Kay said. "I met her at a party once. I think she and Gordon are meant for each other. They're both social butterflies."

"Oh, you girls and your men." Kul picked up her wineglass. "Still, what's sauce for the goose is sauce for the gander, I suppose. Let's drink to Gordon's happiness, if there's such a thing left in this world."

Kay's marriage to Gordon Summersby had been a dazzling three-year whirlwind of idle days, late nights, and weekend house parties: all the doomed gaiety of life before war put the lights out. But for Kay it had quickly become frivolous and empty, too fragile a thread to bind a marriage together, and she saw it now for what it had been: a silly, impetuous mistake. Thank heavens she and Gordon were agreed on that, and neither minded terribly when the war put paid to it.

Gordon had gone first to Egypt and then to India, and a friend had recommended Kay to Worth's in Hanover Square, where the sales manager took one look at her figure and face and hired her as a model. The job didn't pay well, but it brought her back to her first love: fashion design and costume. She hung over the drawing tables and watched the dresses evolve from the first sketch through construction and the final fitting, often on herself. Since she had a "Worth's" figure, she was encouraged to wear the gowns to parties, where they (and she) were much admired.

But that world, too, was quickly doomed by the war. Hitler's armies were marching across Europe, smashing city after city under the hobnailed heels of their jackboots. When England declared war and began to worry about a German invasion, Kay walked out of Worth's and—with Evie, who had left her office job—joined the MTC. They were assigned to the ambulance service and reported every day to their command post, the old schoolhouse in Lambeth, near the docks on the south shore of the Thames.

That was where Kay learned about waiting. Waiting with nothing to do all through the year-long "phony war"—what the papers called the *Sitzkrieg*—until the Luftwaffe arrived like angels of death in August of 1940 and the war became terrifyingly real. Blood and guts and horror and death were the almost hourly order of business during the Blitz, day after day of piloting her ambulance through the burning streets, a Charon ferrying the dead and dying across the Styx. After the Blitz ended, it was back to waiting again, mostly at the American Embassy, where British drivers, skilled in navigating through ruined streets and unmarked lanes and the blackout, were preferred to American military drivers, who were forever getting lost—and getting into accidents, because they tended to drive on the wrong side of the road.

After supper and the washing up and a rubber of three-handed bridge, Kay reminded her mother that she had to pick up her Yank at nine the next morning, *sharp*, so she needed to be off. She and Evie said their goodnights and made their way to their flat through the cave-like darkness of the blackout, keeping to the sidewalk between the white stripe painted on the curb and the comforting brick walls of the buildings.

Kay had never quite gotten used to the utter dark of the wartime streets. This one was lit only by the glowing tips of cigarettes, evidence that a few other people were out and about, their voices and footsteps surreal in the silent night. The only vehicles on the street were a few official cars and trams and lorries, their headlamps pointed downward and masked so that only cat's-eye slits of light shone through—a dangerous situation, since it was easy to step off the curb in front of a car that lunged at you like a panther out of the blackness. There were other dangers, too. She had read just that morning of a man who got out of an unlit train at what he thought was his station and fell eighty feet over a viaduct rail. Accidents happened in the dark.

And it was mostly in the dark that the Luftwaffe came. One of the last bombs of the Blitz had fallen just a block from their building. Kay still remembered the screaming *whoosh* and the terrifying, rocking crash, like a massive earthquake. Every window in their flat had shattered. She had never ceased to be grateful for the current hiatus in the Blitz, but she didn't trust it. Now that the Americans were in the were in the war and bombing the bloody hell out of Hamburg and Rostock and Essen, the Germans were supposed to be too busy to bomb London, but you never knew, did you? The planes could come back any night, groaning with their lethal cargo. The sirens would wail like banshees and she and Evie would grab their pillows and blankets and run through the dark to the shelter a block away, where they would huddle together and try to sleep until the all-clear sounded.

As they climbed the stairs to their flat, Evie said, "This two-star you've got—I suppose he's yours for the duration? You can't trade him to one of the other girls?"

"I don't see how." Kay turned the key in the lock. "He's badly outranked, so nobody else will want him. I'm afraid it's going to be a long, dull week."

"Well, look at it this way," Evie said practically. "Somebody at the bottom of the heap can't be important enough to go very far. He'll probably just have you shuttle him back and forth from Claridge's to the embassy, and that'll be that. Boring, but not very difficult."

They were both wrong.

CHAPTER TWO
The General

London
May 27–June 2, 1942

The two-star nobody with the German name had been sent to England by President Franklin Roosevelt and Army Chief of Staff George Marshall. Ike was there to take a hard look at what the Americans and the Brits were doing to prepare for joint action against the Germans. The news from London had been bleak, and he had been worried enough about the situation before he left Washington. When he came downstairs for breakfast at Claridge's on Thursday morning, he was even more worried. The day before, he'd had long talks with both the American ambassador and General James Chaney, the commander of the U.S. Army Forces in the British Isles. He didn't like what he'd heard.

The British had been at war since September 1939, while America-First sentiments had kept the United States out of the increasingly desperate European conflict. But the Japanese attack on Pearl Harbor was followed just four days later by Hitler's declaration of war against the United States. American citizens had been galvanized by FDR's "Day of Infamy" speech and a newly fired hatred of Hitler and his "Nazi monsters." Since then, the General and other U.S. military planners had been trying to respond to Japan's fierce aggression in the Far East, at the same time trying to develop an Allied challenge to the Germans that would relieve the pressure on the sagging Soviet army—the "second front" that Stalin wanted. It was a damned complicated business that required everybody's cooperation, and it didn't look like that was going to be easy to get.

It didn't look like he was going to get any hot coffee, either, and Ike put down his cup with a scowl. Claridge's was supposed to be the best goddamned hotel in London, and if lukewarm coffee was the best they could do, it didn't bode well. Clark was upstairs on the phone, so he attacked his bacon and eggs alone, glad for the chance to have some private thinking time.

He had plenty to think about, mostly the difficulties involved in getting everybody to agree on an overall command structure and a common set of assumptions—much easier said than done. The schedule was heavy and tight, with one meeting after another, scattered over the whole goddamned country. Today, he had to get to Montgomery's field exercise in Kent, back to London to the War Office to meet with General Sir Alan Brooke, and over to Grosvenor Square for another meeting with Chaney and his team. Then down to Dover, back to the War Office again to talk to Mountbatten, and over to Number Ten Downing Street for a late conference with the Prime Minister. There wasn't much time between meetings in far-flung places. He'd better be able to count on that driver, who hadn't impressed him yesterday.

Eisenhower sat back in his chair and looked around. The dining room was palatial, its eighteen-foot ceilings, crystal chandeliers, and ornately carved columns far too sumptuous for his simple taste. In fact, it was still pretty hard for him to believe that he was actually here. His wasn't the first name that would naturally come to mind—on either side of the Atlantic—to deal with the British military establishment. He was just a country boy from Abilene, Kansas, a staff officer who had never commanded men at war, unless you counted that disgusting sortie that MacArthur had ordered ten years before against the Bonus Army veterans.

In fact, Eisenhower's life as a peacetime soldier had, in his own estimation, been as dull as a slow game of bridge. He'd been an uninspired student at West Point, distracted by the booty he got from playing poker with cadets who had family money in their pockets. Worse, he had suffered a knee injury that ended his football career midway through his first year. He had missed the Great War by a matter of months. After that, he'd been assigned to coach football teams, dispatched to Panama to keep an eye on the canal, sent to Europe to write a tourist guide to the battlefields, assigned to Washington to serve as MacArthur's aide, and posted to the Philippines to create and train a Filipino army with little equipment and less support. He'd had the good luck to be mentored by the smartest men in the interwar army—Conner, Pershing, MacArthur, and now Marshall. But his most satisfying duty as a real soldier had been commanding troops in the Louisiana war games the summer of 1941. For that, he had earned his first star, just three months before Pearl Harbor.

The second star had come—unexpectedly—three months after, when George Marshall handed him the damn-near impossible job of figuring out how to cobble together an Allied fighting force of Yanks, Brits, Canadians, and Free French and develop plans of action for both the European and the Pacific theaters. But two stars didn't count for much, not over here, where he was outranked by every goddamned man he was scheduled to meet with.

Clark pulled out a chair across the table from him and sat down. "Got the schedule reorganized. Dover tomorrow morning. Saturday afternoon open—by that time, we're going to need a break." To the waiter, he said, "What he's got," nodding at Eisenhower's plate.

Eisenhower held up his cup. "And see if you can find us some *hot* coffee."

Clark put his elbows on the table. "Pretty fucking discouraging," he muttered. "That meeting with Ambassador Winant yesterday. Chaney's been sitting on his hands and the Brits think we're wet behind the ears. Looks like trouble ahead for the poor SOB who'll be running this show."

"You said it," Eisenhower replied emphatically. When he got

back to Washington, he intended to recommend Joe McNarney to replace Chaney, and Clark for command of the first corps to be sent to England. Chaney and most of his men would be sent home—on a slow boat with no escort, if Eisenhower were writing the orders.

The American ambassador had laid out the difficulties. The big brass in Churchill's war cabinet were opposed to Sledgehammer, the American plan to land troops on the coast of France, and to its alternative, an operation in Norway—both designed to draw the Germans into a western front and relieve the pressure on the Soviets. Instead, the Brits were pushing for a landing in North Africa, followed by a drive up through Italy, a stab, as Churchill put it, "into the soft underbelly of Europe." Eisenhower was there in part to promote Sledgehammer and in part to measure the resistance to it.

Right now, though, it looked like Chaney and his Observer Group were here for a picnic. Eisenhower, for whom the war had already become an around-the-clock assignment, had been irritated to see that the two dozen members of Chaney's group wore civvies, worked a leisurely eight-hour day, and had forgotten everything they'd ever known about military discipline. No, irritated wasn't the right word. He'd been mad as hell, and it had cost a tremendous effort to conceal his anger at Chaney for encouraging the disgraceful sloppiness. It wasn't his command, and he wasn't in charge here, so Eisenhower was biting his tongue. But he would make it clear to Marshall that the nest of U.S. lounge lizards had to be swept out before the British Chiefs of Staff would believe that America meant business.

Breakfast over, Eisenhower looked at his watch, saw that it was 9:25, and pushed back his chair. "That driver better be out there," he growled. He wasn't used to women in uniform—the President had just last week signed the bill that created the Women's Army Auxiliary Corps. The British drivers, he understood, were volunteers, which was commendable. But while Summersby was certainly decorative enough, she had been out to lunch yesterday when she should have been waiting for him in front of the embassy. He wasn't expecting much today.

But when he went outside, the Packard was parked at the curb and Summersby snapped to attention and opened the car door smartly. And although her salute left something to be desired, he learned over the next several days that she was unfailingly punctual and an exceptional driver, for which he was grateful. She knew where she was going and how to get there on time, which in itself was remarkable, since the Home Office, worried about the very real possibility of a German invasion, had long ago ordered the removal of every street sign and highway marker. She was fearless in the nightly blackouts and the notorious London fogs, navigating in conditions that Eisenhower wouldn't have ridden a horse in. London had grown up in the Middle Ages before city planning was on anybody's horizon, and the streets were a labyrinthine maze. He had heard that cabbies had to study for a couple of years before they could pass the license test—the Knowledge, it was called. Summersby seemed to have the Knowledge tucked into that pretty little head of hers. What's more, she was impeccably uniformed and gloved, with her auburn hair neatly brushed back under her garrison cap, something that counted with Eisenhower, who tended to judge a soldier's military discipline by the condition of his uniform.

He was especially struck by something that happened after a frustrating session with Bernard Montgomery, a jaunty little prick with a swagger stick who dressed him down for lighting a cigarette during his briefing. As he got back in the car with Clark, he could feel the veins in his temples throbbing. He fired off a barrage of blazing curses that smoked the air.

But when he looked up, he saw that Summersby was watching him in the rearview mirror—with a kind of comradely amusement, as if the two of them were sharing a private joke. He had the idea that she knew something about Montgomery and asked her, later, what it was. She told him that Monty was said to complain that the British Army was staffed by too many chaps who were too fat to be fit and smoked too much to be healthy. He liked to rattle off one of Kipling's quatrains in support of his view:

> Nations have passed away and left no traces
> And History gives the naked cause of it,
> One single, simple reason in all cases:
> They fell because their peoples were not fit.

Her recitation didn't endear Monty to Eisenhower, but as he lit another cigarette, he was glad to better understand the man.

In fact, as one day followed another in a grueling parade of stuffy officials, airless, windowless offices, and a frustrating lack of cooperation, Eisenhower grew to appreciate Miss Summersby's observant understanding of the British—who were *not her* countrymen, she was quick to point out.

"Irish," she said, in answer to his question. "Near Skibbereen, in County Cork." He could hear the attractive burr in her throaty voice. But she had lived and worked in England for some fifteen years. She had an insider's knowledge and an outsider's perspective at the same time, with the advantages of both.

The day she drove him and Clark to inspect the coastal defenses at Dover was a case in point. When he asked, she said that the London-Dover highway was part of the area known as Bomb Alley, and pointed out some of the hundreds of ruined buildings.

"It earned the name during the Blitz," she said, and Eisenhower caught her glance in the mirror. "When the German Heinkels and Junkers had the RAF on their tails and were in a hurry to get home, they dumped their bombs along this road."

Suddenly curious, Eisenhower leaned forward. "And you? What were you doing during the Blitz?"

She slowed for a cyclist in the lane ahead of them, a tow-headed boy with a basket of garden vegetables lashed on the back of his rusty bicycle. Over her shoulder, she replied, "I was an ambulance driver in the East End, down by the docks. My sister Evie, too. We drove makeshift vehicles—Ford V-8s with the rear end chopped down so there was room for four stretchers and a rider. Twenty-four hours on, twenty-four off. Bombs every night, fire and ruined buildings and dead people everywhere." She picked up speed again. "Bad time, the Blitz," she added in a matter-of-fact voice. "My mum was a bomb spotter. Still is, since we never know when the bombs will be back."

Ambulance driver, Eisenhower thought. That's why she handled the big Packard with such skill. Would've taken a lot of courage, though. He'd seen newsreels of the horror in which those drivers worked.

"Bomb spotters?" Clark asked, his attention caught as well.

"Incendiary bombs fall on the roof, in the back garden, any-where. They're only about a foot long, but if you let them lie, they blaze up. Next thing you know, the whole block's afire. Mostly happens at night. Mum and the others pick them up, drop them into a bucket of sand, and carry them to a disposal depot. The next morning, they wash their faces and off they go to work." She chuckled. "You've seen the posters? 'Keep calm and carry on.' It became our family slogan after our flat was bombed."

"My God," Eisenhower said softly. He was thinking of Mamie, how shielded she was from the war, as all American women were. Not their fault, of course, that's just how it was, and how he wanted it, how any red-blooded American man would want it. Still, he couldn't imagine his wife—Mamie's health had always been frag-ile—having the courage to pick up a bomb and haul it to a disposal depot, or pilot an ambulance through blazing streets, or carry on calmly after her apartment got bombed. And here was a whole family—mother, daughters, sisters—doing just that, putting all they had into the war effort.

At the wheel of the Packard, Kay caught Eisenhower's glance in the mirror again and was surprised to see the compassion in it. She was finding this American backseat passenger to be much different from others she had driven. The stiff, formal British officers kept quiet so as not to reveal their ignorance. Americans and Canadians were free with their innuendos and their hands. General Clark was not inclined to talk. She thought he was shy.

But Eisenhower, easy and comfortable and entirely natural, peppered her with curious questions about the landscape and the people and their reactions to the war and to the American soldiers who were beginning to arrive by the boatload. He seemed especially interested in what women were doing, so Kay told him what she knew about women acting as air-raid and Home Guard officials and serving in the auxiliary forces—the WRENs, the WAAFs, the ATS, and of course, the MTC.

"We're not just cooks and clerks and telephone operators and typists." She added proudly, "We're also drivers, mechanics, armorers, searchlight operators, radar technicians. Why, I have a friend who operates an anti-aircraft gun in Hyde Park."

"Just what we need," Eisenhower said to Clark. "They'll release the men for combat."

"Excuse me, sir," Kay said firmly, remembering the gun emplacement that had been blown up in Wormwood Scrubs, killing several women. "Driving an ambulance, operating anti-aircraft guns—that *is* combat. People die." She looked in the mirror. "Women die, sir. Women die serving."

Eisenhower cleared his throat. "Noted, Miss Summersby. Thank you." She was still Mrs. Summersby, but not for much longer. She didn't correct him.

The harried days were packed with meetings and conferences from early morning until late at night, and Kay noticed that her passengers were losing the spring in their step. She was feeling the effort, too, since getting them where they needed to go, on time, was something of a challenge. On Saturday, after a long morning's meeting at the War Office, Eisenhower collapsed in the backseat.

"The war can do without us for a few hours," he said. "Clark and I are playing hooky for the rest of the day, starting—" He looked at his watch. "Starting now. Where's a good place for lunch, Kay?"

She was caught off-guard by the General's deliberate use of her first name—how had he learned it? But she knew the answer.

"You'll like the Connaught, sir. It may be the only place in London where you can get a halfway decent piece of fish."

"Eating high on the hog, huh?" he said with a grin. "Let's do it."

She frowned, puzzled. "Ham? Yes, I suppose, but—"

"That just means we're aiming to have a good meal," Eisenhower said, and grinned again. "You know. Two countries divided by a common language."

Kay had to laugh. When they reached Mount Street, she got out and opened the door for the two men, then started to get back into the car, as usual.

"Where are you going, Kay?" Eisenhower asked. "You've earned a good lunch. Come on and join us." He pulled his brows together. "That's an order."

Kay was dumbfounded. She had been driving the War Office top brass for almost a year, and she had never heard of generals taking a driver to lunch. But she tucked in her chin, saluted, and parked the car.

In the elegant Connaught dining room, the maître d' seated the three of them at a table covered with snowy-white damask, studded with silver and crystal, and centered with a bowl of white roses. They decided on a green salad (a real luxury for Kay), poached salmon, and for dessert, strawberry tarts.

"A bottle of your best house white," Eisenhower said to the hovering waiter. As the wineglasses were filled and refilled and the salads came and went, he and Clark traded funny stories from their military past while Kay laughed with them, surreptitiously watching the man she'd mostly seen in her rearview mirror. He had alert blue eyes, a hearty laugh, and a vibrant, resonant voice that he used with authority. His hands as he talked were emphatic, underlining his points. His baldness somehow made him more masculine, and his grin was enormously appealing, especially as the meal went on and he relaxed in the congeniality of Clark's friendship.

But the two men didn't leave her out of the conversation. They invited her to share in the stories and the laughter, so that diners at nearby tables frowned—until Eisenhower turned that infectious grin on them and they succumbed to what Kay was now calling his natural "charm." She had met enough officers to know that the general across the table was someone special—a man's man with the kind of personal authority that could compel attention and respect from those under him without frightening them into whimpering ninnies. A man who somehow made every other man in the room a little less . . . well, manly.

On the other side of the table, Eisenhower was having the time of his life. He had always enjoyed the company of pretty women. Like Marian Huff, the woman who had been his frequent golf and bridge partner in the Philippines—so frequent that Mamie (who was still back in the States) heard the gossip and figured she'd better join him.

But Kay was even prettier than Marian. In fact, when she took off her cap and fluffed up her auburn hair, he saw with pleasure that she wasn't just pretty, she was beautiful, with a fey Irish beauty. Of course she *was* young, he thought with something like wistfulness, probably young enough to be his daughter. She was pert and playful and lively, with that lilting Irish accent and some unusual—to his ear—Irish turns of phrase. When dessert was served, she stared down at the luscious-looking strawberry tart on her plate and reverently whispered, "Jeanie Mac."

When he asked, she laughed. "It's short for 'Jesus, Mary, Joseph, and all the Holy Martyrs'—a way of saying 'Jesus Christ' in front of the nuns, and getting away with it."

Wondering how Mamie would react if he suddenly came out with "Jeanie Mac," Eisenhower gave a rueful chuckle. His wife was forever nagging him about his profanity, which was perhaps why it felt good to let loose with it when he was with the men, or with someone who took it lightly, like Kay. If he'd stopped to think about this, he might have recognized that the freedom he felt in this woman's company was due to the fact that he saw nothing judgmental in her eyes or in her light laugh. Just pleasure and perhaps, something of surprise. Recognizing *that*, he might have retreated to the safety of a uniformed formality.

But instead, when they'd finished dessert and coffee, he found himself saying, "We've seen nothing but military installations on this trip, Kay. How about showing us an English village or two?" He turned to Clark. "What do you say, Wayne?"

Clark shook his head. "Got something else in the works. You two go on."

"Kay?" Eisenhower asked.

"Sure, and that'll be wonderful!" Kay's smile grew even brighter and her eyes seemed to dance. "We'll go north into Buckinghamshire—all the cobbled lanes and lambs and thatched cottages you've ever hoped to see."

It seemed natural to Eisenhower, since this was an informal outing, to get into the front seat beside Kay, where he could better hear her tour-guide descriptions of the sights they were seeing. They drove through charming little villages that looked as if they were right out of an eighteenth-century painting, with spired churches, red roses tumbling over mossy stone walls, and, yes, thatched cottages and lambs playing in the meadows. They stopped in West Wycombe, where Eisenhower somewhat belatedly thought to visit a quaint shop and ask Kay to pick out a brooch for Mamie. He pulled a handful of unfamiliar coins out of his pocket and held them out on the flat of his hand so that she could choose the right ones to pay the proprietor. He might have asked himself why he noticed that her fingers were cool and deft and her hair whispered of fresh lavender, like the sheets in his mother's linen closet. But the pleasure was too startling and too brief and Eisenhower wasn't accustomed to asking such an intimate question of himself. He let it go.

And he didn't ask himself why he was delighted when Kay pulled up in front of a pub, turned to him, and asked, a little shyly, he thought: "Would it be too outrageous if I suggested that it's a gin-and-tonic sort of day?"

"Not at all," he said, happy to extend the afternoon. "I should have thought of it myself."

So they sat outdoors with their drinks, across from the village's Memorial Green and its statue honoring the dead of the Great War, decorated now with wreaths for the dead of *this* war. The glimmering day slid into dusk and the little village folded itself away for the night. He asked Kay about herself and learned of Inish Beg, where she had ridden and sailed and tormented her governesses, and of her forays into acting and modeling. There had been a marriage and a separation and now a divorce in the offing, and he wasn't at all surprised to learn that there was also a man, an American captain in Chaney's Observer Group, and that they were to be married when both of them were free.

But of course there was a man, he thought. She was beautiful and brave and young, and while he couldn't acknowledge the sharp thrust of envy he felt when he thought of the other man, he could smile and say that he wished the two of them well. And he could even feel quite relieved as he said it, for he had the feeling that he had been standing on the brink of something forbidden and undoubtedly foolish, from which he had been saved by this young American captain.

All that lovely afternoon, the war had seemed like a bad dream barely recollected. But the next day Eisenhower met with Churchill and the war was back with a vengeance, a pack of angry wolves snapping at him from all directions. After Churchill it was another day with the Chiefs of Staff, and then the mission was over and he and Clark were scheduled to fly back to Washington.

But fog had set in again and the flight was delayed until the next evening, so Miss Summersby—Kay—had driven them back to the hotel. The following morning, as he was shaving and trying to decide how to spend the extra day, the phone in his hotel room rang. When he picked it up, he heard a breathless Irish voice say, "I was wondering, sir—since you're grounded, p'rhaps you'd like a tour of London. I'd be glad to do the honors."

He felt it then, a quick, warm surge of pleasure, overlaid with a shadow of guilt. He understood what it meant and was grateful once again to the young captain, who made it possible for him to say, "Clark is off somewhere, but I think it's a fine idea, thank you, Kay. If you're sure you've nothing else to do—"

"No, nothing." There was a quick chuckle. "At least, nothing I'd like better. Twenty minutes? Out in front?"

❧

Afterward, Kay wondered where in the world she got the appalling nerve to ring up Eisenhower. She caught her breath as he picked up the phone, realizing how brazen she must sound and bracing herself against a terse "Sorry, I'm busy." When he agreed, she was flooded with relief and so delighted that she gave a little skip as she put down the phone and hurried to brush her uniform jacket.

They spent the morning being tourists. She took him to the Tower of London, Westminster Abbey, Buckingham Palace, and the Guildhall, as well as Fleet Street—the home of most of the British newspapers. Pulling up to the curb opposite an imposing building in Bryanston Court, she pointed out where Wallis Simpson had lived when the Prince of Wales was pursuing her.

"You were here then," Eisenhower said. "What was it like for you? That abdication business, I mean."

She thought about that for a moment. "It seemed quite an intriguing romance. Edward was immensely popular among the people, you see. He was modern and democratic, very unlike the old king. We ordinary people, we didn't want him to abandon the throne. We thought the church and the royal family ought to stop being so old-maidish and stuffy about Mrs. Simpson's divorce. Which was, after all, a bit of a cock-up, the way the law is written. Let him have her, if that's who he needed to help him do his job."

She laughed a little, thinking of her own divorce, which was rather an embarrassment. The only acceptable grounds were adultery, and Gordon was off in India, where she couldn't charge *him*, even though he and Nancy were sleeping together whenever they were in the same country. So by mutual consent and in order to get it done, she had agreed to be the adulteress.

She pulled herself back to the conversation. "The abdication was terribly romantic, I suppose. A crown in exchange for a lady. But still, we were all a little hurt when he preferred Mrs. Simpson to the lot of us."

"The King should have remembered his duty." Eisenhower's mouth was a hard, flat line and his voice was chilly. "Especially at a time when Europe was clearly in such jeopardy."

Kay felt an odd jolt of something like disappointment, but of course you couldn't expect an American general, however sympathetic and likable, to understand a king who had lost his heart.

"Well, I suppose that's why Queen Mary gave old King George a couple of spares, in addition to the heir," she said, chuckling. "Anyway, everybody loves our new King George. He never wanted to be king but he tries *very* hard to do it up right. He's absolutely devoted to us, which is heaps of comfort in the mornings after the bombings. He and the Queen come out of the palace and climb through the rubble and commiserate with people, which counts for a great deal, really. I doubt Mrs. Simpson—the Duchess, as she is now—would do as much." She put the car in gear and pulled away from the curb. "Where next?"

Eisenhower lit a cigarette. "How about showing me where you were stationed during the Blitz."

She glanced at him, surprised. "Why? There's not much left."

"I haven't seen many signs of the war in what we've visited so far," he said. "Either the area wasn't bombed, or it's been cleaned up. I want to see the worst." He looked at her. "Do you mind?"

"No, of course not," she said, although that wasn't quite true. She didn't like going back to the bad places. There were too many horrible memories. But she drove him across Vauxhall Bridge to Lambeth, and along the river. She stopped in front of a heap of burned-out brick and timber, a building that had been leveled on the last day of bombing.

"This is where I was stationed," she said. "My group of ambulance drivers practically lived here during the Blitz. It was Armageddon every night." She pointed toward the Thames. "The oil depots at the wharves went up in great pillars of fire and black smoke, and the streets were so full of rubble we couldn't get our ambulances through." She shuddered. "No light, of course, only the fires. And no sounds, except for exploding bombs and the anti-aircraft guns. And the horrible cries of people who were trapped and burning in the collapsed tenements." She closed her eyes, then opened them again. "It was hell." Her voice broke. "Pure *hell*."

Eisenhower looked down at her, not smiling now, his blue eyes dark and very serious. "And you were driving through that, with the bombs still falling?"

"I had to," Kay said simply. "I was needed. *We* were needed. So we did it. I don't know how, but we did it, all of us." She closed her eyes and saw it all again, wishing that he could see it too, so he would understand—he and all the Americans who thought that war was something that happened somewhere else, to someone else. This war had happened at *home*, to her and her family and their friends, and she could never forget it—or forgive Hitler for causing it.

She shivered and felt the General's big hand on her shoulder, comforting, as if she were a child remembering a bad dream. She took a breath and went on. "The worst was one night when we ran out of bags for the bodies and piled the corpses in the back of the ambulance, with location tags tied to their ankles. When I got the load to the mortuary—" She gulped. "When I got to the mortuary, there was no room. They sent me to another mortuary, but it was full too. They sent me to a half-ruined warehouse that had nothing in it but dead bodies. Stacks and stacks of dead bodies. And the stench—" She put her hand to her face, remembering how it had smelled, and how the bombing had gone on and on and there had been no end to the dead filling her ambulance, to be delivered to morgues that were already full. "As if I were . . . Charon," she whispered.

"The ferryman of the dead," Eisenhower said. His fingers tightened on her shoulder. "Sail upon the wind of lamentation, my friend, and pass over Acheron to the sunless land that receives all men."

She raised her eyes and stared at him, surprised. "Yes," she said. "Yes."

Eisenhower dropped his hand and pulled out a cigarette. "That took courage, Kay."

"London is full of courage," Kay said.

"So I see," Eisenhower said. "Thank you."

℘

The next morning, Kay drove the two generals to the RAF aerodrome at Northolt, where they would fly to Scotland and then back to the States. They got out of the car and shook hands politely, and General Clark thanked her for driving.

But Eisenhower handed her a box. "For you, Kay."

She gasped as she took it in her hands. Chocolates! "Oh, thank you," she whispered, deeply touched. "How very kind. Mum and Evie will be thrilled."

"Not at all," the General replied with a wide smile. "If I'm ever back in London, I'd like you to drive for me again. Will you?"

"I will, sir," Kay said promptly, and saluted, more precisely this time.

"That's better," Eisenhower said, and laughed.

The minute the men were aboard the plane, she tore the box open, greedy for the first chocolate in months. On top of the candy was a note. "To Kay, with thanks for the glimpse into your war. I won't forget." It was signed DE.

Kay watched as the plane disappeared into the overcast and Eisenhower was gone. She felt a small, unsettling sense of loss. She never expected to see him again.

And again, she was wrong.

CHAPTER THREE
The General's Wife

Washington, D.C.
September 1942

"To be honest, Cookie, I feel like a durn football." Mamie took a cigarette out of her case. "You know the drill. When Ike was ordered to London, I was ordered off the post. I had seven days to move and I'm still bouncing around. I don't have a bed to call my own." She thought of adding, "Which stinks." But she made it a rule not to criticize the army, even to longtime friends. You never knew when a careless word might get back to the commander.

Cookie Wilson clasped her hands under her chin. "I don't blame you for being upset, dear. How many times have you moved just since you got back from the Philippines?"

Mamie gestured to the waiter to take her half-finished plate. She and Cookie were having lunch at Giovanni's, a little Italian restaurant near the Mayflower Hotel. It had been one of their favorite Washington haunts back in the early thirties, when their husbands—Cookie was married to Brigadier General Marv Wilson—were both working for General MacArthur. But this was the first time Mamie had been here in five or six years, and she did not approve of the changes. The restaurant was too crowded, with too many tables jammed too close together, and much too noisy.

"More coffee?" the waiter asked, but not encouragingly. Eager customers were lined up inside the door and he was impatient to get the table cleared and a new pair of diners seated. It wasn't just Giovanni's, though. The war had turned Washington from a sleepy Southern city into a boom town. There was too much traffic and crowds everywhere, with people—half of them boys in uniform—lined up in long queues waiting for a table, a seat in a theater, a pack of cigarettes, a chocolate bar.

"Yes, more coffee, please." Mamie held a lighter to her cigarette, refusing to feel guilty for lingering over coffee with all those people waiting. She wasn't through talking to Cookie and she was *not* ready to fight for a taxi. These days, cabs were as hard to find as nylons (which were nearly nonexistent because DuPont had stopped making stockings and was making parachutes instead). You could stand on the curb and shout for an hour before a cabbie would condescend to notice you. Which, as far as Mamie was concerned, was another reason to stay home.

But it was good to be with Cookie, whom she hadn't seen since she and Ike left Manila in late 1939. As usual, her friend was dressed to the nines in a dark-green serge suit with wide, padded shoulders and a nipped-in waist, topped with a perky lime-green felt hat with a single red feather that swept down over one ear. Her amusing, animated recital of her recent moves, her daughter's wedding, and her husband's assignment to Ike's London headquarters had taken them through the entrée and dessert—cheesecake for Cookie, but Mamie had declined. She didn't eat much these days. "Peck, peck, peck, like a sparrow," as her apartment mate Ruth put it. In fact, she had managed to get down only half of the lasagna, although she had enjoyed that glass of wine. Just one glass, though. That was all she allowed herself when she was out in public.

And now they had arrived at coffee and cigarettes and it was her turn.

"How many times have I moved?" Mamie rolled her eyes. "Oh, golly, I'd have to count. There was Fort Lewis, where we had a lovely four-bedroom brick, but it was terribly grimy with coal soot and the drapes were impossible to clean so I had to get all new ones made. We were there for nine or ten months, until Ike was ordered to Fort Sam Houston—just in time for our twenty-fifth." She held out her wrist, proudly displaying the expensive platinum watch he had given her for their anniversary, and was gratified by her friend's drawn-out *ooh*. "Really, Cookie, such a *gorgeous* house, with five bedrooms and the breeziest sleeping porch. It was such a *joy* to be back in San Antonio. That's where we started out as young marrieds, you know." Thinking of it, she felt terribly nostalgic. Those early days, they had been the very best. Oh, if she could only—

Cookie forked up a bite of cheesecake. "I suppose you still do your bedroom in pink, with green walls?"

"Well, of *course*," Mamie said, pleased that Cookie had remembered. "I adore pink, and the green is so restful—just what Ike needs when he gets home, tired enough to drop." She picked up her coffee cup. "Anyway, he got his first star while we were at Fort Sam, which meant of course that he was entitled to an orderly. We found this young private, as Irish as he could be, who used to be a bellhop at the Plaza in New York." She tapped her cigarette into the ashtray. "Mickey is in England with Ike now, but when I had him, he did the shopping and a lot of the cooking."

"*That* must have been a help," Cookie remarked, a bit arch. "I remember that woman who cooked for you when Ike and Marv were with MacArthur here in Washington. If you don't mind my saying so, Mamie, she was simply *awful*. We were always glad when Ike put on an apron."

Mamie made a face, thinking of all the cooks she had hired and fired over the years, paying them out of the fifty dollars a month her father sent her—and still did—because he knew how terribly hard it was for her to get by on Ike's meager officer's pay. She had been raised like a Southern belle, to do nothing but organize the housekeeping, manage the servants, and entertain. Her mother said that ladies didn't cook, they *hired* their cooks, so Mamie had never learned. Which was why for the first few months of their marriage, she and Ike had spent forty dollars a month to take their meals at the officers' mess across the street from their quarters at Fort Sam. It was also why Ike took over the kitchen back in those early days—self-defense, he said. If he wanted to eat at home, he had to cook it himself. Now, of course, he only cooked on special occasions, and always man-food. Steaks, fried chicken, beef stew, baked beans. He hated "high-falutin' gourmet stuff," as he called it.

There was a commotion at a nearby table as three young men in army uniforms pulled out chairs and sat down. They were in the middle of a conversation about the disaster of the Dieppe raid, which had happened in August, several weeks before. Ike hadn't written to her about it. He didn't share his work, and the censors would have stripped it from his letter if he had. But she had been chilled to the bone when she read the awful stories in the *Washington Post*. The Allied casualties had amounted to nearly sixty percent, which the Germans were treating as an immense propaganda coup. She doubted that her Ike had been part of the planning, though. If he had, she was sure it wouldn't have been the catastrophe it obviously was. Somebody else must have been in charge.

Mamie shut out the soldiers' conversation as best she could and went on. "Anyway, Ike was called to Washington right after Pearl Harbor, to the War Plans office. Our son John was at West Point and there I was, all by myself at Fort Sam and in utter limbo. In the dark, really, not knowing what was happening from one day to the next, until General Marshall told Ike he just had to have him available every minute—of course poor Ike was working just brutal hours—so he was ordered to Washington and we moved to Fort Myer. Quarters Seven," she added carelessly, and pulled on her cigarette. "On Generals' Row."

On Generals' Row. Cookie heard the words with a stab of envy. Of course, she had known about Ike's latest promotion. Everybody knew it by now, unless they had their heads in the sand. She liked Mamie well enough and she wouldn't for the world let her know how deeply she resented those incredibly swift second and third stars Ike was wearing. Why, he now outranked Marv, even though they had graduated together in the West Point Class of 1915 and Marv had made it to full colonel three years faster. Nobody wanted to deny Ike what he had legitimately earned, but really—

She couldn't resist adding just a bit of a barb to her smiling compliment. "My gracious, Mamie. Generals' Row! Whoever could have imagined, after all those years Ike spent as a major and a lieutenant colonel?" She smiled to herself, remembering a funny story going the rounds. It had taken place at a Washington cocktail party when Eisenhower was working for MacArthur. Milton Eisenhower, who was forever promoting his older brother, said to a prominent reporter, "I want you to meet Dwight Eisenhower. He's going places." When the reporter learned that Ike had been a major for sixteen years, he said to a friend, "If that guy's going places, he'd better get started soon."

Mamie's eyes narrowed for an instant, and Cookie bit her lip, hoping she hadn't gone too far. Mamie liked to pretend that she was oblivious to rank, but of course she wasn't. She was now a three-star wife, and she had always been good at manipulating Ike. As long as Marv was in Ike's command, it would not be smart to antagonize her.

For her part, Mamie heard Cookie's barb quite clearly but felt that a little generosity was in order. She knew how much rank mattered to Cookie. And to tell the truth, she was flattered by her friend's envy.

"I was glad that Ike was working directly for Marshall, even though the hours were just *brutal*," she said, blowing out a stream of smoke. "Of course, I would never say this to Ike—he always has too much on his mind. But I don't mind telling you that the Fort Myer house was a headache. Beautiful, of course. But oh, so *big*! Twenty-some rooms and no help but Mickey to get things settled. Its saving grace was the gorgeous view of the Capitol dome and the Washington and Lincoln monuments across the river. I could have spent all my time just gazing out the window."

"Oh, I'm *sure*," Cookie said. She raised her voice above the soldiers' conversation, thinking that she should try to mend whatever damage might have been done with her little barb. "But I bet you didn't spend any time at all at the window. You are such a hard worker."

"Oh, you're right, of course. I had to close down the San Antonio house and get the army to move everything, *again*. More than sixty crates just for the china, and—would you believe?—fifteen tables and all the rugs." Mamie laughed ruefully. "Ike says I missed my calling. I could have made a career as a quartermaster, or the manager of a moving company. But maybe I wouldn't be so lucky with other people's things. I've got our belongings trained to jump into their crates all by themselves." She snapped her fingers to illustrate. "All I do is give the order."

Sixty crates of china? Cookie couldn't imagine acquiring that much dinnerware. How could Mamie afford it, on Ike's pay? And how in the world did she imagine she'd ever use it? But to each her own. And since Mamie outranked her, she was in no position to criticize. She laughed at Mamie's little joke.

"Well, Ike always used to say you were a pack rat. I don't remember his ever refusing you, if you wanted something. Like those *two* fur coats you bought in Hong Kong." With a slight smile, Cookie picked up her cup. "In fact, I remember Marv saying that your husband let you have anything you wanted."

Mamie returned the smile, a little acidly. As she remembered it, Marv used to say that Ike spoiled her rotten, which was true, at least as far as *things* were concerned. Her husband was never one to talk about love, and he wasn't very free with kisses or cuddles. But from the very beginning, he had courted her with small surprise gifts, flowers, fruit, candy—an unexpected box of her favorite chocolates with a little note tucked inside. After they were married, the gifts got bigger and more expensive—pieces for her silver service, and the platinum watch.

His time and full attention, though . . . well, that was a different matter. She'd often wished she could trade some of the things he gave her for a little more of *him*. But he had made it clear before they were married that his duty came first. She had learned that sometimes there just wasn't room in the day, or in his mind, for anything or anyone else. Except for that year when he was in the Philippines and she was in Washington with Johnny and he found time to play golf and do who knows what else with Marian Huff.

But she firmly closed the lid on that ugly, jealous jack-in-the-box thought, and put on a bright smile. "Well, it's nice to be appreciated by your husband," she said modestly.

Cookie put her cup down. "But you're not at Fort Myer now," she went on, just to remind Mamie that while she might outrank her, the Eisenhowers no longer lived on Generals' Row. "You're 'bouncing,' I think you said?"

Mamie fluffed her bangs. It wasn't pity she heard in Cookie's voice, was it? Well, she certainly knew how to handle *that*. "Yes. Ike made a quick trip to London in May while I finished getting us settled at Fort Myer. But just a few weeks later, we got the news that he was being transferred to London, as commander of the entire Allied force. In charge of the 'whole shebang,' was the way he put it."

Their son John, a cadet at West Point, had been visiting that July weekend, and Ike had told them both that President Roosevelt had called him to the White House and put him in charge of the European command. Right afterward, he had gone to see Prime Minister Churchill, who was in Washington at the time, and Churchill had said that he'd be in charge of the Allies, too. John seemed stunned at the way his father had leapfrogged over so many men—like Cookie's husband—who outranked him. Mamie herself had been flabbergasted, but she didn't ask how or why it had happened. She had always made it a point never to involve herself in Ike's work. The army was *his* job. Her job was to make a home for her soldier, a refuge from the stress and worry of military life, and boost his career by meeting their social obligations with energy and enthusiasm. She also volunteered hours every week for the Red Cross, the Army Relief Society, the USO, and the American Woman's Volunteer Service. It was all part of *her* job.

She stubbed out her cigarette. Whatever *her* feelings about

Ike's being assigned to London, Mamie knew he was thrilled with his new appointment. All those years he had been stuck behind a desk doing staff work, he had been dying for a command. And now he had the most important command there was, at the most crucial point in the war and— well, it was simply breathtaking, that's what it was.

Breathtaking, impressive, extraordinary, yes, all that. Mamie knew she ought to be proud. Well, of course she *was* proud, really, she was. But if she'd had her way, he'd be fighting this war from the Pentagon. She hated to have her man so far away, the way he'd been in Manila, when he and Mrs. Huff—

She made herself stop. Ike had sworn up and down that there wasn't anything to it, no matter what people whispered (and they whispered a *lot*). But he certainly hadn't seemed keen on the idea of her coming to the Philippines, and his letters were infrequent and chilly. Of course, she herself had led rather a giddy social life in Washington while they were separated. She was a natural flirt and there were always escorts eager to take her out. In fact, on the very day she arrived in Manila, Ike had said, in a frosty tone, "I gather I have reason for a divorce, if I want one."

That had brought her down to earth with a thud. Yes, she had flirted with several men, and allowed several others to take her to parties. But she had done nothing that would warrant such a remark, so she could only think that *he* had. Was it Marian Huff? Was he seriously thinking of divorce? She'd been afraid to ask, and grateful that he hadn't brought up the subject again.

Anyway, there was a different reason to worry now. It was *wartime*, and Ike was in London where anything could happen. He assured her that the bombing had ended, but she had seen the newsreels—so many English cities bombed to rubble during the Blitz, so many buildings burned and people killed—and she knew it could begin again at any moment. Her stomach hurt whenever she thought about him right there with everything blowing up all around him. She reached for another cigarette, her fingers trembling.

"Well, of course Marv and I were simply *thrilled* when we learned that Ike had been given command," Cookie said, smiling. Mamie thought it might even sound like she meant it. "But it's too bad that you had to pack up again. And find a place to live—in this impossible town."

Mamie nodded. "My parents wanted me to come to Denver and live with them, but I'm staying here, where I can get Ike's letters faster. They come in the diplomatic pouch and somebody brings them right over to me so I don't have to wait. And I'm just a few hours by train from John, up at West Point, if he gets sick or something."

She and Ike had lost their little boy Icky to scarlet fever when he was only three, and she had blamed herself for it. If she had only paid more attention when he first got sick, that awful day—but that was the cause of her nearly phobic possessiveness over John, born the next year. He was now a cadet, a sophomore, and quite the young man, but she still hadn't gotten over what Ike rebukingly called her "smother love." He kept telling her she had to let Johnny grow up.

She put that thought aside and went on. "Almost everything is in storage for now. When I find a place of my own, I'll pull out a few more things so I'll have something familiar around me—something that reminds me of Ike. But of course I'm hoping this war will be over soon and he'll be home again."

"Oh, Lord, I hope so too," Cookie said fervently. "When do you suppose that will be?"

"Ike says it may be a very long time," Mamie said. A hard lump came into her throat as she thought of their goodbye, back in early July, at Fort Myer. She had walked out to the car with him. His driver had opened the door and he'd gotten in, then rolled down the window. With that wide, wonderful grin of his, he'd taken her hand and kissed it and said, 'Goodbye, honey.'" A couple of days later, he'd sent a completely unexpected cable. BECAUSE OF YOU I'VE BEEN THE LUCKIEST MAN IN THE WORLD FOR TWENTY-SIX YEARS—LOVE IKE. That was what she held to her heart.

Cookie finished her coffee. "And you're living . . . where, now?"

Mamie pulled her attention back to the conversation. "With Ruth Butcher. We're sharing a kitchenette apartment in the Wardman Park on Woodley Road. Ruth's husband is Ike's naval aide, and they've got a suite together in London. Maybe you remember Butch and Ruth from the old days. They're not military—he's a vice president of CBS when he isn't in uniform."

Mamie didn't much like sharing an apartment, even with Ruth, but there wasn't a lot of choice at the moment. Ike's brother Milton and his wife Helen had invited her to live with them while Ike was overseas. But Milton (who held an important post as associate director of the Office of War Information and knew everything that was going on with the war) liked to "look out for her," as he put it. Mamie, however, always had the uncomfortable feeling that her brother-in-law was watching just a little too closely, counting the number of drinks she had and "reminding" her when he thought she'd had too many. She preferred to be more independent, and sharing with Ruth meant that she could save money.

Anyway, finding a place to live in Washington in wartime was just *murder*. Housing was the very dickens, especially for the multitude of young women thronging to government jobs—five thousand a month, it was reported. "The men may have started this war," Mamie had read in the newspaper, "but the women are running it." The women—"government girls," they were called—were crammed into rooming houses that were more like dormitories, with three women to a room, all living out of their suitcases because there wasn't room to hang up their clothes. Mamie felt she was extremely fortunate to find a place in the Wardman, which was certainly an elite address. Former president Herbert Hoover had once kept an apartment there. And Henry Wallace, FDR's vice president, and his wife lived just down the hall.

She looked at Cookie questioningly. "You're in Arlington, I think you said. Are apartments easier to find in Virginia?"

But she didn't get an answer to her question. Instead, a chipper voice asked brightly, "Oh, Mrs. Eisenhower, is it really *you*?" When she turned in surprise, the woman—short, plump, ginger-haired—crowed, "It *is* you! I *thought* so!" She put out her hand. "I'm Bess Furman, with the Washington Bureau of the *New York Times*, and I just *know* that our readers would *love* a few words from you. We hear that your husband is taking London by storm. How do you feel about him being over there while you're over here?"

Mamie felt her mouth go dry. She had never liked the limelight and over the past few weeks she had developed an intense fear of reporters—an unreasonable fear, Ruth told her, but she couldn't seem to shake it. An AP reporter had somehow gotten the phone number at her apartment and had called several times, asking for an interview. But she kept saying no, afraid that if she talked to one reporter, they would all come flocking. They'd be roosting like buzzards outside the door, just waiting to pounce.

And it wasn't just that the reporters and photographers were a nuisance, although they were. The thing was that she had never in her life had to talk to the press, or see her words or her photo in the newspaper—unless, of course, she was standing beside Ike and they were taking *his* photo. This interview business was something new and she was deathly afraid of making a mistake. She would say too much or say the wrong thing, something silly that would embarrass poor Ike or cause trouble for him. Or maybe she would say the *right* thing but the reporter would misquote her, accidentally or on purpose. Milton always said that you couldn't tell about those people. It was safer not to talk to them at all.

"Thank you, Miss Furman," she said, turning away quickly, "but my friend and I are having a private lunch and I'd really rather not."

"Oh, but *please*, Mrs. Eisenhower," Miss Furman begged. She whipped out a notebook and a pencil. "I read that your husband's home town has just had a 'General Eisenhower Day.' Were you there? It must have been terribly exciting. Won't you tell us how it feels to be married to such a famous man?"

At the nearby table, the soldiers had turned around in their seats, listening avidly, but Mamie didn't notice. She knew she should have gone to Abilene, to stand beside Ike's mother and brothers at the celebration. She felt bad about forsaking the family, but her heart wasn't strong so she *never* flew on an airplane. And railroad trains were so crowded these days, and hot and noisy and dirty—you could pick up all kinds of germs. She wasn't strong and just thinking of the long trip had been enough to tire her out. But of course, she didn't say any of that to Miss Furman, who was watching her, pencil eagerly poised over her notebook. She would prefer to say nothing at all, but she was afraid that the woman wouldn't go away until she got what she was after.

"Being married to General Eisenhower feels . . . it feels . . ." She wanted to say that it felt terribly lonely and that she wished with all her heart that her husband was still just a colonel instead of a general and that there was no war and they could go on living quietly together, just the two of them in that beautiful house at Fort Sam. But she took a deep breath and tried to focus on what she knew Ike—or his brother Milton—would want her to say.

"It feels wonderful to know that people are thinking of him and wishing him well, and of course I am just frightfully proud of him and the job he's doing, fighting for our freedom. But honestly, I am not one little bit different from all the other wives and mothers in this wonderful country of ours. We're all proud of our soldiers. And we're all waiting for the day when our men have won the war and can come home to the families that miss them so very, very much."

"That's perfect." Miss Furman scribbled quickly in her notebook. "Thank you, Mrs. Eisenhower, thank you!" She backed away.

Cookie slanted her an admiring glance. "My goodness, Mamie. I wish Ike could have heard you. You sounded just like you'd been doing that forever!"

Mamie was about to say that she didn't *feel* like she'd been doing that forever when one of the soldiers at the nearby table got up and came toward her.

"Mrs. Eisenhower, we couldn't help overhearing." He turned and gestured to the two other earnest-looking boys at the table.

"My buddies and I—well, we've just got our orders for England. We'll be taking a ship over there in another few days to serve in General Eisenhower's command, wherever it takes us. We know he's new on the job but we've already heard a lot of great things about the way he's taking charge and making things happen so we can get over there and kick those lousy Jerries all the way to hell, where they belong." He reddened. "Sorry—excuse my French. We just want you to know we're gonna do the very best job for him that we can do. For him and for the good old U.S. of A." He stood up straight and tall and snapped a proud salute.

Mamie thought of John and swallowed down a sob. "Thank you," she whispered. "I'll tell the General what you've said. I know he'll thank you too, for doing your very, very, *very* best."

"Yes, ma'am," the boy said. He turned and went back to his table.

"Wasn't that *sweet?*" Cookie said. "Oh, Mamie, what a compliment to Ike." She smiled. "Don't you wish you could be a little mouse in the woodwork and watch him while he's on the job? As long as he didn't know you were watching, of course."

Now, *that*, Mamie thought, was something she could say *yes* to, without even thinking about it.

CHAPTER FOUR
The General's Family

London
July–September 1942

When Kay thought about it afterward, it all seemed quite extraordinary—the way the General's official family came together.

But then, she had never worked with anyone like Eisenhower. When he flew back to Washington in early June, all the Allied war offices were buzzing about his easy American charm, his big grin, his willingness to listen to all sides. And when Kay watched his plane lift off from the Northolt RAF aerodrome, she had felt an unsettling sense of absence—quite silly, really. Their time together had been intense, yes. But it had been only a few days, and she wasn't expecting to see him again. After she and Evie and Kul had devoured his astonishing gift of chocolates, however, she couldn't bring herself to throw away his note: "To Kay, with thanks for the glimpse into your war. I won't forget." She tucked it into her jewelry box as a memento of his generosity and understanding.

Her two-star nobody had been generous in another way, too. She was now driving for hard-jawed, red-haired General Tooey Spaatz, commander of the Eighth Air Force at Camp Griffiss in Bushy Park, outside of London. Spaatz's Yank driver had gotten him lost once too often, and when he asked Kay to drive for him, he mentioned that she had come highly recommended—

by Eisenhower. That pleased her, and as she avidly pursued the war news on the wireless and in the newspapers, she heard his name mentioned often, especially after he was put in charge of the whole European Theater of Operations. He was now Supreme Commander. She heard that he'd gotten another star, too.

At first, she was surprised by his appointment. Most of the brass she knew were egotistical: tough and gruff like Spaatz or petty and often malicious, like Montgomery. She would never have guessed that President Roosevelt and Prime Minister Churchill would give the top Allied job to the friendly, informal man with the easygoing manner who had ridden in the backseat of her Packard. Was he *tough* enough?

And yet, maybe *tough* wasn't what was wanted. She overheard General Spaatz telling British General Sir Alan Brooke that managing the Allied war effort was a goddamned impossible job, but if it could be done, Eisenhower was the man to do it. "He's got the administrative smarts," Spaatz said. And on one of her rare evenings with Dick, he had told her that the Americans who worked at the embassy were deeply impressed by the General's gift for pulling people together, even when they didn't speak the same language and were miles, or oceans, apart.

Dick. Sometimes it seemed that the two of them were miles apart, too. Their divorces were in the queue with the many other wartime divorces taking place on both sides of the Atlantic, and neither would be final for another ten or eleven months. Waiting was hell, but there you were. There was no help for it.

And almost as bad as the waiting was the change in his work assignment. He had been promoted to major and reassigned to General Fredendall's II Corps, which was stationed at a distance from London. Kay was free, since her job with Spaatz didn't take up her evenings. But Dick wasn't. The few hours they were able to spend together were as frustrating as they were fulfilling. There was passion—oh, yes, there was *that*, as natural and irresistible as the powerful tidal currents that ran back home in the River Ilen. Give them five minutes together and they were in one another's arms and his hand was on her breast and—Katie, bar the door!

But while there was plenty of physical passion, there was never enough time—the time it takes to develop the deep, intimate understanding that can hold together two different people from different ends of the earth. She often thought, sadly, that they were strangers moving toward one another through the dark, like two friends on a sidewalk during the blackout, bumping into each other, murmuring *oh there you are, darling*, and hurrying on, deeper into the darkness.

&

Then, quite unexpectedly, Kay's work assignment changed, too.

One afternoon in late July, she drove General Spaatz to Hendon Aerodrome to meet several VIPs who were returning from an inspection trip to Ireland. As the C-47 taxied down the tarmac, the brass lined up at attention. She took her usual place a step behind General Spaatz. The hatch opened and Eisenhower came briskly down the stairs to shake hands with the men. A few moments later, he was extending a hand past General Spaatz to Kay, a mock frown replacing that dazzling grin.

"Ah. The elusive Miss Summersby. Have you forgotten that you promised to drive for me when I came back to London?"

Kay swallowed, uncomfortable at being singled out in front of her boss. She met his eyes. "I didn't know . . . No, of course, I—" She straightened her shoulders and took command of herself. "Congratulations on your appointment, General."

"Thank you." Eisenhower turned to Spaatz. "I've been scouring London for Miss Summersby, Tooey. You've been keeping her under wraps out at Bushy, have you?"

"Don't do this to me, Ike," Spaatz protested. "This girl is the best driver I've got. There's nobody like her."

"Don't you think I know that?" Eisenhower smiled down at

her, and the smile lifted her heart. "Kay, I brought you something from the States. Come over to the office and pick it up. But don't wait too long—it might spoil."

૭૦

Kay hadn't really believed that the General had been looking for her, but when she walked into his office on her lunch hour the next day, she discovered that it was true. His aide, Tex Lee, told her that he had tucked a note under the windshield wiper of her staff Packard in the car park at Bushy, asking her to come to 20 Grosvenor to speak to Colonel Lee. But she had wadded up the note and tossed it. She didn't know any colonels named Lee and she wasn't going to anybody's office without a direct order from General Spaatz.

But now she was here and Eisenhower—the new Supreme Commander—was actually interrupting his work to see her, stepping around his desk with a grin that lightened his blue eyes. Other than the three stars on his shoulders, he looked just as she remembered, and her heart did a curious flip-flop.

"I was hoping you'd come," he said warmly, and handed her a large box of oranges and grapefruit. "I brought this for you."

She looked down at the gift. Undone by the welcome and the sweet, heady fragrance of the fruit, she stumbled over her words. "This is *smashing*! I . . . really, General, I don't know what to say. Heaps of thanks, just heaps. I . . ."

He was laughing at her now. "Consider it a bribe. I'd like to let General Spaatz know that you've joined my staff and that you'll be driving for me. How about it?"

Kay found that she didn't need to think twice. "Yes, sir. Oh, yes." Still holding onto the box of fruit, she managed a salute. "I'd like that, sir. Thank you!"

"Very good." Eisenhower turned back to his desk, which was

stacked with papers. "And now that you're on my team, ask Colonel Lee to help you polish up that salute. It's pretty damned sloppy."

That was how Kay Summersby—Irishwoman, British citizen, and civilian member of the MTC—joined the General's official family, most of whom were crowded into the smoke-filled anteroom adjacent to Eisenhower's small office on the second floor of 20 Grosvenor Square. She quickly learned that it was best to hang around, for the General often needed her quickly to take him to an unscheduled meeting, and he didn't like to wait while somebody fetched her.

After the first few days, Colonel Lee—Tex—suggested that if she was going to be sitting around she might as well answer the phone and pick up a few other office chores. She already knew quite a bit about the British war offices and other institutions— she hadn't been driving the brass for over a year for nothing—and she soon found herself answering questions, giving directions to places that people had never heard of, and interpreting impenetrable messages written in thick British bureaucratese. She saw very quickly that the Americans had something to prove in this war, and whatever it was, it wasn't helping their dispositions. She didn't have anything to prove, so she made it her job to keep their spirits high, sometimes (if that's what it took) playing the bright, bubbly Irish lassie.

Their five-member staff was headed up by tough-talking, short-tempered Beetle. His full name was Brigadier General Walter Beadle Smith, but he had long ago yielded to the inevitable. As Eisenhower's hatchet man, Beetle did the dirty work, firing people the General didn't want to fire, giving orders the General didn't want to give. He was very good at it, too. He barked commands in a way that made you practically jump out of your skin, and he never let anybody get by with anything. The men called him "Ike's sonofabitch." Beetle called Eisenhower *the Boss*, so that's what the rest of the staff called him, too.

Colonel Lee—Tex, a plump, round-faced, bespectacled former automobile salesman from someplace called San Antonio—was the Boss's office manager. A born administrator, Tex kept the paper moving, untied the red tape, and made sure that the Boss (Tex often called him *the Old Man*) got what he wanted when he wanted it. He spoke with a slow Texas drawl laced with words and phrases that made Kay smile: "y'all" and "right quick" and "plumb tuckered out."

Affable Lieutenant Commander Harry Butcher, the General's naval aide, was a former vice president of the Columbia Broadcasting System and longtime Eisenhower family friend and bridge partner. The Butchers and the Eisenhowers were so close, Tex told Kay, that the Boss's wife Mamie was living with Butch's wife Ruth back in Washington, and Butch was sharing Ike's suite at the Dorchester. A natural-born gossip and teller of tales, Butch (who called the Boss *Ike*) was the press liaison, wordsmith and chronicler, in charge of the official diary. But most importantly, he was in charge of keeping the Boss's spirits up, of making sure that he got what he needed when he needed it. Kay had heard Eisenhower say that there were days when he wanted "to curl up in the corner like a godawful sick dog. But Butch won't let me. He keeps me from going crazy."

Butch was also in charge of feeding the newspapermen who hung out at the Hotel Savoy bar, eager to snatch up every crumb of war news or tasty bit of staff gossip. He knew Edward R. Murrow and Eric Sevareid of CBS Radio, which had its studios in the base-ment of the BBC. And Quentin Reynolds, of *Collier's* magazine, and Pete Danielle, London bureau chief of the *New York Times*. Butch said it was important for the Boss to get the best press he could, which was a challenge, because Eisenhower preferred to stay out of the limelight. But higher-ups in Hitler's command read the British newspapers, and while battles weren't won in print or pictures, what the General said—and how he looked when he said it—was important.

And finally, there was blue-eyed and black-haired Sergeant Michael McKeogh, who called himself a proud Paddy from Queens. Mickey shined the Boss's shoes and did the Boss's shopping and wrote regular letters to the Boss's wife, who had asked him to keep her posted. He confided to Kay (Irish compatriots, they hit it off immediately) that he couldn't tell Mrs. Ike *everything*, for she was . . . well, sort of nervous and jumpy, with her husband being so far away. Mickey didn't like to worry her. All she wanted to hear was that her Ike was eating right and wasn't smoking too much and was getting enough sleep and at least some relaxation. All of which Mickey duly reported.

But relaxation wasn't a priority on the General's schedule, as Kay discovered her first week on the job. He hated the stuffy elegance of Claridge's ("That whorehouse-pink bedroom makes me feel like I'm living in sin," he snorted), so he moved to a first-floor suite at the Dorchester with windows looking out on Hyde Park. The Dorchester was supposed to be one of the safest buildings in London, with extra concrete between the floors, but the General liked it, he said, because it "wasn't fancy." Kay met him there with the Packard promptly at seven a.m., seven days a week, and drove him to Grosvenor Square, where he put in a full morning on conferences and paperwork. He usually had lunch at his desk—a sandwich, coffee, peanuts. In the afternoons, she drove him to meetings in London or at military installations outside the city.

The General's night drives were handled by "Lord Gilbey," an upright fellow who affected the aristocratic manner that earned him his nickname. But Gilbey was wobbly and slow and after he ran the car up over a curb in the blackout, the General used him less often. So on Tuesday nights, Kay drove Eisenhower to Number Ten Downing Street for dinner with the Prime Minister, and on Thursday nights to the Treasury building in Whitehall, where the bomb-proof underground Cabinet war rooms were located. If it was late when they got back to the Dorchester, the Boss would invite her to the suite, where Butch or Mickey (both permanent residents) would stir up a quick cup of soup from a powdered mix the General's wife sent from the States. That—with a Spam sandwich and a chocolate bar—was their supper. As the commander of the Allied forces, Eisenhower was deluged with a storm of social invitations, but he turned them all down: "I'm not fighting this goddamned war over tea and crumpets," he'd growl. "We're not here to be wined and dined."

But he couldn't turn down an invitation from Churchill to spend the weekend at Chequers, the Prime Minister's country house, a sprawling brick pile that dated to the late 1400s. He hated to go there, he said, because it was a "goddamned ice box. I wear two suits of underwear and I'm still cold." When the General was staying just one night, Kay stayed, too, to save petrol. On those occasions, she was invited to dinner. The General would be seated to the PM's right, even when he was outranked by other guests, and she was seated to the General's right. But while the setting and service might be quite formal, there was always plenty of laughter, sparked by the irrepressible host himself, who usually wore his "siren suit," a comfortable one-piece affair that could be pulled on quickly if the air-raid siren blew. (Once, he wore one of black velvet, which Mrs. Churchill told Kay she'd had made for him for formal occasions. "It's about as dressed up as he's likely to get, except for the King and Queen," she said ruefully.)

After dinner, the Prime Minister would hurry the General off to his study, where they talked war talk until two or three in the morning. When Kay met Eisenhower with the car the next morning, she saw that he looked tired and haggard. She didn't wonder. The PM was a whirling dervish, always in motion, brandishing ideas like razor-edged swords.

But there were a few relaxing evenings at the Dorchester, which the Boss spent playing bridge with Butch and a few others—often, General Al Gruenther, his deputy chief of staff, who was a world-class bridge player and had written a couple of books on bridge. As it happened, bridge was Kay's favorite game. When they were children, she and her brother and sisters had played bridge on rainy days in the schoolroom at Inish Beg, where their games inevitably ended in a shouting match and tearful accusations of cheating.

Eisenhower's first invitation to play was tentative, as if he wasn't sure she was up to playing with him and Butch. But she took the game seriously and played well, and after a few evenings, she became his regular partner—a great compliment, she thought. Eisenhower was an excellent player. He had an innate ability to conceal his misdirection and deceptions behind his genial glance and the seeming candor of that all-American grin. He appeared so entirely open and transparent and so naturally friendly that his opponents found it easy to trust him, to take him at face value. And then he pounced. Kay found herself studying him intently, watching his face, listening to his voice, warning herself that if she didn't read his signals, she could be as seriously fooled as his opponents.

It was a warning she would remember when it was all over, and think about for a long, long time.

℘

A week or so later, another invitation surprised both of them—Ike even more than Kay, perhaps.

It was a Friday afternoon in late August. He was alone with her in the car on the way back to the Dorchester from the War Office, where he had spent the day in a particularly contentious meeting with the British Chiefs of Staff. They had been working on plans for Operation Torch, which was designed to gain control of French North Africa. American forces would push east into Tunisia and then join up with Montgomery's Eighth Army, which was chasing the Germans out of the deserts of Libya and Egypt. The fall of the Allied garrison at Tobruk in June had been deeply demoralizing, and Rommel was threatening to push on to the Suez Canal, the British lifeline to the oil-producing Arab countries and Britain's overseas dominions.

Ike sighed. Mediating transatlantic disagreements between Washington and London was a goddamned tough job, and the Brits and Americans were still an ocean or two apart on strategy—and fundamental philosophy. Churchill's Chiefs of Staff believed that the Americans had a lot to learn, while the men in FDR's War Department felt that the British had very little to teach them. If he couldn't pick his way through the political and military minefield, it would be impossible to get Torch underway before the Mediterranean winter set in. He sometimes felt like a football coach trying to field a squad of players who didn't speak the same language, refused to read signals, and hated each other's guts. Meanwhile, the Japs had taken the Philippines and Burma and were threatening India. Their navy had been soundly whipped at Midway, but the U.S. fleet had suffered serious losses off Savo Island. Ike knew the Pacific well. It was going to be a long, hard slog.

Glumly, he stared out the window as Kay maneuvered the heavy car expertly and at a fast clip in and out of a roundabout. He had told his old friend George Patton that the past six weeks had been the most trying of his life, and that was one hell of an understatement. When he was a kid, his mother had given him *Pilgrim's Progress* to read. These days, he sometimes felt like that poor clown, Christian, slogging through the Slough of Despond with the White House and Number Ten Downing Street on his shoulders, and that new monstrosity, the Pentagon, piled on for good measure. FDR and Churchill both thought they were military geniuses, but both were swayed by political pressures at home. Operation Torch itself—strung out across three different landings along the coast of North Africa—was a desperate undertaking. He put the odds of success at no better than fifty-fifty. If the weather turned against them or the French decided to resist, it would be more like forty-sixty. Or worse.

He sighed again, thinking ahead to his evening meeting about air support with Air Chief Marshal Tedder, the commander in charge of the RAF in the Mediterranean. He raised his voice. "I have to be back at the War Office at eighteen thirty, Kay. You're welcome to come up and have supper in the suite. Butch can rustle up something for us."

"Gilbey will be driving tonight, sir," she said over her shoulder. "My sister Evie is working in Manchester this month and I'm spending the evening with Mum." She added, "Sorry, sir. I hope you don't mind. It's the first night I've had off in a couple of weeks."

"No, of course not," Ike said quickly, and felt an odd twinge of something like disappointment. He should be the one to apologize. The young woman—a civilian volunteer—hadn't missed a single day since she joined the team. Her ability to navigate the labyrinthine British bureaucracy made life easier for all of them, and she did what she was asked without complaint. Just the day before, he'd heard Butch remark that the office needed more like her.

Ike agreed. He had already put in a request to Colonel Oveta Hobby, the new WAC commander, for as many WACs, trained as typists and stenographers, as she could give him. Five or six, she'd promised, maybe more by the time they'd established their headquarters in Algiers, where they'd be moving in November, if all went according to plan.

Kay was no WAC and her typing wasn't the greatest, but she was making a difference in the office—and making a personal difference to him, too. She was well informed about British politics and history and usually had an answer to his questions about current political issues. What's more, she was witty and funny, with a sense of humor that livened the long hours they spent in the car together, but not in the least featherheaded. He had to admit to wanting to have her around.

And that was when that surprising invitation occurred. He wasn't a man to act on a whim, but he found himself leaning forward, one arm across the back of Kay's seat.

"Speaking of your mother, I've been thinking that I'd like to meet her, Kay. Tomorrow's Saturday. Butch will be gone for the evening and there's nothing on the calendar. How would it be if I invited the two of you to the suite for dinner? Nothing special, just hotel room service, but we'll have a bottle of wine." He paused, now rather astonished by what he had just said and uncertain about whether he should have said it.

Behind the wheel, Kay was as surprised as Eisenhower. She kept her eyes on the road unspooling ahead of them, giving herself a moment to think. The Boss wanted to invite her and her *mother* for dinner? When just last week he had turned down Lady Astor's invitation to dine with the inimitable George Bernard Shaw? Surely it was an unusual invitation, especially now, when he was struggling to resolve a host of touchy issues between the Americans and the British over Torch. The mission was top secret, but she couldn't help overhearing discussions of it among the officers who came in and out of headquarters and rode in the backseat of her car.

She had to consider something else, too. She and Dick had agreed that they would keep Saturday nights free, on the off chance that they might be able to steal a few hours together. But she hadn't heard from him all week, so it was probably safe to assume he wouldn't be available tomorrow. And then, with a shiver of recognition and a sharp stab of guilt, she understood that, even if Dick was available, she would rather spend the evening with Eisenhower. The realization was . . . unsettling.

And the Boss himself? What was in *his* mind? But he was settling back in the seat and when she met his eyes in the rear view mirror, she could see nothing in them but the usual friendliness. He had been under a lot of stress lately. Maybe what he needed was a quiet evening in the company of people who had no special agenda, who weren't trying to push him to come up with a plan of action that would take the troops of two nations into endless bloody battles. It must be terribly difficult for him, so far from home, with so much riding on his decisions. From that point of view, she told herself, a quiet dinner and conversation were simply part of her job, with her mother along to keep the conversation moving. If Dick asked, which he wouldn't, she could tell him in good conscience that she had to work.

She took a deep breath. "I'm sure Mum will be pleased," she said, and gave him a bright smile. "It'll be fun. Thank you, General."

"Very good," Ike said, and went back to staring out the window, thinking about what he'd just done. Or rather, calculating. As a kid, he had learned to play poker from a fifty-year-old mountain man who had drilled into him that the game was nothing but percentages and probable outcomes, and he had trained himself to think that way about all the decisions he made, military and otherwise. Dinner with Kay Summersby . . . What were the probable outcomes?

But he found that he wasn't able to answer this question in his usual logical and coherent way, and he almost spoke up to withdraw the invitation, or at least put it off. He had made it impulsively, out of a desire to—a desire to what? Perhaps he simply wanted to talk, person-to-person, with Kay's mother, who had soldiered valiantly through the Blitz and understood what the ordinary citizens of London (not the BBC or the big brass in the War Office or even the Prime Minister) thought about how the war was going. As for Kay, he had always taken a personal interest in those who served under him, making sure they had what they needed: help with housing, personal time off to attend to family, that sort of thing. An informal dinner was a convenient way of getting better acquainted.

Back in Abilene, of course, such an evening would earn a gasp of disapproval. But this was cosmopolitan London, where (according to Butch, that indefatigable gossip), Ambassador Gil Winant was having an affair with the Prime Minister's married daughter, Sarah. And the Prime Minister's daughter-in-law, Pamela—the wife of the Prime Minister's son, Randolph—was sleeping with Averell Harriman, the American in charge of Lend-Lease. Not that Ike condoned that sort of thing, of course—he didn't. But he was securely married to Mamie (in spite of that little flirtation with Marian, which had not gone nearly as far as his wife feared) and Kay was engaged to Major Arnold (who was *not* in his direct line of command). And her mother would be present. Surely there wasn't anything terribly improper about the invitation.

Was there?

∞

On Saturday evening, Ike found that he was able to push his misgivings (whatever they were) to the back of his mind and enjoy himself immensely. The food was crappy—steak, underdone and cold—but the wine was fine and the company was excellent. Kay's mother, Kul, struck him as a woman of the world, quite sophisticated but entirely natural. Ike could see where Kay got her independence and her sparkling sense of humor. Kul was a well-educated history buff who had many questions about the battles of the American Civil War, which Ike was glad to answer by lining up coins to represent military formations. Every now and then he would glance at Kay, who was wearing a bare-armed summer dress, white, with scallops of lace, the first time he had seen her out of uniform. He would smile, then, just for her, to show her how grateful he was for the happiest evening he'd had since he left home.

"Thanks for making this such a pleasant occasion," he said, as he saw them to the door at the close of the evening. He reached out to shake Kul's hand, and then Kay's. Her small fingers felt cool, and his tightened on hers involuntarily. The touch was jolting, electric, and he pulled back hastily, smiling to cover his confusion. "Let's do it again, shall we?"

"Certainly, sir," Kay said. She raised her hand to salute, then seemed to remember, with a laugh, that she was in civvies. "Thank you, General. Goodnight." She turned to wave and smile at him as she and her mother went down the hall.

Ike closed the door and stood uncertainly for a moment, thinking, letting the faint scent of the women's perfume settle on him. He had always been a highly disciplined man, holding honor, duty, and loyalty as his highest standards. Certainty was a habit of mind, even in uncertain circumstances. What had happened tonight left him uncertain, conscious that he might be standing at a fork in his personal road. And as he remembered Kay's bare shoulders and the touch of her cool fingers, he suddenly understood which fork he wanted to take and had a tantalizing glimpse of where it might take him.

But that was out of the question—entirely out of the question, impossible. With a shake of his head, he poured himself a stiff drink.

☙

In the car—the Boss's official car, which Kay, out of uniform, found a little uncomfortable—her mother pulled the door closed and settled into the front seat beside her.

"Your Eisenhower is certainly a charming man," she said. "Every inch the soldier and quite . . . masculine." She was silent for a moment, then turned to Kay, frowning. "My dear, sweet Kathleen, are you *sure* you know what you're doing?"

"Doing? I don't know what you mean, Mum," Kay said, glancing over her shoulder, then pulling out into the darkness of the empty street. "What am I doing?"

Her mother laughed her woman-of-the-world laugh. "If you don't know, my dear, you should." She sobered. "But then, your General may not know, either. Which makes it doubly dangerous. One of you, at least, should understand what's happening. Before it does."

Kay's hands tightened on the wheel. She appreciated her mother's concern, but really, the idea was ridiculous.

"Don't be a goose, Mum," she said sharply. "I'm just one of the team—his 'family,' Butch calls us—and I'm only doing my job. The poor man is away from home, he's a target in everybody's shooting gallery, and he needs cheering up. Anyway, he's married to his Mamie, and I'm going to marry Dick. You see?" She raised her voice, lightening it. "There's nothing 'dangerous' about it."

"Perhaps. But do be careful, won't you?" Her mother folded her hands in her lap and fell silent again. "I'm sorry, Kathleen," she said finally. "I shouldn't have spoken. Forget I said anything, will you?"

"Of course," Kay said. "It's forgotten already."

But it wasn't. Later that night, as she lay in her bed in her silent flat, she could still feel Eisenhower's fingers, tightening on her hand. Years later, she would remember the warning and know that her mother was right.

ꜱꜱ

In the office the next morning, Ike had forgotten his momentary confusion. What he remembered was the pleasant evening, relaxed and entirely comfortable. He would like to do more of that sort of thing, but the Dorchester was a *hotel*, it was a goddamned goldfish bowl, like the office. There were always people around, coming and going. What he needed—what the whole office family needed, really—was a cottage in the country, a hideout, where they could get away from the distractions of London, play bridge and poker, have a few drinks, and enjoy some good old-fashioned home cooking, real food, not the room service crap he'd had last night.

"Kay!" He raised his voice. "Hey, Kay, get in here. I've got a job for you."

ꜱꜱ

Kay found the cottage with the help of a lieutenant from the British billeting office. A century before, it had been a station on the telegraph line that linked London and Portsmouth, hence its name: Telegraph Cottage. Located just thirty minutes from Grosvenor Square and another ten from Allied headquarters in Norfolk House, it was an unpretentious Tudor-style slate-roofed house that, to Kay, looked like it belonged on a Christmas card. It stood at the end of a long, winding drive, barricaded behind high hedges. There was a tidy green lawn in back, a vegetable garden, a tall fence, and a path bordered by rhododendrons that led into the woods, through a wicket gate, and onto the thirteenth hole of the Little Coombe golf course—ideal for the General, who liked to play golf. He liked to ride, too, and Richmond Park was not far away.

The reviews were mixed. Eisenhower thought the cottage was ideal, although the rent (thirty-two American dollars a week) was "pretty damned steep." The British generals, accustomed to the grand estates they saw as their wartime entitlements, were collectively appalled that the Commander in Chief was going to ground in a "rabbit hole," as General Sir Alan Brooke put it. The Prime Minister thought the cottage was a good idea, but insisted on having a bomb shelter dug in the garden before the General moved in.

The cottage itself was comfortable, cozy, and relatively warm, with a fireplace in the living room and a coal-burning range in the kitchen. Mickey would manage the place, with two colored orderlies, Moaney and Hunt, to do to the cooking and housekeeping. In the dining room, a round oak table seated six for a comfortable meal (ten if they were chummy and minded their elbows), and a sideboard doubled as a bar. French doors led out onto a flagstone terrace and the rose garden, and a steep, narrow stair led up to five tiny bedrooms and one closet-sized bathroom with a shower. The only telephone was in the Boss's bedroom, a direct line to headquarters, installed by the Signal Corps.

From the beginning, the Boss made it clear that he wanted everyone in the office to feel that Telegraph Cottage was *their* home. The first time she drove him out there to spend the night, he said, "Stay and have supper with me, Kay." Without waiting for her answer, he shouted to Mickey, "Hey, Mick, we're home and we're hungry. Light the fire and rustle us up something to eat. Hot dogs, maybe, with mustard and plenty of onions. Fried potatoes?"

We're home and we're hungry, she heard with surprise. She would always remember the bubble of laughter that rose in her throat and the General's blue eyes laughing down at her. In a moment, the fire was blazing and two overstuffed chairs were drawn up close to its warmth. Ike poured each of them a Scotch and water and Mickey brought the Boss an old woolly brown cardigan and a pair of worn straw slippers—"from Manila," the General said. Kay loosened her uniform tie and they put their feet up on the brass fireplace fender and sat with their drinks and a bowl of salted peanuts for a companionable hour, smoking and talking about the house, the garden, her life as a girl in Ireland, his as a boy in Kansas, about anything except the war. And then Mickey brought in their supper trays and two cold mugs of beer—to Kay's delight, because American beer was impossible to get these days.

Before she left that evening, Ike said, very seriously, "Everybody in our office is working like the devil getting ready for Torch. We need this place, and we need to use it just as often as we can get away. I'm putting you in charge of recreation, Kay. Set up bridge games here for the nights we've got free. Shanghai some players for us—Wayne Clark and Al Gruenther, Tex, Butch, whoever plays a decent game. Dig up a badminton net for the yard and some paddles. A football, golf clubs, anything else you can think of to keep us moving around, get some exercise, blow off steam. I'm told there are horses at Richmond Park, and I'd like to go riding. Make some time for that."

"Riding!" she exclaimed, feeling a flash of exhilaration at the thought of it. "Oh, jolly good fun!"

He cocked an eyebrow. "You're a rider?"

"My father put me on a horse before I could walk," she replied proudly.

"Then get a horse for yourself, too. I don't like to ride alone, and Butch and Tex are both city boys—no point in asking them." He grinned at her, that wide, wonderful grin that made her feel she had known this man for all of her life. "Oh, and tell your mum she's invited for dinner and another of our history lessons. As I remember, she asked about Lee at Gettysburg. I've been thinking about how to explain it to her."

"She'll love it," Kay said, knowing it was true.

"And one last thing," he went on. "When I can work it out, I'll be sleeping over here at the cottage and going to the office after breakfast. It's silly for you to drive back to London at night and out here again early the next morning, so I've asked Beetle to requisition a billet for you at Bushy Park, where General Spaatz's WACs will be billeted when they get here. It can't be more than a ten-minute drive. You can stay there whenever I have an overnight here. Will that be okay?"

"Yes, indeed," she said, thinking how kind he was to consider her convenience, with all the other things he had to think about. "Thank you, General." She smiled and saluted smartly, as Tex had coached her, but the General didn't return her smile, and her heart dropped. Her salute wasn't right *yet*?

He was shaking his head at her, but her salute apparently wasn't what he had in mind. "When we're here at the cottage, we're off the job. The war is off-limits. I don't want to hear any shop talk." He paused. "You're Kay and I'm Ike. Got that?"

"Got it," she said, and dropped her voice. "Ike," she said, carefully, quietly, savoring it.

He nodded, smiling. "Atta girl. See you in the morning, Kay."

She hummed to herself as she drove back to the flat in Kensington Close. And only once remembered her mother's warning. *Dangerous.*

CHAPTER FIVE

The General's Birthday

London
October 1942

"The Old Man has named Irish our official recreation director," Tex Lee announced at the staff meeting the next day. "If any of you have suggestions for ways to cut loose and have fun, let her know. But keep it clean." He aimed a pointed frown at Butch. "No naked dancing girls."

"Hell's bells," Butch grumbled, with a grin. Tex and Beetle might treat Kay's appointment as a joke, but he was all in favor. This was wartime, damn it, and sometimes the war news was nothing but bad. There were days when the morale in the office was so low you had to scrape it off the floor, Beetle was impossibly surly, and Ike was feeling meaner—as he put it—than fifty-two rattlesnakes.

For the past ten years, Harry Butcher had been a vice president of CBS Radio and station manager at WTOP, with studios on the top floor of the Earle Building in downtown Washington. As an experienced press, radio, and public relations man, he knew that morale was important. Important, hell. It was *crucial*. Butch—who had coined the term "fireside chat" for FDR's heartening radio talks and had lured folksy, friendly Arthur Godfrey to CBS from NBC—understood the importance, when times were tough, of putting on an engaging smile and an air of cheerful optimism. It was the sunny image that counted, and in Butch's business, image counted a very great deal.

As far as Butch was concerned, Kay was exactly what the doctor ordered. Her bright, enthusiastic, let's-have-fun-while-we-get-it-done attitude gave everybody a shot in the arm—especially Eisenhower, who was dealing with problems from all sides—the British, the French, the Russians, the Americans. He was increasingly impatient, tired, and short-tempered. He smoked as many as four packs of Camels a day, drank a gallon of coffee, and suffered from insomnia and high blood pressure. No surprise, of course, given the headaches he had to contend with.

So Butch was glad to see that Kay was taking her new job seriously. She stashed a set of golf clubs in the cubbyhole under the stairs at Telegraph Cottage. Under her direction, Mickey set up a shooting range at the edge of the woods and Moaney and Hunt cleared off a badminton court and a quoits pit in the back garden—quoits, Butch figured out, was the British version of the American game of horseshoes. For evenings at the cottage, she rounded up decks of cards, dominoes, a chess set for Beetle, a phonograph, copies of American magazines, and stacks of the Western pulp magazines Eisenhower loved to read. At the office, she instituted the British ritual of late-afternoon tea and made sure that the General got a cup or two to keep him going, along with a plate of tea-time cookies—biscuits, she called them—delivered with a smile.

The golf clubs went into immediate use. The path through the woods led to the thirteenth hole, so Ike and Butch went out to play a few holes whenever they could, and Ike usually asked Kay to play along, since she had a pretty good swing. But when it came to riding, Butch said with a laugh that he had never been on a horse and was too old to start now. So when Ike could find a few hours for riding, he invited Kay. He asked her to shoot with him, too, and Butch noticed how pleased he was when she showed off her skill.

One afternoon when the three of them had spent an hour

with the targets, the Boss surprised Butch—and Kay, too—by giving her a Beretta. "It's wartime," he said. "Keep it with you. You never know when you might need it."

"But this is *England*," she said. "The Nazis won't dare invade us. Especially now that you Yanks are here."

Ike nodded shortly. "Damn right. But you may not always be in England."

Butch raised an eyebrow, wondering what was in Ike's mind, and noticed that even Kay looked perplexed. But she only said "Thank you very much, Ike. I'm glad to have it," and put the gun in her shoulder bag.

Butch was glad to see that on the days when Ike could play a few holes of golf or go riding in Richmond Park for a couple of hours, he looked a great deal more relaxed and happy and his temper evened out. This was Kay's doing, Butch knew, and he appreciated her efforts. But he watched the situation with a growing uneasiness, especially when whispers began flying around the office. Butch wasn't one to make moral judgments—he had never been entirely faithful to Ruth and he didn't fault Ike for being attracted to Kay. She was a beautiful woman. Still, the idea that the press might hear the whispers made him nervous. He thought about it for a while, because he wasn't exactly sure what was going on and he didn't feel comfortable meddling. But if he was going to speak up, better sooner than later.

So one October morning, he went to the coffee pot in the lounge down the hall and poured two cups of coffee. Back in the office, he took them to Kay's desk and put one in front of her.

"Coffee for you, Irish," he said, thinking that she looked especially pretty this morning, her auburn hair softly waved, her skin glowing, her delicate hands moving swiftly over her work. Those hands that had the strength to wrestle that unwieldy Packard along roads where *he* wouldn't want to drive.

Kay looked up from the morning's mail. The General had wanted to come in earlier than usual this morning, so she had gotten a start on the job of sorting it, which seemed to get bigger every day. She was surprised to see Butch. He was usually the last one in the office.

She smiled. "Thanks." She put down the last envelope and picked up the coffee. She liked Butch, but she had never been quite sure what his job was supposed to be, except for the feeding and care of journalists and maintaining the office diary. And keeping the Boss on an even keel, of course. "What did I do to deserve room service?"

"Just a great job, that's all. As recreation director, I mean." Grinning, he pulled out a chair, turned it backward, and sat down. "I've been meaning to tell you that—just somehow never get around to it."

She leaned back, glad for his compliment. Tex was always too busy to notice and Beetle never said anything nice to anybody. "Sweet of you, Butch. I appreciate it."

Butch shook a Lucky Strike out of a crumpled pack. "You know, Ike and I go back a long way—fifteen years, in fact. He keeps his nose to the grindstone longer than anybody I've ever known. But he works best when he can get a break every now and then. And he works with guys all the time, so he likes having a woman around." He put the package back in his shirt pocket and lit his cigarette. "He misses his wife."

Kay wondered whether he meant something by that remark, but before she could ask, the door opened and a corporal stepped in with a thick folder. He spotted Butch, and came over. "From Captain McIntyre, sir. The British newspaper clips you were asking for. And a print of the staff photo *Life* magazine is running next month."

"Thanks, Corporal," Butch said, taking the folder and leafing through it rapidly. "Tell the captain to send the American clips as soon as he has them."

He misses his wife. Kay took out a cigarette. When the corporal had left, she asked, "What's Mrs. Eisenhower like?"

"Charming," Butch said quickly. "Exactly what Ike needs—the making of him, in fact, if you ask my opinion. A man's career in the army depends as much on his wife as it does on him, you know, and Ike is no exception. Mamie's a great army wife, a fine manager, totally devoted to him for twenty-six years and through God only knows how many moves." Grinning amiably, he flicked his lighter to Kay's cigarette. "Although she tells Ruth—that's my wife—that the only way to get along with the guy is to give him exactly what he wants."

"I see," Kay said quietly. She knew she should be glad to hear that the Boss's home life gave him everything he wanted and that his wife was behind him a hundred percent. But something in her, some part of her that she didn't understand, felt obscurely—and mutinously—disappointed. Had she been hoping to hear . . . something else?

Butch leaned back in his chair. "The thing is that the Boss can't go anywhere without being recognized, and you're rather . . . well, noticeable, yourself." He pulled the photo out of the folder and held it up. "See? There you are, right behind Ike. It'll run in the article *Life* is doing on him."

"Nice photo," Kay said, remembering how much the General had resented taking the time to sit for it. He'd thought the *Life* photographer—Margaret Bourke-White—was too pushy. She chuckled. "The Boss looks grim."

"Yeah, but grim is good, as far as the public is concerned. War is a serious business. Photos of us having a good time are bad PR. I'm glad *Life* is running this one." Butch put the photo back in the folder. "Speaking of being recognized, somebody told me that they saw the two of you riding at Richmond yesterday evening." He wasn't looking at her. "I wonder . . ." He let his voice trail off.

"Wonder what?" Kay asked evenly, regarding Butch through the smoke of their cigarettes.

"I'm not suggesting anything, mind you, Kay. I'm just thinking about gossip. About the way things look." He held up the folder of clippings. "You know how the Fleet Street gang is—and the American journalists are even worse. They'd love to jump on the idea that you and the Boss are . . ." Leaving the sentence unfinished, he gave a shrug. "Of course, Ike's brother Milton pretty much runs the U.S. Office of War Information, which screens all the war reports. He's not likely to let anything awkward get into American newspapers. But there's an old military saying. The higher you climb the flagpole, the more of your ass is exposed. And Ike is pretty far up that flagpole right now."

Kay regarded him, feeling prickles of apprehension across her shoulders. Yesterday's ride in Richmond Park had been especially lovely, a quiet and companionable canter through silent woods in the magical hour before sunset. The last sweet light slanted through the trees, gilding the autumn air, and they rode through it as if it were a shower of golden sparks. They scarcely exchanged a word during their time on the trail, but as they rode single-file back to the stable, the General reined in his horse and waited for her to catch up to him.

"Thank you, Kay," he said gruffly. "Best evening I've had for months."

"Best for me, too," she said, and smiled. "Ike."

He nodded and rode on ahead. At the stable a few minutes later, when they had both dismounted, he reached for her reins but instead took her hand and grasped it tightly. He stepped toward her, then stood for a moment, his eyes intent on hers, as if he wanted to speak. Her heart pounding, her throat tight, she held the moment as a child might hold a piece of candy, longing to taste it fully but afraid to lift it to her mouth for fear it might melt—or that it might not taste as sweet as she imagined. But even untasted it was sweet. Nothing, not a word was said, but she could feel the strength of his fingers for moments after he let her go.

Now, she picked up her coffee cup and looked directly at Butch across the rim. "I'm only following orders, Butch. If the Boss asks me to go riding, I go riding. If you think that's a bad idea, you'll have to take it up with him." She was smiling, but she heard the edge of challenge in her voice. She knew that Butch heard it too.

"Yeah, maybe I will," he said, as amiable as ever. He stood up, then reached over and patted her on the head, grinning. "As I said, you're doing a great job. Just keep it out of the newspapers, kiddo. Okay?"

Kay swallowed a retort, nodded briefly, and turned away.

℘

The next afternoon, the General gave her another assignment—one that would change her life in an entirely unexpected way.

She had driven Eisenhower to the depot at Cheltenham, where the supplies and equipment for Operation Torch were being assembled and stored. The General had spent several hours with General Lee—John C. H. Lee, whose proselytizing zeal had earned him the name "Jesus Christ Himself Lee." But Lee had to be Jesus Christ, Ike had said, if he was to organize the millions of tons of materiel that would supply the invasion and arrange its transport to North Africa. "An even bigger miracle than the loaves and fishes," he'd added with a grin.

The General must have seen fewer snafus than usual in Jesus Christ's supply system, for when he got back in the Packard, Kay saw that he was in a good mood. He relaxed in the backseat with a cigarette while she drove through the pretty Cotswold countryside. It was a dazzling day, with an azure sky spread over an emerald landscape of picturesque stone cottages and barns and meadows flecked with grazing sheep and cattle.

Eisenhower rolled down the window and fresh air filled the car. "You know, Kay," he said reflectively, "when this war is over and I've stopped moving from one damned army post to another, I'm going to find myself a place in the country and put down a few roots. I want a garden, and some apple trees. Horses, a couple of cows for fresh milk, pigs, chickens, a dog." He tossed his cigarette out the window and rolled it back up. "I woke up this morning thinking about this dog I had when I was a kid back in Abilene. Flip, her name was. Fox terrier, smart as the dickens, all guts, all glory, all the time. Never knew when to quit, even when she was up against a dog twice her size."

That made Kay smile. "We always had dogs at Inish Beg," she said over her shoulder. "My favorite was MacTavish, a Scottie and black as the devil. Tavvy was feisty, independent as they come. Opinionated, too." Her heart lightened and she chuckled, remembering the little dog. "We always had to give him a job to do, or he'd find one on his own. Digging holes in Mum's rose garden, or managing the geese. Crazy, I know, but I miss him still."

There was a lengthy silence, and what the General said next was so unexpected that it took Kay's breath away. "Well, then, maybe you'd like to have another."

"Another . . . *dog*?" Not sure she had heard him correctly, Kay looked up to catch his glance in the mirror.

"Yes. You've been very kind to me." His smile was warm. "And you're very *good* for me. I'd like to do something for you. A Scottie, if that's what you want, like MacTavish." He chuckled. "President Roosevelt has a Scottie, you know—Fala, his name is. He's an opinionated little fellow, too, knows exactly what he wants. Jumped right up on my lap when I went to see the President."

"A dog," Kay said wonderingly. "A *dog*? Oh, General, a dog would be absolutely—"

"Smashing," he said, and they both laughed. "But there's just one thing about this," he added, sobering. "As far as everybody else is concerned, it will have to be the General's dog. If anybody thinks I'm getting a dog for my driver, I'll catch it six ways from Sunday." He shook his head ruefully, and Kay wondered if he was thinking of his wife.

"I understand," Kay said quickly. "It'll be our dog." She bit her lip. "Our" sounded too presumptuous, as if she were claiming a connection to him that was not hers to make.

But Eisenhower seemed pleased. "Exactly, Kay. *Our* dog—just between us. Officially, it's my dog."

Our dog, she thought. Two very small words, but to her they seemed to signify paragraphs, whole chapters, a book, even, page after page of unspoken possibilities. *Our dog.*

He sat forward and put his right hand on the back of her seat, almost touching her shoulder. "You wouldn't know it from looking at Beetle's sour puss, but he's a dog lover. I'll put the two of you in charge of getting our Scottie—for my birthday. It's coming up on the fourteenth."

"It'll be my very great pleasure, sir," Kay said, and heard the happiness in her voice, not just because she was getting a dog, but because she and Ike were *sharing* a dog. Eisenhower must have heard it too, for the incandescent smile she saw in the mirror seemed to lighten the whole sky.

§

The next morning when Kay went into the office, Tex said, "Hey, Kay, we've got a new project. The Old Man has decided he wants a dog for his birthday. Operation Dog, he's calling it. Seems to be quite excited about it, too." He shook his head. "Although I don't know what in the hell he's going to do with a dog when he goes to—"

He shut his mouth quickly, and Kay knew why. Operation Torch was now just a month away, and Tex was in charge of packing up the office for the move to the St. George Hotel in Algiers, designated as the North African headquarters. But the operation was supposed to be a secret. Eisenhower, with his usual skill in misdirection, had ordered Tex and Butch to put up maps of Norway where visitors to the office—journalists and broadcasters from the BBC and the various American press bureaus—would be sure to see them. The newspapers had been quick to notice and were already beginning to speculate that the thousands of American troops now gathering at Scapa Flow in Scotland would be fighting the Germans in Norway.

Kay didn't answer Tex. She knew as much about North Africa

as he did, but she didn't like to think about it. She was a British civilian, a volunteer, not an official member of Eisenhower's staff. She wouldn't be going with them. She had already said a hasty goodbye to Dick, whose unit was part of the task force that would be landing at Oran, east of Algiers. She swallowed, thinking that she would probably be reassigned to the London motor pool and already feeling bereft and abandoned.

But nobody had left yet, and in the meantime, her job was to find a dog for the General. *Their* dog. She didn't ask herself why that thought made her almost giddy with pleasure. If she had, she might have remembered her mother's caution. *Dangerous.*

∾

Operation Dog got underway immediately and Kay and Beetle (who was really rather nice, when he wasn't being Ike's sonofabitch) began looking for candidates. They found what they wanted at the Duke Street Kennels, near Selfridge's. Two possibilities, actually: a sweet-tempered year-old Scottie named Angus and a coal-black three-month-old puppy, the spitting image of MacTavish. Beetle fancied the older dog because he was housebroken, but Kay fell in love with the puppy because he was so lively and alert.

"Not housebroken yet, though," Beetle said with a frown. "Ike will do better with a dog that already knows his manners."

"Why don't we let the Boss choose?" Kay suggested, and with a shrug, Beetle agreed. They took both dogs to the office, where Angus sat placidly on the General's rug and the puppy piddled on it, then strutted around proudly, claiming the territory as his own.

The General crouched down. "Come here, fella," he said to both of the dogs. Angus, the picture of Scottish dignity and decorum, stayed where he was. But the puppy bounced up to Eisenhower, put both paws on his knee, and boldly licked his nose.

"Some cheek," Kay said with a little laugh.

Ike picked up the dog and held him. "Think I'll keep this one, Beetle."

Beetle nodded. "Yes, sir. Come on, Angus," he said, and tugged on Angus's leash.

"Good job, Kay," the Boss said when Beetle had closed the door. He put the puppy in her arms. "Does the little fellow have a name?"

"Yes, sir," Kay said, so happy she could hardly stand still. "He's got a pedigree a mile long. According to his papers, he is Laird Dougal of Douglas Glen. He answers to Dougal."

"Well, let's see how long it takes him to learn his new name," Eisenhower said. "I'm calling him Telek."

She tilted her head. "Telek?"

"T-E-L-E-K," he said. "As far as the staff is concerned, it stands for Telegraph Cottage. But I'll tell you, privately, that it's Telegraph Cottage—and Kay." He wasn't touching her, but she felt as if his glance were embracing her. "Two things in my life that allow me to bear the rest of it." His voice roughened. "Which is pretty goddamned hellacious right about now."

"Telek." She buried her face in the puppy's fur. "Thank you," she said in a muffled voice.

"No," Ike said. "I'm the one who's thanking *you*." He leaned toward her, so close that she thought for one crazy instant that he might be going to kiss her. Then he seemed to catch himself. He took a step back and retreated behind his desk, where he stood indecisively for a moment, then cleared his throat.

"You know I'm leaving for North Africa at the end of this month," he said abruptly.

She could only nod. Of course she knew.

"The staff will join me in Algiers after the area is secure and stabilized. We'll be there for the duration—as long as it takes to takes to run the Nazis out of the Mediterranean." He paused, then spoke, slowly and distinctly, almost as if he were weighing each word. "This is a . . . personal request, Kay. It's not an order. I would like you to come to North Africa and drive for me, if you're willing." He nodded at Telek. "And take care of our dog."

Her heart beat faster. She felt her throat get tight. "General Eisenhower, I—"

"Wait. Don't answer just yet." He straightened and picked up a handful of papers, turning half away, not looking at her. "Think about it. But let me know your decision tomorrow. I need to get Tex started on the paperwork."

The little dog nuzzling her neck, Kay stared at him, wide-eyed. She hadn't dared to hope that he would ask, but she already knew her answer. Later, she would tell people—and write, in her first memoir—that she was eager to go to North Africa to be near Dick, who would be with General Fredendall. And that was true. *She* did want to be near Dick. Going to North Africa would make it possible to see him, once in a while. But at that moment, Major Richard Arnold might have been on the moon.

"Yes," she said quietly. Then, more loudly, resolutely, "Yes, I want to go, sir, very much. Thank you."

He turned to look at her, his gaze unreadable, and she wondered whether he was surprised by her eagerness. Should she have pretended reluctance, caution?

He gave her a lopsided grin. "Very good. Your young man—he's with Fredendall, is he? No doubt he'll be glad to hear that you won't be too far away."

She pressed her lips together, pushing down her disappointment. She must have misunderstood. "Yes, sir," she said quietly. "I'm sure he will."

He studied her for a moment, as if he wanted to say something else. But he only nodded.

"Very well," he said gruffly. "Now take that dog and get the hell out of here so I can go to work. Don't you know there's a war on?"

After Kay left the office with the Scottie, Ike sat down to the usual stacks of orders. There wasn't much time before the North African operation and there were still hundreds of tasks to be done, tasks he couldn't delegate, decisions only the commander in chief could make.

Commander in chief. His rapid rise still seemed almost incredible to him, although he thought it might also be viewed as providential. He wasn't much on organized religion, but he believed in a God who took care of his own—a righteous God who was watching out for the Allies and was ready to help them kick the Axis powers back to the devil, where they belonged. He smiled, remembering what Georgie Patton, who was something of a mystic, had said right here in the office a couple of weeks before. That the Almighty Himself had given Ike his job and was writing the orders for his promotions. That this was true, Georgie claimed, was demonstrated by Ike's initials, D. D. "Divine Destiny" Eisenhower.

Ike had laughed and told Georgie he could go to hell, but he had to admit that there might be something to it. He had chosen a military career, not out of a sense of higher calling or patriotic duty, but only because West Point offered a free education, which meant that he wouldn't have to work his way through college the way his brothers had. But they'd been successful, where his army career had gone nowhere. As a staff officer, he had stalled out at major—three steps above the rank he held when he left West Point—for sixteen long years. Just thirty months before, he had been a lieutenant colonel who had never commanded so much as a squad in combat. And now he was Commanding General, European Theater of Operations.

But Ike had always been ready to make decisions and shoulder responsibilities, even though there hadn't been much opportunity for either in the peacetime army. *Peace* was what was wrong with the army, in his opinion. The officer corps was made up of tired men, old men, men who were hopelessly inept. It was so thick with deadwood that it was a fire hazard. War was a purging flame, and it was the fire and smoke from Pearl Harbor, like the pillars of cloud and fire that led the Children of Israel out of Egypt, that had finally shown America the way forward. War, with all of its pain and anguish, was what brought out the very best in a man, and in a nation. As a man, as an officer, as the commander in chief, he knew he was ready.

But the challenge was immense. With three task forces leaving from multiple debarkation points and landing at three different points along a thousand-mile front, Torch was unquestionably the most complex operation in military history. It was hard to be optimistic about the outcome. Most of the troops weren't battle-tested, logistics were a nightmare, communication was unreliable, and the Mediterranean weather was a constant worry. Still, he had told Georgie that as D-Day approached, he had never felt better.

"I could lick Tarzan," he'd said, and grinned with all the confidence he could muster.

It was a lie. It was all bravado, an attempt to conceal his never-ending uncertainty about the decisions he was making, about the prospects of victory, about the cost in men and materiel. It was getting harder to concentrate on the job that had to be done. Worst of all, it was getting harder to look self-assured, confident, optimistic.

But he *had* to look confident and optimistic, had to be on top of every situation. He had to keep up the façade, no matter how much effort it took. And that, he confessed to himself, was the reason he wanted—no, he *needed*—Kay with him. Unlike everyone else in his command, she had no expectations and no agenda. Nobody had ordered her to do what she was doing; she had volunteered, and she served without question, criticism, or hidden purpose. He needed the companionship of a woman, especially a vital, spirited, interesting woman whose smile was almost enough to make him forget that there was a war. Never mind the other thing—the powerful physical attraction he could not deny but wasn't quite willing to acknowledge—*that* was why he needed her. She could make him forget the war, and he needed to forget the war.

Which was why he had blurted out the question a moment ago—the question that had been nagging at him for weeks. He wanted Kay with him in North Africa, and he was delighted and relieved that she had said yes, even though he knew she had agreed so she could be closer to that young man she was engaged to.

But there were difficulties. For one thing, she was a civilian, a British civilian, and a volunteer. Attaching her to his command was going to take some doing, and there would be questions. For another, there was the appearance of the thing, as Butch had coyly reminded him just the other day. He knew that the staff had covertly code-named the cottage Da-de-da, Morse for the letter K, and he had caught their knowing glances more than once. But Beetle had no room to criticize, since he was sleeping with that beautiful American nurse, Ethel Westermann, *and* making arrangements for her to go to North Africa with him. Ike didn't intend to sleep with Kay—after all, she was engaged to that Arnold fellow. But people would have their suspicions, and some wouldn't be shy about saying so.

Suspicions. He glanced down at Mamie's photo on his desk, at the eyes that always seemed to follow him as he moved. His wife, whom he loved quite sincerely—but no longer passionately, as he had when they were young—and to whom he fully intended to return when the war was over. He was uncomfortably aware of Mamie's jealous possessiveness, so to avoid provoking her wrath he had omitted any mention of Kay in his letters home. And he was especially careful to assure her at least once in every letter, sometimes twice or three times, that she was the only woman in his heart. Still—

His thoughts were interrupted by a knock at the door, and Tex came in with a document. "Sorry, sir, but this has to go out this afternoon."

Reaching for his pen, Ike said, in an offhand way, "Kay will be joining us in North Africa, Tex. Find out what's involved—the paperwork, I mean—and get it straightened out for her."

Tex's gingery eyebrows went up. He hesitated as if he were about to ask a question, but all he said was "I'll take care of it, sir."

"Good." Ike took the document, scanned it, and scrawled his signature. "What's next?" he asked, handing it back.

"The Chiefs of Staff. At four, sir."

"Right," Ike said. "Tell Kay to get the car. I'll be down in ten minutes."

ॐ

For Kay, the General's invitation changed everything. Before, she had been an outsider in the office, the temporary who would be left behind when the staff closed up shop at Grosvenor Square and moved to North Africa. Now, she was one of them. She was going *with* them—with him!—and she was so excited that she could scarcely breathe.

But in another way, the invitation changed nothing. She couldn't be sure why he had asked her. Was it because he wanted her with him, or because he thought he was doing something nice for her and Dick? *That* seemed more likely, she told herself. Didn't it?

The question—*why?*—hung like a blinking sign on the back wall of her mind, but Kay was too busy to think about it. Beetle had put her in charge of the Boss's birthday party. The big day, October 14, was filled with meetings, and it was early evening before the family could gather at the cottage. Mickey served as bartender and Moaney and Hunt produced a baked ham, sweet potatoes, and potato salad with plenty of mustard and chopped pickles, made from the General's personal recipe. For dessert, Mickey carried in a coconut cake with three red frosting stars and three candles. Tex broke out the champagne and they all toasted the Boss.

And then came the big moment—the presentation of the

General's birthday present. Kay led Telek out, dressed up with a red ribbon around his neck and wearing a funny little mini-harness and parachute that she had gotten from a parachute guy at Eighth Air Force headquarters. Ike read the note tied to Telek's harness, promising that if the Scottie got airdropped into the wrong territory, the finder could return him to the Commander in Chief in Algiers for a thousand-dollar reward.

"A thousand bucks!" Butch whistled. "Jesus, I wouldn't pay that for my *wife*."

That brought a big laugh. Then they broke into nine boisterous verses of a song Butch had written. Called "Send 'Em Ike!" it was sung to the tune of "Yankee Doodle." The General, delighted, sang loudly and wildly off-key, with Telek—obviously thinking himself the star of the show—adding exclamatory barks at the appropriate moments.

> When clouds of war in 'Forty-one
> Came thundering down upon us,
> We had to pick a Man of Steel
> To fight the foe Ger-Manus.
>
> "Send 'em Ike!" arose the cry,
> From the hills and valleys,
> He's the man to track them down
> And stow them in the galleys.

After that, there was poker and music on the phonograph—Ike's favorites, "Beer Barrel Polka" and "One Dozen Roses"—and a great many more toasts. Finally, the party was over and the last guest had either staggered out the door or up the stairs to bed. Ike fixed one more drink and he and Kay sat down in front of the fire.

"Any cigarettes left?" he asked.

Kay took out a pack of Camels. "Just one," she said, holding it up. She was now the official holder of Ike's cigarettes, responsible for trying (without a lot of success) to keep him to a three-pack maximum.

"Well, let's have it, damn it," he said. She took out her own and they smoked as the fire burned down to embers and Telek nestled, asleep, in Ike's lap. After a few moments, he said, "Thank you for the party, Kay." He smiled down at Telek. "And my dog."

"Hey, wait a minute," she objected, teasing. "You said he was *my* dog."

"Our dog," Ike agreed with a chuckle. "Let's take him to the office in the morning." He stroked Telek's ears. "It's going to be a long war. He might as well get used to his job."

"What job?"

"I'm appointing him Morale Officer—second lieutenant." He gave Kay a sideways glance. "Our dog is going to North Africa with us."

Kay exhaled. *Our dog . . . with us.* The way Ike put it, it seemed so easy and ordinary and *right*, as if they were only going up to Oxford for an afternoon's sightseeing. "I'm glad," she replied. "I'd hate to leave the little guy behind—he'd probably forget who we are." She glanced at her watch, then stubbed out her cigarette. "Speaking of going to the office in the morning, it's late. I'd better head for my billet."

Ike stood up, the little dog under one arm. "Telek and I will walk you to the car." Companionably, naturally, as if he had done it a thousand times, he slipped the other arm around Kay's shoulders. She felt its weight and its warmth as though it were wrapped around her heart.

The cottage was dark and quiet behind them and the October sky held a half-full moon and a chilly infinity of stars. Somewhere deep in the silent woods, a nightingale was singing. As Kay opened the car door, Ike turned her toward him, put a finger under her chin, and tipped up her face. His was silver in the moonlight, his expression intent, and she willed herself to remember how he looked at that moment. Her heart was thudding.

Boyishly, almost bashfully, he said, "Would you consider giving the birthday guy a kiss?"

Without a word, she leaned against him. Their kiss was light at first, friendly, perhaps testing. Then he seemed to have decided something, for—still holding Telek—he put his free arm around her, drawing her hard against him and holding her fiercely, his mouth on hers, demanding, commanding. In the dark, her eyes closed, she knew she had come to an entirely new place. She entered it eagerly, gladly, folding herself into the promise of his embrace, until Telek whimpered and squirmed and they pulled apart.

They were both laughing, Ike with a wryly amused chuckle, she with a full, surging pleasure, thinking, *He asked me to go to North Africa because he wanted me with him!* She was sure of it now. On a nearer branch, the nightingale unfurled another song, as if celebrating with them. For years after, she would remember how giddily happy she had been that night.

As if that weren't enough, there was one thing more—something, she thought, that he had just this moment decided. He stepped back and cleared his throat.

"Meant to tell you that we're taking the train to Scotland on Sunday. Just three of us—you, me, and Butch. You'll be driving when we're up there," he added, "so dress warm. I'm told it's pretty cold." He held up the Scottie in both hands over his head, dancing him, the way a man dances a child. "We'd better leave our little guy with Tex. We don't want him to catch cold."

"Scotland," she said, and felt the laughter bubbling foolishly, ecstatically in her throat. The two of them, together: this was how it was now. Not forever, not next year, perhaps not even next week. But *now*, this was how it was, and it was enough. She took a breath. "You continually surprise me."

"That's the way I like it," he said, and dropped a light kiss on her hair. "Surprise keeps us on our toes. Goodnight, Irish."

As she got into the car, he stood watching, holding Telek against him and whistling "One Dozen Roses."

Early on Sunday morning, Kay, Ike, and Butch boarded the General's private railroad coach, code-named *Bayonet*, for the sixteen-hour ride to western Scotland, where the First Division was practicing night amphibious landings. *Bayonet* was new, carpeted and teak-paneled and quite elegant, with a small conference room, an office for Eisenhower, and sleeping quarters for four. Kay had brought along several folders of paperwork and she and Ike settled down to work in the office. But he had a weary look and a raspy cough, and it seemed hard for him to focus.

After lunch in the dining car, they played bridge for a while, intently, as if to shut out everything else. And then Ike put down his cards and said, "I don't know about the rest of you, but I'm bone tired. It's been a helluva week and we'll be up all night with the landings. We'd better get a nap."

In her compartment, Kay took off her jacket and tie and her shoes and lay down in her berth under a light blanket, enjoying the swaying of the car and the rhythmic clickety-clack of the train wheels. She was just dozing off when the door opened quietly and Ike came in. His tie was off, too, and he was in his stocking feet.

"Don't get up," he said, closing the door behind him. "My insomnia's been bad. I didn't get any sleep last night and I can't sleep now. Thought I might just lie down beside you, if it won't disturb you."

Kay concealed her astonishment. "There's not a lot of room, but you're welcome." She turned on her side with her back to the wall, making room for him in the narrow berth, and lifted the blanket. He lay down and turned away from her, fitting his back against her as if they were two spoons in a drawer. She rested her cheek against his back and her free arm over him, and in a few moments, his breathing slowed and he was asleep.

She lay awake for a long time, deeply aware of his male scent of tobacco and Old Spice, thinking, wondering, questioning. Dick's presence in her life, once so vibrant and compelling, had retreated into the shadows. Ike's commanding presence, his *force*, filled her waking hours and her dreams.

But she had no illusions. Whatever this was, whatever it became, it was for the moment only and entirely separate from her relationship with Dick, whom she planned to marry (yes, she did, truly she did) as soon as both their divorces were final. She supposed, too, that Ike's relationship with his wife was an entirely separate thing for him. When the war was over, he would return to her and the two of them would take up where they had left off. Whatever was now was *now*, only. No past, no future.

Still, as she drifted off to sleep with Ike fitted closely against her—the two of them breathing together, their hearts, she thought, beating together—she knew that a line had somehow been crossed. Her last thought as sleep came was her mother's word: *dangerous.* Yes, it was, she thought, yes.

She woke at dusk, as Ike swung his legs off the narrow berth. She stirred and he leaned over her. "I'm sorry, Irish." He bent to kiss her cheek.

Sorry? She lay still, eyes closed, unmoving. Sorry for lying beside her, sorry for leaving her, sorry for kissing her at the cottage? Or sorry for not turning toward her? As he closed the door, she lay awake, hearing those enigmatic words and trying—without success—to summon Dick's face against the encompassing, overwhelming strength of Ike's presence.

At midnight, they reached Kentallen, on the eastern shore of Loch Linnhe. Kay knew the loch must be beautiful, but the night was pitch black and the weather abominable—cold and wet, with near gale-force winds. They were met by Colonel Price of the British Army, who climbed into the front seat of the heavy staff car beside Kay, who took the wheel. With the General and Butch in the backseat and a caravan of eight or nine military vehicles behind them, she followed Price's directions to the first of a dozen landing points. She stayed in the car as Ike and Butch got out in the rain, trudged across wet fields to the headland, and watched men loaded with battle gear jump out of landing crafts and storm the beach. Then back in the car and on to another beach and another flotilla of landing crafts.

Kay was accustomed to driving unfamiliar staff vehicles on unfamiliar lanes, but this drive tested her to the limit. Between midnight and sunrise, she drove some ninety hellish miles. Blackout was rigidly imposed, the roads were little better than cart tracks, and it was sometimes impossible to know whether she was driving on the road or in the verge. Finally, as dawn broke on the bleak, wind-battered shore, they came to Admiralty House in the village of Inveraray, where the Royal Navy's Admiral Hewitt gave them breakfast.

Ike let everyone know that he wasn't happy with the disorganized chaos he'd seen on the beaches that night. He was worried about the untrained men and—worse—the inexperienced officers, who didn't seem to know what to do with the men after they were ashore. In a matter of weeks, they would be landing on the beaches of North Africa, possibly under hostile fire. "If they don't sharpen up by D-Day, they'll be sitting ducks," he said. After observing another couple of daytime landings at Inveraray, he was even more glum.

Their train left at four in the afternoon. The three of them had sandwiches and shared a bottle of wine. Then, exhausted, they went straight to their berths. Kay wondered whether Ike would join her again, but he didn't. The train pulled into Euston Station at 7:30 a.m., where Tex was waiting with the car—and Telek, who greeted them exuberantly. At the office, Ike said nothing at all to Kay about what had happened on the way to Scotland, but the next morning, she found an envelope on her desk.

In it was a greeting card with a picture of a bouquet of red roses. Inside was written just one word, *Thanks*, and the initials *DE*.

The weeks before the top-secret November 8 invasion were a blur of work and worry. Beetle's ulcer kicked up and Ethel, an experienced nurse, insisted that he go the hospital, leaving Kay, Tex, and Butch to carry on without him.

Butch was concerned about the cover story he was peddling to the newspapers to account for Ike's absence from London in early November. He was telling reporters that Ike would be flying to Washington to confer with the President. That part was fine—it was Mamie that Butch was worried about. She was bound to see the story in the papers and would be terribly disappointed when Ike didn't show up. He wished he could get word to her that the story was a ruse to fool the Jerries.

Beetle and Eisenhower were both worried about General Clark, who had boarded a submarine to the Mediterranean to carry out a dangerous liaison mission with Vichy officials and Resistance groups. It was a dicey business, but in the end Clark got back to the sub after a brief skirmish in the surf—without his pants.

And everybody who was in on Operation Torch was worried about the thousands of troops in scores of troopships already underway across an Atlantic crawling with German subs. Churchill was a quivering mass of nerves. Eisenhower had caught cold that rainy night in Scotland; he was pumped up on caffeine and cigarettes and looked as if he hadn't slept for a week. Watching him in the car and in the office, Kay was increasingly worried. Everything depended on him, on one man. What would happen if he got seriously sick?

A few days before Ike was due to fly to the operation's headquarters on Gibraltar, Butch pulled her out into the hallway. Very low and hesitantly, he said, "Kay, I wonder if you could do the Boss a favor."

"Of course," Kay said instantly. "If I can."

"He's not sleeping." Butch pulled on his cigarette. "I've been thinking that maybe you could stay over at the cottage tonight and . . . well, spoon with him, the way you did on the train. It might help him get some sleep."

Kay's breath caught in her throat, but when she searched his expression, she found no judgment in it. "How . . . how did you know?"

"A telegram came for Ike on the train's wireless." Butch grinned crookedly. "He wasn't in his compartment or his office. I knew he wasn't with me, so unless he'd jumped off the train, he had to be with you. I knocked. When you didn't answer, I opened the door a crack and peeked. And shut it again," he added hastily. "I decided that the telegram could wait until he woke up." He cocked his head. "I haven't said anything to Ike about it. Or anybody else. And I *won't*," he added emphatically. "This is just between you and me."

Kay gave him a hard, straight look, angry that she and Ike had been spied on. But at the same time, oddly relieved that Butch knew, and grateful for his silence. It was almost as if they were partners, conspiring to protect the General. But she had to clear something up.

"What you saw was all there was to see," she said firmly. "Just that. Nothing else."

"Don't get me wrong, Kay." Butch dropped his cigarette on the floor and stepped on it. "I've been sharing Ike's suite at the Dorchester for the past three months, and in all that time, I haven't seen him sleeping as peacefully as he was on that train, with you. Maybe he misses Mamie. Maybe it's just the comfort of a warm body." He paused. "I don't know what's going on between the two of you and I don't need to know. I'm just afraid he's going to be a basket case if he doesn't get some sleep."

Kay closed her eyes, fastening on the memory of Ike's body next to hers. She was trying to think how she could do what Butch was asking, what she could say to Ike, what would happen, what *might* happen, what would happen after that.

"I can't, Butch," she said finally. She searched for a way to explain and couldn't find one. Helplessly, she lifted her shoulders and let them fall. "I just . . . I just can't."

He studied her for a moment. "Yeah," he said regretfully. "Sorry, Irish. Dumb idea. Forget I said anything about it."

I'm sorry, too, Kay thought. *I'm really, really sorry.*

❧

Ike wasn't sure exactly what he had intended when he went to Kay that evening on the train, but he knew why he went. Or rather, he knew what he told himself. He hadn't been able to sleep and he was desperately weary. He had simply wanted to be near her, just for the human comfort of it. That was all, nothing more, although that, to his mind, was enough. For a long time there hadn't been anything more than comfort between himself and Mamie—the fragility of her health, her lack of interest, his preoccupation with his work—and just the warmth of her body beside him had always been enough. He was past fifty, for God's sake. Of course it was enough.

But to his surprise, when he had wakened with Kay asleep and warm against him in the narrow berth, he had realized that just being near her might not be enough. He felt the unexpected stir of desire and understood that he shouldn't have come, that if he didn't leave quickly, he might do something that would complicate the situation even further. What in God's name had he thought he was doing? He must have been out of his mind. He had compromised both himself and her. What if they had been discovered? His whispered *I'm sorry, Irish*, to the sleeping girl had been an impulsive testimony to his complicated regret.

And with Operation Torch just ahead, he sure as hell didn't need any more complications. After all the months of planning and placating and appeasing and knocking heads together, the day he'd been working for was about to arrive. Everything that could be done had been done. If he had overlooked anything, if he had miscalculated, it was too goddamned late to do anything about it. They would simply have to muddle along the best they could and trust to luck—to Providence—to carry them through.

His command team was scheduled to leave for Gibraltar in six Flying Fortresses, taking off from Hurn Aerodrome near Bournemouth on Tuesday morning, November 3. But a storm had moved in and the planes were grounded. The flight was rescheduled and the team went back to London.

They spent a rainy Wednesday evening at the cottage, he and

Kay, Butch and Beetle and Ethel. They had supper and listened to music on the radio and tried to pass the time by playing bridge. But they were all nervy and on edge, and nobody could concentrate on the cards. At ten, Butch had climbed the stairs to bed and Beetle and Ethel went to the kitchen for a glass of milk. Kay was headed back to her billet, and Ike went to the door with her.

"I'd walk you out to your car," he said, "but it's raining." The excuse—for that's what it was—sounded flimsy in his ears. He was a coward, he thought, remembering that moment, that stir of desire, on the train. He was afraid not of her, but of himself. Awkwardly, he added, "Hope you don't mind."

"Not a bit of it." She took her umbrella out of the stand by the door. "You've already got a cold. You have to stay healthy, Ike. Everybody's counting on you, you know."

The gold light glinted in her auburn hair and he could smell her perfume, a soft, intoxicating fragrance. She seemed suddenly very dear, and he forgot why he had decided it was better not to go out to the car. He only knew that he wanted desperately to kiss her but had to fight against the desire, conscious that Beetle or Ethel could walk in on them at any moment. Still, there were things he needed to say, and he was going to say them, regardless. The radio was playing a Noël Coward song—"I'll See You Again"—and he lowered his voice under the music.

"Kay, I want to thank you for keeping me sane in the past few months. You've become very important to me." Telek, on the floor, pushed between them and he bent over to pick up the little dog, glad for the diversion. "You and Telek," he said, scratching the Scottie's ears. "If anything should happen to me, I want you to know—"

"Nothing's going to happen." Her eyes darkened and she put a hand on his arm. "Don't say that, Ike. Please."

"Then I won't. I'll just say, I'll see you again—in Algiers." He could feel the pressure of her fingers through the fabric of his sleeve. "You'll be there for Christmas, I understand."

She nodded. "Tex untied all the red tape so I could get my

passport—which includes visas for Portugal and Spain, just in case." She laughed a little, lightly, and pulled her hand away. "Just in case we're torpedoed and end up there, I guess."

His gut tightened. "Don't even think it," he said gruffly. "Don't forget your Beretta." He paused. "Tex says you're sailing on the *Strathallan*."

"Yes, in the company of four thousand men and a bevy of WACs and nurses." She tilted her head, her blue eyes dancing mischievously. "Should be fun, don't you think?"

He chuckled. "Sounds like a party. In the meantime—" He stopped. Drawn by her glance and by the laughter on her lips, he gave up fighting the desire and surrendered, bending forward, kissing her, his mouth on hers as long as he dared.

At last he heard Beetle say something to Ethel in the kitchen and pulled back, feeling clumsy. "In the meantime, don't take any chances. That's an order, Kay. I want to see you—safely—in North Africa."

I'll see you again, whenever spring breaks through again. The words of the song echoed between them. Her eyes were misty and she was smiling.

"You will," she promised. "Yes, you will."

But it was a very near-run thing.

CHAPTER SIX
The General's Family Photograph

Washington, D.C.
October–November 1942

"Ike's coming home!" Mamie cried, dancing into the living room of the comfortable Wardman Park apartment she shared with Ruth Butcher. It was almost noon, but she was still wearing her pink ruffled nightgown and waving the morning edition of the *Washington Post*—just one of the newspapers that were her lifeline to Ike.

"He's on his way to Washington," she crowed, "to confer with the President! He'll be here soon!"

"Oh, gosh, Mamie! That's wonderful." Ruth looked up from the polish she was applying to her nails. Then her expression became skeptical. "Who says he's coming? You know those gossip columnists—they can spin a story out of thin air."

Mamie dropped onto the sofa, her excitement spilling over. "It's not a gossip column, Ruth. It's news, See? Right there!" She put her finger on the headline on page two: EISENHOWER TO RETURN FOR WAR CONSULTATIONS. "The trip was supposed to be hush-hush, but a reporter got wind of it and asked the President at his press conference yesterday. Roosevelt said he couldn't comment on the movements of army officers. He thought it wasn't "appropriate" to report travel, since the enemy might be listening. He sounded pretty huffy about it."

"Well, if FDR was annoyed, it must be true," Ruth said, capping the nail polish bottle. She pushed her brown hair out of her eyes. "Does the *Post* say whether Butch is coming with him?"

"It says he'll be accompanied by 'several of his top command staff,'" Mamie said. "Which must mean Butch."

"Does the article say when they're coming?" Ruth asked, frowning. "Maybe we ought to cancel tomorrow's mah-jongg party. If so, I suppose I'll have to call the girls and let them know."

Mamie understood why Ruth didn't sound all that excited about her husband's return. The war had come at a difficult time for Butch and Ruth. They had been growing apart for several years, and while they had tried to resolve their differences, Mamie knew that the marriage was shaky. She didn't like to be critical of Butch—she understood how much Ike relied on him for support and friendship right now, when he was so far from home and lonely and carrying so many responsibilities. But from what she had seen in the years she and Ike had known the Butchers, Ruth was the one who had given the most to the marriage, managing a big house and raising their daughter. Butch, on the other hand, liked to hang around with journalists—he managed Washington's radio station WJSV—which meant late nights out with the boys. Unfortunately, there were too many husbands like Butch. Mamie pitied their wives and was glad Ike wasn't like that. Apart from that unsettling year when Ike was all by his lonesome in the Philippines, she had always known where his heart lay. She found that reassuring, especially since she was about to turn forty-six. She did all she could to ward off the wrinkles, but she knew they were creeping up on her.

To answer Ruth's question, Mamie scanned the article again. "No, it doesn't say when." She frowned. "How frustrating."

Ruth waved her hands impatiently, drying the bright-red nail enamel. "You'd think Butch or Ike could have written to tell us. Or called."

"It must have been a sudden decision." Mamie folded the newspaper. "I got a letter from Ike yesterday, and he didn't say a word about it." She pulled her brows together. "Gee, I hope everything is okay."

Ike had written that he was pleased at being elected to Honorary Membership in the Abilene Rotary Club and that he'd been smoking too much and had gotten Mickey to ration his cigarettes for him—he was down to three packs of Camels a day. He had added, in a reassuring way, that she was the only one he was in love with. "I've never been in love with anyone else and don't want any other wife."

That unusual assertion had jumped out at her, since he had never written anything remotely like it before, ever. It had made her feel good, of course—what wife of twenty-six years wouldn't want to hear her husband say she was still his one-and-only? But she had puzzled over it, since it was so unlikely. Now, though, it occurred to her that maybe he was already looking forward to seeing her on this trip to Washington and the idea had filled him with an eager pleasure—so eager that it just bubbled over. Ike was his own best censor. He occasionally wrote about the people who worked for him. He'd said that his driver, a man named Gilbey, was called "Lord" Gilbey by the staff because he had an aristocratic British manner, and he sometimes mentioned Mickey and Butch or Beetle. But he never told her what he was doing or where he had been. He never wrote *anything* the enemy might want to read.

Ruth examined her nail polish. "You are a silly-dilly worry-wart, Mamie. Of *course* everything is okay. Other than the war, I mean." She uncapped the bottle again and began to repair a smudge. "Why wouldn't it be?"

Mamie frowned, thinking of all the reasons Ike might have been ordered back to Washington. "Because that's the way they do things in the army," she said, beginning now to feel anxious. "If you're head of a command, they leave you pretty much alone until you do something they don't like. Then they bring you home and call you on the carpet."

She hoped to high heaven that wasn't what was going on. From everything she read in the papers and heard on the radio, Ike's situation over there in London had to be terribly touchy. Of course, he'd never complain about that to her. He'd always said that the home front was *her* job and he didn't want to trouble her pretty little head with the problems on his desk.

But from what she read in the newspapers, he had to satisfy not only President Roosevelt and General Marshall, but Prime Minister Churchill (who seemed to be as bad as FDR about stirring the pot) and half a dozen jealous British generals, as well as the French, who were letting those doggone Germans run all over them and were never *satisfied* with anything. It would probably be a surprise if poor Ike *hadn't* gotten crosswise with somebody.

"I sure do hope he's not in trouble," she said, half under her breath.

"Now, Mamie." There was a touch of impatience in Ruth's voice. "You've got to stop thinking like that. From everything I read, Ike is doing a good job in a difficult situation. Nobody's going to *reprimand* him, for pity's sake."

"I sincerely hope not," Mamie said, jumping up off the sofa. "But now that I know he's coming, I'd better get busy. I need to get my hair done, and Chloe is always so booked up."

"You might ask her to experiment a little," Ruth suggested. "You've been wearing those bangs ever since I've known you. Maybe something . . . a little different?"

It wasn't the first time Ruth had made the suggestion, but Mamie always brushed the advice aside. She liked her bangs—they made her look just like Claudette Colbert. "Oh, and I saw a lovely little pink dress on Garfinkle's sale page this morning," she said. "Five dollars off. Come with me, Ruth, and we'll have tea in the Greenbrier Garden—you know, that new tearoom on the fifth floor."

It wasn't that she actually needed a new dress—her closet was absolutely stuffed and she had a *lot* of clothes in storage. But it would make her feel better. And really, she had been losing so much weight, ten pounds in the three months Ike had been gone. Most of her clothes just hung on her. She needed something feminine and flowery, with lots of little ruffles and flounces to help disguise how *bony* she was. She was afraid that Ike would scold her for not eating enough, which was unfortunately true. She slept so late in the morning that she usually just combined breakfast with lunch and then ate dinner half-heartedly, when she ate at all. But sleeping late—until noon if you could—was good for your skin. One of her doctors had told her so, and she had taken his advice ever since. She knew it annoyed Ruth, who was an early riser, but that couldn't be helped.

"Sure, I'll go shopping with you," Ruth said, standing up and brushing off her skirt. "You've been cooped up here for too long. I'm glad you're getting out."

Mamie frowned. She liked Ruth, but she didn't appreciate her nagging. She didn't go out much these days because, with Ike gone, nothing held much pleasure, and because she didn't like to be recognized, even though most people—except for the newspaper reporters—were usually well-meaning, like the soldiers in the restaurant, the day she ate out with Cookie.

But the reporters were the worst. They had been after her nonstop, lurking in the Wardman's downstairs lobby, even crowding onto the elevator or tagging along after her when she went out. She had started using the freight elevator at the back of the building for just that reason and went out only when she had to.

And she *never* went to a party, although her name seemed to pop up on a great many invitation lists these days. Of course, she was pleased, because the invitations showed that people understood how important Ike was, now that he was a *three*-star general and got his name in the newspaper almost every day. But while she longed to go to the parties, she just didn't dare. She couldn't say yes to one invitation without saying yes to all of them, and *that* would be utterly impossible. Wartime Washington was awash in parties. She didn't want to risk being criticized for picking favorites, because that might cast a bad light on Ike. Worse yet, she might find herself seated with somebody who wasn't on the right side of some political issue she didn't understand. Mamie had never cared two hoots about politics, and she knew she wasn't at all astute, politically speaking. A photograph of her with the wrong person might damage Ike's reputation.

And of course there were the people who'd say that she shouldn't be going to parties at all. Not when all those flag-draped coffins were being shipped back from overseas every day—so many that General Marshall, Ike's boss, had had to stop writing condolences to all the families of soldiers killed in battle and send Western Union telegrams instead. One newspaper columnist had testily criticized a party that priced out at an exorbitant forty dollars a plate, "which would provide 1,180 cartridges for Marine rifles in the jungles of Guadalcanal."

One reason for the plethora of parties was that wartime Washington was an extremely complex social world. There were the old-money cave-dwellers, mostly elderly ladies and gentlemen who could trace their families back to the days when Georgetown was a busy little port city and Washington was nothing but a dreary swamp. There were the rich manufacturing magnates who had come to the city to take dollar-a-year jobs in the government and whose ambitious wives gave the very biggest and best parties with the most star-studded guest lists, based on the calculation that the best way to become a celebrity was to seat one at your dining table.

As well, there was the Congress, with its attention to social rank and etiquette; the Roosevelt White House, with its orbiting luminaries (its luster somewhat dimmed by the fact that it served the worst food in town); and the diplomatic community, where each embassy had its own nation's protocols and practices, which sometimes intersected but more often collided with those of other embassies. No wonder the *Daily News* quoted a popular fellow-about-Washington as saying that he had never, in forty years in the city "seen anything like the parties going on now. Do you know, my dear, I've dined out for ten nights straight, and at least two cocktail parties every night for the last month. It's a *scandal*."

So—since Mamie had been sitting out every party since Ike had been promoted to Allied commander—she was especially glad to put on a nice dress, a hat, gloves, and pumps, and go shopping for a pretty dress to wear when her husband came home. She and Ruth celebrated the occasion with a cup of tea and an egg salad sandwich in the Greenbrier Garden, which was lovely, with potted philodendrons hanging from the ceiling and music piped in. Then they went to the A&P, where they combined their ration points to buy a standing rib roast that Ike and Butch would enjoy. Ruth drove. Gasoline rationing was due to begin the next month, and after that it would be harder to get around. But Mamie, never a confident driver, had given up driving long ago. She had been only too glad when Ike's first star had qualified him for an orderly—Mickey—who could drive her where she needed to go, and she was always glad when Ruth volunteered to take her somewhere. A driver was a very handy thing to have.

But Mamie and Ruth didn't get a chance to serve their husbands that lovely roast. Ruth cleaned the house and Mamie got her hair permed and wore her new pink dress several days running (in case Ike surprised her), but their preparations were in vain. Ruth was annoyed at having canceled the mah-jongg party for nothing, and Mamie was so nervous she could hardly sit still. Finally, she screwed up her courage and called General Marshall's office to ask whether the newspaper story had been true. Not long after, an aide called to tell her that it was all a big rumor and suggest archly that she shouldn't believe *everything* she read.

"That said," he added, "you might want to keep an eye on the newspapers or listen to the radio. You may find an important announcement in the next few days."

So Ike wasn't coming, after all. With tears of bitter disappointment, Mamie hung her dress in the closet, next to the old tweed suit of Ike's that she'd kept when she put the rest of his clothes in storage. She laid the rough sleeve against her face, breathing in the lingering scent of cigarettes and Old Spice, and cried. Then she took a nap.

The next day, Ruth cooked the roast and made a deep-dish apple pie, Mamie set the table with flowers, and they invited their friends Cookie Wilson and Cheryl Sullivan, both military "widows," to dinner and a bridge game afterward. Mamie had only one glass of wine. She felt she could trust Cookie and Cheryl, but she also knew that people loved to gossip, and she had to be very careful.

For the next day or two, Mamie did as General Marshall's aide had suggested. She watched the newspapers and listened to the radio, which she was in the habit of doing anyway. With Ike gone, she suffered terribly from insomnia and seldom managed to get to sleep before the wee small hours. She began and ended her day with the morning and evening papers, and she made it a point not to miss any of the radio newscasts. On Sunday nights, she always listened to Walter Winchell, with his staccato delivery of "Good evening, Mr. and Mrs. America from border to border and coast to coast and all the ships at sea." And every night, on the Mutual Broadcasting System, she tuned in to Gabriel Heatter, who comforted her (and everybody else in America) with "Ahh, there's *good* news tonight!" When he couldn't dodge the bad news, he reported it in a funereal, almost mocking voice.

And then she saw what she was looking for, in Washington's *Evening Star.* AMERICANS TAKE ALGIERS! screamed one headline. ALLIES SEIZE 1000 MILES OF NORTH AFRICAN COASTLINE. And on the same page, the Associated Press reported: HIGH STRATEGY PRECEDES U.S. ATTACKS. PLANS LAID MONTHS IN ADVANCE AND ENEMY KEPT GUESSING. The article credited General Dwight D. Eisenhower, Commanding General of the European Theater, with a "monumental secret planning effort" that involved both American and British forces in a major deception designed to conceal the real targets of the invasion:

> Feints and deliberately misleading information played a
> part in deceiving the Nazi intelligence system, which was
> led to believe that General Eisenhower was traveling to

Washington when in actuality he was settling into Allied headquarters on Gibraltar to oversee landings along the North African coast. German military intelligence appears to have been convinced that the more than 150 Allied ships that sailed through the Straits of Gibraltar were on their way to resupply Malta and sent Sicily-based Luftwaffe squadrons to Malta to bomb the convoy as it arrived. Instead, it was bound for Oran and Algiers. German planes had no targets.

And then Mamie saw how she had been fooled and why, and her disappointment turned to a proud delight as she understood that Ike's stratagems, so cleverly and deceitfully planned, had fooled Hitler too.

∽

A couple of mornings later, Mamie was still asleep when Ruth knocked on the door and shouted, "Mamie, it's eleven o'clock. Come on, get up, lazy-bones! You've got to see this!"

"See what?" Mamie asked drowsily, pulling the blanket up to her chin. She had stayed up very late the night before, clipping articles out of the newspapers and pasting them in the scrapbook she was keeping. *Her husband*, her very own Ike, was being credited with the successful invasion of North Africa. There had been some sort of political disagreement about a French admiral named Darlan that she didn't understand, but other than that, it looked like everything had gone Ike's way. He was being praised in Washington and London. She was very proud.

Ruth knocked again. "You've got to see *Life* magazine!" she said excitedly. "Ike is featured in the Close-Up section—nine whole pages. There's even a photo of you."

"Me? In *Life* magazine?" Mamie jumped out of bed and pulled on a pink ruffled housecoat over her nightgown. Of all the incredible things that were happening, this was really the *most* astonishing.

"Yes, you. Come on, Sleeping Beauty. I've mixed Bloody Marys and I'll make us an omelet. We're celebrating!"

A few minutes later, Mamie was at the table with coffee and a Bloody Mary, leafing through the magazine while Ruth sliced mushrooms and grated cheese. The weekly Close-Up feature was an important section of each issue, reserved for very important people. And there was her husband in a full-page photo, looking incredibly handsome and military, three stars gleaming on his shoulders. The article was subtitled GENERAL EISENHOWER, WHO HATES TO MISS ANY "GOOD CLEAN TROUBLE," GETS SET FOR PLENTY. The writer went on for page after page after *page*, telling Ike's story from his humble beginnings in Abilene to his time at West Point and his staff positions in the peacetime army, praising his genius for organizing and especially his candor—his reputation for "telling the whole truth and withholding no secrets." Which was just a little ironic, wasn't it? The newspapers were still applauding him for tricking the Germans into believing he was doing one thing when he was doing something entirely different. There was a lovely family photograph, with Ike and his parents and his five brothers on the front porch of the Eisenhower family home in Abilene. There was also a photo of him with MacArthur in the Philippines, and—yes—a photo of the two of them, Ike and Mamie, grilling steaks in their backyard. Ike was wearing an apron.

"Oh, what a horrible photo of me!" Mamie shuddered. "Makes me look like a dreadful old hag. I could be his *mother*. I wonder if they used that one on purpose."

"Oh, I don't think so," Ruth said, breaking an egg. "It's probably just one they had in their files."

Cringing, Mamie turned the page. "But this is a very nice photo. 'General Ike's official family,' it says." A grim-looking Ike was seated on a leather sofa, flanked by two officers, with a row of six people, all in uniform, standing behind him. "Look, Ruth, there's Butch, on Ike's right! And that's Tex Lee, on his left. Tex was with Ike in San Antonio, too."

Skillet in hand, Ruth came to look over Mamie's shoulder.

"And there's Mickey McKeogh in the back row, next to somebody named Lord Gilbey. But who's that on the other side of Mickey? That attractive young woman standing right behind Ike?"

"Gilbey is his driver," Mamie said. "Ike says the staff calls him 'Lord' because he has such an aristocratic British manner." She peered closer, trying to make out the fine print without her reading glasses. "The woman's name is Kay something. Summersby, it looks like." She read the caption aloud. "'Pretty Irish girl who drives for General Eisenhower.'"

"Pretty? Well, that's stating the obvious, wouldn't you say?" With a teasing laugh, Ruth went back to the stove. "My goodness, Mamie, that young woman is more than pretty. She's *beautiful*. And very elegant, in that smart uniform. If I were you, I'd be just a tad bit worried about that one. What has Ike said about her?"

Her eyes still on the photograph, Mamie forced herself to echo Ruth's laughter. "She . . . she must not be very important." Quickly, she turned the page. "He's never even mentioned her."

"Never mentioned her?" Ruth went back to the stove. "My dear, that's exactly when I'd worry."

PART TWO

NORTH AFRICA AND WASHINGTON
NOVEMBER 1942–DECEMBER 1943

CHAPTER SEVEN
The *Strathallan*

England, North Africa
November–December 1942

Kay spent the night of the invasion huddled with her mum and sister over the wireless, listening to the BBC's news broadcast, which was intermittently punctuated by the martial melody of "La Marseillaise." The Allies were there, after all, to liberate French North Africa. But there was frustratingly little real information—deliberately, Kay was sure. The full scope of Torch was still secret.

Two days after the invasion, Kay went to the Grosvenor Square office to find out what was really going on. The Boss's door was closed and the place seemed forlorn and empty without his commanding presence. But she heard from Tex—who was in touch via cable with the Allied headquarters in Gibraltar—that things were going more or less according to plan. Patton had taken Casablanca, and while the landings at Oran and Algiers weren't exactly by the book, the troops had managed to pull them off. All three cities were in the hands of the Allies—the first Anglo-American victory of the war, won from the French, not the Germans.

Kay had heard enough talk about the invasion to understand its complicated political context. The troops that the Allies confronted in Morocco and Algeria were pro-German French, under the command of the pro-German government that Hitler had established in Vichy, in the so-called "free zone" of southern

France. The dangerous liaison mission that had cost General Clark his pants had encouraged the Allies to hope that the French general Henri Giraud, recently escaped from a Nazi prison, would persuade the French North African troops to come over to the Allied side without a fight. They didn't, quite, but they didn't have the equipment—or the will—to put up a sustained resistance.

And it wasn't Giraud who turned the trick. The cease-fire was arranged in a behind-the-scenes agreement that Clark negotiated on Eisenhower's behalf with the Vichy French Admiral Darlan, giving Darlan control of North African French forces in exchange for his joining the Allies.

But the agreement had come under heavy fire. The Darlan deal saved lives, Eisenhower insisted, but when word got out, the newspapers called it a deal with the devil. The French admiral was almost universally viewed as a Nazi flunky, and the General was catching flak from both sides of the Atlantic for negotiating with him. "What the hell is this all about?" snarled Edward R. Murrow, the influential American broadcaster. "Are we fighting Nazis or sleeping with them?"

Germany retaliated, sending troops to occupy southern France. The French, afraid that Hitler would seize their fleet, scuttled what was left of it in the French port of Toulon. At the same time, Allied troops had begun to push east through Tunisia, aiming to trap Rommel's Afrika Korps between them and Montgomery's British Eighth Army.

"Like this," Tex said, and took her into the Boss's office to show her the map. "It'll be a cakewalk," he added with a brash confidence that Kay would remember later, when all the costs were counted. "The Germans and Italians are pushing back, but we'll be in Tunis before Christmas."

Looking at the map, Kay guessed that it wasn't going to be a quick or easy victory. And if Eisenhower's command was in for a long campaign, she desperately wanted to be where he was. Tex and several other staffers had finished packing up the office and would be flying out on Ike's B-17 in just a few days. Kay would travel by troop transport, so she would have to wait another few weeks.

"What about Telek?" she asked worriedly. Still a puppy, the Scottie had had a bad cold. "He could hardly avoid getting wet on board a troopship. I don't think a long sea voyage will be good for him."

"The Old Man says he's lonesome for the little guy," Tex replied. "He's flying with me."

"With his parachute, I suppose," Kay said, with a quick laugh. "Let's hope he won't need it."

Tex's eyebrow went up. "If he does, I'm dead. The Old Man loves that dog like he loves his kid. Anything happens to Telek, he'll skin me alive." He gave her a look. "Getting everything done on your end?"

"I'm still working on it," Kay said.

There had been complications with her assignment to Eisenhower's North Africa command. She was a civilian, after all, and the General's order had raised eyebrows both at Whitehall and at Grosvenor Square. But Beetle had pulled strings and the paperwork was finally complete. There were farewells to say to friends and family, goodbyes that were complicated by the fact that she couldn't tell them where she was going.

Her mother guessed, though, and asked once more, and more plaintively: "Kathleen, are you *sure* you know what you're doing?" This time, she added, "I just want you to be safe, my dear. I hate the idea that you might be where there's fighting. I don't want you to be hurt."

Was she sure? No, of course not. Kay had the sense that the war had taken over her powers of decision-making. And anyway, if she was hurt, what of it? A little personal pain didn't seem to matter when she thought of how many people were *dead*.

Kay's communications with Dick had been intermittent. She had decided she wouldn't tell him that she was coming to North Africa. If they couldn't manage to get together, he wouldn't be disappointed; if they could, it would be a lovely surprise. He had written the day after the invasion to say that he was safe. He couldn't tell her where he was, of course (the censors would have blacked that out), but she knew that his unit was in Oran and was scheduled to go to the front at any time. He'd had good news from America, though. His divorce was final and they could get married when her divorce from Gordon went through in June.

"You'll be mine, all mine," he wrote exultantly, "for the rest of our lives." *All mine* was underlined twice.

She read the letter with a curious kaleidoscope of swirling feelings: relief that Dick had gotten through the landing safely and pleasure at the thought that she might even be able to see him before he went to Tunisia. Perhaps they could be married before the summer. And as Dick's wife, her dream of a future in the United States would finally come true. But her pleasure was complicated by the memory of those moments on the train with Ike, his birthday kiss, their goodbye kiss, the way his presence filled not only her waking hours but her dreams. Still, however powerful her attraction to him might be, it held no future. *Dick* was her future. Now that Ike was gone and she was no longer with him every day, it was a little easier to remember that.

So as she packed her suitcases (the same two elegant, brass-bound Vuitton cases she had taken to Europe when she was sixteen), she reminded herself that she was packing for a new life with Dick. It was pointless to try to shop for elegant things in wartime, but her friends at Worth's had made two gorgeous ivory satin nightgowns and three precious pairs of silk crepe de chine panties for her. Those—with her grandmother's diamond earrings, the pearl necklace her mum gave her for her sixteenth birthday, and a tiny bottle of My Sin perfume from Evie—were her trousseau. She also packed Dick's letters and a bundle of family photographs. The rest was all military practicality: her summer uniform, woolly underwear, rayon stockings, an extra pair of regulation shoes, and the Beretta Ike had given her. And her just-issued gas mask and helmet, required accessories for travel to the war zone.

A few days later, Kay kissed Telek goodbye and sent him off

with Tex on the General's Flying Fortress. She was relieved when Tex cabled that the Scottie had arrived safely—and no, he hadn't had to use his parachute.

Kay wasn't so lucky. As it turned out, she had to row part of the way.

ℬↄ

Early on the morning of December 8, Kay went to Euston Station to meet Elspeth Duncan, a stenographer on the Boss's staff, and a contingent of five WACs newly arrived from the States. Together, they boarded a train for the long overnight ride to western Scotland. The next day, at the windswept village of Gourock on the bank of the Clyde estuary, they queued up in the icy rain, waiting to board the small tender that ferried them out to the *Strathallan*, moored a couple of miles offshore.

Built for peacetime pleasure cruises, the *Strathallan* had been designed to carry a thousand first-class and tourist-class passengers from the British Isles to India and Australia. When war broke out, the government had requisitioned her. Now a troopship, she had been repainted regulation gray and armed to defend herself against attack. On this voyage, she was crammed bulkhead to bulkhead with some 250 Scottish nurses from Queen Alexandra's Military Nursing Reserve Service, American WACs, over 4,000 Allied soldiers, and a crew of 862. The convoy flagship, the *Strathallan* was joined by nearly two dozen waiting ships—troop transports, an aircraft carrier, corvettes, and destroyers. They sailed out of the Clyde and headed southeast, plowing through the stormy winter seas north of Ireland in an effort to avoid the German submarines that infested the Irish Sea.

But U-boats were still a looming menace along their route, and the convoy, sailing in formation, set a zigzag course. Lifeboat drills were held two or three times a day—and night. Kay got used to sleeping in her clothes so she could pull on her shoes and coat, grab her already-packed torpedo bag, and make her way to her lifeboat station—No. 12, B-deck, port side, aft—in under five minutes. There, they would stand in unmoving silence for fourteen minutes, exactly the amount of time (if they were ordered to abandon ship) it would take them to climb over the rail and into the boat. The frightening truth was, though, that there were only enough lifeboats for 1600 of the passengers and crew. The unlucky majority—3500 of them—would have to make do with rubber rafts, life vests, and prayer.

Crammed, Kay discovered, was the operative word. Besides herself, there were two other women in her tiny, airless D-deck cabin: Elspeth and Peggy Bourke-White, the *Life* photographer who had taken the "family" photos in London a couple of months before. They slept in a double-decker bunk and on a dirty mattress on the floor. There was no room to sit or dress except on the beds, and because there was no porthole and no ventilation, the cabin air was thick with clouds of cigarette smoke. They spent hours queuing up for meals and the toilets (which were unimaginably foul), doing lifeboat drills, and playing endless games of bridge. Whenever she could, Kay climbed the companionway to C-deck to fill her lungs with the fresh salt air. And every night before bed, she and the others checked their torpedo bags to be sure they had the things they'd need in an emergency: extra socks, a flashlight, candy bars, and whatever personal items they could stuff in. Kay's bag also contained her precious silk undies, her nighties, her bits of jewelry, and Ike's Beretta.

Three days out of port, the convoy ran into a savage Atlantic gale, with mountainous waves and bottomless troughs and rain and blowing spray so thick it hid their destroyer escorts. The *Strathallan* pitched and yawed and heeled at a terrifying angle. A flying sofa broke a nurse's arm and a grand piano careened across a steeply tilted deck and splintered against a bulkhead. Lifeboat drills were reduced to once a day and meals to sandwiches—anyway, most of the passengers were too seasick to eat. Kay kept reminding herself that the storm was actually a bit of luck. A sub surely couldn't hold aim long enough to torpedo them.

After days of rough seas, the weather finally calmed. On the evening of December 21, Kay and her cabin mates climbed up to B-deck for a look at the stars. But something else enchanted them.

"Lights!" Elspeth cried, clutching Kay's arm. "Oh, look, Kay. Lights!"

"Where *are* we?" Kay asked wonderingly. Off to starboard, glittering lights were draped like diamonds along the shoulders of the mountainous coast and pooled in the dark throat of a bay. Lights were a magical sight, after so many long, weary months of blackout.

"That's Tangier," one of the ship's officers told her. "We've entered the Mediterranean."

Dawn brought more magic. A golden sun glazed an azure sea and Kay watched, open-mouthed, as a flock of majestic white pelicans circled over the ship. By mid-morning, though, the sea was churned to a frothy gray by the depth charges dropped by the convoy to discourage a pack of German subs reported to be in the area, and the pelicans flew along the tops of the waves, skimming up fish killed by the explosions. Late that afternoon, the ship's loudspeakers announced that they would be disembarking at Algiers the next day. Kay and her friends happily unpacked their torpedo bags, tucked their valuables into their suitcases, and dashed off to celebrate at a rowdy Christmas party with popcorn, cookies, and a heavily spiked rum punch.

The evening was filled with singing, dancing, and fun—"Swell fun," Elspeth said, "to be one of the few women on a ship filled with men!" It was nearly two by the time they got back to their cabin, all three of them a little tipsy. Elspeth was pinning up her hair, Peggy was writing in her journal, and Kay was pulling off her uniform tie when a dull, thudding explosion rocked the ship, catapulting all three of them onto the floor of their compartment.

We've been torpedoed, Kay thought without surprise. *This is how it feels when a ship is hit.* The *Strathallan* shuddered like a wounded animal and the engines growled to a stop, the silence so immediately deafening that her ears seemed to ring—until it was filled with startled yelps, the clamor of women's voices, and the sudden brassy clang-clang-clang of the alarm gong. The single bulb in the ceiling blinked and went out. The cabin was plunged into utter blackness.

Suddenly sober, Kay fought down the acid fear that rose in her throat. She was a *soldier*, dammit, and the rattle of the ship dying under her feet was no more terrifying than the shriek of bombs that had rained around her in the Blitz. But her hands were shaking as she groped for her flashlight and found her coat, her shoes, and her life vest. Elspeth pulled the pins out of her hair. Peggy scrambled for her cameras, a Rolleiflex and her favorite Linhof, grabbing lenses and film. There was jostling but little visible panic as they joined the stream of nurses jamming the narrow passageway, moving as if in slow motion toward the companionway. Somebody was sobbing. Somebody else growled, "Shut the hell up, Crandall," and the crying stopped.

By the time Kay reached B-deck, the ship was already listing hard to port, and she slid down the steeply angled deck on her way to the lifeboat station. A brilliant moon high overhead illuminated the ships of the convoy, steaming like ghost vessels past their crippled ship. But Kay knew it was too dangerous for any ship to attempt a rescue. The U-boat that had struck the *Strathallan* could be lurking nearby, with others in its wolf pack. They would fire on any that came to help.

Her heart was hammering as she reached her lifeboat station. The last of the convoy slipped past them and Kay suddenly felt the enormity of their isolation, alone on a vast silver sea under a canopy of aloof and distant stars. And yet, she wasn't alone. She was with five thousand others, standing together against the implacable night and the uncaring ocean and a waiting enemy. She would forever remember that moment as the point at which her old life ended and a new life began. *If I survive*, she thought, *I will be different. I will know, always, that I am a part of something larger than myself.* It was a strange new thought—one that had not come to her before, even during the Blitz—and strangely comforting. She carried it with her as she clambered over the rail and into the lifeboat—and into icy water sloshing over the seats. The torpedo that had crippled them had splashed enough water into the boat to fill it.

Their lifeboat was designed to carry a hundred passengers, but because of the weight of the water, the crew began lowering it before all were aboard. As it jerked downward, several of the women grabbed the outboard gunwale and leaned over, peering fearfully at the sea below. The lifeboat tipped and water sloshed. Kay found her voice.

"Goddamn it, sit down!" she shouted. "Sit in the middle of the boat. Don't move unless you want us all to drown!"

It was the General's vocabulary, but the order came from a woman who had grown up on the River Ilen and understood what it took to capsize a boat. Everybody sat down. The lifeboat hit the surface with a giant splash and they were adrift in a sea of moon and stars and bobbing soldiers and nurses who had scrambled down the network of rope ladders that had been flung over the *Strathallan*'s port rail. As Kay watched, afraid to look but unable to look away, a cluster of nursing sisters dropped like grapes from the ropes into the sea and swam toward the fleet of inflatable rafts the crew had tossed from an upper deck.

Amid geysers of exploding depth charges, the nurses and WACs in Kay's boat began pulling swimmers from the oil-slicked water while the crew strained to row them away from the dying ship. With each rescue, their overloaded craft settled further into the water, waves washing over the gunwales. Those who were wearing helmets snatched them off and began to bail, while Kay and others grabbed oars to help the crew.

As she rowed, Kay turned to look over her shoulder at the *Strathallan*. The ship was settling lower in the water, and she knew it couldn't last long. She thought wistfully of her lovely collection of silk undies and satin gowns, her little hoard of jewelry, the family photos, Dick's letters—the last traces of her previous life. *Before long*, she thought, *it will all be at the bottom of the Mediterranean.* Once again, she had the sense that the life she had known was gone, disappearing with the ship that had brought them here, and that the future was an empty horizon.

But they were alive and safe, as long as they weren't swamped and capsized by a depth charge. Lifeboats and rafts began to cluster together, and soon there was a little flotilla of bobbing vessels under a lowering moon. A cold wind came up, and Kay shivered inside her wet coat. After a long while, the stars began to fade and streaks of a pink and lavender dawn brightened the eastern horizon. *Surely we'll be picked up soon*, she thought, and heard a small cheer go up as a British destroyer sliced through the waves toward them. But an officer with a bullhorn leaned over the rail, shouting that it was still too dangerous—they couldn't be picked up until mid-morning. As the ship disappeared, the vast loneliness of the infinite sky and water settled across Kay's shoulders.

Beside her, Peggy muttered, "Drat. I thought they might be bringing breakfast."

"That'll be the next ship. Curbside service." Kay raised her voice. "Okay, everybody, taking breakfast orders. I'm having bacon and toast with three eggs sunny-side up, no yolks broken, please. Yours?"

"Lox and bagel," a nurse said. "Plenty of onion."

From a nearby raft, a voice said, "I'll have what she's having. With a gallon of hot coffee."

"And a pitcher of Bloody Marys," somebody shouted, and laughter rippled around them.

And then, against the dawn horizon, Kay saw a dark shape breaking the surface. A German sub?

"Oh, shit," the soldier beside her muttered under his breath.

"On a shingle," Kay said brightly, and they all laughed.

∞

In Algiers, news of the sinking reached Eisenhower's Allied Forces headquarters early that morning. The AFHQ had taken over the Hotel St. George on Rue Michelet, an ornate alabaster palace of Moorish arches and crenellated red-tile roofs flanked by pink oleander, purple bougainvillea, and statuesque palms. Eisenhower had just settled down at his desk with a doughnut and a steaming cup of black coffee when Butch rushed in with the message.

"Torpedoed!" Ike stared at Butch, his mouth suddenly dry. "Christ. Where? What's the situation?"

Butch shook his head. "We don't know much. The *Strathallan* was the only ship hit in the convoy. They have her under tow now. Happened around two in the morning, off Oran." He looked at his watch. "Six hours ago."

Butch was talking about the ship, but Ike was thinking of Kay. Six hours ago. Six hours. He pulled a pack of Camels out of his shirt pocket. If they had the *Strathallan* under tow, chances were good that the passengers had gotten off. Most of them.

He shook out a cigarette. "Did the lifeboats get away?" But he knew that the crowded troopships never carried enough lifeboats. If there was a sharp list, half would be useless. He felt suddenly cold. "Losses?"

"Like I said, we don't know." Butch gave him a pale smile, meant to be reassuring. "Don't worry, Boss. Must have been a lone wolf—there are no other reports of enemy activity. It's light out there now. They'll be picking up survivors."

Survivors. Eisenhower flinched. The lists of torpedoed ships weren't released because of the need for secrecy and because the government feared the effect of bad news on public morale. But he saw the reports, and the recent disasters—the number lost to German U-boats just since September—hung like albatrosses around his neck. The British troopship *Laconia*, sunk off West Africa with sixteen hundred lost, many killed when the German rescue vessel—the same sub that had torpedoed the ship—was attacked by a B-24 Liberator. The *Nova Scotia*, eight hundred; the *Juneau*, seven hundred; the *Ceramic* the previous month, six hundred on board, no survivors. Just those four ships totaled more than twice the number of losses at Pearl Harbor. What were the odds that Kay had survived?

He struck a match with his thumbnail and lit his cigarette. He knew Butch was watching him, trying to read his expression, to see how he *really* felt. But Eisenhower had learned the importance of looking confident and optimistic, no matter how dicey the operation. Concealing his apprehensions, his personal feelings, was second nature to him now. In the last six months, he had built an increasingly higher wall between his public and his private lives. His old friend Butch now belonged to the public life, the life that was owned by the army. Mamie, too, the quintessential army wife, such an important asset to an army career.

But not Kay Summersby. While he didn't fully understand how he felt about her, he knew without question that she belonged to his private life, to his secret self, to the man whom nobody, not even Mamie (or especially not Mamie), knew. His feelings about Kay, whatever they were, were nobody's goddamned business but his own.

Still, it was difficult to hide his apprehension from Butcher, who had known him for fifteen years and could probably read him pretty well. He got up from his desk and walked to the tall, narrow window of his corner office, feeling Butch's eyes on the back of his neck. Cigarette in one hand, he shoved the other into his pocket and fingered the lucky coins he'd carried during the invasion: a silver dollar, a French franc, and a silver crown piece newly minted with the image of George VI. Luck, luck. They needed it now. *Kay* needed it now.

He stared out across the great crescent of the bay where ships were moored two and three deep at every pier, seeing beyond them to the brilliantly blue Mediterranean, bright under the morning sun. Kay was out there somewhere on the unforgiving sea, and the thought of it made him want to highjack one of those ships—or maybe an airplane—and get out there and join the search. But he couldn't do that, goddamn it. He was helpless to help her. Somebody else had to do it.

He pulled on his cigarette. At least the *Strathallan* had gone down in the Mediterranean, where rescue was more likely than in the Atlantic. But not certain. There must have been five thousand men and women on the ship. They'd be lucky if there were life-boats for twenty percent of the passengers, and that only if they'd all been lowered fully loaded. What were the chances of that?

He pulled smoke deep into his lungs, feeling its acrid bite. In the streets below, the city was going about its ordinary business. The Allies had captured the port facilities nearly intact (although not quite as handily as they had expected), while eager French par-tisans had taken the power stations, police station, Radio Algiers, the central telephone exchange, the Vichy French army head-quarters. But war had scarcely touched the busy, bustling market streets around the St. George. Vendors' awnings shaded trays and baskets of tangerines and grapes and olives and figs. Skinned goat carcasses hung from cedar poles, and wooden bins were filled with bottles of Algerian wine and boxes of the local cigarettes—"Dung d'Algerie," the Yanks called them. The streets were shrill with the metallic drone of electric trolleys, acrid with the stink of the charcoal engines that powered buses and lorries, and crowded with plodding horses pulling hay carts and flat-footed camels laden with bags of market-bound goods. The muezzins' midday calls to prayer were laced with the vivid laughter of the blue-uniformed girls of the École Ste. Geneviève and brightened by the cries of old women hawking red and white and yellow roses. Sunny Algiers, unmindful of war, going about its pleasant business, while out there on the Mediterranean, prowling subs killed ships and people drowned.

Ike turned away from the window. His office suite, four rooms at the end of a first-floor hallway guarded by armed soldiers, was small but functional. Beetle, Butch, and Tex had desks in the adjoining rooms. Kay's desk was there, too, waiting for her, and down on the street, his armored Cadillac had just been delivered, for her to drive. Yes, he had known it was risky to bring her here—a

British civilian, a young and beautiful woman promised to one of Fredendall's engineers, who had come to North Africa to be close to the man she loved.

But while Eisenhower was relatively inexperienced with women, he wasn't naive. He knew damn well that Butch—and Beetle and Tex and probably Clark and Patton and even Churchill, that dirty old man—would think that he and Kay had been sleeping together in England and they would sleep together when she got to Algiers.

Well, they hadn't, by damn, and by damn, they wouldn't. She was dedicated to her young officer. For his part, he wasn't much of a lover. What's more, nothing would make him forget his duty to his wife. Given that resolution, there was nothing wrong with having Kay here, where he could see her smile and hear her lilting Irish voice and occasionally touch her hand.

Yes, he had to admit to a few reckless, adolescent mistakes back in England—lying beside her on the train (how in bloody *hell* had he been so stupid?) and kissing her on his birthday and before he left for Gibraltar. He'd acted like some love-struck kid. But he had already promised himself that there wouldn't be any more of that foolishness. The simple fact was that Kay Summersby made his work easier and more pleasant. He intended to have her with him, goddamn it, and people could think whatever the hell they wanted.

He intended to have her with him . . . if she'd survived the sinking of the Strathallan. He steeled himself against that chilling possibility, and against the guilty awareness that he should have put her on the plane with the rest of the staff. But the newspaper guys hung out at the Maison Blanche airfield. He'd thought that Kay would attract less attention if she arrived by ship, just one of a crowd of nurses and WACs. Unfortunately, Mamie had seen the photo of his official family in *Life* magazine, the one where Kay was described as "the General's pretty Irish driver." Ike didn't want any more photos—or any more haranguing letters like the one Mamie wrote when she saw that *Life* photo. His wife had a jealous streak a mile wide and a mile deep and she had given him Hail Columbia and then some. The truth was that he had put Kay on that ship to keep from provoking Mamie. Wrong, wrong, wrong, goddamn it. But there was nothing he could do about it now.

Butch was waiting. Eisenhower turned and walked briskly to his desk, sat down, and pulled a stack of papers toward him. Without looking up, he said, "Since Kay isn't here, you'll need to line up another driver for tomorrow. You and Whiteley and I are leaving at six a.m. for the front."

"The front?" Butch's voice registered surprise. "How long will we be gone?"

Eisenhower thought of the operation that was planned for his absence, so secret that no one in his command—not Clark, not Beetle, and certainly not Butch—had been told of it. When it happened, he would be meeting his generals at the V Corps command post at Souk el Khemis, four hundred miles from Algiers.

"We'll be back on Saturday," he said. "The day after Christmas. Probably late in the evening. It's a helluva long drive." He glanced up to see Butch giving him a peculiar look. He took a last pull on his cigarette and stubbed it out. "Oh, and let me know when you hear something about the *Strathallan* survivors. If Kay won't be here, I'll need to find another permanent driver."

෨

Resisting the urge to slam the door behind him, Butch left the office and walked down the hall, avoiding a barefoot Arab woman wearing a traditional ivory cotton haik, vigorously brushing dried mud from the mosaic floor with a straw broom. Who the hell was Ike trying to fool, putting on that I-don't-give-a-damn face when he heard that the *Strathallan* had been torpedoed? Everybody in the whole damn office knew how eager he was for Kay to arrive. His calendar was marked and he had dogged the supply guys, making sure that new Caddy was waiting when she got off the ship.

Oh, yeah, that car. Ike had had to pull serious rank to get it, since Fleetwood had built only a handful of Seventy-Fives. The left-hand drive Caddy had a standard flathead V-8, blackout shields on the lights, fine leather upholstery, a siren, flag mounts, and enough armor to bump its weight to nearly three tons. The only spots of color on the olive-drab sedan were the two red plates emblazoned with three stars, mounted front and rear. The Cadillac crest was all over the car, however, every logo intact. Beetle could laugh and tell him he was nuts, but Butch was convinced that the Caddy was Ike's gift to Kay, and a damn impressive one, at that. He hoped the girl would appreciate it. *If* she was still alive, of course.

He crossed the high-ceilinged lobby. Still dignified by imposing Moorish arches, mosaic floor, and gilt chandeliers, it was now crowded with the gray metal desks of the rapidly expanding headquarters staff they hadn't been able to squeeze into the rooms upstairs. Ike had originally wanted to keep the AFHQ to 150 officers: "Am particularly anxious to strip down to a working basis and cut down on all the folderol," he had told Marshall. But that idea had died immediately. Now, just six weeks after the invasion, there were already some 2,000 staff in four hundred offices scattered among eleven buildings on the Rue Michelet. Ike and Beetle were expected to keep track of all the whole motley crew, as well as mastermind the critical Allied push to retake Tunis and Bizerte, currently stalled in rain and mud out there in the desert. It was impossible. Goddamned impossible.

And to make a bad situation worse, the storm over the Darlan deal was still intensifying in both Washington and London. Butch—who was in charge of press relations and had heard a helluva lot more about it than he wanted to hear—couldn't see how the controversy could be defused. Not as long as Darlan was still around, anyway. Too bad there wasn't a way to ship the impertinent little bastard off somewhere. Devil's Island, maybe.

Reaching the second floor, he turned right and followed the bundle of transmission wires and cables stretching down the corridor to the signals office, where he hoped to get some good news about the *Strathallan* survivors. He had known Eisenhower for a helluva long time, but he had to admit that he didn't understand the man. If Ike wasn't worried about Kay, he *ought* to be. She was a sweet girl, smart as a whip and true-blue loyal, not to mention beautiful and sexy. Unless Butch missed his guess (he hardly ever did, when it came to things like this), she was in love with Ike, in spite of being engaged to somebody else. The Boss should have put her on the plane with Tex and Telek and the rest of the official family instead of stowing her on that troopship, hoping to keep her out of sight of the photographers. Butch understood why he'd done that, although he thought it was cowardly. Ruth (Butch's wife and Mamie's apartment mate) had written that Mamie was really ticked off when she saw the photo in *Life* magazine. Ike's little flirtation with that girl in the Philippines had apparently gotten under his wife's thin skin. But then Butch had to admit that he'd never been crazy about Mamie, whom he viewed as a self-absorbed female who bossed everybody around her—including her husband—as if *she* were the three-star general.

He opened the door to the signals office and went in, wincing against the deafening din of the teletypes and typewriters clattering under a thick cloud of cigarette smoke. The setup here was still primitive—the cryptographic machines were located in the bathroom, perched on a piece of plywood laid across a monstrous claw-footed bathtub—but if there was any definitive news about the *Strathallan*, Signals would have it.

No soap. But there was one piece of news. The crippled ship, under tow, had exploded and sunk. It was reported that there were some seventeen lifeboats and an unknown number of life rafts still out there, waiting to be picked up. The HMS *Verity* and several other destroyers were in the area. Survivors would likely be taken to Oran.

And that was it. Glumly, Butch went upstairs to the motor pool to find a driver for the General's Christmas trip to the front. Kay wouldn't be here to drive her new Cadillac.

"I *know* you told the major." The colonel narrowed his eyes suspiciously. "Tell me."

Shivering, Kay clutched her still-damp coat around her. She could usually find something to laugh about in even the most frustrating situation, but she was about to run out of patience—and strength. Her knees trembling, she leaned against the desk.

"Our troopship was torpedoed at oh-two-hundred," she said, reciting the now-familiar line. It was late in the afternoon and she had already told her story to a guard, a lieutenant, a major, and now to this colonel, sitting with a phone at his elbow at headquarters in Oran. "I spent the next ten hours in a lifeboat, floating around the Mediterranean, watching depth charges explode. I was picked up by the HMS *Verity* and disembarked here in Oran. I am a member of General Eisenhower's personal staff. His office will want to know that I am safe and will issue my transportation orders. If you will *just* pick up the telephone and call the AFHQ at the St. George Hotel in Algiers, I would be grateful." She took a deep breath and added, since the colonel appeared to be the boss in this place, "And if you could check and see if there is a Lieutenant Colonel Richard Arnold in this sector, I would appreciate that, as well."

The colonel turned to the major, who was standing by. "Cranston, be a good chap and see if you can find Arnold." He looked up at Kay, frowning over round, metal-rimmed glasses.

She knew how disreputable she looked. Unlike some of the survivors, she still had her shoes, but the hem was ripped out of her skirt, she'd lost her tie and two of the buttons from her blouse, and her hair was stiff with dried salt. She pulled herself up and spoke as briskly as she could.

"*If* you don't mind, Colonel. AFHQ, St. George Hotel,

Algiers. General Eisenhower is probably not available, but you can ask for General Beetle Smith, his chief of staff."

"Uh-oh," the colonel said under his breath, and Kay almost smiled. The Supreme Commander probably seemed safely remote, but Beetle's reputation for unbridled ferocity must have already made itself felt. "Ah, anybody else?"

"Major Ernest Lee," Kay said, more kindly. "The General's ADC. Or Harry Butcher, his naval aide."

The colonel began to put through the call and while they waited, thought to ask Kay if she wanted a chair and a cup of coffee. She accepted both gratefully, clutching the hot mug in both hands and feeling the liquid scald her throat and the weariness invade her bones. She found she was holding herself rigid to keep from trembling.

It took nearly ten minutes, but at last Butch came on the line. "Kay?" he asked eagerly, almost shouting. "Kay, is that really *you*? We got word of the sinking this morning, and we've all been worried sick. You're safe? You're not hurt?"

"Yes, it's really me, Butch," Kay said, hanging onto the phone as if it were a lifeline. "And yes, I'm safe—although I must say, it was all a bit . . . dodgy."

"Wonderful, wonderful. That's very good news." There was a brief flurry of voices in the background. "Hang on. I'm putting you through to the Boss. He's just come in and he wants to talk to you."

Kay felt her heart race. She hadn't expected that Ike himself would—

"Kay," he said gruffly. "Kay, thank God you're not hurt. Was it bad?"

His voice was so unspeakably dear that she wanted to cry. "Let's just say that I'm glad you ordered Telek to go by plane." She made her voice as light as she could. "I had to row. He might have had to swim." She could hear the relief in Ike's chuckle.

"When you get here," he said, "you'll have to teach our boy some manners. He peed in Beetle's hat last night."

"Oh, no!" Kay exclaimed, laughing. "I hope Beetle forgave him." But her heart sang *our boy*.

"He was ready to snatch him bald. But the little guy will sure be glad to see you." Ike's voice deepened, and there was something in it she had never heard before. "I will, too, Kay."

"Thank you," she whispered, holding his words close to her, smiling. "Thank you, General."

There was a moment's silence. Then, briskly, Eisenhower said, "Very good. You tell whoever's in charge there to find you a place to spend the night. Beetle is sending a plane for you first thing tomorrow." He paused. "I'm headed for the front early in the morning. When you get here, I want you to take a day or two to rest. Then we've got work for you to do. A new car to drive, too. And your job as recreation director is waiting. You can start planning the New Year's Eve party." He chuckled again. "We have something to celebrate."

She was still smiling when she handed the phone to the colonel. "Thank you," she said. "General Eisenhower said that he would appreciate it if you could find a place for me to stay tonight. He's sending a plane—"

"Kay?"

That voice. Stunned, she turned. Standing in the doorway, Dick was staring at her as if she were a ghost.

"Kay, what the *hell* are you doing here? Why aren't you back in London? How—"

"I was on my way to Algiers," she said, "but my ship got torpedoed—"

And then Dick's arms were around her and his mouth was on hers, and there was nothing more she could say.

After a few moments, the colonel cleared his throat and stood up. "Arnold, if it's not too much trouble, do you suppose you could find this, er, soldier a billet for tonight?"

"Oh, yes, *sir*," Dick said with a grin. "You damn well bet I can!"

CHAPTER EIGHT
"We've Got a War to Win"

North Africa
December 1942

"I still can't believe you're here," Dick said, as he bundled her into the borrowed jeep. He said it again at least twice as he drove her to the cramped apartment he was sharing with two other officers. He found her some towels and she took a bath and washed her hair, the first time since she'd left London two weeks before. What's more, she was able to lounge in a bathtub filled with hot water right up to her chin, not just the paltry six inches allowed in water-rationed Britain. For those moments, all she could think of was the luxury of hot, hot water and the bliss of being clean.

While she was bathing, Dick had found a pair of pajamas for her, several sizes too large. Then he sat her down at the table while he scrambled eggs with K-ration chopped sausage and served them with toasted *khobz el dar*—Algerian "bread of the house," he said—and a most welcome glass of robust Algerian red wine.

"Eat first," he commanded. "And then you can tell me just how in the bloody hell you managed to get to Algeria."

Under Dick's constant gaze, she practically shoveled in the food, since she'd had only a sandwich and a candy bar since the shipboard farewell party. Once she was finished, she talked and he listened. She told him how Eisenhower had asked her if she wanted to go to North Africa with his command, how she had jumped at

127

the chance to be near the front, where *he* was—Dick, that is—and how she and the others had escaped from the sinking ship. It had all worked out, except that she had lost her trousseau—her nighties and silk undies—when the ship went down.

"If I'd just left everything in my torpedo bag, I'd have it now," she said. "But we were so close to the end of the voyage. I thought we were safe."

"Your *trousseau?*" he asked disbelievingly.

She nodded. "I came to Algeria because I hope we can get married just as soon as my divorce from Gordon is final. That'll be in June." She took a breath. "It's what I want, Dick. It's *all* I want."

It was true. She'd had a lot of time to think on board the ship and later, in the lifeboat. She was attracted to Eisenhower, yes—who wouldn't be? He was charming and charismatic and powerful. But her future lay with Dick. They would be married by summer. The war might keep them apart for a while, but after it was over, they would have the rest of their lives together. She had a lot to say and the words tumbled out.

But Dick seemed unusually quiet, not his normal happy-go-lucky self. In the letters he wrote after the invasion, he said he'd seen some serious skirmishes. He didn't actually say that he had killed anyone, but she supposed he had, and that might have changed him. Mostly, though, he seemed to have trouble believing that she had actually come all the way from England just to be with him. Every now and then, he'd shake his head and mutter that he couldn't imagine that Eisenhower would ask a civilian—a *woman*—to drive him in a war zone.

Finally, he said, "You must be one helluva driver, Kay."

"Well, yes, I guess I am," she said. "The General thinks so, anyway." Like a shadow, the thought crossed her mind that Dick might be jealous. She put out a hand. "Aren't you glad I came?"

"Of course I'm glad," he said defensively. "I'm surprised, that's all. You could have given a guy a little warning."

"Warning of *what?*" she asked. "I was headed for Algiers. If you want to blame somebody for my being here in Oran, blame the German sub that torpedoed us."

"I'm not blaming anybody. Really, I'm glad you're here, Kay. I love you, you know." He looked at his watch. "Sorry, but I'm going to be late for duty if I don't leave right now."

She gave him an appealing look. "You couldn't get somebody to stand in for you—just for tonight?"

He shook his head. "I'm the duty officer. We're shorthanded as it is. Everybody has to do his share. We've got a war to win, you know." He managed a lopsided grin. "Anyway, you need to get some sleep, precious. You're dead on your feet."

It was the word *precious* that undid her. She had held up so far without tears, even when others in the lifeboat were weeping, but now she began to cry.

He folded her in his arms, kissed her softly, and said, "Sleep. We'll work it out, kid. We'll have time. We're on the same continent, aren't we?" He grinned crookedly. "What else could we want—except maybe a few more hours."

She knew Dick had to go, and she had to get some sleep. The General's plane was coming in early. She knuckled the tears from her eyes and whispered, "Yes, you're right. We have time."

Time. As she was brushing her teeth with Dick's toothbrush, she reflected that tonight was perhaps the sweetest time that they had spent together since they met—he scrambling eggs for her, she wearing his pajamas—but they were still a little uncomfortable with one another. That was the thing about wartime romances. She and Dick had only been able to piece together an hour here and a couple of hours there, with long stretches of empty time between the latest goodbye and the next hello. Whenever they came together, it was as if it were the first time, the first tentative touching, the first hesitant kiss, always just getting acquainted, the exhilarating magic of a first encounter lighting up all over again. Even their intimacies had been rushed, the two of them hurriedly stripping out of their clothes and, afterward, pulling them on hastily—no time to lie together, to talk softly, to linger in the sweetness. She had spent many more hours alone with Eisenhower than she had with Dick, and that would likely be true until the end of the war.

And now, pulling Dick's comb through her still-damp hair and looking at herself in his shaving mirror, she realized that it had been naive to imagine that coming to North Africa might allow them to spend more time together. He was in Oran and she would be with Eisenhower in Algiers. On the map, the two cities were only a couple of inches apart. But it was two hundred miles by road, and the road, Dick said, was a nightmare. And anyway, this was *war*. Officers had responsibilities, like his tonight. They couldn't just hop into a vehicle and drive off for a date in another city. What's more, he was doing his best to get a regimental command at the front in Tunisia, which would make things even harder.

The thought of Dick's going into combat made her shiver, but what could she say? He was a career army man, keen to serve where his service would matter most, intent on putting his duty above everything—and everyone, even the woman he loved. And that woman would soon be his wife, an army wife. As long as there was a war to fight, she had better get used to coming in second.

And as she climbed into Dick's bed, she thought that she now knew one important thing among the many uncertainties. She was committed to Dick. She had given him her heart. He was a good man living through a hard time. It wasn't fair to be with him and think of Eisenhower, so she wouldn't. She just wouldn't.

She pulled up the scratchy woolen blanket, making herself a promise. She would put Dick first in everything she thought and felt. That was *her* duty. The General was out of reach and out of bounds. She would do her job for him, and that was all. That was *all*.

She fell asleep thinking that she had to stop thinking about Eisenhower.

ℰↄ

When the Flying Fortress landed on the muddy Maison Blanche airfield outside Algiers the next morning—Christmas Eve—Kay found Tex waiting for her in the misty rain. He was holding an umbrella over his head and an army-issue raincoat over his arm.

"Boy, are we glad to see you!" he said, relief written all over his round, sunburned face. "I don't mind telling you that the office was pretty dismal when we heard you'd been torpedoed. The Old Man plodded around like Gloomy Gus until he got word that you'd been picked up." He draped the raincoat over her shoulders. "You're all in one piece? No serious damage?"

"No damage," Kay said. "Just a little disreputable." Her uniform was a wreck. The only thing about it that could pass muster was the tie. Hers had gone down with the ship and Dick had found one to replace it.

"The uniform we can replace," Tex said, as they walked from the plane to his car. "The Boss told me to take you straight to your billet and order you to get some sleep." He handed her a brown paper bag. "Pajamas and cigarettes. Don't come to the office until you're ready."

"Smashing," Kay said, taking the bag gratefully.

When Tex dropped Kay at her billet, she discovered that she would be staying temporarily in the nurses' dormitory of the Clinique Glycine, a French maternity hospital only a few blocks from AFHQ. She spent the rest of Christmas Eve sleeping in a pair of rough-cotton pajamas on a narrow bed in a spare, chilly, white-painted room. She woke briefly to the sound of women's voices singing a French carol, then fell asleep again.

On Christmas morning she borrowed a comb from a French nurse across the hall—the French she had learned long ago came in handy—and did her best to pull the tangles out of her hair. After breakfast in the hospital dining hall, she walked to the St. George, savoring the strangeness of this new and very foreign place. The morning sun was shining and below her, the alabaster city cradled a blue, crescent-shaped bay. Beyond, reaching to the distant horizon, lay the shimmering waters of the Mediterranean.

The Germans regularly bombed the city, Tex had told her, but they usually hit the harbor area, where she could see several tethered barrage balloons, floating like silver fish in air the color of water. The streets around the hospital, lined with luxurious French villas, had been spared. If there was a war here, Kay thought, there was no sign of it in this peaceful green neighborhood.

But AFHQ was a different matter. The elegant St. George Hotel sat behind a hedged courtyard brightened with hardy white oleanders and red geraniums and centered with a cascading fountain. A café was there, its tables topped by baskets of oranges and lemons, and the fragrance of fruit and sound of bubbling water filled the air. But the tables were empty, guards armed with machine guns stood watch over every entrance, and the place bristled with men in uniform, striding here and there as if the success of the war depended on their getting where they had to be in the shortest possible time. It was the same sort of brisk purpose, Kay thought, that General Eisenhower had imposed on Grosvenor Square when he first arrived. But here, today, she felt a taut wariness in the air, like invisible thrumming power lines, that had been lacking in London. No one was smiling, no words were exchanged. People seemed more than usually apprehensive, throwing watchful glances over their shoulders. Something must be going on, she thought as she went into the lobby and asked directions to Eisenhower's office.

An armed guard stood in the corridor outside the General's office. Because Kay didn't have an official pass, he made her wait until Tex came out to vouch for her. Whatever was going on was serious, she thought, judging from the urgent whispers traded by officers hurrying back and forth. Down the hall, a teletype rattled and quit, then rattled again. In another room, she could see a bank of switchboards lit with flashing lights, and uniformed operators, like stage magicians, deftly manipulating the cords. *What was it?* she wondered uneasily. What had happened? A substantial German advance? An unexpected Allied loss?

None of that, thankfully, but something that provoked an enormous uncertainty: an assassination. When Tex finally emerged, he told her that Darlan—the Vichy French admiral with whom Eisenhower had made what the London newspapers called "a devil's deal"—had been murdered the day before. No one was sure what might happen next. There were rumblings of an uprising among the French military. Would there be other assassinations? Bombings? The Algiers police had quickly captured the assassin—Chapelle, a young Frenchman barely out of his teens—but it wasn't clear who put him up to the murder because the admiral had enemies everywhere. De Gaulle's Free French forces, the Algerian police, the British, even the American OSS (the Office of Strategic Services)—all had plenty of reason to want the man dead. Exactly who was behind the assassination might never be known.

In the meantime, General Clark, who had been involved with Darlan since his secret trip to North Africa back in October, had managed to reach Eisenhower at the front. The Boss would be back in Algiers that evening, Butch said. So, on this Christmas Day, in the midst of the tension that filled the St. George like an electrical storm, there was nothing for Kay to do except get settled. She spent the day getting her papers in order and collecting pieces of her uniform—new skirt, jacket, slacks, blouses, shoes, cap—from a supply depot a couple of blocks down Michelet. She needed a heavy coat, too, for the weather was expected to turn cold. She stood in one queue after another, and it was late afternoon before she got back to the office. She changed into her new uniform and sat down at her desk.

"These are your maps, Irish," Beetle said, dropping a stack in front of her. "Better study up. You start driving tomorrow—and Algiers is a bitch of a place to find your way around in. The roads are like corkscrews, and hubcap-deep in mud. And the Germans are still bombing."

"Can't be any worse than London during the Blitz," Kay said. "And I won't be hauling any dead bodies."

Across the room, Tex gave her a wicked grin. "Yeah, but it's the wrong side of the road for you, kid. You'll have to get used to a left-hand drive."

Mickey, who was in charge of shopping for the General's household, took the ration coupons Tex had obtained for him. "And just wait till you see the armored Cadillac the General's got lined up for you. Bigger'n a Sherman tank." He held up his hand, palm out. "Swear to God, Kay. So big it won't go through most of them narrow streets out there."

"Watch me," Kay retorted cheerfully. "If I can't drive it, I'll fly it." She was smiling. In spite of the worries over the Darlan murder, everything seemed so *normal*. All they were missing was the Boss.

And then, just as she was opening a map of Algiers, the General walked in, with Harry Butcher on his heels. His shoulders were stooped, his shoes were caked with mud, and he looked bone-weary. But his blue eyes lit up when he saw her and his grin nearly split his face.

"Kay!" he exclaimed. "Hey, glad you're here! Stay put until we get this goddamned mess sorted out, will you? Seems to me Beetle said something about a Christmas party at his place tonight." He stopped, frowning. "It *is* Christmas, isn't it?"

"Oh, yes, sir," she said happily. And suddenly, just like *that*, she knew she had come home.

∞

Ike's first order of business was to get Mickey to build up the fire in the fireplace. It was the only heat in the whole damned office and he was glad to have it. His second was to write a note of sympathy to be hand-delivered to Admiral Darlan's widow. His third was to call Beetle in for a briefing.

"Were you surprised?" Beetle asked, after he had run through the homicide reports from the police and the situation reports from Giraud and the Vichy French posts around Algiers.

"Don't ask." Ike took out a cigarette.

"Like that, huh?" Beetle raised an eyebrow.

"Like that." The battlefield was cleaner, but sometimes things had to be handled otherwise. Lies and deception and calculation were the ordinary commerce of war. The swifter the act, the fewer people who knew, the better. A line from a long-ago reading of *Hamlet* crossed his mind. *If it were done when 'tis done, then 'twere well it were done quickly.* It had been done quickly, while he was conveniently out of the city. The mop-up would no doubt be just as quick.

He fished out a cigarette and lit it. "Probably a good idea if the OSS agents left town for a few days." He pulled in a lungful of smoke. "Where's de Gaulle on this? What have we heard from London? I'll need to talk to Clark first. Then get Giraud over here. And coffee. A couple of buckets of coffee. *Hot* coffee." He frowned. "And get Mickey to bring in more coal for that fireplace, will you? All it does is smoke, damn it." Over the fireplace, somebody had hung a large framed photograph of President Roosevelt. FDR's face was already stained with soot.

"Right." Beetle headed for the door, then turned. "We're still on for a late Christmas dinner tonight, if you're not too tired. Patton sent a couple of live turkeys over from Casablanca. Ethel has been planning quite a spread."

"Not tired at all, damn it," Ike lied. He hated it when anybody worried about his health, but the truth was that his chest hurt and he couldn't seem to get rid of the hacking cough he'd acquired in those damned damp tunnels on Gibraltar. He straightened his shoulders. "I hope Ethel has already got the turkeys roasted. I'm hungry enough to eat them both myself." Beetle had arranged for Ethel's transfer to Algiers, and Ike was glad. Beetle was easier to get along with, now that he was shacking up with the attractive nurse. His bridge game was better, too.

Beetle grinned. "You bet she has. I'll get Clark. And coffee."

Clark came, and after an extended discussion, a series of coded cables was dispatched to Washington and London. Giraud arrived, stiffly French and correct as always, and after a twenty-minute discussion, Clark left, taking Giraud with him. By that time, the replies to the cables had come back from Whitehall and the Pentagon, and more cables were sent. There were telephone calls, and more telephone calls, some of them so static-laden that he was forced to shout to be heard.

Finally, just before nine, Ike had done everything he could on the Darlan issue. It was all over but the post-game quarterbacking, although there would no doubt be plenty of that, in every newspaper on the globe. He hated to see his name in the papers. It was usually embedded in a hash of the facts. He drained his third cup of coffee, stubbed out his cigarette, and pushed his chair back from his desk.

"Kay," he shouted through the open door. "Kay, get in here and let me see that you're all in one piece."

The drive to the front had been a long one, with plenty of time to think. The news of the *Strathallan's* sinking had pulled him up short and made him understand just how much he cared about the girl, how much he wanted her here, with him. But nothing was going to make him forget his duty to his wife, and to himself, as an honorable officer. From here on out, he was behaving like Kay's commanding officer. Period. Paragraph. End of story.

He had this resolution fixed firmly in his mind when Kay came into his office and he stepped around the desk to greet her. She stood in front of him, smiling and composed, and he was flooded with an unexpected—and unexpectedly disconcerting—warmth.

"You see?" she said. "All in one piece, and newly outfitted. Getting torpedoed was not much fun and I don't plan to do it again. But no damage done." She snapped him a credible salute. "I'm glad to be here, sir."

"We're glad you're here," he said, steadying himself, surprised by the sudden flare of desire that threaten to undo his resolve. He had never wanted anything as much as he wanted this young Irishwoman, whom he had so nearly lost to the sea. She was even lovelier than he remembered, the light catching in her auburn hair, her head tilted, her mobile mouth curving in a small smile—

He lifted his hand and took an impulsive step toward her

before he was able to check himself. He fumbled in his shirt pocket for another cigarette as if that was all he had meant to do, and turned back to his chair.

"I haven't yet talked to a soldier who's been torpedoed and lived to tell about it," he said stiffly. "You'll be the first. Have a seat and give me the story."

He lit his cigarette and leaned back as he listened to her description of the storm the ship had sailed through in the Atlantic, the torpedo strike in the Mediterranean, the lifeboats and rafts, the night on the open water, the rescue by HMS *Verity*.

"They took us to Oran," she said. "I checked in at headquarters there and called you." She took a breath and met his eyes directly. "And then good luck for me—smashing good luck, actually. As it happened, Dick Arnold was there. Colonel Richard Arnold. My fiancé."

Was her tone defiant? Her glance certainly was. "Excellent," he made himself say. "So you didn't have to sleep on the street. I suppose Arnold gave you a place to spend the night." He heard the dryness in his tone and despised it.

"Yes." She was poised but tense and unsmiling. He had the sense that she had made up her mind to something. To what? She took a breath.

"Actually, it was worth being torpedoed," she said, "if that's what it took to give Dick and me a few hours together."

Eisenhower was lanced by a stab of envy, imagining Arnold— young Arnold, her age, twenty years his junior—making love to this woman, holding her all night in his arms, lying beside her in his bed. *All night.* What would he give for the privilege of—

But he was a goddamned fool. He pulled on his cigarette and—carefully—allowed himself to say part of what was in his mind, editing it from the singular to the plural.

"All of us here had a few bad moments until we heard you'd been picked up. If something had happened to you—" He paused, considered, and said the thing a commanding officer would say. "I'd be the one to write the letter to your mother. I'd sure as hell hate that. Kul would never forgive me for letting you come out here." He pushed his chair back and stood up. "Enough. It's Christmas. Beetle's invited us to his big, fancy house for a late supper—turkey and the trimmings, he says." He picked up a set of keys from his desk and tossed them to her. "Your car." Butch thought it was a gift to her, and maybe that's what he had imagined. But that was foolish, too. He was a foolish old man.

She caught the keys in midair and with a laugh, turned them over in her fingers. "Mickey says it's big as a Sherman."

"Bigger. Meaner, too." He pointed to the door. "Let's see if you can handle it."

The Cadillac *was* big and Ike could tell that the left-hand drive felt awkward to her. But the streets were empty of vehicles and they didn't have far to go. He sat beside her and gave her directions to Beetle's rented hillside villa. It belonged to a wealthy Frenchman and boasted terraces and gardens, mosaic floors, and luxurious furniture. Beetle, in his element, dropped his sonofabitch office persona and played the gracious host. Butch had brought a young Red Cross nurse named Molly (he wouldn't be writing to his wife Ruth about *her*, Ike guessed). And even Mickey had a date—Pearlie, a shy, pretty young WAC who seemed awed by the company of officers.

The table was splendid: traditional American turkey and stuffing and a great many Algerian foods, with an English plum pudding for Kay and plenty of champagne for everyone. As if in defiance of the day's ugliness, there was laughter and singing and more champagne. Somewhere, somebody had found a limp scrap of mistletoe, and the playful kissing was accompanied by loud hoots and cheers as, one after another, the women were enticed beneath it. Ike got in line and to resounding laughter, cheerfully bestowed an enjoyable avuncular kiss on Ethel, Pearlie, Molly, and Sue Sarafian, one of the office stenographers.

And then it was Kay's turn. But when he looked for her, she had disappeared, so that was the end of the game. A little later, she was back again, standing quietly apart from the champagne-fueled merriment. He felt drawn to her, despite his resolution.

But hell's bells, he told himself, it's Christmas. He'd been working hard, damn it, harder than anybody else in this man's army. He deserved a little celebratory kiss. He'd kissed all the others—why not Kay? He waited until the group went out on the terrace to admire the full moon over the Mediterranean, then took her arm and pulled her under the mistletoe.

"Your turn, Irish," he said, brushing his lips lightly against her cheek, then her mouth. He put a hand on her waist. She was slimmer than he remembered, and he was suddenly jolted by a deep, strong hunger. He put his arms around her and pulled her closer. She half-turned her head, but he put his fingers under her chin and kissed her again, his mouth seeking hers. For a moment, she gave his kiss back to him, urgently—and then just as urgently pushed herself away.

"I can't, Ike," she whispered, stepping back. Her eyes were on his, almost pleading, and she let out a ragged breath. "I . . . just can't. You know why."

He dropped his hand, instantly regretting. "I know." He heard himself say the most honest thing he had said yet. "I can't either, Kay. But I wish I could." The words were almost wrenched out of him. "Oh, God, I wish I could." But he couldn't pull his eyes from hers.

Her eyes widened and, half unwillingly, she lifted her hand as if to touch his face. Impulsively, he caught her fingers and kissed them. What might have happened next, he would never know, for a gust of Mediterranean wind pushed the terrace door open and the sound of laughter blew into the room, followed by Butch and Molly. They were chuckling at a private joke.

Ike stepped back. In as normal a tone as he could manage, he said, "There's a small black dog at my house who can't wait to see you, Kay. Will you come over and have breakfast with Telek and Butch and me in the morning?"

"Oh, Telek!" Her hand, her fingers—the fingers he had

kissed—went to her mouth. "Oh, that would be the *best* Christmas present ever!"

"Even better than the Eisenhower Cadillac?" Butch asked with a laugh. "It's got to be the fanciest car in Algiers."

Kay rolled her eyes. "*Infinitely* better. It was love at first sight with that Scottie. It'll take a while for me to make friends with the car."

"Let's hope you can knock some sense into that damn-fool little dog," Ike said wryly. "He's decided he's boss of the place."

"Yeah," Butch said. "And he shows it by forgetting he was ever house-trained. He needs somebody to lay down the law."

"And that's where I come in, I suppose," Kay said lightly. "I get to walk the dog."

Ike put on a grin. "He'll be happy to see you, I promise." He straightened his shoulders, glad now for the interruption. In spite of his resolution, he'd almost lost his head again. Who knows what might have happened if Butch hadn't come in when he did?

ℂℂ

It was very late when Kay got to bed in her room at the clinic, but sleep was slow in coming. The memory of Ike's arms around her was as powerful as his embrace had been. In answer to his wrenched *I wish I could* she had wanted to echo *Oh, so do I. So do I!* But however much she might have wanted that kiss, she had been constrained by her promise to marry Dick, just as—she knew—Ike was constrained by his promise to his wife, by his duty. Still, if Butch and Molly hadn't come in just then, she might have given in to him and to herself. *But then what? One kiss, another, and what after that?* She couldn't answer that question.

When she finally fell asleep, she dreamed that she was in a lifeboat, like the one that had saved her from the *Strathallan*. She was alone in the large boat, oars in her hands, trying frantically to row toward a beach where Dick was standing amid the wreckage of war, his hands out to her, frantically calling her to come to him. But no matter how hard she rowed, a strong offshore wind and current kept pushing her away from the beach, pulling her out to the vast and stormy sea.

℘

At six-thirty, she got up and showered and dressed and drove to Ike's rented villa for breakfast. Built on the lip of a green hill high above Algiers, it bore the apt Arabic name of Villa dar el Ouad—the Villa of the Family. In the same compound as Beetle's house, it was not nearly so luxurious. The place was large—seven bedrooms, she would learn, and a library with a Ping-Pong table, a music room with a grand piano, and a mosaic-tiled bathroom with a tub almost large enough to swim in—and set far enough back from the street to afford a little privacy.

But it wasn't the comfortable privacy Kay had loved at Telegraph Cottage. There was a wariness about this place, for Algiers had only recently been taken from the enemy, and at any moment, the war might invade from the sea or fall from the sky. A vicious-looking spike strip was deployed across the driveway, uniformed guards patrolled the grounds, anti-aircraft guns were dug in at strategic points, and the sentry stationed on the terrace asked to see her identification and searched her bag before she was allowed into the house.

When Kay walked through the door, all that was forgotten. She was met by a bouncing black ball of a puppy, barking with wild delight. She scooped the little dog up in her arms, holding him tight and burying her face in his fur. "I've missed you, funny little boy," she whispered as Telek lavished kisses on her. "Oh, I've missed you!"

Mickey had just served breakfast in the drafty, high-ceilinged dining room, and Telek immediately took his usual place on Kay's lap so he could share her breakfast bacon, just as they had back in

England. In other ways, it was like England, too. The General sat across the table from her, a frown on his face, reading glasses on the end of his nose. He was buried in the *Times*, which arrived daily in the diplomatic pouch. Butch was tossing down a handful of aspirin as an antidote to last night's champagne. Mickey was hovering with a pot of fragrant hot coffee and a plate of toast while Moaney and Hunt rattled pots and pans in the kitchen. A wireless on a nearby shelf was broadcasting a BBC news program, the commentator reporting heavy fighting at Guadalcanal, aimed at driving the Japanese out of their fortified positions on Mount Austen. Under his breath, the Boss muttered something about being damned glad that Vandegrift had gone back to Washington and Sandy Patch was calling the shots in the Pacific.

Kay listened and looked and hugged Telek to her, loving the small, squirming body, the fervent kisses on her nose, the smell of the coffee, the General's muttering, Butch's complaint. Home. Yes, in spite of the frozen-faced guards outdoors and the house's alien surroundings, she was at home, because her *family*—all in uniform and all committed to the same vital purpose—was here. She could have lost it all when the torpedo tore through the hull of the *Strathallan*, but she hadn't. She was here, where she knew she was meant to be.

But still, the distance across the table from the General felt very great, and she sensed a difference in him. Had she offended him the night before? After all, he was only being playful, having a bit of holiday fun. But perhaps he'd had a bit too much champagne and regretted his kiss. Perhaps he was putting her on notice that from now on, it would be strictly business between them. He was her commanding officer. She was his driver. And that was *that*.

And then, as if in answer to her unspoken question, he glanced up across the table. For the first time that morning, he looked directly at her, intent, unsmiling. "Good morning, Kay," he said. Then, folding his paper, he turned to Butch.

"Time we went to work." His voice was sharp, crisp. "Butch, bring that report we were looking at before breakfast. Kay, you bring Telek. Now that you're here, that pup can come to the office and learn to take orders, instead of lollygagging around this place all day, thinking he's running the show." He pushed back his chair and stood up. "Come on, people. We've got a war to win."

"Did you hear that, Telek?" Kay said. "The Boss says it's time to go to work. Let's get a move on."

Telek, always happy to be going somewhere, erupted in a flurry of happy barks. Kay smiled. Yes, truly. Truly, she was *home*.

CHAPTER NINE
"Durn Those WACs"

Washington, D.C.
February 1943

When she thought about it afterward, Mamie would realize that her wartime worries had been spawned, like fierce little dragons, from that first *Life* magazine photograph. That picture of Kay Summersby, a member of her husband's official family, the "pretty Irish girl who drives for General Eisenhower." The girl he hadn't mentioned in any of his letters.

Mamie knew she had always been . . . well, possessive. Very possessive. Her mother said so, her sister said so, even Ike said so, especially after she took him to task about that woman in the Philippines. She had already given him (by letter, right after she saw that first photo) what he ruefully called "Hail Columbia," letting him know that it was not a good idea—for appearance sake, if nothing else—to spend so much time driving around England, alone, with a pretty woman, especially a civilian. He had to drop her from his staff, right now, right this minute. If he didn't, people were bound to get ideas.

To which he had replied soothingly that nobody in the world could ever fill her place with him and that he needed her and loved her—a comforting declaration that she thought of whenever she thought of that photo, which was often. Too often. And even if she had wanted to forget it, her friends wouldn't let her. Everybody had seen it, just *everybody*: the girls who came to the apartment to play mah-jongg, the volunteers at the Stage Door Canteen on Lafayette Square, the army wives with whom she traded letters and phone calls. They all repeated pretty much the same thing, like a phonograph record with the needle stuck in the groove.

Like Cookie, who arrived a little early for mah-jongg one afternoon. "My gracious, Mamie, what a beautiful girl, that driver! Now, tell the truth, my dear. Aren't you just a little bit jealous? Heaven knows, *I* would be. After all, she's a WAC and everybody knows all about *them*."

"But she's not a WAC," Mamie had protested. "She's a British civilian. She's wearing that uniform because she belongs to the Motor Transport Corps, which is like our motor pool, only volunteers. She drove an ambulance during the Blitz."

She had pried that little bit of information out of Mickey McKeogh, Ike's orderly. Mamie had instructed him to write to her regularly—and secretly, since she didn't want Ike to think that Mickey was spying. But Mickey's letters were never informative enough to suit her. He would write things like, "The Boss isn't sleeping real good but he's not smoking any more than usual and he's eating three meals a day. Oh, plus he got a new dog who he likes a lot." When she finally got him to tell her something specific about Kay Summersby, though, he provided an unsettling detail: "Back during the Blitz, she drove a bunch of corpses around in her ambulance while the bombs were falling."

Mamie shuddered. The idea of hauling a load of dead people while bombs were raining down. . . . Well, the woman must have nerves of steel, that's all. No lady that Mamie had ever met would do something like that.

And then, under duress, Mickey had mentioned the other assignment Ike had given Miss Summersby: "She's our rec director," he wrote. "She got some golf clubs for the Boss and told me to build him a shooting range and horseshoe pit, except it's not for horseshoes, it's for something called koyts. She's real good at bridge. Also horseback riding."

Mamie only briefly felt guilty for asking Mickey to tittle-tattle on Ike. She was too bothered by the fact that her husband had appointed the multi-talented Miss Summersby as the staff "rec director." If everybody in his command was as busy as they claimed, how did they find time for golf and horseback riding and koyts, whatever that was?

The more she thought about this, the more anxious she felt, for Mamie had never been an outdoor woman. She'd had rheumatic fever when she was eight. The doctors had told her that her heart might be weak and advised her not to exert herself. Ike had managed to get her on a horse a few times, but it wasn't an experience that either of them remembered with pleasure. She'd taken up golf after that business in the Philippines with Marian Huff, just to keep Ike company on the course, but she wasn't what you'd call good at it. And Mickey's remark about bridge was also troubling. Mamie hated to play bridge with Ike. She just wasn't in his league. She had trouble keeping track of the cards and he was forever losing his temper over her playing.

Mickey, pressed just a little harder, was disappointingly (or maybe tactfully) vague about Miss Summersby's appearance. "Well, I wouldn't say she's pretty, exactly. About average, maybe, sorta. Anyway, we're all too busy to notice. We got jobs to do."

Mamie had reread Mickey's reply several times, then looked at the "official family" photograph again, a flare of jealousy burning hotly in her heart. Mickey was wrong about Miss Summersby. Even in uniform, she was much, much prettier than average. And much, much prettier than Mamie herself. Mamie knew that she was too skinny and that her forehead had slipped back almost as far as Ike's, bless him, so that her Claudette Colbert bangs had become essential camouflage. She had one nice feature—her sparkling china-blue eyes—and her creamy skin was flawless. That was why she wore pink whenever she could, and also why she had such a large collection of clothes.

"You need to work with what you've got," she often told her sister Mike. "I don't have a lot these days, beauty-wise, so whatever I'm wearing has to make up for the lack." Plus, she always insisted on the best quality. Her nightgowns had to be silk and her bedsheets linen or satin, never that awful percale. She liked lots of frilly lace on her dresses, and hats with flowers. She simply could *not* understand how any woman could bear to wear a uniform. The color was horrible, olive drab—nobody could look good in *that*, for heaven's sake. And it was always the same thing, day in and day out. How utterly boring.

But Cookie wasn't finished with Kay Summersby. "Well, if she's not a WAC, what does he want with her? And if she's a British civilian," she added, taking her cigarettes out of her handbag, "why is she in *uniform*? And what exactly is she doing on the personal staff of the Supreme Commander? Besides driving, I mean." She eyed Mamie. "Does Ike say why he insists on keeping her?"

Cookie had always been just a little too nosey, and Mamie sidestepped the question. "Every general has a couple of drivers," she said. "It's especially good that they're British, since they have to drive on the wrong side of the road." She laughed to show that she was making a joke. "Anyway, it's all water under the bridge now. Ike has moved his headquarters to North Africa. She's a civilian volunteer, and a woman. He would never in the world be responsible for sending somebody like that to the war zone."

Cookie turned down a carefully lipsticked mouth. "I'm sure you're right, dear. But there will be others. The WACs are flocking over there by the thousands. *Nobody's* husband will be safe."

Mamie hardly thought that Cookie had to worry. Marv was past fifty, overweight, and terribly unattractive. But she understood. Many of the wives she knew were concerned about the WACs who would be working shoulder to shoulder with their husbands overseas. Proximity was a powerful aphrodisiac, and war only heightened the attraction.

It wasn't just the wives who were opposed to the idea of women in the military. Many people were suspicious, and all kinds of stories about after-hours hanky-panky were going the rounds. The public backlash grew even louder after the *New York Daily*

News ran a front-page exposé, reporting that the War Department was furnishing army women with "contraceptive and prophylactic devices." After that, it didn't matter how hard Colonel Hobby tried to emphasize the "high moral standards" of her WACs. They were branded as loose women.

And even Mamie had to admit to sharing those feelings. Ike hadn't mentioned it, but she had heard from Mickey that the General's staff had celebrated New Year's Eve in Algiers with a party. She was sure Ike hadn't participated—working as hard as he was, he'd probably gone to bed early. But when she wrote to her parents, she mentioned the celebration and added, "Mickey said there were eleven men and five women. I suppose we can guess who the women were. Durn those WACs!"

But this was really beside the point, as far as Mamie was concerned. Miss Summersby was a British civilian and her service in Ike's command had already been terminated. Whatever her driving skills, she was pretty enough to be in great demand, so she had no doubt been reassigned to drive some staff officer around London—and cause trouble in someone else's family. Anyway, Mamie firmly refused to believe that there could have been anything between Ike and Kay Summersby. Hadn't he written, over and over, that he "lived in a goldfish bowl"? He was surrounded by men who watched his every move. Even if he wanted to stray (which she was sure he didn't), he couldn't.

And Mamie had other things to worry about. There was that awful Darlan business, which had filled the newspapers with a cruel criticism of Eisenhower's "deal with the devil." It was all politics, of course, and politics had always bored her to tears. But some of the newspaper columnists had gone so far as to call Ike a fascist and even (Mamie could hardly believe it) a Hitlerite!—because he was cooperating with somebody who had cooperated, even just a little, with Hitler. It frightened her to death to think of her Ike, who liked to call himself "just a simple country boy from Abilene," dealing with such devious people.

And since everybody was talking about Admiral Darlan and

what a snake he was, Mamie simply stopped going places where somebody might ask her opinion, and she actually felt relieved when, on Christmas Eve, the admiral was assassinated. Thank God Ike wasn't in Algiers when the fellow was shot; he had gone to spend Christmas at the front. If he'd been around when it happened, she was sure they would have blamed the murder on him! They found the person who did it, though—a twenty-year-old French boy—and put him in front of a firing squad right away, which turned out to be a very lucky break for Ike. It took him off the hook, politically speaking.

But not entirely. Some people hinted that he knew about it ahead of time, which was why he was out of town when it happened. And Mamie heard that the OSS director got sent to Tunisia immediately after the assassination, so he wouldn't be available for the investigation. People said it was all a little fishy.

There was another problem to worry about. Mamie was awfully fond of Ruth Butcher and grateful that Ruth had invited her to share her Wardman apartment. It eased the financial situation quite a bit and gave Mamie some peace of mind where money was concerned. But even though Ruth's husband, Butch, was serving as Ike's naval aide, the Butchers weren't really military. Ruth had never lived on an army post and didn't understand the pressures of being a career army wife—especially the wife of the Supreme Commander.

The situation had become especially awkward over the holidays. Ruth liked to entertain and had a great many friends, most of them connected with Butch's work in radio and print journalism. There was a lot of drinking and carousing, and while Mamie liked to have fun as much as anybody else, there'd been some pretty wild goings-on, with loud music on the radio and sudden bursts of laughter that could be heard up and down the hall. It made Mamie worry about what the neighbors might think. She had asked Ruth to keep it a little quieter, but that hadn't gone over very well.

What's more, she didn't like the people Ruth invited to the apartment. One night, she was forced to flee to her bedroom when David Brinkley, a brash young fellow from CBS, quizzed her about Ike and Darlan, in her very own living room! And a couple of others asked her about when Ike was going to push into Tunisia. "What's he waiting for?" they asked. "Why isn't he putting Rommel out of business?"

But she couldn't answer because she had no idea. She always got Tunisia and Libya mixed up and of course she had no idea what Ike's military strategies were. Ruth laughed at her and said she was being paranoid, but Mamie had reached the point where she was afraid that any silly little word she said might show up in the next day's newspaper.

There was another problem, too. Ike's brother Milton, who always kept an eye on her, had cautioned her not to drink when she was with a group of people—any people, but especially Ruth's journalism friends, who might happen to mention a little something in the newspaper. "I know you wouldn't want anybody to get the wrong idea," he said. "And you wouldn't want to do anything that might compromise Ike."

Of course, Milton didn't need to lecture her. She knew where her duty lay. Unfortunately, this meant that she couldn't even have a ginger ale, because nobody could tell what was actually in the glass she was holding and if they wanted to think it was gin or vodka, why, of course they would. This was especially hard because at cocktail hour Mamie was used to enjoying a bourbon old-fashioned or two and sometimes even three, if it had been a trying day. But Ruth quite often had unexpected drop-in company, which made things . . . well, awkward. There had been one or two embarrassing episodes which might have led to some rather nasty gossip. Mamie didn't want that to happen again, and naturally Ruth felt the same way.

At the same time this was going on, Mamie was suffering from a flare-up of a problem she'd had for several years. She described it as feeling dizzy and unsteady on her feet. She had been seen by quite a few doctors but they couldn't tell her what was wrong. One said it might be something called Meniere's disease (which nobody seemed to know much about), but most said they thought it was psychosomatic, probably brought on by stress, and a few acted as if they didn't really believe her.

Things came to a head one day in January. She was working at the Stage Door Canteen when she stumbled with a tray and accidentally spilled gravy on a soldier's uniform. "Hey, lady, you better watch what you're doing," he yelled. Her face as red as fire, Mamie hurriedly fetched a cloth and sponged him off, but she knew there was snickering about it, and innuendo. She hated to give up her job because she thought she should be doing *something* for the cause. But she decided to resign as a volunteer, rather than give anybody a chance to say that they had seen her drunk in public, which would upset Milton and be a terrible black mark against Ike.

The situation was becoming decidedly uncomfortable. Ruth began dropping broad hints that it was time for a change, and when the apartment across the hall became vacant in January, she jumped at the chance to move. Mamie was relieved. Living alone might be lonely, but it mean that she could sleep late without anybody nagging, eat whatever she wanted (or not, if she didn't want to), and enjoy her old-fashioneds in peace. Since Ruth was no longer there to do the cooking, she hired a cook-housekeeper. And then, to celebrate, she bought a baby grand piano, using money that her father had given her. She had been an indifferent student in English and arithmetic at Miss Wolcott's Denver finishing school "for ladies of refinement," but she had at least learned to play the piano. She could play popular songs by ear, and the piano was a marvelous place to display her photographs of Ike.

In fact, life was sailing along on a much more even keel, now that Mamie had the apartment all to herself. In February, she was overjoyed when Ike got his *fourth* star—only fifteen months after being a lieutenant colonel, but of course he was doing a splendid job. The promotion brought a huge flood of congratulatory mail, and she spent a couple of hours every day personally answering notes from well-wishers. She looked forward to the little mah-jongg parties with the girls once or twice a week, frequent letters from Johnny and her family, and Ike's regular letters.

She still had her low points, of course, moments when she felt so sorry for herself that she just collapsed in a chair and cried. But she kept to a schedule as best she could. She got up in time for lunch, and in the afternoons (when the girls weren't there for mah-jongg), she listened to her radio soap operas. *Stella Dallas* and *The Romance of Helen Trent* were her favorites, but really, she liked them all. There was cocktail hour and then the little supper the cook had left for her. In the evenings, she read mysteries and romance novels and listened to comedy shows, like *Amos 'n' Andy* and—her favorite—*Burns and Allen*. Mamie loved Gracie Allen and joked that if she ever voted for anybody for president (she hadn't), she would have voted for Gracie when she "ran" on the "Surprise Party" ticket in 1940. (That was a dig at Eleanor Roosevelt, of course, who involved herself much too much in public affairs.)

Other army wives—General Patton's wife Bea and General Clark's wife Maurine—went around the country making speeches and selling war bonds, and General Marshall's wife Katherine raised money for hospitals and servicemen's canteens. But Mamie rarely went out now, except to go to the grocery store. War meant waiting, and she was managing to keep herself occupied and reasonably content while she waited for the war to be over and her man to come home.

Until one evening toward the end of February, when everything just . . . well, it all just sort of fell apart. The cook had left her a bowl of homemade chicken noodle soup and she was eating that with a few crackers and a glass of wine while she paged through the latest issue of *Life* magazine, noticing how much of the magazine was about the war effort, even the advertising. There was a full-page ad for Pond's cold cream, featuring a girl who worked in a war production plant and was engaged to a boy who had enlisted in the army ("She's engaged! She's lovely! She uses Pond's!") There was a two-page ad reminding housewives that "food is ammunition" and that the reason they couldn't buy meat at the butcher shop was that soldiers in training had to have a pound of meat every day to get them ready to fight the Nazis, which Hitler made sure were very well fed. And then her glance fell on an article called "Women in Lifeboats," written by the famous photojournalist Margaret Bourke-White.

Mamie's eyebrows went up under her bangs. Miss Bourke-White was the woman who had taken the "official family" photo of Ike's staff that had appeared in the magazine back in November—the photo that had introduced Kay Summersby. After that, *Life* had named Miss Bourke-White as the magazine's official photographer for the U.S. Army Air Force, the very first woman to hold that accreditation. In early December she had boarded a troopship with some five thousand soldiers, nurses, and WACs, on their way to join the Allies in North Africa. But the ship hadn't made it. It was torpedoed by a German submarine in the middle of the night.

"The torpedo did not make as loud a crash as I had expected," Miss Bourke-White wrote, "but somehow everyone on the ship knew almost instantly that this was the end of her. And possibly, of us."

Usually, Mamie wouldn't read a story about a ship being torpedoed, but this one caught her attention. She had skimmed the first page and was halfway down the second when she stumbled across something that made her catch her breath. By the time dawn broke, Miss Bourke-White wrote, survivors had been pulled out of the water, several of the lifeboats had been roped together, and everybody was singing to keep their spirits up while they waited to be rescued.

"People in the lifeboats were joking now," she reported. "The irrepressible Kay Summersby, Eisenhower's pretty Irish driver, announced her breakfast order. She wanted her eggs sunny-side up and no yolks broken." There was even a picture of Kay in the crowded lifeboat, although it showed only the back of her head.

Kay Summersby? Mamie stared at the page, her heart beating as fast as if she'd just rushed up the stairs instead of taking the elevator. She read the sentence again, and then again. Kay Summersby, on her way to North Africa, on a troopship? But how could that be? She was a British citizen, a woman! She should be driving generals back in London. She—

Mamie read faster now, flying through the paragraphs, looking for another mention of that woman's name. On the next page, she found it. After hours adrift on the sea, the survivors had been picked up by a British destroyer and people were warming themselves on the deck with cups of hot Ovaltine, looking through their pockets to see what they had brought with them when they abandoned ship. A man had saved a pair of keepsake cufflinks. A woman had her rosary. And "the beauteous Kay still had two precious possessions, her lipstick and her French-English dictionary. She's sure both will come in handy at Ike's headquarters in Algiers."

At Ike's headquarters! The words were a knife to Mamie's heart. She closed the magazine and pushed her bowl away. She was too upset to even think about eating. She sat at the table as evening darkened the windows, then got up and drew the blackout curtains closed. It was time for *Amos 'n' Andy*, but she didn't feel like laughing at the Kingfish's hijinks, so she left the radio off. She went into the living room and sat in the dark for a while, trying to tell herself that she was getting upset over nothing.

But a moment later, the telephone rang, and when she picked it up, she heard Cookie's voice. "Mamie, have you seen the latest issue of *Life*?" She went on without waiting for Mamie to answer. "There's an article about a troopship that got torpedoed on its way to North Africa. You'll never in the world guess who was on that ship! Kay Summersby! Here. Let me read it to you." She took a breath. "'The irrepressible Kay Summersby, Eisenhower's pretty—'"

Without saying a word, Mamie very quietly replaced the receiver in its cradle. She closed her eyes and drew in her breath, and when the phone rang again, shrilly, she put it under a sofa cushion. She got up and made herself a drink, which she carried into the bedroom. Ike's photograph—her favorite, taken when he was a West Point cadet—sat on her dressing table, surrounded by her bottles of perfume and nail polish and tubes of lipstick. His face looked out from its silver frame with a frank, open smile. "For the dearest and sweetest girl in the world," he had written under the picture.

She picked up the photograph and stared at the inscription. She had loved Dwight Eisenhower for over a quarter of a century. She had borne him two sons: little Icky who had died so tragically, leaving a void between them that not even their common grief could fill; and sweet, strong Johnny, dear Johnny, of whose achievements and promise they were both so proud. She had supported him in all the ways she knew how, through all the difficult assignments his career had brought: the awful years in the tropical jungles of Panama, the unhappy years in the Philippines, the constant moves, the many homes she'd created.

But in spite of all that, she didn't know her husband. His hours, his days, his thoughts, his plans were separate from her, from anything they had together. She had sometimes—no, she had to confess it—she had *often* been jealous of the energy and time he gave to his work, and of the men he shared it with, men who took him away from home, from her. Now, the war had taken him away. And he was sharing his war with another woman.

She looked at the inscription again. "The dearest and sweetest." Did he still feel that way? He said he did. In fact, in his last letter, he had written, "I'll never be in love with anyone but you!" She had been struck by the force of that sentence, which seemed half-defensive, almost a protest, or a reminder to himself of how he ought to feel. Was he in love with that other woman? Was that why he kept insisting he *wasn't*?

The phone was ringing again in the living room, muffled by the sofa cushion, but she ignored it. Somebody—Ruth?—was knocking at her door. She ignored that, too. After a while, she finished her drink, then picked up the photograph and carried it with her to the bed, where she lay down with it in her arms, cradling it against her, and began to cry.

CHAPTER TEN
The End of the Beginning

North Africa
January–June 1943

After the bleak, wintry wreckage that was wartime London, Kay found Algiers to be a fascinating place, sun-washed, colorful, and lively. Everywhere she went, she saw new and exotic sights: snorting camels burdened with bolts of bright-colored weavings, barefoot young men in turbans carrying bunches of yellow bananas suspended from poles across their slim shoulders, toothless old women hawking fragrant *mechoui*, chunks of spit-roasted lamb wrapped in hot flatbread.

But the colorful sights, scents, and sounds of this foreign city quickly slipped into the background. Kay and the five American WACs who had come to work as stenographers and typists in Eisenhower's office were billeted in a small house a short distance from Ike's villa. The women became friends, and although they were rarely all home at once, they enjoyed sharing their new life. Kay, who had been sleeping in a hospital bed and living out of a paper bag (her luggage was at the bottom of the Mediterranean), was glad to have a couple of bureau drawers and a third of a closet.

In the office, Kay fell quickly into the familiar routine. Every morning, she had breakfast at the Villa dar el Ouad, then, with Telek in the seat beside her, drove the Boss to the St. George. At her desk, she helped with the now-voluminous mail, answered the telephone, and drove the General wherever he needed to go. Each day, the workload seemed to get heavier and the pressure more intense, and she could see that Eisenhower was often exhausted by the time she drove him back to the villa for drinks and dinner, often as late as nine or ten o'clock. On days when he quit earlier, they might have an evening of bridge, although their games were often interrupted by the sound of German planes and the thud of exploding bombs. When they went out onto the terrace to take a look at the action, they could see puffs of light smoke against the dark sky and tracers from the Allied anti-aircraft guns firing at the planes. The searchlights danced, the AA thumped, and the bombs exploded on random targets—ships in the harbor, a convent, a hospital. It was like being in the middle of a colossal Guy Fawkes Night fireworks celebration, Kay thought, with arcs of light and streamers of smoke everywhere.

But this was no holiday celebration. It was war, war, and more war. The Darlan business lingered like a noxious fog, with snarling reports emerging daily in the newspapers in London and Washington, never quite charging Eisenhower with the admiral's murder but blaming him for the whole sorry affair. The alleged assassin had been tried on the same day as Darlan's funeral, the outcome so assured that the man's coffin was ordered before his trial began. He was executed that night by a firing squad, at a moment when the sound of the gunfire was blanketed by the thunder of a German air raid on the harbor.

In the Pacific, the war took a more encouraging turn as the Japanese were defeated at Guadalcanal. In Russia, the Germans were facing defeat at Stalingrad. But in the Tunisian desert, the wet, cold North African winter wore on. Kay heard the grim reports that came into the AFHQ. Allied troops—British, French, Americans—were stretched like a thin rubber band along a bleak three-hundred-mile front. Miscommunication left units stranded and confused, not quite certain who was commanding them. Burned-out vehicles littered the roads, mute testimony to the dangers of daylight driving. German Stukas and Me 109 fighters flew low over the ridgelines, sending men diving into slit trenches that were often filled with icy water. The weather forced Eisenhower to abandon the drive to take Tunis from Rommel, "the biggest disappointment so far," Kay heard him tell Beetle. He had to report to London and Washington that he had failed to push the Torch offensive as far and hard as he had been ordered against the Axis forces in the desert.

Eisenhower hadn't said much to Kay after the Christmas party. His instructions to her were clipped and professional, he said very little in the car, and their bridge-table conversation was focused on the cards. Others might have been fooled by his ready grin, but she knew him well enough to sense that behind that easy manner, he was under a terrible strain. Confronted with the fact that the Axis forces were holding onto territory he was tasked to take, he had to admit that the Germans were better at making war than he was. Another commander might blame the humiliating defeats on the winter rains and the knee-deep mud, or the failure of supplies to get through, or the poor cooperation among the Allied field commanders: the recalcitrant French, the arrogant, know-it-all Brits, the inexperienced Yanks. But Kay could see that the General understood that the losses were *his*, and the knowledge was a bleeding ulcer in his belly. He was chain-smoking, working fourteen-hour stretches, and (according to Butch) his blood pressure was through the roof. He was worried and depressed. Kay often went into his office to find him slumped in a chair beside the smoky fireplace, staring at the maps that covered the walls.

"It's a helluva mess out there," he'd mutter. "No movement, everybody's mired in the goddamned mud. And I've got to face them in Casablanca."

The "they" he had to face were Prime Minister Churchill, President Roosevelt, and the VIPs from the Imperial General Staff in London and the War Department in Washington, meeting in a top-secret conference at the Anfa Hotel in Casablanca. Eisenhower had been called on the carpet to explain, if he could, the humiliating setbacks in Tunisia. It wouldn't be easy. The Allies all spoke

English, but as far as military strategy was concerned, they weren't speaking the same language.

"The Boss has his neck in a noose," Butch told Kay the day before he and Eisenhower left for the conference. "He's in for a serious grilling. If they don't like what they hear, he'll be sacked."

"But he's doing the best he can," Kay protested loyally. "He's on the job from dawn until way past dark. He knows how to deal with these crazy conflicts—the French, the British, the Americans, none of them talking to the other."

"Understood." Butch was somber. "But sometimes the best you can do isn't good enough. There are some who say that *nobody* could manage this war. It's not just being fought on the battlefield, you know. It's being fought in the newspapers back in England and the States. Churchill and Roosevelt read the papers. And Ike's press isn't good right now."

Kay shivered. Butch should know—the press was his business. "What will happen if . . . if he's relieved?"

"He'll be shipped back to Washington," Butch said matter-of-factly. "Somebody else will be sitting at his desk." He regarded Kay, an eyebrow cocked. "One of your Brits. Montgomery, maybe."

"Montgomery's not *my* Brit." Kay snapped. She knew that Montgomery wouldn't tolerate a female driver in the war zone. She'd be sent back to England so fast that she wouldn't have a chance to say goodbye to Dick.

They hadn't been able to spend much time together. There were letters, of course, and she had seen him once in Algiers when he'd come over from Oran for a meeting. All they'd had time for was a quick dinner and a few kisses before he flew back to his unit, but it was enough.

It had to be. It was all they had.

ॐ

As it turned out, Ike almost didn't get to Casablanca. His B-17, long retired from combat duty, lost two engines over the Atlas Mountains. The passengers put on parachutes and stood at the hatches, ready to jump. The plane had limped in on two engines. To get back to Algiers after he made his report to the decision-makers, Ike had to thumb a ride with the Eighth Air Force.

But he wasn't sacked. He was kicked upstairs. He was given a fourth star and named Commanding General of the North African Theater of Operations, while three British generals were given command of daily air, sea, and ground operations. That is, the Brits now had control over what happened at the front. He had been outflanked and he knew it. Ike's fourth star was political, Butch told Kay—and more than a little grudging, because there had been no victories to reward. Roosevelt and Marshall understood that one of the problems the American commander in chief had faced was the fact that he was outranked by the British generals who reported to him. Ike welcomed the promotion, but Kay—who was with him in his most unguarded hours—could see that he was dealing with something close to humiliation. He understood, in a way he hadn't before, that a title was one thing and authority was another.

After Casablanca, General Marshall flew to Algiers for a private conference with Ike. Kay met him at the airport and felt instantly frozen by his glance of glacial displeasure. "*Mrs.* Summersby," he addressed her, with emphasis. She didn't understand—until Butch told her that Marshall had heard from his wife (who had heard it on the army wives' grapevine) that Mamie Eisenhower had seen the *Life* magazine "official family" photograph back in November and was angry and unhappy about it.

"But that's not my fault," Kay protested. "What does he want me to do?"

Butch looked uncomfortable. "Marshall told Ike he should have left you in London."

"Oh, bloody *hell*," Kay said despairingly. "He's not going to insist that the Boss send me back, is he?"

SUSAN WITTIG ALBERT

"That's what he wanted to do, but Ike got stubborn, so he backed off." Butch gave her a direct look. "You have to understand that Marshall is old-school, Kay. The army is his family, and he keeps a close eye on the way his boys behave. If they don't toe the straight and narrow, he lets them have it, both barrels." He chuckled ruefully. "I'm glad I'm in the navy. General Marshall isn't *my* father."

There was more—and it was funny. That evening, Kay drove Marshall and Ike to Ike's villa, where Marshall was to spend the night. Formidably formal, Marshall did not unbend when Telek jumped up to greet him, so Kay took the dog into the sitting room while Ike showed his boss to the elegant upstairs bedroom where he was to sleep. Telek, who always hated to be left out of the action, leaped out of her lap and dashed up the stairs.

Kay got the rest of the story from a pink-faced and sputtering Butch, who carried the dog downstairs a little later. As Ike and Marshall were chatting, Telek had jumped up on Marshall's bed, hiked his leg, and peed on the pillow.

"Just like a kid thumbing his nose at a mean old man," Butch said, trying to smother his laughter. "Ike was red as a beet. I couldn't decide whether he was mad at the dog or trying to keep from laughing."

Kay fought against a giggle. "Bad puppy," she said sternly.

She smuggled the disgraced Telek out of the house and kept him with her until Marshall had left Algiers. When she returned the dog to the villa the next morning, Ike took him with a gruff "thank you." To Telek, he said, "Don't you ever, ever do that again."

Telek licked his nose.

❧

One good thing did come out of the uncomfortable visit. Concerned about Ike's health, Marshall ordered him to lay off the sixteen-hour days and make time for some relaxation.

"What I need is another Telegraph Cottage," Eisenhower said, and Butch immediately went in search of it.

A few days later, Kay drove Ike and Butch to take a look at the new retreat, ten miles outside of Algiers. It was a white stucco farmhouse with a red-tiled roof and three small bedrooms, surrounded by a courtyard fence. Its biggest attractions: a stable, a sandy beach on a quiet cove, a range of open woodland, and a gorgeous view of the Mediterranean from the clifftop. Butch gave it the name "Sailor's Delight"—because, Kay suspected, he and Molly intended to make use of it, too.

The Boss called it "the farm" and ordered Butch to find him some horses. "Get a couple," he added, turning to Kay with the brusqueness that had become typical of his communications with her. "You want to ride too, Irish?"

"That would be smashing," Kay replied, because that was the truth. Then she hoped she hadn't sounded too eager. She didn't want him to misunderstand.

"Good," Ike said. To Butch, he said, "Let's have the horses here next week, when Kay and I get back from the front."

"She's driving you to Tebessa?" Butch slid a questioning glance at Kay. He lowered his voice. "You sure that's a good idea?"

Kay saw the General bristle. "Why not?" he growled.

"Well, because . . ." Butch looked uncomfortable. "She's . . . you know. A woman. She—"

"Cut that crap, Butch," the Boss said shortly. "There are nurses out there. Women have a job to do just like men. It's a fact of life. The sooner everybody gets used to it, the better."

Butch shifted from one foot to the other. "That wasn't exactly what I—"

"I'll leave it up to you, Irish," the Boss said, interrupting again. "This is a combat drive and you're a volunteer. If for any reason you don't want to do it, you're excused. I'll get somebody else."

Kay knew what Butch was getting at. It was the appearance of the thing, especially given what Marshall had said. And she wasn't sure she wanted to make the drive. It would be long and uncomfortable and dangerous. But maybe the General was doing this *because* of what Marshall had said. Maybe Ike wanted to prove—to Marshall, to the rest of them—that she was a soldier, just like everybody else. If that was it, she had to back him up.

"I'll do it, sir," she said promptly.

The Boss didn't say thank you. "Be ready to leave at midnight," he said. "It's a two-day drive."

Kay straightened her shoulders. Good. The long trip would allow her to demonstrate to the General that their personal encounters were behind them, in the past, forgotten. She was a soldier and she was doing a soldier's job. What's more, she was engaged to Dick. *He* was first in her life and in her thoughts, as he should be.

Her determination was strengthened by Dick's almost daily letters. He was still in Oran, and still hoping that Fredendall would give him his own command at the front. And he had news:

> . . . the very best news! I've applied to my CO for permission to marry you and it's been granted. In fact, it went all the way up to Eisenhower and came back with his John Henry on the bottom line. June 22 is the date I put down—which might have to be delayed if the Tunisian campaign drags on.
>
> So there it is, in black and white, my dear. You can't back out now. I love you, Kay, more than I can ever say.

"I love you, too," she wrote back to him, "with all my heart."

And of course she did. A June bride, she told herself, smiling a little. She would be a June bride, and the gang in Eisenhower's office could help them celebrate. The thought of Eisenhower pulled her back to Dick's letter. The General had approved his request to marry—and he hadn't said anything to her about it? That was odd.

But no matter. She *would* be a June bride, Dick's bride. And when the war was over, she would go home with him to America and they would live happily ever after. If she thought with a half-furtive pleasure of horseback riding with Ike at the farm, she quickly pulled a curtain over the thought.

∞

It was a chilly, rainy midnight on February 12 when Kay began her first combat drive. They were taking the Cadillac, which she seldom drove in town because Mickey had been right: it was big and as hard to maneuver as a tank. But it was heavy enough to take the punishment of the mountain roads and armored against attack, so that's what she was driving. She was dressed for the trip in slacks, a man's battle blouse, a fleece-lined leather RAF jacket that had turned up in St. George's lost and found, brown boots, and a steel helmet.

Ike chuckled when he saw her. "Well, we've got the tank," he said, putting a hand on the Cadillac's hood. "All you need are a pair of ivory-handled revolvers and you could pass for Georgie Patton."

"I have *my* gun, sir," Kay said firmly, and pulled out the Beretta that replaced the one she had lost when the *Strathallan* went down. The front was 720 miles away and the two-lane road was known to be dangerous. If there was trouble, she was determined to hold up her end as well as one of the boys.

"That'll do." Ike said. "Let's get on the road, Irish."

The five-vehicle convoy set off. The lead scout car went first, followed by Kay and Eisenhower in the Cadillac, his flag fluttering on the hood. A weapons carrier followed, and a backup sedan (in case the Caddy was disabled), with a second scout car bringing up the rear. The convoy moved as fast as conditions allowed, but the twisting two-lane road was crowded with large trucks carrying equipment and supplies to the front and ambulances carrying the wounded back. Bands of rain and low fog slicked the macadam surface. Kay found herself hunched over the wheel, her attention fixed on the narrow pavement ahead. If her backseat passenger had asked her a question, personal or otherwise, she couldn't have answered him.

The grueling, white-knuckle drive was broken by an overnight stop in the ancient walled city of Constantine, where Brigadier General Truscott had established an advance command post in an empty orphanage. There, in that all-male enclave, Kay found herself the target of a barrage of grins, muted wolf-whistles, and pointed remarks. Eisenhower, hearing it, flushed red, glowered, and muttered about the lack of discipline.

Kay wasn't offended. She knew that the men hadn't seen a woman for months and would whistle at anybody who looked remotely female, even in slacks and a battle-scarred flight jacket. But in one or two of the remarks, she caught an assumption about her and Eisenhower that made her distinctly uncomfortable. She could only hold her head high and hope that Dick wouldn't hear any of it.

That was bad enough, but what happened at Tebessa was worse. The convoy left Constantine at dawn and pushed on through showers of sleet and cold rain toward the front, a couple of hundred miles farther east. Truscott had joined Eisenhower in the backseat and Kay could hear the tension in their voices as they discussed plans to meet a threatened Axis attack. At Tebessa, in the late afternoon, the biting wind that swept down from the highlands was filled with spurts of icy rain. Eisenhower ordered Kay to stay at the command post. He picked up another car and driver and headed out into the desert to the American airfields at Thélepte and Fériana.

Kay could sense a deep uneasiness among the men at the post. The recent action had produced casualties, and the post hospital was full. She overheard low-voiced, edgy talk of intelligence reports of a German attack in the next few hours, although nobody seemed to know where it might occur or how the Allies would respond. She heard a couple of worried officers saying that the danger of ambush was so high that the General should fly back to Algiers, rather than drive. They seemed to be concerned about their four-star guest out on the desert, too—especially after they lost radio contact with Eisenhower's party. And she caught a couple of raised eyebrows and quizzical glances and understood what was behind them. The sentries' code-word challenge, "Snafu" and the counter-sign, "Damned right" summed up the general apprehension.

Kay ate at the officers' mess, then decided to get some sleep in order to be ready for the trip home—or for whatever else might happen. A corporal directed her to the VIP tent, which boasted a pebble floor rather than the usual mud, and a pair of army cots with just enough room for a thin soldier to sidle between them. Fully dressed and still wearing her boots, she climbed into her sleeping bag, pulled it over her head, and went to sleep.

It was pitch black when she was awakened by the General's gruff voice outside the tent. The corporal was saying, "Your driver's in there, sir. Hang on and I'll find her another tent."

"Hell, no," Eisenhower rasped. "*She* didn't dump me in the goddamned ditch. She's gotta get me back to Algiers tomorrow. Let her sleep."

No! Kay thought. What was he *thinking?* She was struggling to get out of her sleeping bag so Eisenhower could have the place to himself, but he had already come in and was snapping the tent flaps. A moment later, he had spread his sleeping bag on the cot next to hers and was climbing in, fully dressed and wearing his battle jacket. Another few minutes, and he was snoring—loudly.

Kay gave up and lay still, hoping that whoever was standing outside the tent could hear the General's snores and understand that nothing else was going on inside.

The next day, she learned that the soldier at the wheel of Ike's car, exhausted from the strain of driving a four-star passenger a hundred blackout miles over terrible roads in enemy territory, had dumped his vehicle in a ditch. She didn't blame the poor guy. She knew exactly how he felt. But she wished that Ike had let the cor-poral find her another place to sleep. The General might be going out of his way to treat her like one of the boys, but she *wasn't*, and the whole camp knew it.

The German attack happened after they left, and they learned the bad news when they got back to Algiers. The Fifth Panzer Army had broken through at Faïd Pass. Tanks of the First Armored Division had run into an ambush of infamous Krupp eighty-eights, high-velocity anti-aircraft guns. "It was murder," an observer wrote. "The First Armored rolled right into the muzzles of the concealed eighty-eights. All I could do was stand by and watch tank after tank blown to bits."

Things would go from bad to worse. A week later, Eisenhower would blame himself for the mauling at Kasserine Pass that cost some ten thousand casualties. The errors of the Allied field commanders—British, French, and American—would be laid at Eisenhower's door, and at a press conference in Algiers, he took full responsibility for the defeat. Then he sat down to study his mistakes—and wait to see if he would be relieved. For him, Kasserine Pass would be one of the lowest points of the war. In his diary, Butch would write that "the proud and cocky Americans today stand humiliated by one of the greatest defeats in our history."

For Kay, the bad news took a different form. One afternoon a couple of weeks after the trip to the front, she was at her desk, sorting cables. It had already been a difficult day. Montgomery was being insufferable and Patton, whom Eisenhower had put in command of II Corps, was wooing the war correspondents with speeches like "Tomorrow we attack. If we are not victorious, let no one come back alive"—not exactly what the mothers and wives back home wanted to hear. Eisenhower was in a rotten mood and everybody in the office was staying out of his line of fire.

His arms full of folders, Tex stopped at her desk. He bent over and said, in a low voice, "Kay, I think you ought to know that there's a lot of gossip going the rounds. About you and the Old Man."

"That's just too bloody bad," Kay said shortly. She took a deep breath. "What kind of gossip?"

Tex shifted awkwardly. "Well, they're saying that out there at Tebessa, you . . ." He coughed. "The two of you slept together."

"Well, for once 'they' got it right." Kay managed a wry chuckle. "We both slept in the VIP tent. But we never got our clothes off." She told Tex what had happened. "And to be honest," she added, "I hope it's the last time I ever have to sleep with that guy. He snores like a one-man artillery bombardment."

Tex shook his head disapprovingly. "The Old Man should have had better sense. It's not right for him to compromise you." He shifted his armload of folders. "I'll pass the word, where I can."

But Kay understood that the real story wouldn't make it very far. Sadly, she reflected that Dick would likely hear the gossip.

Eisenhower was feeling better. The Marines were kicking the Japs off of Guadalcanal. The remaining German forces had surrendered to the Soviet army at Stalingrad. And with the coming of spring, the North African situation had improved. In March, the German army under Rommel and von Arnim—outflanked and outgunned—was pinched between the Allied Eighth under Montgomery and the First under Anderson. There was hard fighting, but the Germans and Italians were cut off from support by their naval and air forces based in Sicily. They were weakening.

Ike was making more trips to the front, flying now, which was quicker than driving. But he had to admit (to himself—he couldn't discuss this with Butch or Beetle) that he was keeping Kay out of the limelight in order to protect her. While it was more or less reasonable (he couldn't decide which) to ask her to drive to the front, it had been unforgivably stupid to bed down with her in the same tent. The event had lit a wildfire of rumor that blazed from post to post along the front. Eisenhower generally put his head down and ignored gossip, but he would have to be deaf, dumb, and blind not to be aware of this story.

In late March, Ike and Beetle flew to Gafsa to confer with Patton, who was whipping II Corps into shape. Beetle went to bed early and Ike stayed up for a few drinks with Patton. Their friendship dated back to 1920, when Ike was at Camp Meade as the second-in-command of the 305th Tank Brigade and George commanded the 304th. Tonight, they discussed the comparative virtues of the heavily armored German Tiger tank, which was designed to knock out other tanks in the front lines, and the American Grants and Shermans, designed to smash through enemy defenses and raise holy hell in the rear—the traditional role of cavalry. In fact, Ike parenthetically reported, Marshall had just disbanded the Chief of Cavalry's office. The horse was out of a job now, replaced by armored vehicles and tanks.

"Speaking of armored vehicles," Patton said, with a great deal of amusement, "that reminds me of a story that's going the rounds out here. You want to hear it?"

"Maybe," Ike said, not sure that it was the right answer.

Patton grinned. "Well, it seems that you and Kay were on your way back from the front late one evening. You were still fifty-some miles from Algiers when that armored Cadillac of yours developed engine trouble. Kay went under the hood to see what was wrong, but wasn't having any luck finding the problem. After a while, you got out, opened the trunk, and took out a tool. 'Screwdriver?' you asked, and handed it to her. 'Might as well,' she said. 'I can't get the bloody thing started.'"

Slapping his knee, Patton roared with laughter. "Get it?" he asked, when Ike stared at him, stone-faced. "Screwdriver. Screw driver."

Ike could feel himself flushing and the veins in his temples throbbed. "Some goddamned idiots don't have anything better to do than flap their goddamned mouths," he growled.

"Hey, sorry, Ike." Patton's laughter faded into a frown. "Hell, I thought you'd find it amusing, after the night the two of you spent in the VIP tent in Tebessa." He eyed Ike, paused, and tried again. "You know, I've met your Irish gal. She's charming, smart as a whip, too. Not only that, she has got to be the best-looking driver in any man's army, anywhere. I don't wonder that you—"

"She is also engaged," Ike interrupted testily. "To one of Truscott's engineers. A colonel named Richard Arnold, whom she is scheduled to marry on June 22." The date—which he had seen on Arnold's permission to marry request—had somehow got stuck in his mind. "In fact, she came to North Africa just to be near him. Her being here has nothing to do with me. As for that night at Tebessa, I was so tired I wasn't thinking straight. I should've found another place to bunk. Bad mistake."

Patton eyed him for a moment, one eyebrow cocked. Then he lifted his glass. "Well, then," he said. "To the happy bridegroom. A man to be envied." After a moment, he added, with unaccustomed delicacy, "Until the wedding, you might consider moving her out of AFHQ. Maybe to Oran."

"Nothing doing," Ike growled. "She's the best goddamned driver I've got. *She's* never put me in the ditch."

While the gossip made Ike feel that he had to protect Kay, it also made him dig in his heels. His mother had always said he was stubborn as a Missouri mule, and by damn, he was going to be stubborn about this. There was nothing between him and Kay Summersby, nothing at all—which would become quite evident shortly, when she and Arnold were married. What's more, the military *needed* women and lots of them, to release men for combat. A female driver behind the wheel of the general's car meant a man with a gun on the front line. So he and Kay were going to drive to the front when that was necessary, enjoy their evenings at bridge, and—now that the weather was decent—get out with the horses for an afternoon's ride. Which was, after all, what Marshall had ordered him to do. Wasn't it? Take a break from the war every now and then?

At Ike's direction, Butch had managed to get his hands on three Arabian horses, gleaming chestnuts with silken, flowing manes and tails, and had them stabled at the farm. Ike had seen a lot of horses in his long army career, but he had to admit that these were quite remarkable. They were massive stallions, strong and high-spirited, and required a rider who had the strength and spirit to control them. The horses that he and Kay had ridden at Richmond had been docile enough for even Mamie to ride, and when he first saw the Arabians, he'd hesitated to let Kay get aboard. But she quickly demonstrated both her strength and her mastery, and the two of them rode together whenever he could get away from the damned desk, sometimes as often as three or four times a week.

The area around the farm was isolated and open, making it ideal riding country. The fields were bright with the blooms of red poppies, orange nasturtiums, and pink wild roses. The air was fresh and clear, and the clifftop gave a marvelous view of the blue Mediterranean, gilded by the late-afternoon sun. Unlike Algiers, where trouble was around every corner, the farm was safe. Beetle had posted sentries at the only entry and assigned a security guard armed with a Thompson submachine gun to ride thirty or forty yards behind them. Ike often thought that if he wanted to yank Kay off her horse and ride off into the sunset with her, like the heroes in his Wild West magazines, the security guard would be watching every move. If he had harbored *any* ulterior motive—a stolen kiss, an embrace, something more—the realization that they were under constant surveillance would have been enough to cool his ardor.

But that was *not* going to happen. He was simply enjoying the girl's lively company, which lifted his spirits and brightened his day. On balance, he reflected, it was probably good that they were watched. Let the rumormongers understand that he and his driver were under the eyes of his staff and his guards every minute of every day. Let Patton and his friends repeat whatever ridiculous jokes they liked. He lived in a goddamned goldfish bowl. They could put *that* in their pipes and smoke it.

The tide had turned after Kasserine, and finally, on May 6, the Allies got what they came for. The British retook Tunis, and American troops reached Bizerte. On May 13, the Axis forces surrendered. The Germans continued their nighttime bombing of Algiers—Mickey had picked up a dozen pieces of shrapnel in the courtyard at the villa, and nearby explosions had cracked the plaster. But it was a minor harassment. The campaign was finally over. North Africa was in the hands of the Allies.

On May 20, the end was marked by a victory parade at Tunis—not something Eisenhower enjoyed, but it was obligatory. Victories had to be celebrated so that the victors could remind themselves—and the vanquished—of their power. As parades go, this one went well enough, he supposed. He and the French and British commanding generals took eyes-right salutes from the twenty-eight thousand troops that marched past the reviewing stand in the broiling desert sun.

The Americans were tough and rugged in dirty, sweat-stained battle dress with steel helmets and weapons at the ready. "Vive l'Amérique!" the spectators cried as Mitchell bombers and Spitfires roared overhead, rocking their wings in salute. The British—Brits and Scots and Kiwis and Aussies and Sikhs—wore khaki shorts and knee socks, with berets or forage caps, their shirts unbuttoned at the throat and the sleeves rolled to the elbow, showing tanned, muscular arms. "They made a marvelous show," Beetle had to acknowledge later. "Better than our guys."

But the French—the Foreign Legion, the Chasseurs d'Afrique, the Tirailleurs, and the Zouaves—stole the show, which was ironic, Eisenhower thought, since they hadn't been particularly effective in the campaign. Sometimes they couldn't even decide whose side they were on. Their exhibition reminded him of a Shriners parade back home: scarlet pantaloons and narrow-waisted blue tunics with crimson and gold epaulets; *les blancs képis*, bright turbans, and black woolen berets; polished knee boots, field boots, sandals, even bare feet. Most extraordinary of all were the bearded Goums in their camel-hair robes with bulging leather pouches, which the American GIs whispered were full of enemy ears.

After the parade, Muhammad al-Amin, the Bey of Tunis, summoned Eisenhower to the palace. The Bey was wearing a dress uniform with gold cuffs and gold epaulets as big as dinner plates and was seated on a gold throne flanked by white-robed attendants. He presented Eisenhower with the highest Tunisian order, the Nichan Iftikhar, the "Order of Glory."

As Ike stood to attention, he couldn't help reflecting that it had been almost exactly a year—just a year!—since he had arrived in London, a two-star nobody to whom the British generals gave the cold shoulder. And here he was, receiving a big silver medal from a foreign potentate who acted like he was some sort of savior. He wasn't letting it go to his head, though. When he got back to Abilene, he and his brothers and their friends would have a big laugh about it. Still, as victory celebrations go, this had been a pretty good one—except for one thing. A small thing, really, and he had tried to dismiss it. But it rankled, and he was still thinking about it as he boarded the plane to fly back to Algiers.

His personal staff had traveled with him to Tunis for the parade, and he'd made sure that they had seats in the bleachers next to the reviewing stand. At one point, he had turned to look for them and had spotted them, sitting all together on the top row. Tex, Beetle, Butch, Mickey, Kay—and seated beside her, a tall, good-looking, dark-haired officer.

Arnold, Eisenhower thought, startled. *Colonel Richard Arnold*. The man Kay was going to marry in just a month. He had a possessive arm around her shoulders and she was looking up into his face and laughing. And then he bent to kiss her.

Eisenhower felt his gut tighten. "A man to be envied," Georgie had said. He was right.

❧

For Kay, seeing Dick in Tunis was an unexpected delight. After the parade, they had found a quiet corner in a little café, where they sat for an hour, talking over glasses of strong Turkish coffee and a plate of date biscuits. There was news: Dick would very soon have his own command, the Twentieth Engineers. If he could get a day or two of leave, he would stop in Algiers and they could have a little time together.

"It won't be much," he said ruefully, reaching for her hand.

"But better than nothing. And maybe we'll be able to talk about wedding plans."

Wedding plans, she thought with a little thrill of pleasure. "Now aren't you glad I'm here in Algeria?" she asked lightly.

"Oh, you bet," he said. He picked up her hand and kissed her fingers. "Even if it means that you're sleeping with Eisenhower."

She stared at him, horrified. She had written to him about the VIP tent at Tebessa, and she'd hoped he would understand. "Oh, Dick," she whispered, "surely you don't think—"

"Right. I *don't* think," he said firmly. "I'm sorry, Kay—I shouldn't tease. That was stupid of Eisenhower, though. That kind of thing just feeds the gossip." He glanced at his watch. "Dammit, I have to catch a plane."

"Ships passing in the night," she said with a regretful laugh. "But it won't always be this way."

"No," he said, "it won't. And June 22 is just around the corner. Kathleen Arnold. I like that." A smile crinkled his eyes. "Mrs. Richard Arnold. I like that even better."

At the airfield, they kissed goodbye and boarded different planes. Dick was on his way to Oran and Kay was flying back to Algiers, where the AFHQ would be hosting a round of visits by Prime Minister Churchill, General Marshall, and (later) General de Gaulle. Tunisia had been won, but the invasion of Sicily lay ahead and planning was already underway for the Italian campaign that would begin in September.

And by that time, she thought, she and Dick would be married and her new life would begin.

The special guests arrived, one after another, over a period of several weeks, and Kay drove Eisenhower to the airfield to meet each of them. Marshall was his usual frosty self and de Gaulle was the unbending aristocrat, both of them militarily proper. But when

Churchill arrived, he bounded across the airfield to greet her, waving his cigar.

"Not a bit surprised to find you here, holding up our banner among the Yanks." His pudgy face wore a cherubic smile. "How do you like driving on the wrong side of the road?" He made sure that she was invited to the dinners at Ike's villa, where she enjoyed bantering with the PM, who wore his siren suit and embroidered slippers just as he did at Chequers.

But for Kay, the most important visitor was a man who traveled in great secrecy, under the pseudonym of General Lyon: King George the Sixth. After several days of frenetic preparation, the King arrived at Maison Blanche airfield in his Lancaster. The plane circled the field twice, then touched down smartly and taxied behind a jeep with a yellow flag to the end of the field, where it came to a stop in front of the assembled brass and a bevy of cameramen from the Army Pictorial Service. A few moments later, the King, slim and stiffly erect in dress naval whites, came slowly down the stairs. After a round of salutes and handshakes, the King and the General got into the Cadillac, with Kay behind the wheel and Butch in the front seat beside her.

I am actually driving the King! Kay thought with breathless excitement. But because of the extra-tight security—nobody was supposed to know that royalty was in town—she had only the usual two-motorcycle escort to clear traffic. She drove up the hill to the villa of General Gale, where the King would be staying, and parked in the curving driveway in front of the impressive house.

Once out of the car, Eisenhower paused to introduce Captain Butcher, his naval aide. Butch stiffened and saluted smartly. The King gave him a thin, aristocratic smile and held out his hand. Then, to Kay's enormous surprise, Eisenhower turned to her.

"Your Majesty, this is Kay Summersby. She is a British subject, on duty at my headquarters as my personal driver. I am grateful for her service."

Kay hadn't expected to be introduced to the King, and she fumbled nervously for the right response. She was wearing an

American uniform, so she couldn't curtsy as a subject; she was a civilian, so she couldn't salute. After a moment's blurred hesitation, she bobbed a half curtsy and hesitantly put out her hand, saying, "How do you do, sir?"

The King ignored her hand, nodded a curt dismissal, and turned away. Kay was chilled by his rebuke. She had been so excited about being with the man whose modest, unflinching courage had won British hearts—and hers—during the awful days of the Blitz. She couldn't help feeling hurt that he hadn't found even a small smile for her. She stayed out of his way at the dinner the General gave in his villa, and for his part, he pointedly ignored her. Of course, while it might be argued that he should at least have been polite, she felt she was asking too much to think that he might have paid her any attention at all. She was only an ordinary British citizen of no special standing, and he was the *King*. She should count herself lucky just to be seated at the same table with him.

And she did. After dinner that night, she went back to her billet and wrote a letter to her mum. "Guess what, Mum!" she wrote. "I had dinner with the King tonight!!!"

Then she sat back and looked at what she had written. The King's visit was top secret and the censor would black it out. She wadded it up and threw it away.

In war, everything was secret. Even the good news couldn't be shared.

§੭

Dick had been disappointed that his command hadn't come through while the fighting was going on in Tunisia, but Kay had been secretly glad he was back in Oran, and safe. And now that the fighting was over, she was delighted, too—and even more, when he was able to stop off in Algiers on his way to his new post in the Tunisian desert.

Generously, Eisenhower gave Kay the day off and sent her

and Dick off to the farm where they could play tennis and swim. Butch loaned Dick a pair of swim trunks and Mickey packed a picnic lunch for them. When Kay opened the basket at the hidden beach, she found a bottle of wine and an unexpected note from the Boss: "Hope you and Dick enjoy your time together." It was signed "DE."

Dick stretched face-down on the blue-striped cotton blanket she had brought. "Gotta say that your general is an all-right guy." He turned his head to face her, opening one eye. "And for the record, I have never believed a single word of all those crappy rumors."

Overhead, a pair of storm petrels sliced through the crystalline sky. Kay leaned over to brush the sand out of his dark hair. "Oh, those rumors. I wish—"

"Just forget them." Dick turned over on his back and pulled her down against him. "The thing is, I *know* you, Kay. Eisenhower is a great guy. He's a powerhouse, and maybe he's made a move or two. I mean, it's pretty obvious that he likes you, and I sure couldn't blame him if he made a try. But I know you'd never go for somebody like him." He ran a playful finger down her nose. "Number one, he's practically bald. Number two, he's old enough to be your father. A guy that age . . . he's probably no good at all in the sack."

Kay thought of New Year's Eve and Ike's arms around her. She pushed herself up and gave Dick a playful slap. "And number three, why would I want anybody else when I have *you?*"

"Damn right. You got the best, right here." Dick flung his arms out, squeezing his eyes shut against the bright sun. "You know, I've decided something, Kay. When this war is over, I'm getting out. I'm leaving the army."

Surprised, Kay sat up straight, pulling up the top of the one-piece bathing suit she'd borrowed from Ethel. "Leaving the army?" She was suddenly struck by the thought that what she knew of Dick was entirely framed by his identity as an army officer. She had never seen him wearing anything but his uniform—and now Butch's bathing trunks. What other life had he led, outside of the army? What other interests? What other hopes and dreams? Who *was* he?

Wonderingly, she asked, "What will you do instead?"

"Dunno, but I'll figure it out. My mother has a place in Florida. Maybe we'll go there. Sunshine and blue skies and palm trees along every street." He opened his eyes and smiled dreamily at her. "Florida, that's it. You'll love it, Kay. We'll have a house with a big green yard—lots of grass to mow—and *kids*. Two kids, a boy for me, a girl for you." He put up a hand and touched her cheek. "Maybe even three, huh?"

"Florida," she mused, clasping her arms around her knees. "Florida." It sounded exotic, wonderful. It reminded her of how much she wanted to go to America, where it seemed to her that the future was just around the corner. "Florida and a house and a yard and . . . and children." She had wanted children, but Gordon didn't. It was one of the wedges that had driven them apart. "It sounds like heaven, Dick."

Dick sat up too, then pushed her down on her back, flinging his bare, sandy leg over hers. "What's heaven for me is *you*, Kay. Being with you, having you." She felt herself arching against him. "Just you, only you, always. You know that, don't you?" His hands were rough on her bare skin and the beach was a gritty bed, but she didn't care.

They swam and ate and then went up to the farmhouse and slept through the heat of the afternoon in one of the little bedrooms. When they woke up, they made plans for their wedding, only a few weeks away. If Dick couldn't get to Algiers, she would go wherever he was, and the company chaplain would marry them in a simple ceremony. That night, the General invited Butch and Molly and Beetle and Ethel and Mickey and Pearlie to a dinner party in their honor, and opened a bottle of French champagne to toast their future. The next morning, Dick left for Sedjenane to take up his new command and Kay—sunburned, content—returned Ethel's swimsuit and Butch's trunks and went back to work.

෩

It wasn't just Kay and Dick who were planning a wedding. At the General's Villa dar el Ouad, things had taken a romantic turn. Butch had made a two-week visit to the States in March, and when he came back, he brought with him another black Scottie, a bride for Telek. Her name was Caacie (short, Butch said, for Canine Auxiliary Air Corps), and pronounced "Khaki."

Telek was smitten but Caacie was no pushover. On their first date, she bit him. But this painful rejection only made the little dog more determined to press his suit, and it wasn't long before he had won his reluctant lady. Two months later, Caacie produced three jet black puppies, the most adorable Kay had ever seen.

The puppies brightened life at the General's villa, which was becoming more easygoing now that the Tunisian campaign had come to an end. The planning for Husky (the code name for the invasion of Sicily, the next part of the Mediterranean campaign) was underway, but there was time for riding in the afternoons and bridge in the evening. To the staff's relief—and especially Kay's— the General was more relaxed and cheerful than he had been since Operation Torch was launched. Not even the scheduled return of General de Gaulle—a difficult, autocratic man who bitterly resented the Allies' occupation of French territory—could darken his mood.

One June day, though, Kay thought that there must have been a military setback that hadn't yet been announced. She knew Eisenhower well enough to read his moods, and as the day wore on, she saw that he was becoming more withdrawn and troubled. The weather had turned threatening, too. The afternoon had been hot and sultry, and now a thunderstorm was gathering. As she drove him back to the villa at the end of the workday, the sky over the sea was glazed with a deep purple and a rumble of thunder echoed against the green hills. He was silent throughout the ride, but as she pulled to a stop in front of the villa, he said, "Come in and have a drink with me, Kay."

He made their usual Scotch and water. Then, glass in one hand, he put the other hand on her shoulder.

"Kay," he said gruffly, "There's no easy way to tell you this, so I'm going to say it straight out. I'm sorry. Dick is dead."

The world seemed to stop. She stared at him for a moment, then heard herself ask, with astonishing calmness, "How? How did it happen? There's no enemy action in the area, is there?"

"No. It was an accident, a week ago—just a few days after he got out there." He dropped his hand, but his eyes were on her face, his own face somber. "General Truscott sent a wire immediately, but it got lost in the message center. Somebody there happened to mention it to Tex, assuming he knew, and Butch tracked it down quick as he could. Dick and another officer were clearing a German mine field. One of them hit a trip wire, and a Teller mine exploded. The other officer survived, but Dick was killed instantly." His mouth tightened. "I am so sorry, Kay. So very sorry."

She closed her eyes tight and stood for a moment, willing herself not to cry. She could feel her heart beating through her skin, echoing with the words in her ears. *Dead, dead. Dick is dead. So very sorry Dick is dead.*

And then the reality of it hit her like a punch in the belly and the room went dark. She heard her glass shatter on the floor as her knees gave way and she sagged. Ike's arm went around her, steadying her as he half-led, half-carried her to the sofa and made her sit down. He sat beside her, holding her as she began to weep, holding her tenderly, as if she were a child.

"Just cry," he whispered against her hair. "I know it hurts, Kay. Just cry. Just cry."

She cried for what seemed hours, as the storm broke around them, thunder crashing against the house and the rain coming down in torrents outside the window. After a while, Ike went to the kitchen and came back with a mug of hot sweet tea. He put it into her shaking hand and made her drink it.

Very quietly, he said, "You're not going to get over this for a while. It's too hard." He handed her a handkerchief. "I want you to go out to the farm for a few days."

"I can't." She blew her nose. "General de Gaulle is coming and you need—"

"Forget about de Gaulle," he said roughly. "We'll manage. Nobody's staying at the farm, and you can be alone out there. Go riding. Go walking. Activity helps." His voice softened and he put his hand on her hair, smoothing it. "Losing someone you love cuts deep. I know—I lost my own little boy. It takes time to deal with it. Take as much time as you need."

That evening, Butch, deeply sympathetic, drove her out to the farmhouse. The rain had stopped and she went out on the terrace to watch the lightning play across the sea as the storm retreated into the distance. At last she went to bed—the narrow bed in the small bedroom where she and Dick had made love—but not to sleep. The window was open to the fresh sea breeze and she lay very still, letting the cool air brush over her, feeling the penetrating loneliness. The man she'd planned to marry was dead, and she was left alone to mourn the empty years ahead, mourn the life they would no longer have together, mourn the unlived-in house in Florida, the unborn children, the unfilled days. But now that the immediate shock had passed, she found that she couldn't cry. She couldn't sleep, either, and when morning came, she was still lying awake, listening to the gulls call as they rode the wind, watching the sun climb the white-washed wall.

She hadn't eaten the night before, so she got up and went into the empty kitchen, where she found eggs and bacon in the refrigerator and coffee and a coffee pot and fresh oranges. And then, sitting at the table by the window, thinking of the lonely, empty beds and unshared breakfasts that stretched out across the days and years ahead, she was quite suddenly angry at herself—an anger that had the startling force of a swift, hard slap in the face.

Why was she *doing* this? She was alive and comfortable, here with coffee and orange juice and eggs and bacon, in the fresh, bright sunshine of an Algerian morning. It was *Dick* who was dead. He was the one who had lost all future mornings, lost all the future, lost his chance to have children, to live in a world that was no longer at war, to find work that satisfied, to lead a productive life. She stared down at her plate. How could she be so self-centered? It wasn't her empty future she should be mourning. She should be mourning his. She should be crying for *him*.

But with this thought came another, even more startling. She couldn't mourn him, she couldn't cry for him, because she didn't really know the man she was grieving. Oh, yes. She could remember Dick's physical presence, remember the feel of his lean, hard body against hers, the urgency of his desire—but theirs had been a wartime romance. They had met and fallen in love and within a month of their meeting they were planning to marry. But days, weeks, even *months* passed when they were apart, and when they did manage to meet, they had only a few rushed hours. She knew nothing about his family or his life back in America, and he had met her mother and sister only once. She had never seen him dressed in anything but his uniform and Butch's borrowed swim trunks. She knew he was a good dancer, but she didn't know what he liked to read or whether he played bridge or snored or preferred his steaks rare. She didn't know *him*. She had spent more time with Beetle and Butch and Tex and Eisenhower—with Eisenhower especially—than she had with Dick. And Eisenhower knew her better and had seen more of her family than Dick ever had.

She washed her few dishes and went out to the stable. The bright morning sky had turned gray and there was the scent of rain in the air, but she didn't care. She saddled one of the stallions and rode—fast and hard, testing herself and the horse—until she was exhausted. But she couldn't outrace the fierce, hard grief that pounded behind her like a demon. She ached for Dick, for herself, for the loss of their lovely dream, for all the sweet years they would not have together.

At last, she dismounted on the secluded beach where she and Dick had lain together and made love on that last, beautiful day.

Now, the clouds and water were the same dull gray and the sea was whipped to a foamy froth by the stiff onshore breeze that flung salt spray against her face. High in the sky, one single gray gull hung, hovering, on the wet wind. Two gray ships, like toy boats, moved along the distant horizon.

She thought of the moment the *Strathallan* had been torpedoed, of the fiery bombs that had rained on London, of the hundreds of corpses she had ferried in her makeshift ambulance during the Blitz. She thought of the war dead—so many, *many* of them, now and in all the days and nights until Hitler would at last be beaten—and the death of one, just one, seemed to shrink into a terrible insignificance.

And at last she began to cry, but now she was crying, not just for one but for all who had already died, were dying today, would die tomorrow and next month and next year. And for the millions of mothers and wives and daughters and sisters—and fathers and sons and brothers and friends—who were waiting for those who would never come home. And only then could she cry for Dick, for *him*, for the man she had not really known.

And that, she realized now, was her greatest sorrow. She had not known the man she thought she loved. She couldn't cling to a memory that was little more than a pale mirage in the desert, seductively hopeful, lovely—but an illusion, a fantasy.

And now she would never know the reality of him, of them, of the truth they might have been, together.

CHAPTER ELEVEN
Carrying On

Washington, D.C.
May–June 1943

It had been a cruel spring. Just twelve months before, Mamie had been excited and happy, moving with Ike into that grand house on Generals' Row and delighted no end when he got that second star so quickly—all because of the war, of course. The war was awful, yes, certainly. But it was also responsible for the good things that were happening to Ike. His third and fourth stars, which made her very proud.

Still, the war, and the fame it brought her husband, was responsible for the bad things that were happening to *her*—especially that Kay Summersby business. The first photo in *Life* magazine's November issue had been bad enough: the photo of Ike's official family, including his "pretty Irish driver." But then, just three months later, came the second photo, revealing that Kay Summersby had been on her way to join Ike in Algiers when her ship was torpedoed. The first photograph had worried Mamie but had prompted only a few calls from her closest friends. The second prompted a tidal wave.

Most of the people who called were longtime friends, army wives whose husbands were serving in North Africa. They were all so sweetly affectionate, so sympathetic, and not at all subtle. One of them might say, with a delicate hesitation: "Mamie, dear, I thought you ought to know—I heard that the two of them go on long trips through the desert together." Or resolutely: "Of course, everybody agrees that the General himself is above reproach, but my husband says it's a scandal, what people over there are saying about that woman!" And impulsively, with feeling: "Mamie, dear, I wish there was something I could do to help. You must be just *sick* about it."

Mamie had never considered herself a distrustful person, but she found herself feeling skeptical about almost everybody. She knew that the women who called were jealous because her husband had four stars and their husbands had just one or two. She didn't distrust Ike, of course. She knew he loved her and would never even think of betraying her for another woman. When she wrote to him about the second *Life* magazine photo and asked him why a British civilian was working for him in Algiers, he replied that she had come to North Africa to be near her fiancé.

"She is head over heels in love with a young American colonel," he wrote. "They're planning a June wedding—if they're both still alive." In response to her charge that he never wrote about what he was doing, he went on, "I'd bore you to death if I told you every little thing that goes on around here." And if anybody hinted to her that her "old duffer" was "fooling around" with a nurse or a driver, she would know how utterly idiotic that was. The war was turning him into an old man.

Of course she trusted him. Just looking at him, you knew it wasn't in him to be deceptive. If nothing else, he was surely too busy with his important duties to fool around. What's more, he had no privacy. He lived in a goldfish bowl, with Butch and Beetle watching every move and faithful Mickey reporting to her every two weeks, although of course Ike didn't know that. And as far as sex was concerned, well, he hadn't bothered her about it for a very long time, so she knew he wasn't interested in *that*. After all, he was, as he said, an "old duffer."

But while she didn't honestly believe he was up to anything, she was deeply annoyed by the fact that he had brought that woman to

North Africa. Couldn't he understand how she—his wife—might feel about it? Couldn't he see how it looked to everybody else? Of *course* he wasn't involved with Kay Summersby, but the appearance of the thing was embarrassing and deeply, deeply humiliating. Her parents and grandparents had always set great store by what other people thought of them. When she was growing up, her mother had warned her and her sisters to wear only clean underwear and stockings without holes, for fear of what the nurses might think if they were run over by a car. And of course in the army, appearances were *everything*—you dressed by a code, you lived by the rules, your life had to pass inspection. The malicious gossip about Ike and his driver, added to the ceaseless whispers about her drinking, made Mamie feel that she was wearing dirty underwear and everyone could see it.

Finally, Mamie felt she was going to snap like a stretched rubber band under the strain of pretending. She packed her suitcases, closed up the Wardman Park apartment, and took the train to San Antonio to stay with her sister Mike. The poor thing had four young children, one of them still a baby, and was overwhelmed by life on her own, now that her husband had been sent overseas. Her sister's difficulties went a long way toward taking Mamie's mind off her own troubles. Mike lived only a few blocks from Fort Sam, where she and Ike had been so happy when they were first married—and very far from Washington. If anybody had heard the ridiculous gossip about Ike and Kay Summersby, they didn't mention it.

And of course, there was the pleasure of being a four-star wife. Mamie wasn't especially fond of the caste system that prevailed on army bases, but she had to admit she liked being treated as if she were somebody special. Everyone seemed thrilled to see her and there were quite a few private parties and dinner invitations. And since San Antonio wasn't Washington and Fort Sam was closed to reporters, she felt free to go out and enjoy herself.

Her health improved while she was there, too, perhaps because she had such a good time playing auntie to Mike's sweet children.

She made them marshmallow fudge—the only thing in the world she could cook, really—and loved to watch them devour it. She found herself thinking often of her lost little Icky and the things she would do differently now. She remembered when they were at Camp Meade and she put him to bed with his shoes on, the laces tied together, to keep him from wandering in the night. She would never do that again. She would be more attentive to her precious boy and more watchful, for she still blamed herself for hiring the nursemaid, the girl who had given him scarlet fever. She wondered if Ike still blamed her too, as he had done at that awful time, for not paying enough attention to their darling. Looking at Mike's dear little family, Mamie sometimes wished she'd had more children, especially a daughter or even two. She would be less alone—and she and Ike might feel more connected to one another. Children created a bond after other bonds were gone.

Now, truth be told, she felt terribly cut off from him, remote and out of touch, in spite of his assurances, repeated in every letter, that he loved her. He was leading a very different life in an alien world quite beyond anything she had experienced or could imagine, and there was so much he would not or could not tell her. "Everything I do, or see, or hear, or even think, is secret," he wrote, which would certainly have worried her if she had imagined that he was capable of carrying on a secret affair. But the idea of the multitude and scale of the secrets he carried—some of them surely world-altering—made her feel even more keenly that he had grown away from her, that he was far beyond her reach. He no longer belonged just to *her* and she felt this keenly. What was worse, Miss Summersby lived in his world.

How many of his secrets did she share?

But the woman wasn't actually *Miss* Summersby. Mamie learned this from Cookie Wilson when she returned to Washington toward the end of May. Cookie's husband Marv (now stationed with Ike in Algiers) had told her that *Mrs.* Summersby had gotten a divorce from a British fellow—Lieutenant Colonel Gordon Summersby—who was serving in India. The charge? (Here Cookie lowered her voice and leaned closer to Mamie over the card table.) Adultery! And the divorce had been filed by the injured husband, no less, naming an American colonel, Richard Arnold.

There was more, and even more distasteful. It turned out that Pamela Farr (a mah-jongg regular whom Mamie had known since they lived across the street from one another at Fort Leavenworth) was acquainted with the American colonel's ex-wife. Pamela reported that the Arnolds' divorce had been "terribly messy," and that it involved charges of adultery with Mrs. Summersby. The Arnolds had been having marital difficulties for some time, but Mrs. Arnold had believed that things were getting better—until this Irishwoman came along and . . . Well, Pamela wasn't going to repeat the details. Suffice it to say that it was *not* a pretty story.

"Luckily, there were no children involved," Pamela added. She gave Mamie a significant glance. "I wonder if Ike knows about this ugly business. If he did, surely he wouldn't want that woman on his staff. Mrs. Summersby, I mean. Her reputation is certainly questionable. She sounds to me like a troublemaker."

"That woman" sounded like a troublemaker to Mamie, too. The minute the girls left, she sat down and shot off a letter right away, reporting what Cookie and Pamela had said.

"Colonel Arnold's divorce is not a pretty story." She let her pen dig into the paper with the force of her feeling. Ike needed to know how important this was. "And really, it's not at all nice to have a scandal—or even the *appearance* of a scandal—in your office."

After the letter was in the mail, Mamie had second thoughts. She didn't usually tell Ike how to manage his staff, and she was afraid he would think she had been a little too . . . well, shrill. But surely he'd see that she was only looking out for his best interests. People always said that where there was smoke, there was fire.

Really, it was *all* about appearances. A man in his position was vulnerable. He couldn't be too careful.

Ike's response arrived not long after. His letter shook her, and her cheeks flushed scarlet as she read it. By one of those uncanny coincidences of war, her letter containing the ugly story about Colonel Arnold and Mrs. Summersby had arrived on her husband's desk at the very same moment as the report that the colonel had been killed by a German mine.

"Your letter said his story was 'not a pretty one,'" he wrote sternly.

> Until I read it, I had no idea there was any "story" at all. I've met Arnold and I liked him. He was thirty-two, commander of a regiment, and scheduled to be married on June 22. Death is a daily event here, and I suppose we are changed by that. But decency, generosity, cooperation, devotion to duty—these things don't change, and out here, they mean a great deal more to us than the way things "appear." I don't know what young Arnold did to deserve your disapproval, and frankly, I don't care. His colleagues and I considered him a valuable officer and a fine person. I am deeply saddened by his death.

Biting her lip, Mamie put down the letter, feeling as chastened as she had once, long ago. She had been young and immature and willful then, "rotten spoiled," as she herself admitted, and given to childish fits of temper when she didn't get her way. Not long after she and Ike were married, she had gotten angry about something—something so trivial that she couldn't remember now what it was. But she would never forget what happened. She had slapped at her husband's hand and her ring struck his West Point ring and shattered the amethyst stone. He had drawn back with a cold, distant look and said, "Are you proud of yourself, young lady? For that display of temper you will replace this stone—with your own money." Of course, he knew she didn't have any money of her own: it would come from the monthly allowance her father gave his indulged daughter. The reprimand had stung even more because of that.

Now, she took Ike's letter into the bedroom and closed it away in her handkerchief drawer. She had the disquieting sense that, in scolding him about Colonel Arnold, she had revealed herself as a lesser person, too concerned with the way things looked to others. She had disappointed her husband, had failed to live up to his high expectations. He had more courage than she did, a stronger, more enduring sense of what it took to do the right thing. Beside his strength, his moral conviction, she felt small and inconsequential. And ashamed.

Blinking back the tears, she went to the bedroom window and pressed her head against the glass, staring at the cars moving briskly along Woodley Road in the bright afternoon. Not many, because gasoline rationing was in full force now, but there was a truck loaded with used tires and bearing a sign: "Slap the Japs with Rubber Scraps." A woman with a baby carriage waited to cross the street. On the other side, a sailor in naval whites strolled along the sidewalk, his arm around a pretty girl. People going about their ordinary lives on an ordinary day in wartime Washington, far from the battlefields of North Africa and the South Pacific.

She leaned her forehead against the cool glass, and a new thought—unwelcome, prompted by the sight of the sailor and his girl—pushed into her mind. Like so many other women caught in the cataclysm of this fearful war, Kay Summersby had lost the man she loved, the man she had been planning to marry. How would *her* life be changed?

And then, with a sense of relief so swift and sharp that she felt ashamed, it occurred to her that Mrs. Summersby would likely go back to England. With her fiancé dead, there would be nothing to keep her in North Africa. She would *want* to go home. And if she didn't, surely Ike would see the wisdom of sending her home instead of letting her hang about headquarters, giving idle tongues something more to wag about.

Yes. She was sorry to hear about Colonel Arnold, but his death settled the matter. And if Ike himself didn't see it, she would suggest it. Not right away, perhaps, but soon. Soon.

CHAPTER TWELVE
Secrets

North Africa
September 1943

Afterward, Kay would wonder how she had managed to live through that awful summer of loss and pain. But in the end, it was work that had been her refuge, her answer to Dick's death. And with the invasion of Sicily underway, work had been constant.

The people at home were impatient for the Allies to crush the Nazis, and Operation Husky—the invasion of Sicily—might have seemed to them like a sideshow. But Husky was strategically important, the largest amphibious operation in history and a dress rehearsal for the invasion of Europe, which the planners were saying would happen in eight or nine months. Everybody at head-quarters was keyed up and anxious to see how the troops would perform against the Germans and Italians. Montgomery and his British Eighth Army had gotten unexpectedly bogged down in the rugged hills south of Mount Etna, but Patton pushed the U.S. Seventh with his usual cocky audacity, forcing the Germans off the island and rolling into Messina in advance of the British.

The Sicilian invasion meant a summer on the move for Kay and the rest of the staff, flying back and forth from Algiers to Ike's advance command post at Amilcar, on the Bay of Tunis near Carthage. Tex, charged with finding a place for the General and his staff to stay, had appropriated the imposing villa previously occupied by Rommel at El Marsa. La Maison Blanche, the White House, hardly looked like a field camp with its high-ceilinged rooms, intricate mosaic floors, and open terrace with a wide view of the sea. Ike objected that it was much too large and grand. But even he had to admit that its palatial dining room and many bed-rooms came in handy when they hosted important guests, like the Prime Minister and, later that year, President Roosevelt.

The alternate headquarters, code-named Fairfield Rear, was an hour's drive. Kay regularly drove Ike between Amilcar and Fairfield, a harrowing trip over narrow roads congested with supply vehicles ferrying fuel and bombs to the Tunisian airfields. If she didn't want to drive the General into a ditch, she had to pay careful attention to the road. The work helped to keep her mind off what she had lost and what lay ahead.

For the first few days after she learned of Dick's death, Kay had groped through a despairing fog, trying to come to terms with what had happened. She had always been strong, able to deal with setbacks and obstacles, and she had become stronger and more self-reliant during those awful days of the Blitz. But Dick, who had once been her wide, wonderful future, was now her past. He was gone, and she faced the future alone: no lover, no husband, no children, no Florida, no America. Instead, she would go back to whatever was left of civilian life in chilly, bleak London and try to make a place for herself there.

But not right away. On her first day back in the office, Eisenhower had offered to release her from her service as a civilian with the American army. "I know how hard this is for you." He was shuffling papers on his desk and didn't look up. "I'm sure there's war work to be done in London, Kay, and I know your mother will be happy to have you home. I'll be glad to speak to the Prime Minister. He'll find you a place."

"That's very kind of you, sir," she said, "but I'd like to stay—if you want me."

He raised his head, looking at her over the tops of his reading glasses. He was silent for a long moment, his eyes searching her face as if he was trying to gauge the depth of her intention. "You're *sure*? You're a civilian, for chrissake. Nobody's going to criticize you for going home."

"Yes, sir," she said firmly. "I'm sure."

She had already thought it through. Butch and Beetle and Tex and Mickey were like brothers to her, while the WACs in the office— Sue, Margaret, Ruth, Louise, and Nana—were not just roommates, but sisters. All of them, the whole team, shared the certainty that what they were doing was vitally important, not just to them or their countries but to the world. They had a purpose and a mission. This work, this war, these *people*, were the center of her life.

And there was Ike. She couldn't leave him—although what that meant, exactly, she wasn't quite prepared to say, even to herself.

"Well, then." Eisenhower took off his glasses. "If you're staying, I've got a new job for you. The WACs manage the military correspondence, but the mail from the public has gotten beyond anything I can handle. I want you to keep on driving, as usual. But when we're here in the office, I'd like you to serve as my personal assistant, answering those letters and dealing with the gifts. How about it?"

Kay didn't have to think. "I'd love to," she said eagerly. "When do I start?"

She had already helped him with his personal correspondence, even typing a letter to his wife after he'd sketched out what he wanted to say. "This is perfect," he'd said when he read it. "You've made me sound like I'm enjoying myself, for a change." He'd added a few quick lines with a pen, and Kay had sent the letter off to Mrs. Eisenhower. It had made her angry, though.

"She gave me what-for," Ike said ruefully. "She wants me to write in longhand, so we can't do *that* again."

But there were plenty of other letters to be written, and as the Sicilian campaign continued through July and into August, Kay dug into her new assignment, glad to stay busy and grateful for the work. The Boss got a basketful of mail every day: letters from anxious wives who hadn't heard from their soldier husbands; from a mother asking the General to make sure that her son was wearing his long underwear; from someone complaining that a husband or boyfriend was overdue for a promotion; from people in England or the United States wanting a signed photograph of the General. There were also gifts—dozens of hand-knitted scarves, mittens, and socks; cartons of cigarettes; magazines and books and boxes of candy, mostly homemade fudge, which Kay sent out to the troops. Letters that required investigation or some official action, Kay handed over to Tex. She answered everything else, some with a short note, others with a more detailed response, all of them over the General's signature.

For the first few weeks, Kay took the letters and photos to Ike to be signed, but that soon became impossible. He told her sign the letters that went out over his name. It wasn't long before she was able to reproduce his signature so skillfully that nobody in the office could tell it from the real thing. She loved seeing his name flow out of her pen and earning an approving nod when he saw the stack of envelopes ready for the mail pouch.

And if her thoughts went back to the afternoon on the train to Scotland, or their goodbye at Telegraph Cottage or the Christmas kiss from which they had both pulled back . . . well, what was wrong with that? Richard Arnold had been her lover, the man she planned to marry. She had loved him and been loyal in all the ways that mattered. But he was gone and she was alone. There could be no harm in holding to herself those moments with Ike—those few moments, still as intensely vivid as lightning in a black sky and as fleeting and unsustainable. She thought of Dick and the little time they had had to love one another. In war, *everything* was fleeting and unsustainable. Nothing was permanent. You could only seize what was offered and hold on to it until it was gone.

In war, nothing lasted, nothing.

Not even love.

ร๛

The door opened and Butch put his head through. "Busy, Ike?"

Eisenhower looked up from Omar Bradley's report about the worn-out artillery, especially the 155 mm Long Toms, he'd had to work with during Husky. Some of the barrels were so badly worn, Brad wrote, that the shells were exploding right out of the gun. The barrels had to be relined or the guns replaced before they could be used in the upcoming Italian campaign. The guns would have to be dealt with, he knew, but it wouldn't be Bradley's job. Marshall wanted him for the Allied invasion of Europe, planned for the following spring.

Ike put the report down. "What's on your mind, Butch?"

"Got a swatch of that material you wanted." Butch put a foot-square piece of olive-drab wool on Eisenhower's desk. "Tropical-weight worsted. Farouk—he's the tailor—guarantees the wear. He can take your measurements tomorrow at the villa and have everything ready for fitting when you get back from Sicily." He grinned. "Patton recommended him, so we know he's good."

Eisenhower nodded wryly. Georgie was a fanatic about his uniforms, always the best, money no object. But the fabric was exceptionally nice: soft, supple, densely woven, better than anything that came from America these days. It should do quite well.

He leaned back in his chair. "I'll want two full uniforms." He lit a Camel, then added casually, "Any chance you can get enough of this same fabric to make up a couple more?"

"Probably." Butch gave him a sly grin. "But if I'm the one getting new uniforms, it'll have to be navy blue."

Ike grunted. "Just check it out, will you?"

Butch eyed him curiously, and Ike knew that he guessed. But that was no surprise. Butch was his closest friend and confidante. He understood.

"Yessir." Butch gave him one of his snappy navy salutes. "Give me twenty minutes and I'll get back to you on that."

Ike went back to Bradley's report, thinking that it wasn't just the artillery that had to be replaced. There was Alexander's C-47, which the maintenance crew called "Patches" because that's what it was—nothing but patches. The plane was pretty much held together with baling wire and had to be grounded. Hell, everything was falling apart. But that was war. You couldn't expect things to last forever. People fell apart, too. Look at Patton, losing control and slapping those shell-shocked soldiers, something that wouldn't have happened if he hadn't been exhausted. Battle fatigue—that's what the people back home didn't understand and couldn't appreciate. During a military campaign everybody, even the staff behind the lines, was pushed to the breaking point and beyond.

Butch reported back. Ike thought about it for a few minutes, his fingers tented under his chin, and then buzzed for Kay. She came in with her notebook and pen and stood in front of his desk. Her rich auburn hair was pulled back smoothly behind her ears, emphasizing her high cheekbones. Her face looked thin, he thought, and shadowed. She had lost weight, poor kid, in the nearly three months since Dick Arnold had been killed. He knew she was working long hours. He guessed she wasn't eating right.

He looked at her critically. "I've been noticing that uniform of yours, Irish. Seen better days, hasn't it?" Her uniform was a replacement for the one that had been ruined by seawater when she was torpedoed. The jacket elbows were worn nearly through and the skirt had a glossy shine on the seat from sliding in and out of the car.

"I'm afraid so, sir." She smoothed her skirt ruefully. "The quartermaster says it's hard to get anything decent right now. The material—well, you've heard what they say when you ask for something." She smiled, and a dimple came and went in her cheek. "'Don't you know there's a war on?'"

"I hear that every so often," he said with a chuckle. "So how about this?" Still seated, he opened a drawer, took out the fabric swatch Butch had brought, and pushed it across the desk. "I'm having a couple of uniforms made for myself. Butch has rounded up a tailor, the best in North Africa, according to Georgie Patton. Do you like this fabric?"

She turned the material over in her fingers. "Do I like this fabric? Of *course* I like it. It's absolutely—"

"Smashing," he said with a grin.

"Yes." The dimple came and went again. "Smashing."

"Very well, then. I'll tell Farouk—he's the tailor—to make a couple of uniforms for you while he's at it. Jackets, skirts, slacks. He can measure you tomorrow."

Her eyes widened. "But, sir, I can't afford to . . . I mean, I don't have the money to—" She took a deep breath. "I'm sure your material costs heaps more than I make in a year. And a tailor—" She shook her head. "I know I must look rather seedy. I don't think there's a jacket to be had in all Algiers, but I'll go back to the quartermaster and see if he can find a decent skirt for me, at least."

"Hang on." He raised his hand. "You don't have to pay for it."

Eisenhower knew exactly how much she was making, which was less than half of what the lowest-paid American clerk earned—and, as a civilian, she didn't qualify for a uniform allowance. She needed to look presentable when she was out with him, especially when the brass came to town—the Prime Minister, for instance, or Lord Mountbatten or the American Secretary of State or the Ambassador to Moscow—as well as Hollywood luminaries. She needed a decent uniform and it pleased him to make it happen. Easy as that.

"Don't . . . have to pay for it, sir?"

"It's a gift, Irish. From me to you. Because you make my life easier and more pleasant and I'm grateful."

"A gift!" Her face lit up. "Oh, sir, what a lovely—"

And then the light faded.

"But I don't think . . . that is, I . . ." She pulled in her breath. "I'm afraid I can't accept."

"Can't accept?" He scowled. "What the hell is *that* supposed to mean?"

She dropped the square of fabric on his desk. "I'm sorry, General. Truly sorry. It's a lovely, lovely offer, and I appreciate it more than I can tell you. But I . . . I just *can't*."

"What do you mean, you can't?" He pulled on his ear, not understanding. "I'm getting Long Toms for Bradley to replace his worn-out guns, and another C-47 for Alexander, because the wings are about to fall off his. That's what I'm here for, to see that people get what they need so they can do their jobs." Now fully irritated, he smacked the flat of his hand, hard, on the desk. "You want the damned uniforms, don't you? You *need* them—right?"

"Yes, of course, I want them. And yes, I need them." She pulled herself up straight, shoulders back. "But some people are bound to see them and think—"

"Some people?" He pushed back his chair and stood up, feeling the frustration mounting. All he wanted to do was give this woman something she obviously needed—this *little* thing, not half as important as that dog he'd given her—and she was making a federal case out of it. "I don't get it. Why in the hell would you turn down a new uniform? And what's this about 'some people'? Who? What the hell business is it of theirs?"

Coloring, she ducked her head. "Maybe it's different in America, but in Ireland—and in England, too—a woman doesn't accept personal clothing from a man unless they're . . . well, you know. Engaged. Or something. And damn it, sir, you're my commanding officer." She took a breath. "People already seem to think I'm . . ." Her voice trailed away.

And then he understood. "Ah, *hell*," he said, remembering Patton's screwdriver joke, a joke he would have laughed at if it had involved anybody else but Kay.

She was looked straight at him, her blue eyes shiny-wet, and then half-turned her head, blinking hard. "Sorry," she muttered. "Didn't mean to tear up like that. I love the thought, truly I do, General. You've been so kind to me. First Telek, and letting me come to North Africa, and then . . . well, it's all very . . . generous of you." She swiped the back of her hand across her eyes. "But no."

He stared at her, gut-wrenched by the sight of her tears and furious at himself for being the cause of them. Yes, of course she was right, and he was stupid for not thinking of it. Some people would see her new uniform and his and jump to the wrong conclusion. But he was suddenly angry at the idea that he should be denied the pleasure of giving her this inconsequential gift—something she needed and deserved and was within his power to give—because some people might think they were sleeping together.

Well, they *weren't*, dammit, although to be perfectly frank, he wished they were. Patton bragged about his affair with his wife's niece. Beetle slept with Ethel and never minded who knew it. Butch didn't give a damn what people said about him and Molly. Even Mickey had his little girlfriend. And Patton and Beetle and Butch were as married as he was, with wives at home. Here was *he*, the good soldier who had followed other people's rules his whole goddamned career, the staff officer who always did what his boss ordered, who tried to play the game the way his superiors thought it ought to be played. Yes, he'd been good. And good had gotten him where he was. Four stars and Supreme Commander.

And now that he was here, by damn, he was going to do this little thing for this helpful young woman, no matter how it looked. And "some people" could stick their dirty jokes and their stupid conclusions where the sun didn't shine.

Feeling the anger pound in his temples, he stepped around the desk toward her. "You're getting measured for those uniforms, Kay," he growled. "You're getting measured *tomorrow*. That's an order. You're going to have what you need and I don't give a damn what anybody thinks. If they ask, we'll come up with a cover story. If they don't believe it, they can go to hell."

She stared at him, her lips trembling, eyes wide and brimming over, the tears bright on her cheek. "I . . . I can't—" Her voice broke.

"Don't." He was moved by her vulnerability. His voice softened. "Don't cry, Kay, please." He put up his hand and with his thumb gently wiped the tears away.

And then suddenly, without any intention, without a single conscious thought, he had swept her into his arms and was crushing her against him, kissing her hungrily, his mouth on hers searching, demanding, in an uncontrollable explosion of desire. Her arms were around his neck and she was meeting his demand, answering his desire with a feverish desire of her own that aroused an urgency in him he hadn't felt in years, an urgency he had thought was long since dead. Another kiss and then another, and he was lost to himself in the scent of her, the closeness of her, lost in her unrestrained response.

He took a breath. "Oh, God, I'm *crazy* about you, Irish." The words, too, came without intention or conscious thought. They surprised him with their force, but they didn't say all he meant. He took her face in his hands. "I love you, Kay."

There was a burst of male laughter in the hallway. Its reality stopped him like a splash of icy water in his face. He dropped his arms.

She looked at him. Her hand went to her mouth, then dropped to her throat. Her fingers were trembling. She said something, but her words were blotted out by another raucous laugh in the hall.

A second splash of cold water, and he was himself again. He straightened his shoulders and took a step back.

"I'm sorry," he said. Kissing this woman, telling her he loved her—it was nothing short of a loss of control, as unpardonable as Patton slapping those soldiers, and no doubt a result of his own battle fatigue.

"I'm sorry," he repeated stiffly. "That shouldn't have happened. I'm a goddamned fool. Forget what I said, Kay. And forget about the uniform. I can't let you become the target of loose talk. It was a bad idea."

She stared at him for a moment. Then she shook her head with a sudden vehemence, her eyes flashing in a burst of Irish temper.

"No!" she exclaimed fiercely. "No, I won't forget it, and I won't let you forget it, either. If you're a damned fool, so am I. For over a year, we have spent more time with each other than with anyone else on earth. We have taken care of one another, we have cheered one another up, we have worked and worried and played together."

She clenched her fists. "Dammit, Eisenhower, I love you, too. And I don't give a damn what people think."

Her words hung in the air between them like a brilliant light, and he was almost blinded by their power. He reached for her. "Kay, I—"

She pulled out a handkerchief. "There's more to say. But not now, General. You're wearing my lipstick. And somebody might come in." She put up the handkerchief and scrubbed his mouth. "There. Entirely presentable."

He felt as if the earth had shifted on its axis. Trying to compose himself, he turned and retreated behind the safety of the desk.

"Helluva mess," he muttered. "I want what I have no right to want. I want things to be different. I wish . . . I wish we didn't live in a goddamned goldfish bowl." He looked at her and his voice softened. "I wish I could offer you something more, Kay."

She smoothed her hair. "Thank you," she said, very softly. Her lips quirked in a smile. "And now that we've got all that straightened out, I take back what I said. I accept your offer of the new uniforms, with pleasure. I'll report to the tailor tomorrow." There was a tap at the door and she pulled her shoulders back. "Will that be all, sir?" she asked crisply, as Tex came in with a folder in one hand and a cable in the other.

"That's it for now," he said, and sat down, feeling that nothing at all had been straightened out. It was a *helluva* mess.

But there wasn't time to think about it. The cable was from London and required an answer. When he'd scratched it out and handed it to Tex, Beetle was at the door with a message. Patton had assembled the First Division—all eighteen thousand men of the Big Red One—on the bank of the Palma River and had given them a twenty-minute speech.

"Supposed to be an apology for the slapping incidents," Beetle said. He made a wry face. "But he apparently used so much profanity that nobody could figure out what the hell he was talking about. The men were ordered not to boo him, but they sat on their hands when he was done talking. Stony silence. No applause."

Ike frowned. "Tell Patton to keep his head down and his mouth shut until this is done. He's the army's best general. He has to be saved for the cross-Channel invasion."

It was a cover-up, top to bottom. Ike had to keep the press from printing the story until it was time to use it where he could make it count. But that wouldn't be easy. Quentin Reynolds, the war correspondent for *Collier's* magazine, had told him that there were fifty thousand American soldiers who would shoot Patton on sight if they had the slightest chance.

"You know what the troops call him," Reynolds had said. "It's not 'Old Blood and Guts.' It's 'Our Blood, His Guts.' There are sixty Anglo-American reporters in Sicily and North Africa, and they all want to write the story of the slapping incident. If you'll fire Patton, we'll keep it under our hats."

Eisenhower had turned up the charm and Reynolds had agreed to keep a lid on the story until he was told to release it. But if one of that sixty—just *one*, damn it—wrote about it now, the game would be up.

"Everything I do, or see, or hear, or even think, is secret," he had written not long ago to Mamie, and it was the truth. He spent half the damned time trying to keep the right people informed about what was going on with this war and the rest of his time keeping the wrong people in the dark.

He sat there after Beetle left, thinking about cover-ups—but not about Patton. Now, he was thinking about Mamie. He had been married to her—and faithful, except for that brief flirtation in Manila—for twenty-five years. But she wasn't the lively, curious, vivacious girl he had married. She suffered from claustrophobia and wouldn't fly. She rarely walked more than a block or two, stayed in bed until noon, was prostrated by heat and cold, and had stomach problems. Her frailty and her disinclination to sex had diminished desire, and he thought of her not with passion but with a protective brotherly fondness. Mamie didn't seem to mind; in fact, she liked to laugh about the two of them getting "too old for that kid stuff," as if they had arrived at the natural and rather pleasant conclusion of a quarter-century of married life, when desire had run its course. When they were together, they slept in the same bed and never failed to share an affectionate goodnight kiss. But that was as far as it had gone for . . . how long? Six years? Seven?

And now. . . . He took out a cigarette and lit it. Until Kay, he had almost forgotten what physical desire felt like. Well, maybe it was kid stuff, but he felt it *now*, just as he could feel his gut tighten as he remembered that kiss and the feel of the yielding woman in his arms. He didn't want to hurt Mamie, and he wouldn't. He knew how greatly his wife depended on him, how firmly her identity was tied to his, how much he owed her for twenty-five years of marriage. At the end of the war, he would go back to her, to their affectionate, friendly comradeship. What he felt for Kay was different and separate and *not* a threat to Mamie. It was another thing that happened in wartime, one of the dozens of secrets around which his work revolved. As long as Kay understood that, they would be fine.

He glanced at the clock. Time to shift gears. He had twenty minutes before his next appointment. He was in the habit of beginning a letter to his wife and adding to it as the opportunity arose. It was getting to be a chore to think of something to say to her, and he was afraid that his letters were beginning to seem stale and repetitive. Nevertheless, he picked up a pen and pulled a sheet of paper toward him and began to write:

> Dear Mamie,
>
> So much work, so many knots to unravel—and it's making an old man of me! You cannot imagine how often I think of you and of what we'll do after the war. Retire to some quiet place where we can be lazy and contented. I'll fish every morning and you can sleep as long as you—

On his desk, the phone rang. He put down his pen and picked it up.

"Eisenhower," he said. And he was back in the world of men and action once again.

CHAPTER THIRTEEN
Six to the
Maximum Power

North Africa
October 1943

"Very spiffy." Butch cocked his head. "Turn around and let me get a good look."

Laughing, Kay struck an exaggerated model's pose, turned and struck another. "Do I pass muster?" she asked playfully.

Butch gave an approving whistle. "Ooh-la-la," he said. "Très chic, mademoiselle. Farouk is a first-rate tailor. I'll have to get him to make a new uniform for me. Navy blue, though. Olive drab just ain't my color." He picked up his drink and motioned with his head. "Let's go out to the terrace."

The October twilight was falling over the green hills behind the General's villa, spilling purple shadows across the city below. Kay settled into a chair facing the Mediterranean, drinks and a shared ashtray on a small table between her chair and Butch's. Telek trotted after them and jumped into Kay's lap.

Butch fell into the other chair, took a last Lucky Strike out of a crumpled pack, and lit it. "Well, now that Naples and the rest of southern Italy is in Allied hands, it's on to Rome." He leaned back, contemplating the sunset over the sea. "I may be optimistic, but I'm thinking we'll be there by Christmas."

Hoping would be a better word, he thought. Salerno had been bad, very bad. There had been blunders, mistakes, miscalculations, and so many casualties that the medics had to radio their commander, "On what beach shall we put our dead?" It had taken three weeks to push through to Naples, and they'd taken the city thanks to the help of the Neapolitans who had staged a bloody—and successful—uprising against Kesselring's occupying troops. And now the Germans were digging in across the belly of Italy. It was likely to be a long, hard slog up the peninsula. Longer and harder, he thought, than any of them wanted to think.

Somewhere upstairs, Caacie gave a short, sharp bark. Telek perked up his ears and jumped down from Kay's lap, trotting off to look for his mate and their puppies. Butch lit his cigarette and stretched, savoring the respite from the crazy rush of the day's work. He grinned ruefully, remembering a joke that was going the rounds. A platoon leader had learned that his battalion commander's radio call sign was Big Six, which meant that to talk to the division commander, he should ask for "Big, Big, Big Six." And to reach Eisenhower, it would have to be "Six to the Maximum Power."

"Six to the Max." That cut both ways, of course. The man at the top had all the power. But he also took all the crap from everybody up and down the fucking chain. Today, the phone had never stopped ringing and the cables had never stopped coming. It had been one bloody calamity after another. Butch didn't know how Ike stood the pressure. But he seemed to thrive on it. In fact, he'd been in a better-than-usual mood lately—and Butch knew why.

Beside him, Kay took out her own cigarette and he reached over the table to light it for her. The evening was growing cooler. Overhead, a pair of black-headed gulls shrilled scolding cries in a lavender-tinted sky. Down in the harbor, a deep-throated ship's horn sounded, low and mournful. In the kitchen, Moaney and Hunt rattled pans as they cooked dinner, the appetizing smell of *merguez*—the spicy lamb sausages that Butch liked—wafting through the open window. Almost time for dinner.

But he had something else on his mind. Trying to think of a

way into what he knew he needed to say, Butch cleared his throat. "This afternoon, Sue Sarafian asked me about your new uniform. She said she'd heard a rumor that the Boss had it made for you. She wanted to know if it was true."

Kay picked up her drink. "What did you tell her?"

"I said I didn't know."

Which wasn't true, because Ike had told him how Kay had first turned down the offer of the uniforms and then, after what Ike called "a little gentle persuasion," had agreed. In fact, he and the Boss had had quite a long and surprisingly candid conversation on the subject, man to man—which was why Butch understood about Eisenhower's good mood. Mostly, it had been Ike talking and Butch listening, nodding at appropriate points and pouring another drink when the glasses were empty. Ike often used him as a sounding board when it came to military matters, not looking for advice, but simply laying out options, talking through possible outcomes. Butch was used to keeping the cigarettes coming and the whiskey flowing.

This time, though, the subject had been deeply personal, a confession, really. Ike had spoken not only about his attraction to Kay (not a surprise: Butch had long since known *that*), but also about his frustrations with Mamie. Listening to Ike, Butch understood and deeply sympathized. Hell, he and Ruth had plenty of their own marital difficulties, but not *that* kind. He belonged to the use-it-or-lose-it school of thought. He couldn't imagine being celibate for six months, let alone six years. Six to the maximum power, hell. The man must be made of titanium.

The situation with Mamie wasn't exactly news, either. Butch's wife Ruth, who had gotten so fed up with Mamie's manipulations that she'd decided to move out, had told him that Mrs. General Ike was completely self-engrossed and totally spoiled. She stayed in bed half the day. She played sick as a way of controlling people. Her refusal to eat—Ruth gave it a fancy name, anorexia or something like that—was another control thing. And so was her habit of keeping her husband on an allowance, which Butch already knew about. If Ike wanted a little extra money in his pockets, he won it at the poker table.

In his humble opinion, Butch felt it was good for Eisenhower to have Kay in his life, as long as he was discreet about it. But that didn't mean it was good for *Kay*. And while Butch's natural allegiance was to his longtime friend, Kay was a very sweet girl. She didn't deserve to be hurt. Hence this conversation.

He blew out a stream of smoke and added, "I told Sue she'd have to ask *you* about that uniform. Did she?"

"Not yet. But I've come up with an explanation." Kay gave him a look he couldn't read. "A lie."

"We don't call it a lie, Irish." Butch chuckled. "We call it a cover story. In war, you know, nothing is what it seems. Everything is secret, always from our enemies but often from our friends. We couldn't run the war without cover stories." He put out his cigarette in the ashtray. "What are you going to tell her?"

"That the General didn't want to waste whatever fabric was left on the bolt after his uniforms were cut, so he was happy to let me buy it. And that my mum saw a photo of me and was appalled by how shabby I looked, so she sent me enough to pay the tailor."

"Sounds right." Butch stretched again, getting the kinks out. It really *had* been a helluva day. "Tell you what. You give me a five franc note. I'll drop it into the General's petty cash box. Payment for that fabric."

"Thank you," Kay said dryly. "Then I won't be telling a whole lie—just half a lie."

"Half a cover story." Butch dug in his pocket and pulled out a fresh pack of Luckies. "Look, Kay, I hope you don't mind my butting in. But maybe you remember what I said to you, back in the Grosvenor Square office, after you and the Boss went riding in Richmond Park."

"Remind me." Kay looked out over the sea, half-smiling, and Butch thought, not for the first time, how utterly lovely she was. And how utterly transparent—and, he thought, naive. No, not naive, exactly. She wasn't trusting or innocent. Maybe she just didn't care what people thought. In any event, it was clear to Butch (and probably everybody else at headquarters) that she was a woman in love. With the Boss. With Six to the Maximum Power.

Wherein lay the problem—one of them, anyway. "I told you to keep it out of the newspapers, kid." He stripped off the cellophane from the top of the pack. "It bears saying again."

Kay looked offended. "You think I'm shouting from the housetops?"

"No. But your eyes give you away." He paused. "He's not exactly hiding it, either." Which was true. He probably ought to have this conversation with Ike.

She sighed. "Maybe we should start wearing dark glasses."

He tapped a cigarette out of the pack and stuck it in his mouth. "Look, Irish, I'm concerned about you. Whatever you and Ike are up to is your own private business. I won't pry and I'll always do my best to cover for the two of you. That's my job. Beetle and Mickey, same thing."

She was taken aback. "Beetle . . . and Mickey?"

"Sure." He wanted to say *You think they don't know? You think they're blind?* Instead, he said, "Look. What I'm trying to say is that this relationship may not be good for you. And while it's good for Ike in one way, it's not good in another. Gossip, I mean. People talking."

Kay's eyes flashed. "Look, Butch, we have done *nothing*—"

"That's irrelevant." He flicked his lighter. "You two are constantly together. Everybody can see he wants to have you with him. Everybody can see that you adore him. For most people looking on, this situation falls into the category 'where there's smoke, there's fire.' And where there's fire, Irish, *you* can get burned. Ike, too."

Kay gave an ironic laugh. "Listen to the pot calling the kettle black. You and Molly—"

"I'm not the Supreme Commander, Kay. I'm just a lowly naval aide. When this war is over, I'll marry Molly and go back to being just a radio guy."

"Marry Molly?" She was startled.

"Come on. You don't think I'm a skirt-chaser out for a little fun, do you?"

"Sorry," she muttered, coloring. She gave him a sidelong glance. "You're going to divorce your wife?"

"It's already in the works. Ruth's decision as much as mine. She's got other fish to fry." He picked up his drink. "Anyway, as I was saying, I'm just a humble peon who can carry on as much as he likes and nobody notices. Ike, on the other hand, is the equivalent of royalty. In fact—" He leaned closer and lowered his voice. "Do you remember when the King was visiting, and you were upset when he pretended you didn't exist?"

Kay rolled her eyes. "Of course. I was terribly disappointed."

"Want to know why that happened?"

She frowned. "Do *you* know?"

"I can offer an educated guess. You're a Brit. You probably know how the royal family feels about Wallis Simpson—the Duchess of Windsor, I mean."

"They *hate* her," Kay replied promptly. "King George and Queen Elizabeth and the Queen Mother. They were appalled at the idea of abdication, and they blamed Mrs. Simpson when Edward left the throne. If he hadn't fallen in love with her, he would have done his duty. Instead, he insisted on—" She stopped, staring. "Butch! You're not saying that the King believes that *I*—"

Butch shrugged. "I don't know what the King believes. But if you ask me, it's entirely likely that he's heard all about you and Ike, probably from your PM. I wouldn't be a bit surprised if he's drawn the comparison."

Kay folded her arms, scowling. "It's utter nonsense, that's what it is. Ike isn't Edward the Eighth and I'm not Mrs. Simpson. What's more, we've done nothing—"

"What you've done or haven't done is beside the point, Irish. This is about what some people *think* you've done—and are doing." Butch pulled on his cigarette. "And it's about what other people are planning for Eisenhower."

She looked at him, frowning. "I don't—"

He held up his hand. "I heard it when I went back to Washington in March. After this war is over, Ike is going to be a hero. A *huge* hero—bigger than anybody can imagine right now. Why, they're already saying they want him to run for president. They're telling *him* that, too. A group of his old buddies from Camp Colt, for instance. Arthur Capper, the Republican senator from his home state of Kansas, for another. George Allen, on the Democratic side. There are others. And there will be more."

That got her attention. She turned to him, her blue eyes wide and disbelieving. "President?" she scoffed. "You're joking! Of course he could do it—Ike can do anything he decides to do. But he *hates* politics—all those backroom schemes and intrigues. He calls it the work of the devil. He doesn't even like the administrative work he's doing here. He would much rather be out with the troops."

Butch paused, wondering how much he should tell her. In one sense, her life would be simpler and easier if she didn't look too deeply into the man she loved, if she just lived through it day by day and took from it whatever comfort she could. On the other hand, the more she knew about Eisenhower, the better prepared she would be when it was over for her.

"He won't run next year," Butch said thoughtfully. "The war likely won't be over then—and the war is his job to finish. People are saying that FDR will run for a fourth term. But there's forty-eight and fifty-two. My money's on fifty-two."

She waved him off, as if he were a pesky fly. "He's not a politician, Butch. He's a *soldier*."

Butch shook his head. "There's something you're not seeing, Kay. Under that easygoing manner and that charming, disarming smile, Eisenhower is a hugely ambitious man. But not in the way you might think. He's not out for glory or fame, personally, I mean. He's simply driven to make things happen—the right things, in his judgment. Show him a job that has to be done, tell him it's his duty to do it, and he'll go after it, flat out. The harder the job, the more he'll dig into it." He paused. Now was the time to say this. "After this war, there'll be no room in his life for you."

But she didn't seem to hear him. "I simply can't believe that the General would actually consider running for president. It's out of the question."

He tried again. "Look, Kay, all I'm saying is, don't bet on Ike for the long haul. I know he cares about you." He winced at the way her face brightened, and hurried on. "But he'll go back to the States when this is over. You'll be the girl he left behind. Keep that in mind. Don't burn your bridges."

He leaned closer and lowered his voice in his best Humphrey Bogart growl. "And keep it out of the newspapers. You got that, kid?"

The silence was broken by the brassy clang of a bell from the direction of the kitchen. Mickey was letting them know that the cocktail hour was over. Dinner would be on the table in fifteen minutes.

છૅ

Kay had heard the concern in Butch's voice and appreciated it— and *him*. Butch had been a brother to her, and she knew that Ike spoke confidentially to him in a way that he spoke to no one else. She was glad that Butch felt comfortable speaking confidentially to her.

But he seemed to assume what everyone else (even King George!) evidently did: that she and Ike were sleeping together. She supposed that was natural, especially when he and Beetle and Patton made no secret of their women. The irony, of course, was that it just wasn't true: no matter how willingly she might have yielded, there had been no opportunity for more than a few sweet, stolen kisses. She didn't even know how Ike felt about this, for while he was charmingly adept at small talk, he was slow to reveal the man inside.

"It's always been hard for me to talk about the things I feel most deeply," he said to her one afternoon as they were riding their horses at a walk along the headland. "That doesn't mean I don't feel them. It's just . . . Well, I grew up with five brothers. I stayed out of trouble by keeping my mouth shut. I've lived in the military all my life, and military men don't talk about what's closest to them. But you know how I feel, and how I would show it, if I could." He gave her a questioning glance. "Don't you, Kay?"

"I think so," she said, guarded. But she guessed that his reticence wasn't entirely a matter of having spent his life with men. It was a way of defending his inner self from the intrusions of others, especially when he felt conflicted. And surely he did. Surely he still loved his wife. It might be difficult for him to admit, even to himself, that he could love both of them.

He shifted the reins from one hand to another. "I've lived this way for a long time, and I don't think I'll ever change. But I want you to know that I love you—and that I've loved you since the very beginning, back in England." He grinned. "That first day, when I came out of the embassy and saw you running toward us, I thought you were the most beautiful woman I'd ever seen. And the day I learned that the *Strathallan* had been hit, I went through bloody hell. If you'd died, it would have been my fault."

She wasn't sure she'd heard him right. "*Your* fault?"

"Hell, yes. If I'd flown you to Algiers with the rest of the staff, you wouldn't have been on that ship. It was pretty damned simple: I wanted you here, but I knew that the minute you got off the plane, the photographers would be shooting and you'd end up in the newspapers." He chuckled wryly. "So I put you on the *Strathallan*. I didn't count on *Life* magazine running your photo when the damn ship got torpedoed. What a stroke of fate. Made me wish that Peggy Bourke-White's cameras had gone down with the ship." He was silent for a moment. "And Mamie has given me holy hell ever since she saw it," he muttered.

Kay almost laughed. She had spent ten days on the ship and gotten torpedoed because Ike didn't want his wife to know she was coming to North Africa? It would have been funny if it weren't so . . . ironic.

"The best laid schemes o' mice an' men," she quoted, "gang aft agley."

Ike laughed, then sobered. "I never intended you to know, Kay. I expected you and Arnold to get married and that would be the end of it. But if there was ever any question in my mind about how I felt about you, that day—the day the *Strathallan* went down—gave me the answer." He glanced at his watch. "It's late. I need to get back to the office. There are cables coming in this evening."

Kay lifted the reins and fell in behind him. It would always be like this, she thought. There would be moments when he could be open with her, could be himself. Then it was back to the desk, to the battle, to the war. She reminded herself of Butch's warning: that when it was over, she would be the girl Ike left behind. *Keep that in mind*, Butch had said. *Don't burn your bridges.*

But she didn't want to think of that now. She only thought *What we have is today, and today is all I need, all I want.* That knowledge was a talisman, a secret truth that she carried with her everywhere, hidden in her heart.

It *was* her heart. Her whole heart. Today.

CHAPTER FOURTEEN
"Things I Could Say"

North Africa—Egypt—Jerusalem
October–December 1943

Years later, when Kay recalled the autumn and early winter of 1943, it seemed to her that those were the sweetest of all the months that she and Ike had together. It was a time of veiled glances and quick, soft touches. His hand on her shoulder at her desk, her fingers brushing his when she handed him papers to sign, an urgent kiss in the stable after they'd ridden together. His handwritten notes on tiny slips of paper, like this one: *How about lunch, tea & dinner today? If yes: Who else do you want, if any? At which time? How are you?* Or this one: *Thinking of you, hope you're thinking of me.*

The August invasion of Sicily was followed by the September Italian campaign, and the days had been chaotic. But they managed to work out ways to be together outside of Allied headquarters. Yes, they were often alone in the car, but the driving was a challenge that required Kay's attention, and the General was usually deep in thought. What's more, his safety was paramount in everyone's minds. Wherever they went, they were accompanied by three or four motorcycle guards and followed by a jeep carrying several armed MPs.

It was easier to talk when they rode horseback at the farm and in the quiet cocktail hour at Ike's villa, where they sat together on the high-backed French sofa in front of the fire, sipping drinks, smoking, listening to records, holding hands, even stealing a kiss or two while they listened warily for Mickey, who whistled as he came down the hall as if to let them know that he was there. Kay remembered what Butch had said about Mickey being in on their secret. But she kept it to herself, feeling that Ike might not appreciate the idea that she and Butch had spoken—or that Mickey knew. And she was aware that their desire was sharpened by the apprehension of discovery. It lent a shivery excitement to their relationship, their *secret* relationship, and pulled them closer. It was a bond they shared, just the two of them, with no one else in the world.

At least, that's how Kay felt. She was never sure about Ike. As articulate as he was when it came to giving commands, he fumbled for words to describe what he was feeling. Often, he would say, "I'm not very good at this sort of thing, but you know what I would like to tell you." Or "You know what I can't say, don't you?"

"Yes, I know," she would murmur, and she did. She could read his heart in his expression, in the softening of his mouth and the sudden warmth in his blue eyes when he looked at her. He had grown up within an austere Victorian moral code that valued vows and placed a premium on fidelity and trust. Discovering love outside of his marriage to Mamie must have stirred a storm of inner conflict in him.

And in spite of her efforts to focus on *today*, always *today and just today*, a dark undercurrent tugged at her, too, for she was increasingly aware that their wartime world could soon be pulled apart. Operation Torch was over, Sicily had been retaken, and the Italian campaign was underway, although it wasn't the cakewalk everyone had expected. The taking of Rome was still a likely eight or nine months away, and the Germans had twenty-four divisions south of the Alps.

But Italy was now a secondary focus and attention was shifting to the invasion of Europe. The top-secret code name for the cross-Channel operation was Overlord, and Eisenhower had already been compelled to contribute seven divisions, three strategic bombing groups, and two of his best generals—Bradley and Patton—to the buildup in Britain. The operation would be managed from a base somewhere in the south of England. The question on everyone's lips was, who would command it? And when would the commander be named?

Tex had a ready answer. "It's gotta be the Old Man," he said. "He's the only logical choice."

The staff agreed. Out of all the national agendas, the professional competition, and the petty personal jealousies, Eisenhower had created a unified Allied command. He had made it and babied it and pushed it through three Mediterranean campaigns. He could do the same thing in Europe. But in Washington, the smart money was on General Marshall, according to Beetle, who had just come back from the Pentagon. People in the know were saying that Marshall's appointment would be announced sometime after the upcoming conferences in Cairo and Tehran. When that happened, Ike would be recalled to Washington to take Marshall's job as Army Chief of Staff. As October slipped into November and November became December, the rumors of Ike's imminent return to Washington were as thick as the cloud of black flies that hovered over roasting *mechoui* in the bazaar.

It was the autumn of Ike's discontent. He clearly hated the thought of going back to Washington and bristled whenever it was mentioned. One morning in the office, he exploded. "I've had a bellyful of this goddamned crap," he stormed. "People coming in here to congratulate me for being shipped back to a desk at the Pentagon. If that's all they've got to say, they can goddamn well keep it to themselves and leave me alone. I've got work to do."

For Kay, the thought sliced like a knife. If Ike went back to Washington, she would never see him again. His official family—Butch, Beetle, Tex, and the WACs—would be going with him. She was a British civilian. She would be left behind in Algeria, or shipped back to England.

But there were bright spots in those weeks, too. The Prime

Minister was a frequent visitor to Algiers, and Kay was always invited, with Ike, to the dinner parties. Guests came through Algiers regularly now, and Kay served as the General's hostess. Lord Louis Mountbatten was always welcome; he and the General were "Dickie" and "Ike." Averell Harriman, the new ambassador to the Soviet Union, stopped on his way to Moscow; he brought his daughter Kathy, whom Kay had known and liked in London. And a galaxy of popular Hollywood stars dropped in on North Africa to perform for the troops. Eisenhower always invited them to the villa for a buffet supper. One week it was Bob Hope and Vivien Leigh (who had been unforgettable as Scarlett O'Hara in *Gone with the Wind*), the next it was Kay Francis and her USO troupe, and then Noël Coward. At an evening show for officers and enlisted men, Noël sang "Mad Dogs and Englishmen" for Ike, who roared with laughter all the way through and asked to hear it again.

And then, for Kay, Noël sang "I'll See You Again." One of the lines—*And what has been is past forgetting*—reached into her heart.

Yes, Kay thought. *Past forgetting*. This will all be gone, all of it, but I will never forget.

In the dark, while she struggled to blink away the tears, Ike reached for her hand.

℘

For Kay, the highlight of those uneasy weeks was the picnic with the President of the United States.

It happened in late November. Kay drove to El Aouina Field outside of Tunis, where the General was flying in from Oran with the President, who had arrived in North Africa on board the USS *Iowa*. As she always did, she drove around to the landing area to wait with the car for her passengers. But Mike Reilly, the head of the Secret Service detail, stopped the armored Cadillac and ordered her out of the car. In his Irish brogue, he barked, "No female is going to drive the President while I'm on the job." He slapped the roof of the car with the flat of his hand. "Certainly no *Limey* female."

Kay was steaming—and even angrier when she had to show the American driver how to handle the gearshift on her car. But she followed Reilly's orders. Later that evening, in Amilcar, she met the President in the library at Eisenhower's villa, where FDR was spending the night. When Ike introduced her, Roosevelt shook hands, then frowned.

"Why didn't you drive me today?" he asked. "I'd heard about you and I was looking forward to it."

"Secret Service orders, sir," Kay said, not daring to wonder just why the President of the United States might have heard about Eisenhower's driver. She lowered her voice and in her own Irish brogue, growled roguishly, "No female is going to drive the President while I'm on the job." She smiled. "Begorrah, by damn."

FDR threw back his head and laughed uproariously. "Well, child, lucky for both of us, I outrank Mike Reilly. *I* say you're going to drive me tomorrow, on our tour of the battlefields. It'll be just you and me and General Eisenhower." He pulled down his mouth in theatrical disappointment. "Plus a couple of dozen armed guards. They never let me get away with a thing, damn it."

Child. Kay chuckled, not so much at the triumph over her fellow Irishman as at the name the President gave her. No one had ever called her *child* before. And later that evening, she and Mike Reilly buried their Irish hatchets over a beer in the kitchen. He was nervous about the President's planned driving tour through the battlefields of the Medjerda Valley. Kay tried to tell him that the enemy had already surrendered and the area was secure and quiet, but he wasn't easily reassured.

The next morning, Kay met Eisenhower and Roosevelt with the Cadillac to drive the President on his tour. Their cavalcade was impressively military, with a radio car and a couple of jeeps full of armed MPs ahead of them and halftracks and weapons carriers behind, flanked by eight motorcycle outriders. As she held the car door open for Ike, she whispered, "Alone at last. Won't we have *fun* today?" and Eisenhower chuckled.

As usual, Kay had brought the General's Scottie to Amilcar. When they left the villa, Telek sat on the front seat between her and a Secret Service agent armed with a submachine gun. But they were barely underway when Telek decided to scramble over the seat and into the President's lap—perhaps because FDR's jacket carried the scent of his Scottie, Fala.

"Exactly what I wanted." The President beamed, stroking Telek's black ears. "All the comforts of home." The little dog rode on FDR's lap for the rest of the day, as they drove past one battle site and then another and Eisenhower described the hard-won fights of the previous year at Tébourba and Medjez-el-Bab and Longstop Hill, at Mateur and at Hill 609, where the untried American troops had redeemed themselves.

Mike Reilly had given Kay a copy of the schedule they were to follow, with the time and location for the President's picnic lunch (packed in a basket in the trunk of her car) clearly marked. But forty-five minutes and twenty miles from their planned destination, the President pointed to a grove of eucalyptus trees on the north bank of the Medjerda.

"That's a pretty place for a picnic," he said. "Let's have our lunch there."

Kay swung off the road. The jeep behind them followed and the vehicles in front screeched to a stop and made a quick U-turn. In a moment, the MPs had piled out and encircled the Cadillac, backs to the General's car. The Secret Service man got out. Kay got the picnic basket and began to open it. But Ike said, "I'll do that, Kay. I'm pretty good at passing sandwiches."

To Kay, the President said, "Come back here, child, and have lunch with a dull old man." He patted the seat beside him.

Ike grinned. "Go ahead, Kay. I don't think he's propositioning you."

"I'm disappointed," Kay said, and the President chuckled.

Kay and Ike traded places. Eisenhower handed out their sandwiches—ham, with cheese and lettuce—while the President asked her about driving ambulances in London during the Blitz and her life in Algiers. He had the gift, she realized, of seeming genuinely interested in the small details of an ordinary person's life, and she found herself telling him about London, then working at Allied headquarters in Algiers and living with the WAC officers. "Your American WACs are wonderful women," she said. "They work so hard and contribute so much."

"Indeed," the President said, around a mouthful of sandwich. "Well, then, why don't you come over to our side? You'd make a fine WAC, my dear."

This was a question Kay had already thought of, but when she had asked Beetle, he'd told her it was impossible. "It's a tempting invitation, sir. But your rules make it rather difficult. I'm a British citizen."

"So I understand. But rules can be broken, you know. Especially when the President says so." FDR leaned forward. "General, is there any dessert in that basket, or will I have to wave my magic wand?"

But Mike Reilly was approaching. "Mr. President, we've been here longer than I like." He cast an apprehensive glance over his shoulder. "We should move on now."

"Nervous Nellie," FDR muttered. He grinned at Kay. "You're lucky, child. You have only one boss to please. I have dozens."

Kay drove the President to the airfield, where they said good-bye and he was put aboard the airplane for his flight to Cairo. As they drove back to the General's villa, Ike said, "I'm flying to Cairo tomorrow evening, to meet with the President and the Prime Minister." He paused to light a cigarette. "General Marshall will be there, as well."

"Oh, dear," Kay said, half under her breath. "Do you think they'll announce . . . I mean, will they tell you—" She looked up to catch his eyes in the rearview mirror. "About command of Overlord, I mean."

"They might." Ike gave her a lopsided grin. "When it comes,

it's likely to be a big, formal announcement. The British, the French, the Russians—they're involved, too. Cairo would be a good setting, especially with Marshall there."

A man was leading a camel loaded with sacks of oranges along the edge of the road and Kay moved over to pass. "It sounds like you think they're going to name General Marshall." Her heart felt as dark and heavy as a chunk of lead.

"It seems likely. But who knows?" Ike pulled on his cigarette. "Anyway, there's no point in worrying about it. We'll find out eventually. And in the meantime, why don't you go to Cairo with me?"

"That would be smashing!" Kay exclaimed. Then, cautiously, she added, "But how can we? I mean, won't it look—"

"No, it won't. I'll ask a couple of the WACs, too. Not to work," Ike added quickly. "You girls can go shopping and have some fun."

So that's why Ruth and Nana were with Kay, Beetle, Mickey, and the Boss when they boarded a four-engine C-54 for the night flight from Tunis to Cairo. They flew at night because daylight flights were too risky, and the General didn't want to have to run a fighter escort all the way to Cairo. The workday had already been long and demanding, so after the plane took off, Mickey served drinks while they played a few rubbers of bridge. Then the pilot turned the lights down and everyone took their seats and fell asleep, lulled by the loud drone of the engines.

But not Kay and Ike. They sat together in the darkened rear of the plane, whispering, touching, kissing. For a brief hour, they were just two people in love in the midst of war, holding on to each other as the world threatened to pull them apart. Kay stopped thinking of Overlord and Ike being returned to Washington, and lost herself in the sweetness of his kiss.

After Ike had gone to sleep, Kay moved to the seat facing him, where she watched him with a deep, yearning tenderness, thinking how wonderful it would be if she could wake beside him every morning—even as she reminded herself that all they had was today. *Today, not tomorrow. Just today.* Years later, she would remember the bittersweet contradictions of that hour with a poignant longing. And she would think that what she and Ike had shared in each other's arms in the back of the darkened plane was an act of love as deeply intimate as a physical encounter.

It was all they had. It was enough.

ॐ

Eisenhower woke that morning to one of the world's most memorable sights: sunrise over the pyramids. The pilot of their C-54 was flying low, giving his passengers—those who were awake—an incredible birds-eye view of the ancient Egyptian monuments to the power of dead kings.

But the sight didn't lighten Eisenhower's mood. He lit a cigarette and leaned back in the seat, thinking of what lay ahead at the conference in Cairo and far to the north, in Italy, where the Fifth Army under Mark Clark was pounding the so-called Winter Line. Meanwhile, Monty was pushing his Eighth Army up the east coast of Italy, aiming to swing in behind the Gustav Line toward Cassino. It would mean bitter fighting across mountainous terrain, pushing men and equipment through cold rains, freezing mud, and icy snows. It wouldn't be quick, and it wouldn't be easy.

To do the job right, Eisenhower knew that Clark and Alexander would need more men and more equipment, and more and then *more*, and that Churchill would back their demands with the full force of his authority. Some reinforcements were about to be deployed: mountain-trained Algerian and Moroccan troops were scheduled to arrive in Naples before Christmas, and Ike himself was planning to move to a new forward headquarters at Caserta, where he could be closer to the front and to the real challenges of the war.

But his task here in Cairo was not to argue for more troops and equipment for Clark and Alexander. He intended to report that the short-term purposes of the Italian campaign had already been achieved: the capture of the Foggia airfields and the port of

Naples, important for the resupply that would ensure the taking of Rome. Now, all available troops and equipment must be dedicated to the cross-Channel invasion—the "second front" that Stalin demanded. And the commitment had to be made as speedily as possible, so the commander of the cross-Channel invasion would know what resources he had to work with.

Eisenhower stared out the window, feeling the tension rise in his gut. In his career as a professional soldier, he had become accustomed to waiting for orders, waiting to learn what the future held, or just . . . waiting. He had moved from place to place and rank to rank, not by his own volition but at the will of the men to whom he reported. Oh, he gave his share of orders; the Mediterranean campaign had gone forward under his direct command. But war, he knew, was waged between two poles: the possible and the probable. Its outcomes were always contingent, never certain. No general ever forgot, as Patton had once put it, that he was entirely the pawn of the fickle gods of battle. Whatever planning he did could be undone in the blink of an eye by the weather, by an inept subordinate or an unexpectedly adept enemy, or simply by some goddamned rotten luck. All a man could do was soldier on, take whatever came, and make the best of it.

That was what he would do, he supposed, for Churchill had let him know what was coming. A few days before, Ike had flown to Malta to meet with the Prime Minister and his Chiefs of Staff. There, Churchill had made it clear that he was supporting General Marshall as the commander of Overlord. Ike had tried to mask his bitter disappointment. If he couldn't have Overlord, he would much rather remain as Allied Commander in the Mediterranean, where at least he'd be close to the fighting in Italy. He had said as much to Butcher, whose journalist buddies all predicted that Ike would be going to Washington. Where, Butch said confidently, he would be "the very best Chief of Staff the army had ever had."

Ike was sour. "They'll bury me at Arlington in six months."

"Nah," Butch said. "You won't like it, but you'll do it because you'll have to. You'll do *whatever* you're asked to do because you're a good soldier." He'd given Ike a slantwise look. "And it'll make Mamie happy. No doubt about *that*."

Mamie. Eisenhower pulled on his cigarette. Butch was right. She wanted him back in Washington. She wanted the two of them to move into the army chief's big house on Generals' Row at Fort Myer, where she could unpack her crates of china and crystal and put up new curtains and drapes and manage the household staff and a full social calendar. He'd be sitting behind a desk at the Pentagon, hating every goddamned minute, and she'd be bustling around in her element.

Mamie, he thought again, and sighed. If he tried, he could sometimes still see her as the vivacious young girl he had courted in San Antonio, when he was young and self-impressed and eager to find a wife who would be an asset to his army career. He'd been looking for a beautiful young woman who was above him socially (at the time, that had seemed important) and yet would devote herself unquestioningly to him and his work. Mamie had done that and more, and he was grateful for all she had given him.

But he was more likely to think of her now with a half-puzzled, half-ironic detachment, as if she were the wife of one of his brothers. She still sparkled and charmed, but with a shallow girlishness that wasn't entirely attractive in a fifty-year-old woman. He loved her, he supposed, but they had no common interests except their son, and John was a man now, with his own life. If Mamie had ever been interested in his work, it might have been different. But she had set down a firm rule that he was not to bring the army home with him. In all their years together, he had never shared as much of his work with Mamie as he had shared in the last months with Kay.

Kay. He glanced at the seat opposite him, where she was still sleeping, her head tilted to one side, her mouth softly relaxed, her hair an auburn aureole around her delicate face. He had never gotten into the habit of putting words to feelings, except when he was writing to Mamie and managed to call up a few scraps of romantic endearments from the westerns he liked to read. The thought of his letters to his wife made him uncomfortable, for he knew very well that they were meant to placate and reassure her. But what he wrote in the letters weren't lies. He was only leaving a few things out, that's all. He and Mamie had been married for over a quarter of a century, for chrissake. She was his wife, the mother of his son. He wasn't lying when he said he loved her. Of *course* he loved her.

But not in the way he loved Kay. His glance lingered on her face. He knew how much he would miss her constant companionship, her deep interest in his work, her readiness to listen as he talked out problems. Even more, she was a desirable woman and willing. He knew that she would give herself to him without a second thought, simply because she loved him. All he had to do was ask.

The plane was losing altitude now, lining up for the approach to Payne Airfield, south of Cairo, and he took one last, deep drag on his cigarette. Well, if he thought he could handle it, he might ask, if they were ever able to find a private moment.

But maybe he wouldn't. It wasn't that he didn't want Kay, because he did. He wanted her like bloody hell. He wanted her more than he'd ever wanted a woman, even Mamie, back in the beginning. It was because he wasn't sure he could handle it. He was long out of practice, and wanting might not be enough to make it happen. He sometimes thought he didn't know himself at all, but he knew himself well enough to know *that*.

He put out his cigarette in the ashtray in the seat's arm rest. Most of all, he wouldn't ask because he was about to leave Kay's life. Today or tomorrow or next week, Marshall would be named to Overlord and Eisenhower would be named to Marshall's job. He would go back to Washington, to his wife. Another man might have exploited Kay's willingness *because* he knew he was leaving. But that wasn't the way he did things, and it wouldn't be fair to her. Whatever was between them now would end in a few weeks. She would get on with her life, and he would get on with his.

His gaze lingered on Kay's sleeping face. Then he turned to

look out the window again, at the desert that hid the secrets of so many dead kings.

∽

In Cairo, Kay found herself, with Ruth and Nana, assigned to a private suite in the luxurious villa where the Boss was staying. Ike went off to the conference and the girls went shopping, astonished to see so many wonderful things available in the shops, as if there were no war. They were saving their money to splurge on a fine dinner, but it was fun to window shop. Later that evening, Eisenhower dined with General Marshall, while Kay and the girls went out to a nearby restaurant. Kay had *gambari mashwi*, whole grilled prawns, and *roz bil molokhia*—rice with a green vegetable cooked with garlic and coriander. It was simple but delightfully exotic, she thought.

She had just gotten back to the villa when Mickey knocked at the door. "The General would like you to join him in a nightcap," he said.

Ike was waiting in the long, high-ceilinged drawing room, drinks on a table between two chairs. "Come here, Kay." He held out his arms. She ran to him and he held her close for a long moment, his arms wrapped around her, his cheek on her hair—not a passionate embrace, just a sweet and loving closeness, and she reveled in it.

After a moment, he let her go and stepped back. She searched his eyes. Was he about to tell her that he was going back to Washington? She pulled in her breath and held it, waiting, dreading what she might hear.

But it wasn't what she expected. "The conference is over and FDR and Churchill will be leaving tomorrow for Tehran, to meet with Stalin," Ike said. "General Marshall has decided that I look 'weary' and need a little vacation." He made a wry face, and Kay remembered that he always blew his top when anybody told him he looked tired. "Tedder has offered a C-47 for a trip to Luxor, for a tour of the Valley of the Kings. He's even arranged for an archaeologist to be our guide. I'll be gone for a couple of days. Will you come along?"

"Would I!" she exclaimed happily. "Of course I would."

"We'll be chaperoned." He grinned ruefully. "I'm inviting the staff. And Elliott Roosevelt—the President's son—wants to come with us." He leaned forward to whisper in her ear. "I think young Roosevelt has a crush on you. And the President, too."

Kay rolled her eyes. "Well, they're out of luck," she said with a laugh. "Because I've got a crush on *you*."

"That's what I wanted to hear." Ike pulled her back into his arms. After a moment, he said, in a lower, more somber tone, "I just wish things were different, Kay. If I knew I wasn't going to Washington, I would love to . . ." He shook his head. "I hope you know what I'm trying to say."

"I know." Her breath caught in her throat. Was this "little vacation" a prologue to the announcement she was dreading? She wanted to ask, but she didn't want to hear the answer. She put her hand on his face and drew his mouth down to hers.

Their kiss tasted like sadness.

∞

In hellish heat, they landed the next afternoon in Luxor, checked into the famed Old Winter Palace Hotel, and walked through the streets, which were built on the site of the ancient city of Thebes. It was cooler in the desert evening, and after dinner, they strolled out in a group to see the temples, along what had once been a broad avenue lined with hundreds of human-headed sphinxes. In the shimmering moonlight, ruined statues of pharaohs, like pale stone ghosts, guarded the west bank of the Nile.

On their way back to the hotel through the darkness, Ike reached for Kay's hand. "You have to know how much it means to me to see this with you," he said. "I wish—" He broke off. "Sorry," he muttered.

"Let's not be sorry." She gripped his hand and turned to smile at him. "This is what we have. This is *now*. It's enough." She said the words bravely, but she wasn't sure she believed them.

Back at the hotel, the group had a nightcap together and then said goodnight. She had her own room and had thought—no, she had hoped—that he would come to her. Everyone seemed to be in a different part of the hotel, so there would be little danger of discovery.

But that isn't what happened. As they walked down the hall to their rooms, he slipped a piece of paper into her hand. *You know what I am thinking*, he had written. *Good night. Sweet dreams.*

She lay awake for a long time, hoping he might change his mind. Finally, she drifted to sleep, thinking that he must know he was going to Washington. He was keeping the truth from her to spare her feelings. This was his way of saying goodbye.

The next day, they drove across the Nile and into the Valley of the Kings. It was blazing hot, and the old cars in their caravan often boiled over. When that happened, they got fresh water pumped from wells where water buffalo plodded in circles. In the villages, donkeys hung their heads out of doorways, and clouds of flies swarmed over goat carcasses hanging in the bazaars. But when they reached the great valley in the hills behind Deir el-Bahri, all these sights were forgotten. There, sunk deep into the stone of the mountain, were tombs of pharaohs, designed with descending corridors that opened out into pillared chambers. At the end of the main corridor was the burial chamber: the royal mummy in its stone sarcophagus, surrounded by all the things he would want in the next world. The walls were covered with pictures of the dead king and with illustrated texts to help him find his way through the underworld.

It had been a long, hot, hard day, but Kay would never forget a moment of it. Back at the hotel that night, all they wanted was a cold drink, a quick supper, and a warm bath. Ike kissed Kay quickly in the hall and went to his room. She was sure of it now. This was all they would have, ever. Was it enough?

No! she cried into her pillow. *No, not enough, not nearly enough!* But it was all. All there would ever be.

℘

On the last day of their trip, the group flew to Jerusalem, where they had lunch in the grand King David Hotel, strolled through the bazaar, and walked through the Garden of Gethsemane. The garden was closed to the public, but Ike's four stars opened the gate for the two of them, and they strolled along the quiet paths, away from the noisy crowds. In a remote corner of the garden, behind a gnarled olive tree, he bent to kiss her quickly, impulsively—and almost reluctantly, she thought, as if he had been trying all day *not* to kiss her and had finally given in. She felt inexpressibly sad.

Leaving the garden, they stopped at a crowded bazaar, where she admired a small olivewood box with a hand-carved lid and Ike bought it for her. That night, back at the villa in Cairo, he handed her a postcard he'd bought in the bazaar. It had a photograph of the Garden of Gethsemane on one side. On the other, he had written, *There are lots of things I could say—you know them. Good night.*

In the room she was sharing with Ruth and Nana, she slipped the card into the little olivewood box. That night she dreamed that Ike came to her in the dark and made love to her, a love so sweet and slow and altogether lovely that she awoke, breathless, her heart beating fast, her skin tingling. The urgency of the dream had been so powerful that she could almost convince herself that the experience had been real. But the moments of imagined intimacy were sharpened by her waking awareness that Ike would likely be returning to his wife very soon, and she began to cry—silently, so as not to wake the others.

It was a long time before sleep came again. It brought no more dreams.

Back at Allied headquarters, there was still one more important visit to prepare for. The President would be arriving in Tunis on December 7, on his way back to Washington from his conference with Churchill and Stalin at Tehran. When they met his C-54 at El Aouina Field, Kay thought he looked terribly gray and tired and years older than when they had said goodbye just two weeks before.

But his cigarette holder was still cocked at a jaunty angle and he was still flashing that Roosevelt smile. "Ah, Kay," he said. "I've given orders that you're to drive me, so don't let Mike Reilly pull any of his Irish tricks."

"Yes, *sir*," Kay said happily. "Thank you, sir!"

Eisenhower joined the President in the backseat of the Cadillac. "I trust that the Tehran conference was a success, sir."

"A mixed bag, as usual," FDR said. He raised his voice over the roar of their motorcycle escort as Kay swung into the cavalcade of vehicles. "Stalin got that second front he's been demanding. We committed to the cross-Channel invasion in May." He hesitated. "I don't suppose you've got the news yet, have you?"

"What news?" Eisenhower asked, and Kay, at the wheel, half-turned her head to listen.

"Well, then, I see you haven't," the President said briskly. "So let me be the first to congratulate you, General Eisenhower." He raised his voice—deliberately, Kay thought so that she could hear him. "You will have full responsibility for Operation Overlord and for the liberation of Europe from the Germans. Your title will be Supreme Commander, Allied Expeditionary Forces. You will be based in London for the planning phases of the operation. I will be making the joint announcement with the Prime Minister as soon as I get back to Washington." He thrust out his hand. "Congratulations, Ike."

Ike seemed stunned. He looked up and Kay met his eyes

in the rear view mirror. "Congratulations, General," she said. "Wonderful news."

"Thank you, sir," Ike said to the President. "I'll do my best. My very best." His grin was so wide it nearly split his face, and Kay was unspeakably happy for him and for herself. The Allied command was the capstone of his military career, what he had wanted, what he had dreamed.

For her, it was a breathtaking reprieve. Ike would be going to London. And she would be with him.

They would be *together.*

CHAPTER FIFTEEN
Things Not Mentioned

Washington, D.C.
July–November 1943

In Washington, the wilting heat of the summer had continued well into the autumn. Whenever they could, housewives sat in front of electric fans draped with damp towels, sipping glasses of iced tea. Men took an extra white shirt to the office and changed after lunch. People who had showers showered twice a day, and those with a front porch sat on it in the evening, hoping to catch a breeze.

There were other challenges in this second year of America's war. A shortage of cigarettes forced smokers to roll their own or smoke a pipe, when they could find tobacco. (The Anti-Cigarette Alliance helpfully suggested chewing gentian root instead.) Sugar was hard to get and coffee even harder—unless your neighbor was secretly selling it out of his basement. Chocolates were next to impossible. And even cars with an "A" sticker were limited to four gallons of gas a week.

If people had known the truth about the war—the heavy price paid in human lives and equipment for every foot of ground gained against the enemy—they might have stopped complaining about the shortages. But they knew only what the government told them, and that wasn't much. Every scrap of war reporting was filtered through the Office of War Information, where Ike's brother Milton was in charge.

The OWI controlled the content of newspapers, magazines, radio broadcasts, and films. Readers, listeners, and viewers heard the good news—the bad news (and there was a lot of it) went deliberately untold. For instance, Americans read that Operation Husky was a swift summer success that ended with the taking of Sicily from the Axis. True enough. But the full cost—the Allied wounded, missing, and dead—wasn't tallied in the newspaper reports. And what wasn't reported until after was the fact that 110,000 Axis troops managed to escape the island, taking with them ten thousand vehicles, forty-seven tanks, ninety-four guns, and eleven hundred tons of ammunition. They retreated to Italy and dug in to oppose the Allied advance to Rome. Americans also heard that General Clark had successfully landed at Salerno. But they didn't hear that the Allied divisions under his command—the British Forty-Sixth and Fifty-Sixth and the U.S. Thirty-Sixth—had hit a beach defended by a full-strength panzer division, and that the Allies had barely gained a toehold.

Milton made sure that Eisenhower was given plenty of space in the papers, and when he faced the press, the General was bold and confident: "The time has come to hit the Germans where it hurts. Our object is to trap and smash them." But Ike was concealing what he knew about his army's terrible vulnerabilities. From his headquarters at Amilcar, he cabled the Combined Chiefs that Clark's landing at Salerno had been touch and go, with many losses. "Our greatest asset now," he wrote, "is confusion."

Even the reporters who covered the actual fighting did their part in hiding the truth rather than telling it. After the war, John Steinbeck—then a correspondent for the *New York Herald Tribune*—would write:

> Our obsession with secrecy had a perfectly legitimate
> beginning in a fear that knowledge of troopship sailings
> would and often did attract the wolf packs of subma-

rines. But from there it got out of hand. . . . We went along with [the effort to keep things secret], and not only that, we abetted it. Gradually it became a part of all of us that the truth about anything was automatically secret and that to trifle with it was to interfere with the War Effort. By this I don't mean that the correspondents were liars. They were not. . . . [But] it is in the things not mentioned that the untruth lies.

As in every war, the things not mentioned far outnumbered the mentioned, and untruths and lies were the order of the day.

But back home, Americans didn't seem to mind. Perhaps, like the journalists, they agreed that secrecy was important or feared that the truth would be too painful to face. Or maybe they simply wanted to go on about their business and not be reminded that their brothers and sons and husbands were facing disaster and death on the other side of the globe. In any event, most seemed buoyed by faith in their military leaders—in FDR on the home front, Eisenhower in the Mediterranean and later in Europe, MacArthur in the Pacific. Americans knew their armed forces had never lost a war. They weren't going to lose this one.

By the autumn of 1943, however, the Roosevelt administration had begun to realize that keeping the public in the dark was not an entirely smart idea. The uninformed populace was becoming too complacent to dedicate itself totally to the war effort. The Office of War Information was directed to lift the ban on images showing the real cost of war.

The change was immediate, graphic, and disturbing. In the September 20, 1943, issue of *Life* magazine, readers saw photographs of American corpses, ravaged and bloated, sprawled on a New Guinea beach. These images were the first real truths about the terrible price of victory that American civilians had seen in the twenty-one months since Pearl Harbor. A few months later, the War Department produced a documentary film called *With the Marines at Tarawa*, which contained footage of actual combat scenes more horrific than anything Americans had ever viewed. There were too many mutilated bodies to clear the Hollywood censors, and only FDR could grant permission for the film's release. He asked the advice of Time-Life photographer Robert Sherrod, who had been at Tarawa.

"Our soldiers on the front want people back home to know that they don't knock the hell out of the enemy every day of every battle," Sherrod told the President. "War is a horrible, nasty business. To say otherwise is to do a disservice to those who died."

FDR agreed to release the film uncensored, a triumph for truth.

But that was the exception that proved the rule. Deception was still the name of the game, and most Americans knew very little about what their generals were up to on the other side of the earth.

℅

Mamie Eisenhower was in the dark, too.

But at least she was cool. At her insistence (her vehement insistence), the management of the Wardman Park had installed an air conditioning machine in the window of her bedroom. The machine's mechanical whir was irritatingly loud, its motor turned itself on and off with a shuddering thunk, and it produced a musty odor that Mamie so detested that she sprayed the machine with perfume. But air conditioning transformed her apartment into a cool, dark cave—a refuge from the debilitating heat and humidity that blanketed Washington.

For Mamie, the idea of the cave was more than a fanciful metaphor. She had fled to San Antonio to escape from the nerve-rattling gossip about her husband and Mrs. Summersby, and her weeks away had allowed her to regain at least some of her equilibrium. She had Ike's letters and his repeated protestations of love to bolster her confidence. She trusted him to do the right thing—didn't she?

And what difference would it make if she didn't? All she could do was worry, and she was already doing that, constantly. Determined to put the best face on the situation, she took the train back to Washington. She would simply stay home, stay out of sight, keep her head down and ignore the gossip, and all would be well.

Easier said than done. While it might be difficult for the ordinary American to hear real news of the real war, the army wives' gossip network was humming. Through summer and into the autumn, Mamie's telephone rang almost daily with concerned calls from friends who wanted to let her know that their husbands had spotted Ike and his "pretty Irish driver" in Algiers, or Tunis, or Amilcar, or Constantine. They had been seen driving together, riding together, boarding an airplane together, boarding a ship. Together.

From all reports, Mrs. Summersby did not appear to be in mourning for her dead fiancé—although Mamie thought that particular social standard was probably relaxed at the front. The woman seemed to lead a remarkably active social life, and in star-studded company, at that. Audrey Hamer (whose husband was with the Army Transportation Corps in Algiers) called to report that Ike's driver was a regular guest, with Ike, at dinner parties where the celebrities included Prime Minister Churchill, Lord Louis Mountbatten, Secretary of State Cordell Hull, and Averell Harriman, the U.S. ambassador to Moscow—not to mention Bob Hope, Vivien Leigh, Kay Francis, and Noël Coward. Why, she had even driven King George and the President of the United States!

Most distressingly, Maria Ayers (her husband was the co-pilot on the General's C-54) phoned to tell Mamie that Mrs. Summersby had flown with Ike to Cairo. In fact, she had stayed in the very same luxurious Cairo residence to which Eisenhower had been assigned. When the conference was over, Ike and Kay had flown to Luxor to see the Egyptian temples—and then to Jerusalem, spending the nights in the same hotel. "I'm sure there was nothing at all improper," Maria said judiciously. "But it does seem that somebody should have thought of *appearances*."

Mamie was undone. She had always wanted to see the pyramids, and touring Jerusalem was also high on her list—and now Ike had been there with *that woman*. But she could only murmur, "I'm sure they were part of a group, Marie. The General is always very careful about such things." She took a deep breath and changed the subject. "Now, tell me about that new grandbaby of yours. You must be very proud."

In addition to Mrs. Summersby's exploits, she appeared to be the lucky recipient of several gifts. Janice Cooper, whose husband was serving with Patton in Palermo, reported that Mrs. Summersby had visited there and that Patton had poured some very fine champagne for her and had given her a bottle of Arpège.

And then there was the distressing matter of the uniform, which Cookie mentioned at the mah-jongg table one afternoon. "I suppose you've heard that your husband created quite a sensation with his new jacket design. It's waist-length. They're calling it the 'Eisenhower jacket.'"

Mamie hadn't heard it, and was pleased. "Oh, really? I can't wait to see it. Ike looks so handsome in his uniform."

Cynthia frowned. "I heard that Mrs. Summersby has one exactly like it. Made of the very same material, too. Marvin said it came from what was left on the bolt after the General's uniforms were cut." She cast a half-guilty, half-triumphant glance at Mamie. "Oh, Mamie, *do* forgive me, please! I didn't mean to suggest . . ."

Mamie pushed her chair back and stood up. "Who would like another glass of iced tea?" she asked brightly.

Except for the friends who came in to play cards, Mamie was alone. Every day, she spent several hours answering letters from Ike's friends, admirers, and those who wanted a favor. She kept the radio on, listening to daytime soap operas, evening comedies, and the news on WTOP at noon, six, and ten. And she worked on Ike's scrapbook, which was rapidly filling with newspaper and magazine articles. At the OWI, Milton was obviously doing a good job promoting his brother. EISENHOWER: "ALLIES READY TO GO AGAIN" trumpeted one newspaper, describing Ike's confidence that the Italian campaign would be a short-run affair. TROUBLE-TORN ITALY WEIGHS EISENHOWER BID FOR PEACE said another. And yet another: BOND BUYING AIDS WAR EFFORT, REPORTS EISENHOWER. In that one, Ike was quoted as saying, "The success of the third war bond drive will be proof of every American's devotion to our cause."

Mamie cared for the cause, of course, but it was the commander who was nearest her heart. She added fresh flowers and a candle to the arrangement of his photographs on the top of her piano, a shrine to her valiant soldier. But no matter how hard she tried to keep his image real, it had become elusive, a shadow fading into some distant realm where she was not welcome. At night, her loneliness often became so great that she cried herself to sleep. On other nights, she was pierced by stabs of bitter jealousy—not just of Kay Summersby (although she would have cheerfully wrung that woman's pretty little neck) but of each and every member of Ike's official family. They were there, with him, and she was here, by *herself.*

It wasn't fair. It was just not *fair!*

In November, Mamie heard a new rumor that was beginning to ripple through official Washington, even reaching her Wardman Park cave. The Allies were planning the long-anticipated cross-Channel invasion of Europe, the "second front" that was supposed to take the pressure off the Red Army. The central question: who would be named Supreme Commander? General Marshall was the most senior officer in the American army. If he got the nod, Ike would be brought back to Washington to take Marshall's place as Army Chief of Staff. And Mrs. Summersby, Mamie thought with satisfaction, would be left behind. There was no place for a British civilian in the Pentagon.

Mamie knew very well that her husband would prefer the top

field command to the top staff job, and she knew that she ought to be rooting for him. But she couldn't help praying that Marshall would be named and Ike sent home. He would be once again with *her*. He would hold the highest position in the Stateside army and they would move back to Fort Meyer, into the Marshalls' big house on Generals' Row.

That hope expanded like a gaudy helium balloon, filling all her thoughts. In her imagination, she began to unpack her china and crystal and silver, for there would be entertaining and parties and gala times. She would wear her frilly dresses, and Mickey and two or three others would manage the cooking and housework and drive her where she wanted to go.

But when she asked Ike about it in a letter, he replied that he had no idea what might happen or when. "We'll find out soon enough," he wrote, with an infuriating calmness. "Until then, I can only do whatever job they give me to do, wherever it is, as well as I can do it. I hope you will do the same." Mamie felt she had been rebuked, but that didn't dampen her eagerness.

And then her friends began reporting that General Marshall had secretly been named to the job. He was said to have sent his executive desk to Allied Headquarters in London, while his wife was packing up the house on Generals' Row and moving the furniture to their country house in Virginia.

"Really, Mamie, it's a sure bet," Cynthia told her. "Katherine Marshall told General Richard's wife that she'll be glad to turn over entertainment duties to you. She said that since you have *sixty* crates of china, you deserve to use it."

"I don't know about that," Mamie said uncomfortably. It was true, of course, but it didn't quite sound like a compliment.

"Well, *I* do," Cynthia said. "The Marshalls haven't entertained since the war started. I'm sure you'll change that, Mamie dear. I can't wait for your first party!"

Mamie couldn't either. In fact, she had already planned the guest list for Ike's welcome-home celebration, and the menu was almost complete in her mind. She tried once again to get Ike to give her *some* clue to when he was coming back to Washington. But he didn't, or couldn't, or wouldn't. So she was completely in the dark.

Until the day before Christmas.

ॐ

John—now a cadet sergeant in his third year—was down from West Point for the holiday. He was standing on a chair, attaching the traditional golden angel to the top of their traditional Christmas tree, when Mr. Bracegirdle, the Wardman Park manager, knocked at the door.

"There's a big crowd of reporters in the lobby, Mrs. Eisenhower," Mr. Bracegirdle said with great excitement. "They're asking to see you."

Mamie frowned. "It's Christmas Eve, for pity's sake! *Whatever* can they want?"

Mr. Bracegirdle's bow tie bobbed over his Adam's apple. "They're saying that the President has named General Eisenhower Supreme Commander of Allied Expeditionary Forces, that's what! They want to know what you think of it."

"Supreme Commander?" Mamie whispered. But General Marshall already had that job. Ike was supposed to come home—to *her*.

"Supreme Commander?" John jumped off the chair and grabbed Mamie's hands, swinging her around. "Wow! Isn't that swell, Mother! Just swell! Dad must be so pleased."

"Stop, John," Mamie said crossly. "You're *pulling* me." So Ike would be managing the European invasion from London. And he would need a driver.

"Supreme Commander." Mr. Bracegirdle beamed. "What do you think of that, Mrs. Eisenhower?"

There was a long silence.

Finally Mamie spoke. "I . . . I think it's wonderful," she said, wondering how many times she would have to tell that lie. She straightened her shoulders. "But you can send the reporters away. It's Christmas. I don't want to talk to them today. Or tomorrow, either." She picked up a package of silver tinsel. "Here, John. Put this on the tree."

"I'm sorry." Mr. Bracegirdle looked downcast. "They'll be so disappointed."

"That's just too darn bad," Mamie snapped. "Now you go tell them."

But seven hours later, a young woman from one of the wire services was still perched on a chair beside the elevator. As each hotel resident approached, she said brightly, "If you happen to pass Mrs. Eisenhower's apartment, please let her know the Associated Press is still waiting."

Tired of answering her doorbell to yet another relay of the reporter's persistent message, Mamie had to relent. There were the usual questions, of course, ending with "You must be very proud of the General."

"Oh, yes," Mamie said, trying to look pleased. "From the first, he has been in there to finish the job, and he always does his duty. But I didn't expect *this*," she added, lapsing into candor. "I wasn't in on the secret."

Eyes widening, the reporter looked up from her notebook. "You mean, it was a surprise to *you*?"

"Of course." Mamie forced herself to laugh. "When it comes to my husband, I'm always in the dark."

&

Which was not quite true. A few days after Christmas, General Marshall's secretary called to alert Mamie to expect a visitor. Ike would be arriving secretly, to confer with President Roosevelt and the Joint Chiefs and spend a few days with his family. Mamie could hardly wait see him, of course—it had been eighteen months since her husband had kissed her goodbye and left for London and a whole new life on the other side of the earth.

But if she had dreamed of a romantic homecoming, she was disappointed from their first and very brief embrace, which was interrupted by the frisky black Scottie puppy her husband had brought. Junior, one of Telek's puppies, was all done up with a Scotch-plaid collar and leash and intended as her late Christmas gift. But the puppy piddled on Mamie's prized Oriental rug before Ike even got his coat off. As she ran for a towel, he pooped on her pale green velvet sofa, and then threw up on her pink-and-green chintz bedroom chair.

Mamie managed a shrill little laugh, but she couldn't help being annoyed. What in the world made Ike suppose that she wanted a *dog*, of all things? A dog that wasn't house-trained, in the Wardman? What in the world was he thinking? She shut Junior in the bathroom, where he whined and cried and scratched at the door. Ike—at Mamie's insistence—called his brother Milton, who agreed to adopt Junior.

Ike, as it turned out, wasn't quite house-trained, either. He had gained a few pounds and his face was lined and weary, but there was much more to it than that. The man she had loved for nearly thirty years—her sweet, affectionate, gentle husband—had disappeared. In his place was a stranger who barked orders with the confidence of a commander who was used to being obeyed, promptly and without question. He was restless and edgy, pacing back and forth, scattering ashes from the cigarettes he chain-smoked. He asked staccato questions and—when he bothered to answer at all—was terse and abrupt. He had no patience with small talk, but what else was there? Even in peacetime Mamie had never wanted to know about his work, and now it was all so secret. He talked a little about the Algerian farm—"Sailor's Delight," he called it—and the Arabian stallions he rode as often as he could get away from the office. He mentioned that he had seen the President and that he had attended an important conference in Cairo, taking a day or two off to tour the tombs in Egypt's Valley of the Kings and visit the city of Jerusalem. He didn't mention his driver, and Mamie didn't dare ask.

It wasn't long before they ran out of conversation altogether. Mamie was relieved when, after a few stiff, uncomfortable hours, Ike was called to the White House to meet with the President. He spent the next day going over war plans with the Joint Chiefs at the Pentagon, and that evening, Mamie went with him to a dinner party with the chiefs and important congressmen and their wives. Ike was at ease, affable and assured, but Mamie felt nervous and uncertain. She managed to laugh and chatter gaily, but she couldn't help scrutinizing each face for hints that the person she was talking to had heard the rumors about Ike and Mrs. Summersby. And of course she saw what she was looking for and felt as if she was being measured against the "beauteous Kay."

The next day, they took General Marshall's private Pullman car to West Point to see John—also an uncomfortable visit. Ike was as terse with Johnny as he had been with her. In fact, she was so dismayed when Ike spoke curtly to their son that, for the first time, she protested. "Really, Ike. Must you be so abrupt?"

Her question provoked a dark look, only half-masked by a crooked grin. "Hell," Ike growled. "I'm going back to my command where I can do what I want." Johnny laughed, but Mamie could only turn away and swallow her hurt. She knew Ike wasn't joking.

After West Point, General Marshall arranged for them to have what he genially called a "second honeymoon" at the Greenbrier Hotel in White Sulphur Springs. But for Mamie, it was nothing short of a disaster. Ike was preoccupied and the wary stiffness between them never went away. When she said "I love you, Ike," he returned it with an absent, almost automatic "I love you, too, honey," although once he added, "I hope you know how much I've missed you." She hadn't expected any intimacy (that hadn't happened for years) and his goodnight embrace—while it was still affectionate—felt more like habit than desire. She comforted herself with the reminder that theirs was a mature marriage, and that affection was more important than sex. But she wasn't sure she believed that.

And then he called her Kay.

The first time, she whirled on him in an uncontrollable, high-octane rage. "That's not my name!" she cried. "*That's not my name!*"

His apology was sheepish. It meant nothing, he said. He was just tired, just inattentive. Kay Summersby was always in the office. He was used to telling her to do this, get that, go there. He was sorry. It wouldn't happen again.

But it did. Twice. Each time, she wanted to scream at him, to beat him with her fists. But everything inside her had turned to ice, and she could scarcely catch her breath. She knew she ought to confront him with her fears—they spun like a black whirlpool in her mind, pulling her down and down, drowning her. But she simply did not dare. If he dismissed the rumors as idle gossip and malicious lies, would she—*could* she—believe him?

But worse, she was afraid that he would say it was true. That he was in love with Kay Summersby. What would she do then? Offer him a divorce?

But that was as unthinkable as hearing him say that he *wanted* a divorce. Better to leave the question unasked than to risk an answer that would utterly destroy her. Better—far better—to live with deception than to lose him, lose their marriage, lose her place in the world. Lose everything that gave her life meaning.

She was relieved when—after just a day and a half at the Greenbrier, he left her and flew to Kansas to see his mother and brothers. The trip lengthened into an unexpected several days. He said it was because his mother was ailing but Mamie thought it was because he didn't want to be with *her*. And when he came back to Washington, he was summoned to another long round of meetings at the Pentagon, a routine checkup by a couple of army doctors, and one last evening appointment with the President.

When it was finally time for goodbyes, she found she had just one thing to say. She squared her shoulders, met his eyes, and said it as stoically as she could.

"Don't come home until the war is over, Ike. This is just too . . . difficult, for both of us."

He held her then, and kissed her forehead. "I'm sorry," he said, and brushed his lips across her cheek. "Goodbye, honey."

Then he was gone, and Mamie was left alone, drowning in her whirlpool of fears.

$$\mathcal{SO}$$

At first, Ike found his visit with the President disconcerting. Wearing striped pajamas, FDR was in bed, propped against pillows and ill with what his secretary, Grace Tully, called influenza. But his shoulders were slumped, his face was gray, and the famous Roosevelt grin was missing. Eisenhower had heard rumors of a cardiac condition, even cancer. But he knew that the truth of the President's health, whatever it was, would be concealed—from the media, from the nation, perhaps even from his family. In war, lies were the name of the game, deceit the cardinal rule. Ike understood that the Commander in Chief couldn't let his enemies—or his friends, or even his family—know he was sick.

The President's blue eyes had lost none of their glint, however, and his voice held its accustomed authority. "Pull up a chair, Ike. I trust you've had a good visit with your family."

Eisenhower placed a straight wooden chair beside the bed and sat down. "Yes, sir, I have," he lied. If Marshall hadn't ordered him, he wouldn't have taken the time to come to the States. On balance, he had enjoyed the visit to Abilene, seeing his mother and brothers. But Mamie—he caught himself. Mamie was another story. "Yes, a very good visit," he lied again. "It's been great to be home."

"Excellent. You look fit and ready to go back to work." FDR slipped a Camel into his long plastic holder and offered one to

Eisenhower. "Do you have an idea of what you need, once you get to London?"

"I do, sir." Eisenhower took the cigarette, lit it, and lit FDR's. "We need landing craft. LSTs, LCTs—as many as we can get. And we need more men. On the double." *This was January, damn it. D-Day was planned for early May. There was no time to lose.*

"You're going to have to arm-wrestle MacArthur for both," the President said matter-of-factly. "We're supplying two theaters of war, you know." He pulled on his cigarette. "I'll do the best I can, of course. War production—" A fit of coughing interrupted him, and he paused to wipe his mouth. "Our war production program is going great guns. We're inducting two hundred thousand men a month. But there's a limit, you know. We all have to do the best we can with what we've got."

Eisenhower knew damned well that there weren't two hundred thousand men a month in the pipeline, but he wasn't going to correct the President. "We'll take whatever we can get," he said somberly. "We have to hit those Normandy beaches hard enough break through the German lines." He knew his mission by heart: "You will enter the continent of Europe and, in conjunction with the other Allied Nations, undertake operations aimed at the heart of Germany and the destruction of her armed forces."

Well, it was a damned long way from the Channel beaches to Berlin, the heart of Germany. The landings would open a door to the continent, but if they didn't make it through on the first attempt, it would be slammed in their face. They needed all the help they could get. "Men *and* landing craft," he repeated emphatically. "Anything less than—"

"I hear you, Ike." The President sighed. "I hear you and I'll do what I can." He quirked an eyebrow. "Now, tell me about General Patton. I understand that he's being brought in from the woodshed. You have a new assignment for him, I'm told."

Eisenhower was aware that Marshall had briefed FDR on the slapping incident (recently leaked in the American press by Drew Pearson) and knew why Patton had been sidelined in Sicily for the past four months. Now it appeared that he knew about Operation Fortitude as well.

"That's right, Mr. President. His new command—Fortitude South—is part of Operation Bodyguard. Do you know about—?"

"Oh, you bet." That brought out the famous FDR grin. "Winston is so pleased with his pet project that he has to tell me the latest twice a week." The President blew out a stream of smoke. "I understand that Bodyguard is designed to deceive the Germans about the timing and the location of the Normandy landings." He paused, reflecting. "The name comes from one of Winston's own speeches, doesn't it? 'In wartime, truth is so precious that she should always be attended by a bodyguard of lies.' I've been tempted to steal the line myself. It could come in handy with the folks in the Congress. They are under the misapprehension that a president ought to tell them the whole damn truth."

Eisenhower returned the grin. Bodyguard was the umbrella code name for a series of major ruses that the Allies came up with when they began planning the cross-Channel invasion. Directed out of a half-dozen different agencies, the complex operations involved spies, double agents, false radio and signal communications, and misleading information and lies leaked to the newspapers. Operation Bodyguard was designed to make the Germans think that the American and British fighting forces were much larger and better equipped than they were and that the landings on the Normandy beaches, when they occurred, were only a feint. Hitler was meant to believe that the *real* invasion, planned for a few days later, would be aimed at the Pas de Calais, 150 miles to the north. If the trick worked, that's where he would position most of his force, leaving the beaches more lightly defended.

"Patton's not going to like it," Eisenhower said, "but he's being put in command of a paper army—FUSAG. First United States Army Group, a fictitious force of fifty divisions and a million men. It has to be Patton, because our intelligence tells us that the German High Command—the *Oberkommando der Wehrmacht*—is convinced that he is our best Allied general. They're sure he'll be the spearhead for the invasion. So we're giving him a phony army and aiming him at Calais. His real job won't begin until after D-Day."

"I can see why Patton appeals to the Germans," the President said dryly. "The man has a definite megalomaniacal streak. Which suits him to this task, I suppose."

Ruefully, Eisenhower agreed. "We'll pretend to 'hide' Patton in the south of England, but we'll encourage him to strut his stuff boldly enough to catch the attention of German intelligence. All a fiction, of course."

"Everything in war is a fiction of one kind or another," the President said. "Now, tell me what you think of—"

They talked for another half hour about the progress of the war, and especially Eisenhower's relationships with the British and the French. As always, Ike was impressed with the President's grasp of the overall situation, and he felt better when he got up to leave. The Commander in Chief might not be a well man, but he was still very much in command.

"Oh, before you go," the President said, "I have something for a friend of yours. The very lovely Miss Summersby." He took a photograph of himself, picked up a pen, and autographed it. "Give it to her when you see her," he said, holding it out. He looked up, catching Eisenhower's eye. "You *will* be seeing her, I suppose."

"Yes, sir," Eisenhower said evenly. "My staff has flown to London while I've been here in the States."

The President held his glance. "Well, then, give her my very best regards." There was a moment's silence. "I suppose you know about the gossip."

Eisenhower was tempted to put him on the spot by asking "What gossip?" But he only nodded. "Yes, sir. I know."

Milton had given him an unvarnished version of the talk that was floating around Washington—talk that Mamie had undoubtedly heard. He hadn't been surprised or even offended, although he had been rather startled by his brother's moral objections. He had been quick to interrupt what promised to be a sermon on the subject with "I haven't slept with her, Milt, if that's what you're getting at."

Which was true, strictly speaking, although—having grown up with a religious mother—Eisenhower was well aware of the Bible's stern warning against lusting after a woman in his heart. Of that, he was certainly guilty. In fact, now that he knew he'd be spending the next few months with her in England, he had nerved himself to a discussion with one of the medical officers he had seen the day before. The problem was likely related to his high blood pressure, the doctor had said, adding drily, "I don't suppose it would do any good to tell you that if you want to have sex, you should steer clear of high-stress situations."

"Is that your only advice?" he had asked. He was a goddamned commander. If his job wasn't stressful, he wasn't doing it right.

The doctor shrugged. "No silver bullets, General. If you want to make it happen, lay off the booze. And take it slow. A little patience can go a long way."

The President cleared his throat. "I'm in no position to make judgments, of course," he said wryly. "Just reminding you—and myself—that sometimes the personal gets pulled out into the public. Things we don't think should be mentioned in polite society—well, they are. When that happens, it's usually the woman who's blamed. And in your case, as Supreme Commander, there's an extra burden. I'm not overly worried, but I should tell you that Winston is concerned about blackmail. He—"

There was a light knock at the door and the First Lady bustled in. "Oh, General Eisenhower," she trilled, in her fluttery, flyaway voice. "So *very* good to see you!" She put out her hand. "I want you to know that the fervent prayers of *every* American will be with you in this *tremendous* endeavor of yours. The fate of the world is in *your* hands. We're trusting *you* to save us."

Eisenhower stood. "Thank you, ma'am." He saluted the man in the bed. "And thank you, sir. I'm grateful for your confidence."

"Right-o." The President leaned back against his pillow. "But I imagine you'd be a great deal more grateful for a few extra landing craft."

PART THREE

EUROPE AND WASHINGTON
JANUARY 1944–NOVEMBER 1945

CHAPTER SIXTEEN
One and One

England
January–June 1944

Hands in the pockets of her coat, Kay stood waiting in the chill, foggy darkness. Ike had been expected to fly in from Washington, but another of London's infamous pea-soupers had engulfed the city, and all flights were canceled. The *Bayonet*, the General's railroad car, had been dispatched to Prestwick to pick him up, and Beetle had sent Kay to meet the train at Addison Street Station.

Kay had lived in London for nearly twenty years, and she thought she'd seen fogs. But this was one for the history books. She had driven the General's olive-drab Packard through Mayfair at a snail's pace, threading a perilous way between the abandoned cars and taxis that littered the streets. The occasional pedestrian emerged like a pale ghost out of the swirling fog, then vanished again. And on the Strand, she saw a double-decker bus inching along behind a man with a flashlight in one hand and the other on the fender, guiding the bus as if it were a blindfolded horse.

The Supreme Commander's staff had flown to London a few days before, on his new B-17. Beetle had put them to work at 20 Grosvenor Square, catching up on the cross-Channel invasion planning that had gone on in London while they managed the Mediterranean campaigns. Now, hunching her shoulders against the January chill, Kay found herself missing the warmth of sunny Algiers, with its fragrant orange and lemon trees, its bougainvillea and mild Mediterranean breezes. But London was home—or at least, it would be when Ike arrived. He was the center of her life now. With him, her days had purpose and meaning. Without him, emptiness.

It was after eleven when the train finally arrived with a hiss of steam and the squeal of metal wheels on metal track. Eisenhower alighted and came through the gloom toward her, flanked by Butch and Mickey. Kay wanted to run to him and throw herself into his arms, but that was out of the question. She saluted smartly. "Welcome to England, sir."

"Jesus H. Christ," he exclaimed, as Butch and Mickey went to gather the luggage. "I've never seen such a fog. You *drove* in it, Kay?"

She smiled. "I did, sir. I'll get you home in it, too."

"You never fail to surprise me." Eisenhower frowned. "Where's Telek? I thought you'd have him with you."

Kay made a face. "Afraid he's in solitary. Government-ordered quarantine for all dogs coming into England. The Ministry of Agriculture and Fisheries—don't ask—has detained him for six months, along with Caacie and Beetle's spaniel. Not even the PM could get us out of this one. I asked."

"Six months?" Eisenhower was shaking his head. "Jeez. He'll go stir-crazy, penned up all by himself."

"And no time off for good behavior." Kay grinned ruefully. "He's having to face the most appalling truth of his entire life. He is actually a *dog*."

"I'm sure he's lodged his complaints with the management." The General chuckled. "Well, just get us home tonight, Kay. Tomorrow we'll go visit our little guy." He paused. "Butch and I aren't in the Dorchester again, are we?"

"No, sir, we're not," Butch said emphatically, coming up with a trolley full of luggage. "We've been upgraded. We have a town house."

Ike's new London home was Hay's Lodge, an attractive, nicely furnished two-story townhouse in Chesterfield Hill, not far from Grosvenor Square. Getting there was a problem, though. The fog had thickened while Kay was waiting for the General's train to arrive, and driving through the mizzly brown murk was like trying to swim underwater in a muddy river. In Brompton Road, she turned the steering wheel hard to avoid a lorry and ran the Packard up on the sidewalk, narrowly missing a red callbox. A couple of blocks further on, she had to get out of the car and creep across the curb to a doorway, where she could see the street number and be sure where they were.

At last, she found her way to Hay's Lodge. Tex had left the lights on, laid a fire in the sitting room fireplace, and stocked the bar and the kitchen. They took off their coats and jackets. Ike fixed drinks while Mickey got the fire started, then made cheese sandwiches and went upstairs to bed.

The conversation ran the gamut between the situation they'd left behind in Algiers to the problems the new headquarters was encountering in London and the issues Ike had confronted in Washington. Kay was energized by the talk, feeling herself at the heart of what had to be the most important work in the world. And—even though she knew the enormity of the task ahead—feeling bolstered by Ike's quiet confidence.

After a second round of drinks, Butch yawned, put his glass down, and said, "I've had enough fun for one day, Ike. I'm turning in. Goodnight, Kay."

Kay reached for her shoulder bag. "I think it's time I—"

"Hold on a minute, Kay," Ike said, as Butch took the stairs. "I have something for you in my briefcase."

It was the President's photographed, autographed to her. "Oh, lovely," Kay said, admiring it. "I'll write a note to thank him."

"And these." Ike handed her a thin box. "I had to move heaven and earth to get them for you. They're scarce as hen's teeth back home."

She opened the box. "Nylons!" she cried joyfully. "Oh, thank you. You know the way to a woman's heart, Ike."

"I hope so," he said quietly. He took the box out of her hands and put it on the table.

She looked up at him. "I'm very glad to have you home, General." It had been only two weeks since they said goodbye at the airfield outside Algiers, but it seemed an eternity ago. The war loomed ahead of them like a dark, threatening forest, full of unseen perils. But she felt safe in the fortress of his strength, believing—no, *knowing*—that he had the wisdom and power to push all of them through to the end. And in the end would be victory, she was sure of that.

"No gladder than I am," he said gruffly. He put his hands on her shoulders, then bent and kissed her, his lips lingering on hers. He pulled her to him. "God, Kay, I've *missed* you. Two weeks away from you—it felt like exile."

He held her for a moment, stroking her hair, then gently pulled her down onto the sofa, where she fitted herself into the warm, familiar curve of his arm, feeling as if *this* were home. Not this place, not London, not even England. Just the two of them together, wherever in the world they happened to be. She felt unaccountably contented. Which was strange, because nothing but uncertainty lay ahead.

He turned off the lamp beside the sofa and they watched fire die down to embers as he told her what had happed at the apartment. "The puppy turned out to be a rotten idea," he said, with a rueful laugh. "Junior disgraced himself before I even got my coat off. Mamie locked him in the bathroom and I had to find another home for him."

"I'm sorry it didn't work out," Kay said. "He's such a sweet little fellow."

Ike was silent for a moment. "That wasn't the worst of it," he said finally. "The worst was when I . . . when I called her Kay. Not just once, either." He shook his head. "I caught old Billy Hell, I'll tell you. I've never seen that woman so angry."

"Oh, dear," Kay whispered, and said "I'm sorry" again.

But she wasn't. Or more accurately, she was sorry that Ike had been troubled by this small thing, when he had so many more consequential matters on his mind. At the same time, she couldn't blame Mamie. If she were Ike's wife, she wouldn't feel it was a small thing to be called by another woman's name. She would raise old Billy Hell, too.

He went on. "Most of her friends—*all* of her friends, I suppose—are military wives. They love nothing more than a bit of tittle-tattle. They've likely made sure that she's heard the gossip that's going the rounds. About . . . us, I mean." The words came slowly, and Kay understood how hard this was for him. "She didn't bring it up, but my brother did. And so did the President."

The President? "Oh, dear," Kay said again, adding, again: "I'm sorry. I hope you weren't terribly uncomfortable."

Surprisingly, *she* wasn't. Rather, she felt freer, somehow, and special, very special. The acknowledgment by others felt like a declaration of sorts. It was as if she and Ike had crossed together into a new territory, where their relationship—which they would still pretend was a secret—was an *open* secret, guessed by his wife and his brother and the President of the United States. By the British Prime Minister, too, she thought. And Ike's official family, and most of the generals who worked with him. *They* knew, and instead of making her feel guilty or ashamed, the awareness was somehow reassuring.

But Ike obviously felt differently. "It made me very uncomfortable. I'm not used to people looking into my private life. I hate it." He pulled her closer. "But more to the point, it reminded me that I've put you in a difficult place. *You're* the vulnerable one. Men walk away from something like this without a scratch, while women—they're the ones who get blamed. Who get hurt. I don't want you to get hurt."

She was grateful, but she had already weighed the pain she knew would come, and was resolved. "I don't care about that, Ike. I only want—"

He put his finger on her lips, stopping her. He turned her so that they were face-to-face. His voice was husky. "I have to be honest with you, Kay. I've been . . . wanting you for months now. But I felt it wasn't fair to begin something in Algiers, when it seemed likely that I would be sent back to the States. Now I know that's not going to happen. We can be together until this is over, if that's what you want."

"That's what I want," she said. A flame flickered in the fire-place. Shadows danced in the corners of the darkened room. "Just to be with you, wherever you are."

He shook his head. "There's more, Irish. This thing—it will end when this war ends." He spoke, she thought, with a kind of sad finality. "When that happens, I'll go home to whatever duty I'm assigned to, and to my wife. At some point, I may have to say that our relationship never existed, that you only worked for me. That you and I meant nothing to one another. That will be a lie and unfair, but that's the way it is." He held her eyes. "I'm leaving it up to you, Kay. You can say no and end it now. Or we can go forward."

It was so like him, she thought, to offer her the chance to strike her colors and make an honorable retreat. But that wasn't what she wanted.

"Yes," she said firmly. "I want to go forward, with you. Beside you, behind you, wherever you need me, whenever you want me." She took a breath, remembering that she had loved Dick and lost him to the war. Remembering that uncounted others had lost the ones they loved. That life itself was fragile, fleeting, impermanent. That in spite of what she knew was to come, she wanted to love *this* man.

She put her fingers on the flat of his cheek. "Everything ends, Ike. Nothing is always. Always is . . . never. All we can do is take whatever loveliness we're offered and hold onto it until it's gone. And then learn to live with whatever is left."

"That's what I wanted you to say," he whispered. "But I'm not a practiced lover, Kay. It's been a long time since I—"

"Shh." She touched his mouth, silencing him. Whatever his doubts, his reservations, she would push them away. No words, no promises, no vows. Only touches, kisses.

His mouth came down on hers. Then his hands began to move, searching her body, and she felt a pulsing, singing energy. Something sparked in the darkness, like light, like fire, like an explosion inside her, like bombs raining down, like fireworks shooting up, leaving her breathless, incoherent, desperately eager. Their ties came off, their shirts, everything. He bent over her. She arched toward him as he kissed her bare shoulder. In a moment his whole body was beside her, their loving urgent, muffled, frantic.

And then, not.

They lay very still. He buried his face in the hollow of her shoulder. "I'm sorry, Kay. So sorry. I can't love you the way I want to. It's because—"

"It's because you're tired," she whispered, holding him close. "You were on that plane for . . . what? Thirty-six hours—and on the train for another twelve." She shouldn't have let it happen, she thought. Not tonight, not here. "A *sofa*, for heaven's sake." She chuckled. "Not even a real bed, behind closed doors. Next time will be different."

He stirred. "You're willing to . . . try again?"

"Don't be daft. Of course I am." She pushed herself away, just far away enough to see his face. "But not tonight, dearest." She slipped out of his arms. "Tonight you need to get to bed. And sleep."

He retrieved his pants from the floor where he had flung them. "What about you? Where are you going?"

"Ruth and Mattie Pinnette and I have a flat in Park West. It's just up the Edgeware Road." She was buttoning her shirt.

He turned on the light. "You're sure you can find it in the fog?" he asked doubtfully. "I don't want to let you go, damn it. I wish I could ask you to stay."

"Don't worry." She debated whether to put on her tie and decided she'd better do it. She didn't think the townhouse was guarded, but she couldn't be sure. "Really. It's just the other side of Kensington Gardens. There won't be any traffic."

"That's because nobody else is fool enough to be out in that crap at—" He eyed the ormolu clock on the mantel. "Jesus. Two a.m."

She slipped into her shoes. "Exactly. What time would you like me to pick you up tomorrow?" In front of the mirror, she raked a comb through her hair and settled her garrison cap on her head. "Today, I mean. In the morning."

He put his arm around her shoulders and walked with her to the door. "I told Mickey to have breakfast ready for us at seven. We'll check in at Grosvenor Square first, so I can get things squared away, and then we'll go to that kennel and explain to Telek why he has to pretend he's a dog for a while. And then we'll drive out to Telegraph Cottage." He pulled his brows together. "We do have the cottage, don't we?" he asked quickly. "It's still ours?"

"It's still ours," she said with a delighted laugh, loving the sound of the words. "It's still *ours*."

෴

And so they settled into the routine that would carry them toward D-Day, now only four months away—an impossibly short time to do all the things that had to be done to put a million-and-a-half men on the European continent.

Before the week was out, Eisenhower had decided that there were too many distractions in the city, where after-dark London, with its endless round of cocktail parties, restaurants, the theater, and all-night pub crawls, was too temptingly available. He had also been warned by British intelligence that the Germans were about to aim their new and still secret Vergeltungswaffen—long-range artillery V-weapons—at the city. In Grosvenor Square and Norfolk House, personnel and records were packed together like sardines in a tin, and he worried that a single hit on either place could set the invasion back by weeks or even months.

So the General ordered SHAEF (the official acronym for Supreme Headquarters, Allied Expeditionary Force) to move to Bushy Park, near Teddington—which also had the advantage of being just a few minutes' drive from Telegraph Cottage. Partially enclosed by a high wall, the entrance guarded by white-gloved, white-helmeted MPs, Bushy Park had belonged to the Eighth Air Force and even had its own landing strip. The hurriedly assembled Nissen huts, PX and mess buildings, and tents were ideal for the three thousand SHAEF workers. Quartered together, working together, they quickly developed a close relationship that made collaboration easier.

Eisenhower's staff—Kay, Beetle, Tex, Butch, and the WACs—had their offices in Building C, a corner shack with a tin roof covered with a dingy green-brown camouflage netting. There was never enough heat, the cement floor was damp, the overhead fluorescents flickered and buzzed, and a haze of tobacco smoke hung in the air. The General's modest, windowless office had a thin brown carpet, utilitarian sofa and chairs, a swivel chair, and a gray metal desk equipped with two telephones: the same red six-line phone he had used in North Africa and a scrambler, designed to baffle enemy eavesdroppers.

Kay (who was billeted with the WACs in a house in nearby Stanley Lane) for the first time had an office all to herself, adjacent to Eisenhower's. He had asked her to serve as his appointments secretary, as well as handle his personal mail. This would relieve Tex for other tasks and was exactly the right job for her, since she knew everyone the General knew and understood everything he was working on.

Which was everything under the sun and then some. One hour the Boss might be closeted with Under Secretary of State Stettinius, visiting from the States to discuss the politics of a liberated Europe. The next, he might be telling Patton to shut his goddamned mouth about the Russians and stay out of trouble.

Or he might be listening to Montgomery's continual complaints about American generals. Lunch could be peanuts and a candy bar alone at his desk, or a hot plate of spaghetti and meatballs that Kay brought him from the mess. Once every two weeks, he had a formal luncheon with the British Chiefs of Staff, and twice a week, sometimes more, a lunch at Number Ten Downing Street.

When Eisenhower got in the car after an hour with the Prime Minister, Kay could see the strain on his face. Churchill had made a sort of peace with Overlord, but he wasn't optimistic about its outcome. He would accompany Eisenhower out to the Packard, lean on the door, and say, "My dear General, liberate Paris by Christmas and you will make a believer out of me."

To Kay, the Prime Minister would add, plaintively, "Take good care of this man, Miss Summersby. The two greatest nations on earth have an incalculable investment in him."

"I will, sir," Kay would reply. She would drive the General back to SHAEF for a session on the complicated Free French situation, an emergency meeting about a suspected security breach, or a discussion of Overlord's airborne support, which Eisenhower passionately defended against the British generals who believed that the operation was heading for an aerial catastrophe. Or conferences on the two-thousand-plus ships and naval craft required for the Normandy assault, the C-47s needed for the airdrops of the 82nd and 101st, and the demand for parachutes—some ninety thousand had been earmarked for Overlord—not just for dropping men behind the lines but for dropping provisions and equipment. And once, he had to step into a squabble between the British Chiefs of Staff and the Munitions Board to insist that four million barrels of 130-octane aviation fuel be reserved for Normandy.

Evenings, there were dinner meetings with whatever general hadn't been available during working hours. Often, after dinner, Kay would go into the office to find the Boss on the phone or writing a letter or sending a cable, pleading for more landing craft. And more and more and then more. He was worried that there weren't enough landing crafts to deliver enough men to take the beaches and break through the German lines. There could never be enough.

And sometimes, late in the afternoon, the General might put down a paper and say, "I can't take this goddamned crap one more second. Let's go for a horseback ride." They would go to Richmond Park, ideal because it was closed to the public and there was no need for guards to keep an eye on them. Richmond was a "Starfish" site, designed to lure enemy bombers away from London. Inside the park, British engineers had built a phony "decoy town"—one of 630 such sites around England. This one had plywood buildings and make-believe "factories" surrounded by cleverly designed fires that could be lit at night to make it look like an industrial area targeted by bombs. Kay and Ike avoided the decoy "streets" and stayed on the bridle paths that wound through the springtime woodland, carpeted with bluebells and violets and graced with wild cherry blossoms. It felt private enough, but they never knew when one of the Starfish maintenance men might be around.

Once or twice a week, Eisenhower and Kay drove to the kennel—Hackbridge Kennels, in Surrey—to visit Telek. Kay had taken him an old handbag, and for the next six months, the Scottie slept with his head on it. The little dog was wild with delight when he saw them coming; when they left, he lay with his nose between his paws, utterly bereft. Ike felt just as bad. "I feel as if I've locked up part of my heart," he said sadly. Telek's empty place was partially filled by Shaef the cat, who did something Telek couldn't: she cleared the mice out of the cottage.

Telegraph Cottage remained their refuge. There was something about the little house, Kay thought, that invoked intimacy and trust. They were never quite alone there, but they had moments of privacy in the garden, which was gloriously alive with azure, purple, and red rhododendrons, and on the secluded stone bench at the edge of the woods. They held hands and occasionally kissed, but mostly they just talked—sharing their stories about their lives outside of England and the war, about her marriage to Gordon Summersby and his to Mamie.

Her marriage, she told him, had been a mistake from the beginning, built on nothing but a silly, shallow enjoyment of people and parties; when it broke up, there was nothing left and little to mourn.

His marriage, he told her, had been deeply damaged by the death of their son Icky at three—"The one disaster," he said, "from which I will never recover." He still harbored the awful feeling that if Mamie had tended to the little boy earlier, he might have survived. But she had stayed in bed with a headache that day, so Icky didn't get to the doctor until Ike got home. "Or if I had paid more attention in the morning," he said, and shook his head. "John was our antidote to the loss of Icky. Maybe if we'd had more children . . ." The marriage had been dying for years, he said, and with it, desire. "We don't even have anything to talk about."

For her, the hours of conversation held an intimacy as sweet and all-embracing as physical lovemaking. But he spoke haltingly, painfully, as if he had never spoken such words aloud before, and Kay wondered whether he had perhaps not consciously thought them. Perhaps he was giving voice to new thoughts, a new way to see himself and his marriage. It couldn't be easy. But while they talked about the past, they didn't talk about the future, honoring their tacit agreement that this hour, this day, was all they had.

Ike had said he'd like to try his hand at oil painting, so Kay asked Betty Baker, a friend in the American Red Cross, to put together a kit and give him a lesson or two. He set up an easel in the garden and began to paint the cottage. One afternoon, Kay looked over his shoulder to discover that he was sketching its floor plan, with an addition.

He held out the pad to her. "Look at this, Kay. The kitchen could be turned into a big dining room, and then a new kitchen added on, with a maid's room over it. And maybe enlarge the garden—put in more roses and a place for vegetables. A run for Telek, too, don't you think?"

"I think it all sounds utterly wonderful," she murmured.

Sternly, she reminded herself of what he had said at Hay's

Lodge in January: that their relationship would end when the war ended. But the little floor plan looked like a sketch of a possible future together, and she couldn't extinguish the flare of hope that lit her heart. What an enormous gift it would be to live *here*, with him, for the rest of their lives, sharing peace after war and the tranquility of a quiet English life. Impossible, of course. But the thought was a sweet refuge in the midst of the unrelenting preparations for D-Day.

৪৩

Hay's Lodge proved to be a refuge, too. Ike often had to attend a late dinner and an early meeting the next day, and the Lodge was a convenient place to spend the night. It was there, one night in late February, that he asked Kay to stay with him.

The day had included an early lunch with the Prime Minister and a long meeting with the British Chiefs of Staff that went until well after five. A storm had blown in along the Thames estuary that afternoon, and rain was lashing the streets and backing up traffic.

"We're not driving to the cottage in this crap," Ike said. "Let's have supper at the Lodge. Maybe the storm will let up later." He frowned. "But if we go to a restaurant . . ."

Kay knew what he meant. They couldn't eat out in peace, because the General's face and uniform were instantly recognizable. He'd be barraged with requests for autographs. And somebody would be sure to have a camera.

"Let's get take-away," she said. "There's a pub in Tottenham Court Road. The food won't be fancy, but—"

"Who cares about fancy?" Ike asked. "Take-away is fine."

Usually, when they were at the Lodge, others were with them. But tonight, the place had the feel of an empty house. Ike built a fire in the chilly sitting room, while Kay uncorked a bottle of white wine and spread out their supper—fish and chips, wrapped in the traditional newspaper—on the coffee table in front of the sofa.

They ate sitting close together before the fireplace, with soft music on the wireless.

"Almost as good as my fried catfish," Ike said appreciatively, licking his fingers. "I'll have to fix it for you someday, Kay. I soak it in buttermilk for an hour, then dunk it in cornmeal with lots of paprika and fry it in hot peanut oil." He grinned. "Best damn catfish in Kansas, especially when it comes with mashed potatoes and a big spoonful of catfish gravy. But you gotta catch the fish in the Smoky Hill River. That's what makes them good."

Kate sipped her wine. "In Ireland, fish and chips are called 'one and one.'"

"What's that supposed to mean?" Ike asked curiously.

"The first fish and chips in the country were sold in Dublin, by an Italian immigrant. His wife didn't know any English, so when a customer went to the cash register to pay, she would point to the menu and ask, 'Uno di questo, uno di quello?' 'One of this, one of that?' So that's what we call fish and chips. One and one."

On the wireless, Vera Lynn was singing "The White Cliffs of Dover," a song that Kay loved. Outdoors, thunder growled. Ike turned his head, listening to the gusty wind and the rain rattling against the windows.

"The storm is getting worse," he said. After a moment, he spoke again. "You're not driving in this weather."

"That sounds like an order, sir." Kay picked up the newspaper wrappings and began feeding them to the fire, humming the melody to "The White Cliffs of Dover." *Love and laughter and peace ever after.*

"Come to think of it, that's what it is. An order." He pushed himself out of his chair and put his arms around her. "Come here, Irish."

Fifteen minutes later, they were upstairs in his bed. An hour later, she was lying beside him, feeling the weight of his arm across her, watching him sleep, his face soft, the lines erased, his body utterly relaxed. He had been a strong lover, urgent, eager, but tender—all that she could have wished. It had happened easily, naturally, sweetly, exactly as it was meant to happen. And it gave them both the confidence that it could happen again, *would* happen again. *One and one*, she thought, in perfect synchrony. Whatever pain lay in the future, she would always have that memory to hold against her heart.

After a while, she slipped out of bed, gathered her clothes, and went quietly toward the door. He stirred, awoke, and said, "Where are you going?"

"To the guest bedroom." She smiled in the dark. "If I'm asked, I want to be able to say, 'I have never slept with Dwight Eisenhower.'"

He chuckled, turned over, and went back to sleep.

Eisenhower hadn't meant it to happen.

That is, he hadn't been consciously planning to make love to Kay when he directed her to drive to the Lodge on that stormy night. Instead, he had been thinking of how hard it was raining, and how tired he was and about the prima donnas he'd had to deal with at the afternoon meeting and the bitter disagreement he'd had with Montgomery. He hadn't even been thinking of it when they finished eating and the storm seemed to become worse.

In fact, he hadn't actually *thought* of it at all. He had simply gotten out of his chair and reached for her and there she was, in his arms, soft and willing. What had happened next had seemed easy and uncomplicated and right. It was exactly what he had needed, at the moment he needed it most. Now that it had happened, he knew it would happen again—now that he knew he *could*. Funny how that worked.

But it might be a very long time before it happened again. Preparations for D-Day occupied every waking hour of Eisenhower's day. He knew a commander's visit could lift the men's morale (as it lifted his), so he filled the calendar with troop inspections.

Taking Butch and Kay, he went by train with Bradley and Patton to Portsmouth to inspect the Fourth and Twenty-Ninth Infantry Divisions, where he talked personally with small groups of soldiers—no newspapermen allowed. A week later, with Montgomery and Air Marshal Tedder, he visited the Sandhurst cadets, then the Scottish Highlanders and the American Second and Third Armored. Then it was on to Salisbury, Newbury, Winchester, and the amphibious landing exercises that took place on the beaches at Slapton Sands, near Dartmouth, which did not go as planned.

By this time, England was groaning under the weight of arms, ammunition, and troops—a million Americans alone—and a joke made the rounds: The only things keeping the island from sinking into the North Sea were the huge silver barrage balloons that held it up. Convoys rumbled through the quiet countryside all day and through the night, moving heavy equipment from the north to staging areas in the south. Tanks, amphibious "Ducks," fog-burning FIDOs, concrete and steel breakwaters, Mulberry and Gooseberry prefabricated harbors—all these and more were parked and piled along the Channel coast. Soldiers' leaves were canceled. Civilians were banned from the military zone from the southern beaches ten miles inland. Most of the locomotives and coach cars had been requisitioned for military service, so the queues at the stations got longer and longer. Everywhere, for everyone, security had never been tighter. Which posed a difficult challenge for Eisenhower, from an unexpected direction.

Butch and Beetle brought it to his attention. The problem, they said, was Kay. She was a security risk—and a substantial one, at that.

They had the conversation in Ike's office in Building C, one afternoon when Kay was out on an errand. It was raining again, and chilly, and Eisenhower had caught cold during the trip to Northern Ireland. He wasn't in the best of moods, especially not for *this*.

"It's not a new problem," Butch added. "There was some concern about her back in North Africa, but she didn't have as much access there as she does here. And the stakes in this operation are a lot higher."

"Dammit," Ike said testily, "I don't have time for this crap today."

"Sorry, Boss." Beetle looked him straight in the eye. "You need to hear this."

Ike blew his nose. "Okay. But make it snappy. Bradley will be here in—" He looked at his watch. "Eight minutes." Bradley was always on time, unlike Patton, who always ran late

Butch nodded. "Everybody likes Kay and accepts her—on a personal level. Most men have their own private friendships and other arrangements. They understand."

"You better believe it," Ike muttered. "You've got Molly." He looked at Beetle. "You've got Ethel." Pots calling the goddamned kettle black.

"But Molly and Ethel don't work at SHAEF," Beetle replied steadily. "They don't have access to the Supreme Commander's private correspondence, his telephone calls, his daily logbook. They don't go with him every time he inspects the troops at top-secret locations. Or drive his car, with top-secret discussions going on in the backseat." He leaned forward, his thin face serious. "It's Churchill who's raising the question, Ike. He's afraid of the consequences if the Germans find out about her—especially Goebbels."

"Goebbels?" Ike stared at him. "What the hell—" And then he understood. Goebbels was Hitler's propaganda minister. Churchill was afraid he might publish the story as a way to discredit the Supreme Commander. Or maybe just threaten to publish it. Ike remembered the President saying something about blackmail.

Butch cleared his throat. "I don't think we've got much of a problem with Goebbels. He's got a mistress, a Czech actress. He's not going to blackmail us when he knows we'll counter."

"Anyway," Ike said, "the OWI won't let a story like that get into American newspapers." He looked at Beetle. "What else have you got?"

"She's Irish. Which means they won't put her on the BIGOT list."

"Ah," Ike said, now really steaming. "I suppose you heard that one from Montgomery."

BIGOT stood for "British Invasion of German Occupied Territory." The BIGOT list contained the names of the personnel who were cleared to know the details of Overlord—especially the time and place of the invasion—and cleared for contact with other BIGOTs. Ireland was technically neutral in the war, so people born in Ireland were barred from the list and from any contact with invasion secrets. In Ike's view, this was totally idiotic. Fifty thousand Irishmen were serving in the British Army, and there were several Allied installations in Northern Ireland.

"Yes, Montgomery," Beetle said. "He's raised it several times."

"BIGOT is a British list, not an Allied list," Ike said stiffly. "I'm not obliged to abide by it. I have absolutely no doubt of Kay's loyalty. To me, or to the Allied cause, or the British crown."

"It's not a matter of her loyalty, as I understand it," Butch said. "The question is, what if the Germans should kidnap her? What secrets could she reveal?"

"Well, hell, Butch," Ike growled. "What if the Huns should kidnap *you*? If they started pulling out your toenails, can you guarantee that you wouldn't spill your guts?"

Beetle spoke. "Patton, too, has raised serious concerns about—"

"I've heard all I want to hear from George," Eisenhower snapped. Patton was a public relations liability with a big mouth. In Ike's opinion, Patton was a much greater security threat than Kay.

"That's it, Boss." Butch stood up.

"Just thought you ought to be informed," Beetle said, standing as well.

"I'm informed," Ike growled. "Dismissed."

Then it was June. Everything that could be done to prepare for the invasion—the largest amphibious landing in history—had been done. Now, all attention was focused on the south coast, near Portsmouth, where Eisenhower had set up his advance command post: a trailer for his office and sleeping quarters, surrounded by a tent encampment. Kay had a tiny desk in the corner of the trailer, where she kept up with the correspondence while she monitored the telephone. The WAC stenographers and typists had been installed in nearby Southwick House, an elegant Georgian mansion that had been requisitioned by the Royal Navy at the beginning of the war. Planning sessions and staff meetings were held in the war room there, too. Nerves were taut and security so tight that even the Supreme Commander was given a badge to wear.

The invasion was set for Monday, June 5, and ships from as far away as Scotland were already on their way. Scheduling was tricky. The landing craft (there still weren't enough) required an early-morning incoming tide, and only a few days fit that requirement. The airborne assault required clear skies, but the weather was increasingly problematic. By Saturday, June 3, a thick blanket of clouds shrouded the Channel and the barometer was falling rapidly. Late Saturday night, SHAEF's chief meteorologist, RAF Captain John Stagg, joined Ike and his command team in the Southwick war room to report that Monday's weather would be "unflyable." His forecast sent a disappointed groan rippling around the room, and Eisenhower grimly ordered that D-Day be postponed for one day, to Tuesday, June 6. Afterward, Kay heard him muttering that if he had to postpone again, the invasion forces would have to be held for two whole weeks for favorable morning tides—and that was damned difficult. His greatest fear, she knew, was that if the invasion were delayed, the Germans—who so far seemed to be deceived by Patton's Fortitude—would guess their real target. A delay would give them time to reinforce their lines behind the Normandy beaches.

The storm arrived on Sunday, with high seas and winds that lashed the rain into horizontal ribbons. But the late-night group meeting in the Southwick officers' mess heard a better forecast. As Kay served coffee, Captain Stagg predicted that the cloud cover would lift on Monday night, making the weather "flyable." But the winds would be unpredictable and the seas would still be rough. The airborne drops and the beach landings would be risky.

Pacing across the front of the room, Eisenhower asked for input from his commanders, but Kay knew that the decision was entirely up to him. The full weight of success or failure—and the loss of thousands of young men on a foreign beach—rested entirely on him.

"We'll go on Tuesday," Ike said at last. There was a muted cheer. Cups clattered and chairs scraped as the commanders hurried off to their headquarters to issue final orders, and he was left in an empty room.

Watching, Kay thought that a moment before, he had been the most powerful man in the world, the fate of a million men in his hands, the future of nations weighing on his shoulders. But the moment he said "Go," he became powerless. What he had set in motion could not be altered or halted, not by him, not by anyone.

He turned to Kay. "I hope to God I know what I'm doing," he muttered.

It was still raining the next morning when Kay drove him to South Parade Pier in Portsmouth to watch hundreds of British soldiers clamber into dozens of landing craft for what promised to be a rough trip across the Channel. But by evening the skies had cleared, and she drove him to an airfield near Newbury, where he shared a cigarette with the men of the 101st Airborne, bulky parachutes and weapons strapped to their backs, their faces blackened with burnt cork and cocoa. He told them they had the best training and the best equipment and urged them not to worry—they had a job to do and they were going to do it. A sergeant said, "Hell, General, we ain't worried. It's the Krauts that ought to be worrying."

Afterward, Kay went with the General to the roof of the division headquarters to watch the big C-47s, white and black "invasion stripes" painted on their wings and fuselages, lumber down the runways and lift slowly into the sky, lit now by a full moon so bright that Kay could see their shadows. Overhead, clusters of planes circled like great flocks of wheeling birds, then peeled off for Normandy. Kay held her breath, knowing that she would never see anything like it, ever again.

Ike thrust his hands into his pockets. "All those brave, brave men," he said.

Kay saw that his eyes were bright with tears.

CHAPTER SEVENTEEN
The Beginning of the End

England—Washington, D.C.—France
June 7–August 27, 1944

The first reports were encouraging. The landing had been successful. A hundred and fifty-five thousand men took the beaches of Normandy. There had been heavy fighting, but the losses—twenty-five hundred casualties, mainly at Omaha Beach—were lighter than predicted. The Atlantic Wall had been breached and the Allied army had taken its first step on the long journey to Berlin. Everyone could smile—and breathe out the collective breath they'd been holding for weeks.

Kay felt her own relief as she saw the General's tension easing and the worry lines fading from his face. He looked even better after he crossed the Channel and went ashore at Juno Beach to talk to some of the commanders. They hadn't achieved all of their initial objectives, but he was pleased with what he had seen. "The beginning of the end," he said, clearly relieved.

There was another reason for the General's good mood, Kay knew. His son John had graduated from West Point on D-Day, and Ike had arranged for the newly commissioned second lieutenant to fly to England for his two-week leave. John was a fine-looking officer—tall, slender, ramrod straight, politely deferential, and very young. Kay was fascinated by the relationship between father and son. She drove them where they needed to go and spent evenings at Telegraph Cottage with them. John was eager to please his father and clearly overwhelmed by the General's evident importance. For his part, Eisenhower was often critical; he would snort and exclaim, "Oh, for Godsake," when John ventured an answer to a military question. But the son took the father's curt words good-naturedly and despite the frequent awkwardness, there was an obvious bond between them. Lucky, lucky Mamie, Kay thought enviously, to have such a double treasure.

But while the pre-invasion tensions had eased, there was a new and terrifying danger. The Germans were retaliating for the Allied invasion by firing V-1 flying bombs: *buzz bombs*, people called them. "The devil's own contraption," in Ike's words. V-1s announced themselves with a shrill, whining drone that grew louder and louder and then stopped so abruptly that ears rang in the silence. The next thing people heard—and felt—was the explosion. The chief target was London, where a hundred buzz bombs sometimes crashed into the city in a single day. But the Germans also directed their long-range artillery fire to the area around Bushy Park, which included Telegraph Cottage. While John was visiting, they spent several nights in the bomb shelter that Churchill had built—Ike, John, Kay, and the house staff. Close quarters, hot and stuffy, but a welcome refuge.

A few days before John was due to fly back to the States, Ike surprised Kay with an offer. "I'm sending John home in my B-17. Tex is going, too, on an errand for me at the Pentagon, and a couple of the WACs. How would you like to go? You could spend some time in Washington, go up to New York—see how you like the States, come back in a couple of weeks."

Kay's eyes widened. Washington, New York, America, her long-ago dream, for two whole weeks! "But I don't want to leave you," she protested. "You need—"

He put a hand on her shoulder. "You've been working twelve or fourteen hours a day since you signed on, Kay. You deserve some time off. Anyway, I'm going to France to get a look at the situation there, and I can't take you." His voice softened. "I'll worry about you and John on the same plane, though. Putting all my eggs in one basket."

She smiled. It wasn't very romantic, but she understood what he was trying to say and was touched.

෪

In a few days, Kay found herself with John and Tex boarding Ike's Flying Fortress, almost breathless with anticipation. She had thought that her dream of going to America had died with Dick Arnold, and here she was, making the journey on General Eisenhower's personal airplane. But while the plane was much more comfortable than the usual air transport, the flight was long and tiring. They arrived at Bolling Field in a dizzying July heat wave—worse, Kay thought, as she got off the plane, than the Egyptian desert she and Ike had visited. There, the heat had been dry, crisp; here, the humid air was thick and oppressive.

Kay hadn't expected Mrs. Eisenhower to greet them at the airfield, but there she was. She was perky and stylish in a flowered hat, spotless white gloves, and white patent leather pumps. But Kay was shocked at how thin she was. She hugged John and—obviously surprised to see Kay—offered her the tips of her fingers.

"I'm glad to meet you at last, Mrs. Summersby." Her words were gracious, but her blue eyes were probing and her voice was chilly. "I've heard so *much* about you."

"And I've heard so much about *you*," Kay replied, remembering what Ike had told her about his wife's anger when he called her Kay—and the other things he had said, haltingly, about their marriage. "The General speaks of you often."

"Mother," John said eagerly, "I think it would be swell if we invited a few friends of yours and Dad's to the apartment to meet Kay. Let's do that tomorrow, shall we?"

Kay felt a flutter of alarm. "John, I'd really rather not impose. I—"

"I'm sure Mrs. Summersby will have many other interesting things to do," Mrs. Eisenhower cut in. "I wouldn't want to place any demands on her time."

John wasn't deterred. "Oh, but I'm sure—"

"I've got us a cab, Kay," Tex said, coming up to them. "I thought we'd check in at the hotel first. It's not fancy, but it's affordable." He turned to Mamie. "It's great to see you again, Mrs. Eisenhower. Seems like a couple of centuries since the old days at Fort Sam, doesn't it?"

Kay was grateful to Tex for the interruption, and glad to follow him to the taxi, congratulating herself on escaping from a very sticky wicket. But she wasn't going to get off so easily. A telephone call from John awakened her in her hotel room the next morning.

"Mother would love to have you over for drinks this afternoon," he said. "She's invited a few friends. Do say you'll come, Kay. It's very casual."

Kay remembered what Ike had said about the Washington gossip, and the flutter of alarm became a stab of panic. Obviously, John wasn't aware of the stories that were going around, and—being nice, or perhaps thinking it would please his father—must have pressured his mother into extending the invitation. She shuddered, thinking that Ike would *not* want her to do this.

Uncomfortable, she said, "Thank you, John, but I'm sure your mother wants all your time. And I really don't want to put her to any trouble. Let's not—"

"Oh, but I *want* you to come, Kay." John's voice was earnest. "It'll do these ladies good to meet a woman in uniform and hear just how much work goes on over there and how difficult it is. And of course it's no trouble at all. My mother is a born hostess. She *lives* to entertain."

Kay knew it wasn't as simple as that, but she couldn't think of a reasonable excuse. She put the receiver down, feeling trapped.

The Wardman Park was quite a sumptuous residential hotel, and given the oppressive heat, the air conditioning in Mrs. Eisenhower's elegant apartment was welcome.

But for Kay, the afternoon was a nightmare. The guests—all women—were beautifully coiffed and daintily pretty in their pastel summer suits and Kay, in her olive-drab uniform, rayon stockings, and brown leather service oxfords, felt awkward and clunky in their company. She usually enjoyed the light, lively banter of cocktail parties, but she had nothing in common with these women, who were talking about movies they had seen, parties they had been to, things they had bought and how much they'd paid. Her only topic of conversation was the war, and most of that was secret. And even if it weren't, she couldn't chatter about what she and the General did every day—together. Thankfully, only one or two people asked her about him. Most seemed to want to avoid the subject as much as she did.

John brought her a Scotch and water and a plate of beautifully made hors d' oeuvres, assembled from a sumptuous table loaded with beautiful foods that Kay hadn't seen since before the war. It was all utterly marvelous, and if she hadn't felt so out of place, she would have indulged herself. But as she was introduced to the wives, she couldn't help thinking of their husbands, some of whom she knew had their own wartime companions. They were polite, but she could tell by the narrow-eyed scrutiny and the uneasy glances that they wondered just what and how much she knew about what their husbands were up to.

And while Kay might want to avoid mentioning Mrs. Eisenhower's husband, she saw that he was very much in evidence. In fact, Ike seemed to be everywhere, in a room that was a photo gallery entirely dedicated to *him*. There were seven elegantly framed photographs of him on a piano in the corner, spanning his career from West Point cadet to four-star general. The walls were hung with photographs taken in Panama, Europe, the Philippines, London, North Africa—always with him in the center of an admiring group. The glass shelves in a curio cabinet were filled with small souvenirs of various places he had visited, including (Kay saw with a start) an olivewood box identical to the one he had bought her in the Jerusalem bazaar. A leather-bound scrapbook lay on a table, open to a pasted-in newspaper clipping with a photo of Ike receiving his fourth star. On the table was a framed photograph of Ike with King George. Ike was looking uncomfortably serious as the King hung a sumptuous gold medal around his neck.

Kay looked around for any evidence of Mamie's interests in the room, but aside from the piano (did Mamie play?) she couldn't see any. Uneasily, she remembered that Ike had said his wife put her family first, but this was more than that. It was as if the General was Mrs. Eisenhower's very own special trophy, and that her merits—whatever they were—were derived from the fact that this hero had chosen her as his wife. Dwight Eisenhower wasn't just the center of her life; he was the whole of it, its entire sum and substance. She felt cold. The same thing could be said of herself, couldn't it?

Suddenly she was aware that Mamie was standing beside her, an orange old-fashioned in her hand. She gestured to the photograph. "That was taken in Algiers," she announced brightly. "And that's King George the Sixth, of course, awarding some sort of medal to my husband." The words "my husband"—smug, possessive, proprietary—staked her claim. And perhaps they were also meant as a not-so-subtle warning: *Hands off. This man is mine.*

Kay couldn't help herself. "Yes," she said gently. "I was there. It's the Knight Grand Cross." She turned to smile at Mamie. "Afterward, the General gave a dinner party for King George at his villa. It was an intimate gathering, small, but quite splendid. He must have written you about it."

Mamie met her eyes briefly. "I'm sure it was quite the affair," she murmured. A woman was standing nearby, and she raised her voice. "Cookie, isn't it wonderful?" she trilled. "Mrs. Summersby was just telling me that she was *there* when the King hung that enormous gold medal around Ike's neck. She actually *saw* it happen!"

"Ooh, lucky you," the woman purred. She leaned forward,

regarding Kay with something like professional curiosity. "Do tell me, please, Mrs. Summersby. Have you met the Duchess of Windsor—the former Mrs. Simpson? I understand that she is not very well liked in Britain. For making off with your king, I mean."

"I haven't met her," Kay managed, and escaped as quickly as she could.

The afternoon dragged on interminably. Kay wanted desperately to leave, but she felt that to be the first would be an admission of defeat. At last, to her great relief, two of the guests left together. As she found Mrs. Eisenhower to thank her and say goodbye, John came up to them.

"I'm taking Kay sightseeing around Washington tomorrow," he announced to his mother.

Kay was flustered. "Oh, thank you, John," she said hurriedly. "Really, you don't have to—"

"But I want to." He stepped back, grinning boyishly at Kay. "And then we're going up to New York to see *Oklahoma!*"

"*Oklahoma?*" Kay stared at him, wide-eyed. "But I hadn't expected—"

Mamie broke in. "John, I am *quite* sure Mrs. Summersby doesn't want to go to New York in this terrible heat. She—"

"Of course she does, Mother," John said easily. "Anyway, it was Dad's idea. He arranged for the tickets. Wasn't that thoughtful of him?" He slipped an arm around his mother's shoulders. "Of course, we'd love to have you go along, but I know you don't like crowds. I'll be sure to bring you a program, though."

At the mention of Ike, Mamie seemed to wilt. "Of course, if it was your father's idea . . ."

"If you're leaving now, I'll give you a lift to your hotel, Kay," John said. "I'm going downtown to meet some friends."

"Thank you," Kay said. She couldn't wait to get away from Mamie and her photo gallery—and the uncomfortable realization that, in at least one important way, she and Ike's wife were very much alike.

෪

"Well!" Pamela said, after Kay and John had left. "That woman is certainly a looker, even in uniform." Critically, she added, "John obviously has no idea what's going on. But then, he's still just a boy."

Cookie nodded, agreeing. "I wonder if that's the uniform she got from—" She turned around to make sure that Mamie was out of earshot. "From Ike," she concluded, in a lower voice. "The one he had made for her when they were in North Africa."

"I understand that the General intends to have her commissioned as a WAC officer," Diane Bracken said, picking the olive out of her martini. "My sister Rachel works in Colonel Hobby's office in the Pentagon—you know, the WAC commander." She popped the olive into her mouth. "Eisenhower's request is apparently causing quite a flap over there."

"Commissioned?" Cookie rolled her eyes. "That's ridiculous, Diane. Mrs. Summersby can't be a WAC officer. She can't even *enlist* in the WACs. She's not an American citizen."

Pamela took a cigarette out of an engraved gold case. "She's not a British officer, either, you know. She's just a civilian volunteer." She closed the case with a snap. "And Irish, to boot."

"Colonel Hobby is strongly opposed, Rachel says," Diane replied. "She told General Marshall that it was a *very* bad idea. But Marshall got a note from the President, supporting the request."

"The President!" Pamela and Cookie exclaimed in unison.

"That's right," Diane said. "It turns out that there's no law that says a WAC officer has to be an American citizen. What's more, there's a precedent. Three of them, actually," she added drily.

Pamela tapped the tip of her Winston against the back of her hand. "Really?"

"Really." Diane tipped up her martini glass and drained it. "Last year, General MacArthur commissioned three Australian women—civilians, like Mrs. Summersby—as WAC officers. He didn't even ask permission. He just did it."

"Well, if MacArthur got his WACs, Marshall will let Eisenhower have his," Cookie said in a matter-of-fact tone. She flicked her lighter to Pamela's cigarette and then lit her own. "Although you'd think he would see the request for what it is—simply a way for Ike to keep that woman on his staff, wherever he goes." She blew out a stream of smoke. "Maybe he'll even bring her here to Washington when the war is over."

"Oh, come now, Cookie," Pamela scoffed. "You don't *really* think Ike would do such a thing, do you? Not with his wife—"

"Actually, I *do* think," Cookie said. She lowered her voice again. "My Marv is working in Marshall's office now, and he hears all the latest gossip. He says that Commander Butcher—Ike's best friend—intends to divorce his wife and marry that American girl he met in Algiers. Molly, her name is."

Diane tilted her head. "I hadn't heard that. How interesting."

"Oh, poor Ruth!" Pamela's hand went to her mouth. "She and Butch have been married forever. Whatever will she *do*?"

"Ruth can take care of herself," Cookie said. She tilted her head toward the wall of Eisenhower photos. "But can you imagine what would happen to Mamie if Eisenhower divorced her to marry Kay Summersby?"

"She would have nothing left to live for," Pamela said in a pitying tone. "She's already thin as a rail—why, she'd simply stop eating and waste away to nothing."

Diane gave them both a knowing glance. "Don't you believe it, girls. I've known Mamie Eisenhower for twenty years. The woman may look like a fragile pink flower but she is made out of steel. If Ike tries something like that, she'll fight tooth and nail. Kay Summersby is the one we should feel sorry for. She doesn't stand a chance."

Cookie regarded her thoughtfully. "You may be right, Diane. Mamie certainly knows how to get her way."

Diane looked into her empty glass. "To tell the truth, the

whole thing makes me glad that I'm no longer married. Now, if you'll excuse me, I think I'll have just a teensy one for the road."

∞

New York was sheer delight. Kay had always been enchanted by musical theater, but she had never seen anything like the energy and power of *Oklahoma!* After her work with the Worth dress designers, she thought she knew a little about costumes, but these fit the characters and moved with the dancers in a completely new and quite thrilling way. As she watched, she thought how wonderful it would be if, after the war, she could find work in the theater again.

In contrast to bleak, gray, war-weary London, New York brimmed with delights, and over the next several days, Kay indulged in as many as she could, devouring chocolate and fresh fruit and shrimp (shrimp!) and thick, juicy American hamburgers and rich chocolate milkshakes. The skyscrapers were impossibly tall, the streets incredibly clean, the people amazingly plump and well dressed, and nobody had to flee from buzz bombs. Kay shopped, buying a silk blouse for her mother and filling the orders given her by her the WACs she lived with—orders for little luxuries impossible to find in England: nail polish and lipstick and perfume; scented shampoo; thick, creamy writing paper; a filmy scarf, even a girdle. For Telek, she bought a red dog collar. And for Ike, his favorite fountain pen, a Parker 51, green, with a gold cap.

Kay loved New York. The city's vitality was infectious. She found herself walking faster, smiling at strangers, even humming under her breath. Standing in Times Square, she promised herself that whatever happened, whatever future lay ahead, when the war was over she would come to New York.

But it wasn't long before the abundance that had so pleased her began to seem oppressive. She couldn't help thinking of the empty shops of London, the buzz bombs falling on people's homes,

THE GENERAL'S WOMEN

the soldiers hunkered down under wet French hedges, eating cold rations in the chilly rain. She thought of her MTC friends driving ambulances during the Blitz, the nurses struggling in the water around the torpedoed *Strathallan* or slogging through the mud at Kasserine Pass, the WACs working long, weary hours in the days before D-Day—while the women she had met in the Wardman Park sipped martinis and nibbled hors d'oeuvres and gossiped. For Americans, the war was safely "over there," while for her and Ike, it was their work, their life.

She was ready to go home.

&

It was Saturday when Kay got back to Bushy Park. She went straight to headquarters, took off her cap, and opened the door to the Boss's office.

"Doesn't anybody ever knock around here?" he barked. Then he saw Kay and was out from behind his desk in an instant. Kay closed the door and flew into his arms.

That night, they celebrated her return with champagne, then sat in the garden talking late into the evening. She shared the events of the trip, and then—because she thought his wife might mention the party in a letter—said, "John suggested to his mother that she invite me to meet a number of friends. I felt I had to accept."

Ike frowned. "I didn't think of that possibility. I hope it wasn't too . . . trying."

"I didn't enjoy it, to tell the truth," Kay said honestly. "Mrs. Eisenhower was very nice to me, although I—" She stopped. She didn't want to tell him what she had learned about his wife from the photographs in her apartment—and about herself. It wasn't something she wanted to think about. "And John, of course, was an absolute angel," she went on. "He took me all around Washington, and then to New York. *Oklahoma!* was—"

"Smashing," Ike said.

287

She laughed. "Yes, it was, truly. It made me see musical theater in a whole new way. After the war, I want to do theater again. But perhaps backstage this time, in costume design. I loved the costumes in *Oklahoma!*"

"After the war," Ike said, "I want to go fishing." He put an arm around her shoulders. "How would you like that?"

"I love to fish," Kay said simply. She didn't ask him what he meant by the question.

℅

There was another joyful homecoming a few days later, when Telek was released from his imprisonment at the kennel. When Kay picked him up, he jumped into the front seat of the car without an instant's hesitation, as if he had done it just the day before. At the cottage, he ran straight to Ike, rolled over on his back, and begged to have his belly scratched. Then they took Telek outdoors and sat with their drinks as the little dog—wearing his new red collar—scurried happily around the garden, hunting for the bones he'd buried before he went to North Africa.

"Just look at him," Kay said with a laugh. "He's like a little boy, home after his first year away at school."

"It's damned wonderful to have him with us," Ike said. "You're right. He's just like a little kid." He was silent for a moment, watching Telek chase a butterfly. "Do you ever think of having children someday?"

Kay turned to him. He had often talked about the fun of growing up with a houseful of brothers, and he'd said that he'd wanted a big family—four children, he thought, was about right.

"I've always wanted to be a mother," she replied. And then, impulsively, quickly, "I'd love to have your child."

He met her eyes. "Would you?" he asked gravely.

"Yes," she said. "Yes." She thought of Ike with a little boy on his lap, Ike with a boy on a horse. Of the three of them, father and mother and son, riding across a wild Irish moor—they *would* go to Ireland, wouldn't they? Of fishing for brown trout in the River Ilen. And then coming home to a simple cottage where they would eat and talk and read in front of the fire until the child fell asleep and Ike carried him to bed in his arms. It was a lovely dream, an enticing, treacherous dream. And only a dream.

"But I know it's impossible," she said quietly. There was Mamie, waiting for her husband, the walls of her elegant apartment lined with his photographs. A child—hers and Ike's child—was out of the question. Surely he knew that.

"It's impossible now," Ike said, and reached for her hand. "But after the war . . . You never know, Kay. Things may be different after the war." He picked up her hand and kissed her fingers.

There was nothing at all she could say to that—except hold it to her heart like a fragile, fugitive treasure. In the meantime, there was *now*.

∽

In the United States that summer, Franklin Roosevelt—despite national worries about his health—was nominated for an unprecedented fourth term as president. In the Pacific, American troops liberated Guam and captured the Mariana Islands. In Italy, the Allies retook the city of Florence. In France, after heavy resistance, British troops freed Caen, on the left flank of the Allied advance. And in Germany, an assassination plot failed to kill Hitler and overthrow the Nazi government. In retaliation, some five thousand people were executed.

In England, Eisenhower was moving his headquarters from Bushy Park to Normandy, where he would be closer to the fighting. Kay was helping to pack the office equipment and necessary files when she found the note in the General's office log. While she was in the States, Ike had made the entries in the blue leather-bound diary that she usually maintained for him. *PM for lunch*, he had written on July 3. On July 5, *Buzz bombs chased us to cover 6 times during afternoon.* Later: *Must go to Portsmouth. Wish I could get time to see Telek.* And in another entry: *Lee in Washington to talk to Hobby about K and WACs.*

She stared at the entry for a moment, her heart hammering in her throat. *Talk to Hobby about K and WACs?* She picked up the diary and ran into the General's office.

"'Kay and WACs'?" she demanded, holding up the little blue book. "What is this, Ike? What's going on?"

He looked at her over the tops of his reading glasses. "I won't be in Europe forever, you know. When the war is over, I'll be going back to America. If you're a WAC officer, it'll be easier to take you with me. So I've started the process. I sent Tex to the Pentagon, and a note to the President. If you'll recall, he promised to help." He frowned down at the stack of papers in front of him, and then up again at her. "I hope that's what you want. To go to Washington with me."

"I do," she breathed. "Oh, Ike, I do!"

There wouldn't be a child; she knew that. He was married to Mamie. There would never be a child. But becoming a WAC and going to America with Ike—*that* was beginning to seem possible, and the hope of it made her heart hammer.

∞

SHAEF's new home was an apple orchard in Normandy. Eisenhower worked and slept in his trailer (the same one he had used at Southwick), and the rest of the house and office staff worked and lived in tents. They were only about twenty miles from the British front lines, and Kay could hear the artillery pounding away and every now and then, feel the thud of it beneath her feet. The General made his inspection trips by car, so she was behind the wheel of the big armored Cadillac nearly every day, piloting it through the narrow Normandy lanes toward the fighting. The roadsides were littered with burning tanks and the corpses of dead soldiers, sickening sights that made Kay want to retch, and frequent shelling made the trips dangerous. But the General was going, and she adamantly refused to let anyone else drive.

August was a month of quick combat successes: the invasion of southern France, the taking of the port at Marseilles as well as Avignon and Toulon. Ike was impatient with Montgomery's delays and petulant demands for more men and more supplies, but heartened by the crossing of the Marne and the bold advance of the American Third Army, now under Patton's command. And then the event they had all been waiting for: the liberation of Paris— undamaged, despite Hitler's orders to burn the city.

They went to Paris on Sunday, August 27, just two days after the Germans surrendered the city. In a convoy of military vehicles, weapons carriers, and motorcycle escorts, Kay drove Eisenhower and Bradley down the Champs-Élysées, which looked just as it did when she had last seen it in 1939. The crowds of celebrating Parisians, drunk on freedom and French wine, spilled around the barricades and into the streets, tossing flowers and shouting "Vive la France! Vive la France!" Allied tanks and other armored vehicles filled the avenues, the Free French careened through the streets firing guns into the air, and young boys on bicycles were everywhere, attended by delirious dogs. Music filled the air, flags hung from all the windows, and the French tricolor, a joyful symbol of victory, hung from the Arc de Triomphe.

Kay's heart thrilled as she saw the flags. *Freedom*, they sang to the skies. *Free once again!* She knew there would be plenty of hard fighting before Hitler surrendered, but now that the City of Lights had been freed, the end of the war was at last in sight. The end of the war, and with it, a return to normal life. She could glimpse it here, on the streets of Paris.

The General's jeep had four stars on its red license plates and American, British, and French flags fluttering on its hood. By the time the convoy reached the circle around the Arc de Triomphe, people had recognized the car, and Eisenhower and Bradley were mobbed when they got out to pay their respects at the Tomb of the Unknown Soldier. The air vibrated with the hysterical cries of the crowd, and shouts of "Eisenhower! Eisenhower!" rang like a cannonade. Bradley managed to escape in a jeep, and a dozen MPs fought to clear Ike's way back to the car. When he finally fell into the backseat, his face was smeared with lipstick, his tie was askew, and the sleeve of his jacket was ripped.

"My God," he gasped. "I didn't think I'd get out of that alive."

Kay met his eyes in the rearview mirror. "They love you," she said.

"Nobody needs that kind of love," he replied shortly. "They were holding on to me like grim death." After a moment he leaned forward and put his hand on her shoulder. "Thank you for being here with me today, Kay—and for standing with me through all the hard work it took to get us here. There were times I doubted we'd make it."

"I didn't doubt it," she said, very quietly. "I never doubted it for a minute."

She felt the tears welling in her eyes and knew that today was a day she would never forget. The day she drove the Supreme Commander into a free Paris. The day she understood what the war was about.

And glimpsed its end.

CHAPTER EIGHTEEN
The End, But Not Quite

France
September 1944–May 1945

For Kay, events moved faster that autumn, like a speeded-up newsreel, the frames flashing past so quickly there wasn't time to see them, much less to think about them. Within a couple of months, Brussels, Lyons, Antwerp, Ghent, and Luxembourg were liberated. Operation Market Garden failed disastrously, and with it the hope that the war would end by Christmas. But in Eastern Europe, the Red Army rolled into Bulgaria, Poland, Hungary, East Prussia, Romania. To the south, Allied forces landed on Crete, and Athens was liberated. In the Philippines, the U.S. Third and Seventh Fleets won the Battle of Leyte Gulf over the Imperial Japanese Navy in the Philippine Islands.

But it was hard for Kay to see the big picture. There was simply so much to be done and she was too busy doing it to look up. Ike wanted to be close to the action, so after a couple of weeks in the apple orchard, the staff moved SHAEF to the seaside village of Granville. Mickey set up housekeeping in a comfortable little villa overlooking the water, with a breathtaking view of the ancient abbey of Mont-Saint-Michel, high on its island rock. He found and appropriated two placid Normande cows, spotted black and white, named Maribell and Lulabell. They provided milk for the General's mess and cream for the fresh butter that Moaney churned with an eggbeater. Telek was there too, and Caacie and her pups, and Shaef the cat. The General's family was more or less complete again.

But in early September, Eisenhower was grounded by an accident that could easily have killed him. He had flown to Versailles to confer with Bradley and Patton. When his B-25 was grounded with engine trouble, he and his pilot grabbed a single-passenger Stinson L-5 "Flying Jeep" and started back to Granville, ignoring warnings of bad weather. Short of fuel and unable to see the airstrip in the pelting rain, the pilot made an emergency landing on a sandy beach a couple of miles from the villa. The landing was successful, but when Ike was helping the pilot pull the plane above the high-tide mark, he wrenched his knee in the soft sand. A doctor flew in from London, set the knee in a plaster cast, and ordered him off it for a week.

Ike was a terrible patient, short-tempered and surly, fretting about being away from work, snapping at the doctor who put on his cast. And even though he was flat on his back, the traffic didn't stop: Beetle and Tex were in and out every ten minutes, updating the maps that papered the walls of his bedroom, while the telephone rang constantly. Still, the enforced immobility had a silver lining, Kay thought, for he had slowed down a little. She brought papers from the office that had to be signed, and they chatted as he worked. Telek was there too, curled up on Ike's bed. Evenings, they played bridge with Beetle and Ethel.

Then the General was on his feet again and back to nonstop, sixteen-hour-days. Kay drove him to Brussels and Luxembourg, to Nancy, to Aachen—to wherever the armies were on the move, liberating village after village, pushing the Germans back to the Rhine. They flew to Portsmouth and she drove him to London to confer with Churchill or to Bushy Park. Once or twice they found time to visit Telegraph Cottage, where they stole a precious hour or two for themselves. *One and one time*, Ike called it with a chuckle. But Kay knew that the war was always on his mind and was content simply to be with him, wherever he was, helping him do whatever he needed to do to win through to the peace.

Today, she reminded herself. No tomorrows, only today.

☯

Granville was comfortable but the communications there were terrible, so Eisenhower's command post moved again, this time to Versailles, just outside of Paris. There the headquarters staff took over the luxurious Trianon Hotel. The ornate Clemenceau Ballroom (where the Allies had negotiated the Treaty of Versailles) was turned into a map room, forests of radio antennae were planted in the royal gardens, and black-tie waiters served K-ration lunches on gold-rimmed plates.

Kay's office, where she handled the calendar and the bushels of letters and gifts that came to the General, was partitioned from Ike's with army-issue blankets hung from wires stretched across the room. She was billeted with the WACs in a flat above what had once been Louis XIV's great stables. Ike lived four miles away at Saint-Germain, in an eighteenth-century chateau that had recently been vacated by Field Marshal von Rundstedt. The mansion was huge (ten bedrooms), ornate, and uncomfortably furnished with fragile antique furniture.

"Makes me feel like a goddamned bull in a china closet," Ike grumped to Kay.

The garden was lovely, though, and Mickey found pasture for Maribell and Lulabell in a nearby field, so they had fresh milk and enough cream for butter. And there was room to entertain the parade of VIPs eager to enjoy the newly liberated Paris. Churchill came, of course, and the British top brass, as well as Marshall, congressional visitors from the States, and a star-studded troupe of American entertainers, including dancer Fred Astaire, crooner Bing Crosby, and comic Bob Hope.

It was Crosby who caused Kay all the trouble. He told the

General that he was headed back to the States and would be glad to send him anything he'd like. "Just tell me what you want and I'll get it for you," he said.

"Hominy grits," Ike replied promptly. "You know, I haven't had any grits since I left home—and I miss it."

"On its way," Crosby promised, and it was. He mentioned it on his Stateside radio program, and the result was a deluge of hominy, arriving in bags and boxes and case-lot cartons. "Jesus Christ on a mountain," Ike exclaimed when he saw the stacks in the hotel hallway, and vowed to never again tell anybody what he wanted, for fear he might get it.

Mickey took a dozen cans for the General's breakfast. The rest of it was Kay's problem. For weeks, she was kept busy dispatching hominy to refugee camps, hospitals, and orphanages—compliments of Bing Crosby and General Eisenhower. She wondered if they knew what to do with it.

ℬ

On October 14, Ike turned fifty-four. Kay drove him to Liège, where he had lunch with King George, who gave him another medal: the Order of the Bath. That night, General Bradley and his staff threw a surprise birthday party for him, with an enormous cake with four stars and the SHAEF insignia and plenty of French champagne. Late into the night an orchestra played songs that took them away from the war, while Kay and Ike danced together in a dark, quiet corner.

"The best birthday ever," he whispered, and she felt his arms tighten around her. Afterward, he came into her room for an hour.

He left before they could fall asleep. "If I'm asked," he said, as he shrugged into his shirt, "I want to be able to say that I've never slept with Kay Summersby."

ℬ

In late October, Kay (still a British citizen) became a WAC officer—a great relief to her, since her presence as a civilian in Eisenhower's headquarters in North Africa, England, and France had caused enormous headaches for everybody.

But the process hadn't been easy, Tex told her, and some in the Pentagon had gotten quite fussy about it. It was only General Eisenhower's persistence, a note from President Roosevelt, and the lucky precedent of three Australian women recently commissioned by MacArthur that forced Marshall's reluctant approval. In a five-minute office ceremony, Kay stood up beside her desk to swear allegiance to the United States of America and Ike pinned the gold bars on her shoulders.

Then Second Lieutenant Kay Summersby went back to work— not, however, as the General's driver. Ironically, now that she was an officer, she could no longer drive Eisenhower's car. But winter was coming to northern Europe, and she was thankful that she didn't have to push the big vehicle through the narrow, icy lanes. She had breakfast with Ike as usual every morning, rode with him to and from the office, and traveled with him when he flew to England or went on troop inspections. But now they sat together in the backseat, where they could talk face-to-face and occasionally touch hands.

All this ramped up the gossip, of course. Concerned, Butch came to Kay with the latest tittle-tattle. She listened, then shrugged and said, "I'm following the Boss's lead."

"You don't care what people say?" Butch asked, frowning.

"I care about Ike," Kay said simply. "Everybody else can go to hell."

"Funny." Butch gave her a crooked grin. "That's exactly what Ike said, when I talked to him about it."

❧

Mid-December was memorable for many reasons. On the fifteenth, American band leader Glenn Miller disappeared during a cross-Channel flight from England to Paris in a single-engine Norseman. It was a shock to the office staff, because the General had asked Miller to head up a joint British-American radio production team to perform for troops and record for broadcast back home. Everybody loved Glenn Miller, and his death was terrible news.

But the same day also brought good news, when the General learned that President Roosevelt had nominated him for a fifth star. He had spent sixteen years as a major and had risen from lieutenant colonel to General of the Army in forty-five months. He and Kay celebrated that night by playing five rubbers of bridge with Beetle and General Bradley.

The next day, Sunday, they went to a wedding. Ike's long-time orderly, Mickey McKeogh, married his Pearlie in a beautiful ceremony in Marie Antoinette's chapel in the palace at Versailles. Pearlie (the young WAC from Minnesota whom Mickey had met in Algiers) was attended by Margaret and Sue, two of Ike's WAC secretaries. Kay arranged the reception at Ike's chateau, with a towering French wedding cake and enough champagne to float the USS *Missouri*.

The staff saw the bride and groom off to Paris for a week's honeymoon and then went back to the champagne. After all, there was plenty to celebrate. The Allies had now freed Rome, as well as Paris, Belgium, North Africa, Sicily, Crete, and Greece. The war wouldn't be wrapped up by Christmas, but the game, Ike told Kay, was just about over.

But Hitler had one final hand to play. While the SHAEF staff was celebrating Mickey's and Pearlie's wedding and the General's fifth star, the Führer made his move. Thirty German divisions—a quarter of a million men, with tanks, assault guns, and artillery pieces—thundered across an eighty-five-mile Allied front, from southern Belgium to the middle of Luxembourg. The massive counterattack was planned and supervised by Hitler himself. A complete surprise, it was designed to split the Allies and compel the Americans and the British to settle for a separate peace, independent of the Soviet Union.

The Americans bore the brunt of the attack. In some places along the thin forward line, they were outnumbered ten to one, and their immediate losses were massive. By Christmas, the German offensive had pushed some fifty miles into American-held territory. For nine interminable weeks, what came to be called the Battle of the Bulge raged through towns and villages, up and down narrow lanes, across the dense woods and hilly terrain of the Ardennes Forest.

The situation was worsened by the weather: it was the nastiest winter in memory, with below-zero temperatures and driving snow that reduced visibility to ten or twenty yards. Truck engines had to be run every half hour to keep the oil from turning to molasses, and tank treads froze to the ground overnight. The men were dressed for the autumn campaign, and frostbite became a stark reality. Some of the wounded, pinned down in foxholes, froze to death.

But the Americans, stoically determined and fighting on sheer gut, pushed the Germans back to the east. As the enemy literally ran out of gas, German losses grew to somewhere between eighty thousand and one hundred thousand men. By the end of January, the original line been restored, the Allies were regaining their balance, and the push toward Berlin was underway.

ℂℂ

In January, Kay went with Eisenhower to Bastogne and Houffalize. Everywhere in the snow she could see evidences of the great fight the airborne troops had put up there, and what it had cost the Allies and the enemy. The fields around Bastogne were dotted with snow-covered mounds, bodies of dead soldiers—and sometimes a frozen arm upraised, as if reaching for help, or hope. Blackened hunks of tanks, smashed-up C-47s, and broken gliders—used to deliver combat surgeons, gasoline, and ammunition to the besieged towns—littered the ground. At Houffalize, where the armies of

Montgomery and Patton had met, there was literally nothing left. The Germans were in full retreat.

And there was good news for Kay. Ike told her that Churchill had recommended her for the British Empire Medal, "for meritorious services." She was astonished, but the recognition was welcome, especially from Churchill, for whom she had a great admiration. Her King might snub her, but the Prime Minister had always been both kind and attentive—perhaps because (as she remembered), he had stood up for King Edward when he wanted to marry Wallis Simpson. Churchill was a deep-dyed romantic.

At the end of January, Ike turned down the President's invitation to go to the Yalta Conference because he didn't feel he should leave his command. He sent Beetle instead. When Beetle got back, they moved the SHAEF command post to Rheims, in the heart of France's champagne country. The offices were set up in a large red-brick schoolhouse on the main convoy route. The General's office was the size of a closet, but his residence, the Brown House, was a large chateau owned by a local champagne baron. Mickey rounded up a record player, and Kay found an album of West Point songs that Ike could play in the evenings. He loved them.

෨

On February 24, in Rheims, Kay's life changed again. Ike promoted her to first lieutenant and she became his aide. And because Eisenhower was now a five-star general, she had become the first female five-star aide. Her new rank came with a new insignia, a blue shield decorated with five stars and topped with an eagle. In Ike's office, when he was pinning the shield on the lapel of her uniform jacket, she said, "Is this part of your grand master plan?"

"You bet it is." He kissed her quickly. "The war will be over in a few months, and it's anybody's guess where I'll go after that. Berlin, maybe, to get things sorted out with the Russians. Eventually, Washington." He put his hands on her shoulders. His voice was deep, deliberate, full of intention. "Wherever it is, I want you to be there, too, Kay. With me."

She was elated, buoyant. She wanted to say, *Wherever you are, that's where I want to be.* She had already looked into the process of becoming an American citizen. But the requirements—three years' service in the U.S. military or five years' residence in the States—seemed daunting, especially when she was trying so hard to focus on *now.*

Instead, she thought of Mamie, secluded for nearly three years in her apartment, barricaded behind her husband's photographs, surrounded by images of him. It was a cautionary reminder of the exorbitant price sometimes exacted by love.

And for herself? She wanted love, but she didn't want to be love's chattel. And even though Ike might want to take her to America, could he? *Would he?* It wasn't a matter of trusting or not trusting him, for experience had taught her that life often took matters out of the most willing hands.

He might want to take her with him. But she didn't dare tie her dreams to his desire.

જી

Throughout March, the Allies gained new ground every day. Bradley's Ninth Armored Division unexpectedly seized the railway bridge at Remagen, and over the next two weeks, nine divisions crossed that bridge. Allied bombers from Britain, Western Europe, and Italy pounded German cities hard, over and over again. SHAEF began making plans to move the headquarters staff to Frankfurt. It was the end, everybody said. It was only a matter of time now—of days, not months. At the most, of weeks.

But Kay and Beetle were increasingly concerned about Ike. The knee he had wrenched in the airplane crash in September was giving him trouble again. He suffered through one cold after another and then the flu; he had to have a cyst cut out of his back.

Most of all, he was exhausted. He had been constantly on the move during the nine months since D-Day, juggling the demands and needs of commanders, trying to outguess the enemy, and anticipating the political situation after the war. When he went out in public, he could muster the energy and spirit to flash that confident Eisenhower grin. But in the office, he let the pain show on his face, in his slumped shoulders, and in his temper—which, as Kay could testify—was increasingly terrible. He had a quarter-inch fuse, and the slightest thing set him off like a bomb.

"He's going to have a nervous breakdown if he doesn't get some rest," Kay said worriedly, and Beetle agreed. Both of them pushed him, and finally he gave in. A wealthy American family had offered the use of a villa on the Riviera, so in the middle of a cold, wet March, Ike and Kay took off for a five-day rest in a luxurious villa called Sous le Vent, overlooking the Mediterranean. Beetle and Ethel went along, and General Bradley flew in the next day.

Ike was supposed to relax, play bridge, watch movies, and sit in the sun on the villa's private beach. The first two days, he did nothing but sleep, waking late in the morning and limping outside to the sunny terrace that looked out over blue sparkling water. He would eat there (the villa had a marvelous cook), drink a couple of glasses of wine, and go back to bed until dinner. After forty-eight hours, he was well enough to concentrate on bridge. Every day, he became more like his old self, and on the last day, he was Eisenhower again. Kay was with him every moment, thinking as she often did that the future was her enemy, that the present time, the *now*, was her dearest friend. There was grace in that knowledge, she told herself. All the grace she needed.

And now, so far away from curious eyes and surrounded only by friends they trusted, they even slept together, in a giant bed in a room that looked out over an azure sea. "Nobody's going to ask," Ike said to her the first night, "but if they do, we'll just lie."

"Just lie?" she asked, fitting herself against him as she had done on the train to Scotland, so many months before.

He was silent for a moment. "Nobody's going to ask," he

repeated. "If they do, don't answer. It's nobody's goddamned business."

છ

On April 12, Kay and the General met Bradley at Patton's Third Army headquarters at Bad Hersfeld for a tour of the Nazi treasure hoard hidden away in the Merkers Salt Mine. A rickety wooden elevator took them a half-mile down. At the bottom, corridors opened out into vaulted caverns filled with pallets of gold bullion and bales of paper currency, art treasures pillaged from museums and homes of wealthy Jews, and endless rows of suitcases filled with watches, jewelry, and gold-filled teeth—all that was left of their murdered owners. The Merkers mine was in what had been agreed as the Soviet zone, and plans were already in the works to move the hoard to American-held Frankfurt, where the occupation forces were headquartered. It would be transported in thirty ten-ton trucks guarded by two MP battalions and seven infantry platoons, with air cover provided by P-51 Mustangs.

Dinner that night was lively—Patton had invited two Red Cross girls to join them. Afterward, Kay went to her room in the guest house to which she'd been assigned, knowing that the generals would sit up late, discussing strategy over drinks. It was well after midnight when Ike knocked on her door—with bad news.

He had just gone to bed when Patton woke him. Patton had noticed that his wristwatch had stopped, so he turned on the BBC to learn the time. What he heard was a news bulletin. Franklin Roosevelt was dead.

Kay's breath caught in her throat. America without FDR—it seemed impossible. The sixty-three-year-old President had appeared so well at their picnic in Tunisia. But she knew that the war was a killer, not only of troops on the ground but of the men who were responsible for those troops. She put her hand on Ike's arm. He was nine years younger than the President, but the war had aged him. He looked like a man in his sixties.

"A goddamned shame," Ike said softly. "He didn't live long enough to see the victory. And it's so close now. So close. So close."

He sat down on her bed, put his head in his hands, and wept.

☜☞

A few days later, in the middle of April, Kay and Ike flew to London, where they had dinner with the Churchills. Ike attended a Cabinet meeting, and then he and Kay hosted her mother at an informal picnic lunch in the garden at Telegraph Cottage. Kay had visited with Kul on several of the trips back to England, but this was the first time the three of them had been together since late 1942—which seemed, Kay thought, like a century ago.

The roses and rhododendrons were in full bloom and the garden was lovely. Ike had gone for a walk and Kay and her mother were left alone.

Kul put her elbows on the table. "Do you remember what I asked you after we had dinner with your General Eisenhower in his rooms at the Dorchester?"

"I'm not sure," Kay said evasively.

"I asked you if you were sure that you knew what you were doing."

Kay sighed. "I remember," she said, wishing her mother would let it go.

"It's true now, too, Kathleen. Perhaps even more true. I hope very much that *both* of you know what you're doing."

Kay looked away. "I'm afraid that things are too much of a muddle to know anything for certain, Mum. The war—"

"We know all about the war, dear." Her mother's voice was sympathetic. "He's still married, isn't he?"

"Yes." Kay thought of Mamie, barricaded behind her photographs. "Please don't ask, Mum. I don't have any answers."

Her mother regarded her, a frown between her eyes. "He's *theirs*, Kathleen. They've made him. They'll never let you have him."

Kay frowned. "I don't know what you mean. He just won this bloody war. *Nobody* can tell him what to do—especially in his private life."

"Oh, my dear." Her mother shook her head pityingly. "You don't know what you're up against."

Kay smiled. "You think my heart will be broken, then?" she asked lightly.

"I'm sure of it, love. Are you ready for that?"

Kay thought of what had happened since the beginning of the Blitz, the unending horrors she had seen, the countless lives lost. What was a little personal heartbreak compared to all that?

"Yes, I'm ready." She smiled. "But if that's what comes, it won't be the end of the world, you know."

"I see." Kul was silent for a moment. At last, she nodded. "I think I'll stop worrying about you, my dear."

❧

On April 27, Benito Mussolini and his mistress, Clara Petacci, were apprehended in an attempt to escape north to the Swiss border. They were both executed.

❧

On April 30, Adolf Hitler, hiding in his bunker in Berlin, shot himself. Eva Braun, his longtime companion and wife of forty hours, died of cyanide poison.

❧

On May 7, at 2:41 in the morning, the surrender documents were signed in the red-brick schoolhouse in Rheims. The war in Europe was over.

Immediately after the Germans left, General Eisenhower and his staff posed in the General's office for the official photograph. A jubilant Ike, grinning, was holding up a pair of pens in a victory V. Kay was standing behind him and to his right, smiling happily over his shoulder.

When the photograph was published, her image had been removed.

CHAPTER NINETEEN
"The Woman Who Knows More Secrets of the War . . ."

England—Germany—Washington, D.C.
May–November 1945

Two days after V-E Day, Ike, Kay, and Ike's son John flew to London. Kay and Ike visited Telegraph Cottage again, played a couple of holes of golf, and sat on their bench holding hands, relishing the quiet time. That evening, they drove to London, to the Dorchester Hotel, for a cocktail party in General Bradley's suite. Kul was invited, and John and his date (a friend of Kay's, a WREN). Afterward, the six of them went to the Prince of Wales Theater to see *Strike a New Note*, a light-hearted song-and-dance revue. A box had been reserved for their group, and when the audience saw Ike come in, they exploded in applause.

At last, to stop them, he stood and spoke a few words about how glad he was to be back in England: "a country," he said, "where I can *almost* speak the language." When he sat down, he gestured to Kay to sit beside him. She took her seat defiantly, even proudly. To her, it felt like a declaration, although of what, she scarcely knew—or was reluctant to imagine.

After the theater, they went to Ciro's, where the orchestra

played "For He's a Jolly Good Fellow," to Ike's delight. They had a late supper and then Kay and Ike danced together for the first time in public, among strangers. And then again, and again.

"I love you, Kay," Ike said, resting his cheek against her hair. His voice was deeply serious.

"I love you too, Ike," Kay said. "So much, so much."

She could feel the curious eyes on them as they danced. Ike seemed to be throwing off all attempts at discretion, to be making a public declaration of their relationship. But she had seen the official V-E Day photograph that had appeared on the front page of the *Stars and Stripes*. She knew that she had been erased. She remembered what her mother had said.

He's theirs, Kathleen. They made him. They'll never let you have him.

She buried her face in his shoulder and felt his arm tighten around her.

℘

If the last months of the war had been like a speeded-up newsreel, the first months of the peace were even more frantic. Every day brought some new change that required Kay to bend and stretch and reach to meet it. And each change not only altered the present but the future as well, so that it became even more impossible to tell what lay ahead. All she knew was *today*. Just *today* and *today*. Never tomorrow.

Telegraph Cottage was permanently closed on the last day of May. Sadly, Kay pinned a photograph of it to the wall beside her desk in her office at Frankfurt. The little house seemed more like home than anywhere she had ever lived, and her throat ached every time she looked at it.

Ike, who had been appointed the Governor of the American Zone of Occupied Germany, was showered with honors. In Moscow, the Russians gave him the Order of Victory. In Paris, de

Gaulle pinned the Compagnon de la Libération on his uniform and the French gave him a triumphant parade along boulevards jammed with cheering crowds. The British gave him the Order of Merit—the first to go to an American. But the award that he cared about most was the Freedom of the City of London, and he worked hard on his acceptance speech. Kay and Ike flew back to London for the award ceremony, which took place in the ancient Guildhall. That evening, there was a dinner for both of them at Number Ten Downing Street, with the Prime Minister and Mrs. Churchill.

And then Ike was off to the States, for a tour that General Marshall had arranged for him. While he was gone, every morning, over her eggs and coffee, Kay read newspaper stories about his triumphal progress. He had been greeted at the Washington airport by his wife and a crowd of some thirty thousand well-wishers. There were reports of his address to a joint session of Congress, dinner at the White House, a ticker-tape parade in New York and victory parades in cities across the country. Mrs. Eisenhower was with him in almost every photograph, beaming and waving and blowing kisses to the crowd, whose eager hands reached toward them, toward both of them. Some were carrying signs: WE LIKE IKE! and IKE FOR PRESIDENT!

Kay stared at the photographs, hearing her mother's voice. *He's theirs, Kathleen. They made him. They'll never let you have him.*

And now she understood.

☙

Their time together wasn't quite over—not yet. When Ike returned from the United States, he settled into his new command: managing the American occupation forces in Germany from headquarters in Frankfurt. He expected to be there until Japan was defeated, and he wanted Kay with him.

But there was some time for actual vacationing. They spent a precious week at Sous le Vent, where they slept together every night, not caring who knew it. In August, they went fishing with Beetle in Bavaria. Later that month, they visited Mark Clark in Salzburg and went to see Berchtesgaden, Hitler's mountain hideaway. There were always photographs snapped on these trips. Kay had learned to stay out of camera range, but now Ike insisted that she stand beside him when the photographers wanted photos. She wondered if he had seen the official photograph of V-E Day and wanted to somehow make up for what had happened—or perhaps to defy whoever had taken her out of the picture.

And one afternoon, back in Frankfurt, he offered her a gold and platinum Cartier cigarette case decorated with a ring of five sapphire stars and a sapphire-studded clip. It had been given to him by General de Gaulle after V-E Day. Inside the case, de Gaulle's name had been engraved, in his own handwriting.

"The sapphires match your eyes, Kay," Ike said. "It was a personal gift, so it's mine to give."

It was on the tip of Kay's tongue to say *Oh, yes, thank you! What a wonderful gift!* But instead, she heard herself saying "I'd love to, Ike, but I don't think I ought to take it. It's too valuable. And if de Gaulle ever found out, he'd be insulted."

Ike scowled at her. "You have the damnedest way of turning down my offers," he growled, and she knew he was thinking of the uniform. He thought for a moment, then nodded. "I suppose you're right. Now I'll have to come up with something else for you."

It was a summer for traveling. Ike flew to Berlin and back every day during the Potsdam conference—and the new American president, Harry S. Truman, came to visit the General's Frankfurt office in the huge IG Farben Building, where Kay and the rest of the staff were personally introduced to him. After that, Ike was off again, this time by himself, to Luxembourg, Warsaw, Belfast, Brussels, Moscow, Amsterdam, and Prague.

While the Boss was gone, Kay traveled, too, with Averell Harriman, the U.S. ambassador to the Soviet Union, and his daughter Kathy, who was by now a good friend. The three of them visited Copenhagen, Vienna, Budapest, and Moscow. In Moscow, she attended the world-famous Bolshoi Ballet, visited the Kremlin, and heard the Red Army men's choir sing "It's A Long Way to Tipperary" in Russian, just for her.

Tipperary was not far from Inish Beg, and the sweet, remembered melody made her homesick for Ireland. But she had indeed come a long, long way. She had no idea where the future was taking her or what kind of life she would lead. But she knew she couldn't go back.

℘

She had just returned from Moscow when Ike called her into his office and told her she was going to Washington.

"Washington?" she asked in surprise. "Why?"

He grinned at her, obviously pleased with himself. "You wouldn't take the cigarette case when I offered it to you. But you can't turn this down, Irish. I'm sending you to Washington to take out your citizenship papers. The State Department will expedite your application."

"*Citizenship* papers?" she squeaked.

He took off his reading glasses and leaned back in his chair. "Marshall is retiring at the end of the year, and I'm to take his job as Army Chief of Staff. I want you with me, Kay. It'll be easier to keep you on the staff if you've already applied to be a citizen." He gave her an intent look, hesitating, measuring his words, speaking deliberately. "I want you to come with me. Will you?"

Kay was trembling. She did indeed want to become an American—had wanted that for a very long time. But she wasn't a naive young girl, venturing out into the world for the first time. She knew what Eisenhower was saying. He intended to stay with his wife, for (she thought) good and honorable reasons, reasons she knew and understood and, yes, *respected*. He was a good and honorable man, but he was also ambitious. He was obviously a rising star in the American political world. He could be anything he wanted to be. *We Like Ike. Ike for President.* Yes, that too, if he chose.

But he also loved *her.* He wanted to continue being what they had been, together. He wanted her to continue to work with him, to be his lover. There would be no marriage, no children, and if there was a cottage hidden away somewhere, their visits would be brief—and secretive. Would she go with him, under those terms?

She thought of everything they had done together in the past three and a half years—all the victories, the losses, the triumphs, the disappointments. Of the thousands of miles they had driven and flown together, many of them in desperately difficult conditions. Of the thousands of hours of work, the too-brief hours of intimacy.

She thought of today, today, and today. Did she dare to think of tomorrow?

She thought of all that, and then nodded. "Yes," she said.

He bent to kiss her.

↾↽

On November 1, Kay flew from Frankfurt to Washington in the General's Skymaster, traveling with Ambassador Robert Murphy and General Lucius Clay, the deputy military governor. This time, the schedule was less rushed, the weather was decent, and there were no uncomfortable parties with army wives. She went to the State Department and applied to become a citizen, saw a few friends, and took a quick trip to New York for some shopping. Everywhere, she was as discreet as she could be. She didn't want any attention from the newspapers.

But somebody in the State Department must have leaked the news about her application. It caught the attention of political journalist Doris Fleeson, who wrote a daily column for the Washington *Evening Star* that was syndicated to newspapers around the country. Fleeson's November 5 column was headlined WAC AIDE OF

EISENHOWER FLIES TO U.S. TO SEEK CITIZENSHIP. Kay sat on the bed in her hotel room, smoking one cigarette after another as she read and reread it, feeling more and more vulnerable.

"The woman who knows more secrets of the war than any other member of her sex is in this country exploring the possibilities of becoming an American citizen," Fleeson wrote. She reported that Eisenhower was expected to return to the Pentagon to become Army Chief of Staff. "Presumably, like other secretaries, Lt. Summersby is eager to take steps in time to hold on to her good job when and if her present employer changes stations. But it would be an unlikely situation that would find a British subject holding a post as administrative assistant in Washington to an American Chief of Staff." In an acerbic aside, Fleeson added that Kay held the rank of a WAC lieutenant. "Just how this was managed WAC headquarters here cannot say and they have no record regarding it."

It was a hurtful piece. Kay was dismayed at its sardonic assumption about secretaries' ambitions—and about the suggestion that there were hard feelings in WAC headquarters about her commission. That, she feared, might be very real, although it surely wouldn't cause trouble for Ike. When he became Chief of Staff, he'd be the most powerful man in the army, second only to the Commander in Chief.

But when she thought about it, what troubled her even more was the possibility that Mamie—and perhaps even General Marshall—might read the column. But surely not, she thought, trying to comfort herself. It was so obviously one of those tittle-tattle gossipy pieces, designed to make the writer look as if she were in the know. In London, such things appeared all the time. Lots of people read them, yes, and they sold newspapers. But nobody took them seriously.

Still, Fleeson's column spoiled the rest of the trip. She ordered room service for supper and stayed out of sight until it was time to go to the airport. She was anxious to return to Germany, and Ike.

৪৩

Back in Frankfurt, Ike was also having a difficult time. In fact, he thought the goddamned war was easier to manage than the unmerciful hell he'd been going through for the past few months. From the time he had been able to admit that he loved Kay, he had told himself that it was only a wartime romance. Yes, she was an extraordinary woman, and their relationship had been a comfort and a refuge for him. It had kept him sane, during pressure-filled months when he'd thought the lid was going to blow off the whole crazy world. But his loyalty belonged to his wife, to Mamie, and he had fully intended to return to her after the war. He had assured her of that almost every time he wrote—because he really meant it, damn it. Meant every word of it.

But in the weeks just after V-E Day, when the war pressures eased up and he had to make decisions about the future, he had begun to reflect how deeply he loved Kay, how much he needed her, how goddamned much he hated the idea of giving her up. What he wanted, more than anything else, was to marry her and have a baby—hell, two babies, three, however many the good Lord saw fit to send them. To live somewhere quiet where he could fish and write his memoirs and put the war behind him—maybe in England or Scotland. He'd have to retire from the army, but wasn't it time for that, anyway? He'd given his country the past thirty years; surely to God he could lay his own claim to the next thirty. He deserved that, didn't he? Hell, yes, he deserved it, and then some. Kay made him happy, happier than he had ever imagined he could be. She made him more of a man, too, than he'd been in nearly a decade. And that was no small thing, for chrissakes.

But he was a military man, and however much he might yearn for a comfortable retirement, he had the feeling that he'd pretty quickly get bored. Even writing and fishing and a houseful of babies might not be enough. And there was the unavoidable business of making a living. He didn't know much about divorces and alimony, but he knew he'd have to support Mamie—she certainly wasn't capable of supporting herself and he couldn't leave her out on a limb. He'd been in the military so long that he had no idea how much a civilian life might cost or how far his pension would stretch, especially with a chunk of it going to Mamie. So maybe he should plan on staying in the military, at least for another five or ten years.

And then he considered something else. Divorce in the military could be a tricky business. If he intended to stay in the army, he'd better find out how a divorce would affect his career. In a situation like this, a soldier went to his commanding officer for advice. Which for him meant Marshall. His best course of action was to let the Old Man know what he was considering and see what he had to say. Then he'd be able to think a little more clearly about his options.

So he had written a letter—he had handwritten it, because he sure as hell wasn't going to send it through the secretarial pool. It was very straightforward, offering no explanation, no apologies, just a request for information. He put it in an envelope, marked it "eyes only," and sent it to the Chief. And waited for the response.

ॐ

When Kay got back from Washington, she was surprised to find that Ike—although he was suffering from another very bad cold—was preparing to leave for the Pentagon.

"Things have gotten a little complicated in the past few days," he said grimly. "Truman has decided he wants to send Marshall to China to try to broker a coalition between the Nationalists and the Communists. I've been ordered to take over the Chief's job, effective immediately." He coughed. "I'm flying to Washington tomorrow, damn it."

"Are you sure you should be flying with that cold?" Kay asked worriedly. She knew that he never liked to be reminded that he was ill, but she felt she had to ask.

"I wouldn't if I didn't have to, Irish. Orders are orders."

Kay smiled gamely. "I hope it's a comfortable flight. When do you expect to be back?"

"In a couple of weeks. Certainly before Christmas." He put an arm around her shoulders. "This is just a preliminary visit, to get things set up in the Chief's office. Let's have a quiet dinner tonight and spend the evening by ourselves. When I get back here, we'll pack things up and head for Washington." He shook his head. "God, I hate Washington. Politics, politics, all day long. Nothing but snipers and back-stabbers everywhere."

Kay thought about Fleeson's column in the *Evening Star*. Should she mention it to Ike? No, she decided. There was no point in worrying him when there was nothing he could do about it. She only said, "I'll be glad when everything is settled."

"So will I." He bent to kiss her. "And then we'll go to Washington. You, me, and Telek—together."

"Wonderful," she murmured, her cheek against the rough lapel of his uniform. "That's wonderful, Ike."

CHAPTER TWENTY
The Real Story

Washington, D.C.
November 10, 1945

Cookie Wilson put a tray of snack crackers and thin-sliced ham and cheese in the center of the card table in her spacious Arlington living room. "Here, girls," she said, "we can snack on these while we're waiting for Mamie. She's stuck doing a newspaper interview." She added a stack of cocktail napkins. "She said if she wasn't here in fifteen minutes, we should go ahead and start without her."

"Poor Mamie." Pamela Farr picked up a cracker and topped it with bits of ham and cheese. "I'm sure there are lots of those interviews, now that Ike has turned into a big muckety-muck."

"So true." Diane Bracken pursed lipsticked lips. "The Eisenhowers are in *all* the papers these days. Mamie must hate it."

"I'm not so sure about that," Cookie said archly. She found her cigarettes and sat down at the table. "Mamie wouldn't do it if she didn't like it, you know. She's in charge."

"You may be right," Pamela said. "Personally, I find her a trifle overbearing these days. All those ticker-tape parades have gone to her head." She popped the cracker into her mouth. "But I didn't say that, did I? I'm *sure* I didn't say that."

Cookie patted her friend's hand. "You didn't say that, dear. Or if you did, we didn't hear you."

SUSAN WITTIG ALBERT

"Speaking of newspapers," Diane said, "did you happen to read Doris Fleeson's column in the *Evening Star* on Tuesday? The piece about Kay Summersby applying for citizenship, I mean." She tilted her head. "Rather cynical, I thought. And full of insinuations."

"Cynicism is Fleeson's middle name," Pamela said. "A few years ago, she wrote an article about Missy LeHand—she used to be FDR's secretary, you know—for the *Saturday Evening Post*. She didn't actually *say* that Missy was sleeping with the President, but she certainly left that impression." She patted her lips with a napkin. "I hope Mamie didn't see Fleeson's piece about Kay Summersby. It would give her heartburn."

"But she did *see* it," Cookie said. She clapped a hand to her mouth. "Oh, stupid me. There I go, opening my big mouth. Forget I said anything, girls."

"She saw it?" Diane asked avidly. "What did she say? Come on, Cookie. Do tell."

Cookie looked away. "I don't think I should—"

"Cookie, my dear," Pamela said, "you know something, don't you? What is it?"

Cookie picked up a cracker and added cheese. "Well, if you *must* know. Yes, Mamie read Doris Fleeson's column. And yes, she was terribly upset. Wouldn't *you* be, if you found out—from the *newspaper*—that your husband was bringing his British secretary to work for him in the Pentagon?" She popped the cracker in her mouth.

"Oh, I *would*," Pamela said.

"That's why I don't have a husband," Diane murmured. "Men are such louses."

"But I have to hand it to Mamie," Cookie said. "She handled it very well. Very professionally."

"Professionally?" Diane asked.

"What did she do?" Pamela wanted to know.

Cookie frowned uncertainly. "I would really rather not—"

"Oh, well, if she made you promise." Diane examined a fingernail.

318

"No, it wasn't like that. In fact, she doesn't know I know."

"Well, then . . ." Pamela said suggestively.

Cookie took out a cigarette and lit it, very deliberately. At last, she said, "She telephoned General Marshall."

"Telephoned General Marshall!" Diane put her glass down with a thump. "I would never have thought Mamie could be so . . . devious!"

"That's not devious," Pamela said. "It's forthright. General Marshall has always encouraged his commanders' wives to tell him if they have a problem. Remember when General Akers' wife was thinking of getting a divorce? Marshall heard about it and called her. Whatever he said to her must have changed her mind. She's still married to her husband. And he—the husband, I mean—got a promotion." She looked at Cookie. "I suppose you heard about Mamie from Marv."

"Of course she did," Diane said knowingly. She reached for a cracker. "It's very convenient to have a husband who works in the Chief of Staff's office. He probably brings home all sorts of wonderful stories."

"Actually, Marv was impressed," Cookie replied, pulling the ashtray toward her. "He said that Mamie handled the situation very well. She was very calm and self-contained. She simply telephoned the General and asked him if he'd read the column. When he said he hadn't, she read it to him."

"*Read* it to him?" Diane and Pamela said, practically in unison.

Cookie nodded. "And then all she said was, 'I'd really appreciate it if you'd look into this, General Marshall. As you can guess, it's terribly painful for me. And of course, it's embarrassing for our son John.'"

"Good for Mamie!" Pamela said. "I'm proud of her."

"That certainly took chutzpah," Diane said. "To call up your husband's boss and—" She paused, looking at Cookie. "But I'll bet there's more, isn't there, Cookie?"

Cookie nodded slowly. "Yes. There was a letter—" She broke off. "But perhaps I shouldn't—"

"Of *course* you should!" Pamela exclaimed. "We promise not to breathe a word." She looked pointedly at Diane. "Don't we, Diane?"

"Promise." Diane crossed her heart. "Cross my heart and hope to die."

Cookie tapped her cigarette into the ashtray. Finally, she said, "Well, it seems that Ike wrote a letter to General Marshall, asking what would happen to his military career if he divorced Mamie and married that woman. His secretary, I mean. Kay Summersby."

"*Divorced* Mamie?" Pamela cried, her eyes widening.

Diane leaned forward. "Really, Cookie? You're *serious*?"

"Really," Cookie said. "Marv didn't actually see it, of course. Ike sent it 'eyes only.'" She pulled on her cigarette. "But he did see the cable." She blew out a stream of smoke.

"What cable?" Pamela asked.

"General Marshall's reply to Ike, in response to the letter. He told Marv to code it and then take it down to the communications officer."

"How *convenient*," Diane said archly.

Cookie gave her a look. "It's part of his job, Diane. My husband is very discreet, you know. *Very*."

"What did the cable say?" Pamela leaned forward. "Hurry up and tell us, Cookie. Mamie may show up any minute."

Cookie lowered her voice. "It said that if Eisenhower divorced his wife to marry that girl, General Marshall would relieve him from duty and personally see to it that he would never draw another peaceful breath on this earth."

"Oh, my God," Pamela breathed. "Marshall said *that*?"

Cookie nodded.

"And then—" Diane prompted.

"And then General Marshall went straight over to the White House to see President Truman. Of course, Marv doesn't know what they talked about. But when Marshall came back, he had new orders. He's going on a mission to China. And Eisenhower has been ordered to come back to Washington and take Marshall's job. Immediately."

"What did Eisenhower say?" Diane asked.

"In response to the cable?" Cookie replied. "He didn't say anything. But he's on his way to Washington, so—"

"So he gave in," Pamela said. "He won't be divorcing Mamie to marry that woman."

"So it would seem," Cookie said, with a kind of grim satisfaction. "The man could stand up to Hitler, but he can't stand up to General Marshall."

"Or maybe he's decided he wants to be president someday," Pamela said with a shrug. "And of course he couldn't, if he's divorced. No divorced man will *ever* be elected president, I don't care how many wars he's won. Being divorced is even worse than being Catholic—if you want to be president, I mean."

"But what if he brings that woman here anyway?" Diane asked. "Without divorcing Mamie, I mean. I suppose he could get by with it." She frowned at her friends' raised eyebrows. "Well, Wendell Willkie did. Don't you remember? When he was running for president a few years ago, all the newspaper people knew about his romance with Irita Van Doren—and he was married. But they didn't say a word. Not one word."

"And don't forget about FDR and his secretary," Cookie said.

"But that won't work for Eisenhower," Pamela said definitively. "There's been too much talk already. If he brings that woman to Washington, it'll be all over the newspapers."

"There's something else," Cookie said. "Diane, don't you remember how much resentment there was in the WAC office about Mrs. Summersby's commission?"

"I certainly do," Diane said emphatically. "My sister Rachel said there were several WACs in Eisenhower's command—American citizens—who could have served as Ike's aide. Instead, he got the British civilian commissioned as a WAC and gave it to *her*. And on top of that, he gave her a Bronze Star. Rachel says there are several WACs in Ike's office with very ruffled feathers. One of them might be very glad to spill a few tidbits in front of a gossip columnist. In front of Doris Fleeson, for example."

"He gave her a Bronze Star?" Pamela trilled a disbelieving laugh. "What in the world *for*?"

"'For meritorious service in a combat zone,' Marv says." Cookie paused. "To be fair, she probably deserves it. She drove Ike to the front many times in both North Africa and France, under enemy fire."

"And who knows what else they did, out there on the front," Pamela said darkly.

Diane frowned. "Mamie isn't aware of the letter her husband wrote to Marshall?"

"Not so far as I know," Cookie said.

"It's better if she doesn't know the real story," Pamela said. "That way, she doesn't have to *pretend* that she doesn't know."

Diane laughed lightly. "How very true, Pamela. Where men are concerned, it's better not to know." Her laughter faded. "But *we* do."

"We do what?" Cookie asked.

"Know the real story," Diane said uncomfortably. "So *we* have to pretend."

The doorbell gave a cheerful ding-dong. "There she is." Cookie pushed her chair back and stood. "Remember, girls. You promised. Mum's the word."

"Our lips are sealed," Diane said.

"Oh, positively." Pamela smiled. "You can trust us."

CHAPTER TWENTY-ONE
"Dear Kay . . ."

Frankfurt, Germany
November–December 1945

"When do you expect to be back?" Kay had asked him.

Before Christmas, he had said. "And then we'll go to Washington. You, me, and Telek—together."

But he didn't come back before Christmas. He didn't come back at all.

❧

The General had been gone for only a week when word reached the Frankfurt office that he was checking into Walter Reid Hospital. The cold he'd had when he left had turned into bronchial pneumonia. Kay only worried a little—she was mostly glad that the doctors had been firm enough to send him to the hospital, where he would be forced to get some rest. He had been working much too hard, on top of all the travel. She wished she could write and tell him that she missed him, but letters between them were impossible.

Meanwhile, a flurry of telexes had begun arriving with directions for moving important files and documents to the Pentagon. Cries of celebration rang through the office—"We're going home!"—and everyone started getting things ready to go. Then came an order to the General's personal staff: they were to prepare to leave for the States on December 1. By that time, though, there were mostly WACs—and Tex, of course. Mickey and the house staff had already left. Beetle and Ethel were back in Washington, where Ethel was working as a nurse. She had written to Kay that President Truman planned to name Beetle ambassador to the Soviet Union, to succeed Averell Harriman. Butch had left Ike's command months before and was already back in the States, with Molly. They would be married as soon as Butch's divorce was final.

Kay was clearing out her desk drawers when Tex came into her office, a telex in his hand. "I'm afraid there's a problem, Kay." He handed her the telex. "I don't know what to say. I have no idea what's going on."

Kay took the telex. As she read it, her heart thudded twice, then seemed to stop. It was brief, telegraphic, to the point. Lieutenant Summersby had been dropped from the travel roster. She was being ordered instead to Berlin, where she would be working for the Deputy Governor, General Clay. She looked at Tex, blinking hard to hold back the sudden tears.

"Just this?" She swallowed hard. "No message from the Boss?"

"No." Tex touched her shoulder. "Sorry, Kay." His voice was rough with compassion. "You don't deserve this."

It felt as if an axe had fallen into her life, severing the yesterdays from the tomorrows. "No," she said. "I don't."

Without another word, she picked up her bag and left the office, walking blindly through the bomb-ravaged streets of Frankfurt. Its wreckage was like the burned and broken London where she had driven her ambulance during the Blitz. It was like the wreckage of her life, shattered and desolate now. Ike had told her that she'd be going with him to Washington. He had *promised*—and he had never broken a promise to her. Had he changed his mind? Had somebody else changed it for him? She bit her lip until the blood came. She knew him well enough to know that he wouldn't have done this unless he'd been ordered to do it. But why? Did it have anything to do with the "complications" he had mentioned when he was getting ready to leave. What complications? Why? *Why?*

At last she went home, where she lay down on her bed, pulled Telek against her, and began to cry. The little dog licked her nose and nuzzled close against her. Seized with a crippling despair, she cried herself to sleep.

∽

Three days later, the letter came. It was typed; Ike had obviously dictated it. *Dear Kay,* he began: *I am terribly distressed, first because it has become impossible to keep you as a member of my personal official family and secondly because I cannot come back to give you a detailed account of the reasons.* He went on to say that there would be opposition to someone who was not a completely naturalized American citizen working in the War Department. He would not try to express the depth of his appreciation for her unexcelled loyalty and faithfulness. He was distressed that their valuable association had to end, but it was by reasons over which he had no control. He wanted her to keep Telek, asked her to stay in touch, and offered to help her find a suitable job if she came to the States. He signed himself, *With lasting and warm regard, Sincerely, DDE.* A handwritten postscript added that he was in bed with a bad cold. *Take care of yourself,* he wrote. *And retain your optimism.*

Optimism! She stared at the word, dumbfounded. What a ridiculous thing to say! How could she be optimistic about anything when he had allowed them to cut her off in such a brutal way?

And the postscript—was he trying to tell her that he was too damned sick to pick up a pen and write a proper letter? Or that he was being held captive in a hospital somewhere, his letters scrutinized by an evil-eyed censor determined to let nothing but the most brutal messages get through?

She laughed bitterly. Yes, that was it. General Marshall had put his war hero to bed and locked the door so he couldn't get out.

Her mother had been right, damn it. *He's theirs, Kathleen*, she had said. *They'll never let you have him.*

Clutching at one last fragile hope, she read the paragraphs over again, remembering that Ike was accustomed to working with deceptions—Darlan's death and Fortitude were just two examples of the dozens of clandestine operations he'd been involved in during the war. Many of his messages to Washington and London had been written in code. Was there some secret meaning encrypted in this one?

But if there was, she couldn't decipher it. And even if it meant only what it said, what did it *mean*? "By reasons over which I have no control." If the reasons weren't his, whose were they? Who was in a position to make this man obey? Mamie? General Marshall? President Truman? Who? *Who?*

Or perhaps it was something much simpler. Perhaps they—this nameless "they"—offered him something he wanted more than he wanted her. Still, he had already held the most powerful command in the world. What more could they offer him? The Chief of Staff job? No: he didn't want that. What else could it be? The presidency? Surely they hadn't offered him *that*—had they?

But no matter how many questions she asked of the letter, it refused to answer any of them. Bland and inert, speechless, it lay like a dead thing on the desk in front of her. That evening, back in her room, she folded it into a small square and tucked it into the olivewood box Ike had given her in Jerusalem. In the box, she found the card he had also given her that day.

There are lots of things I could say, he had written. *You know them.*

Yes. He hadn't had to speak, then: she had known what he meant to say. Now, she had no idea. Now, it was all a terrible mystery.

Beside her, Telek was wagging his tail eagerly, begging to be taken for a walk. "Let's," she agreed. "It'll be good for both of us." The November air was chilly, so she buckled his plaid tartan coat around him.

"Come along, funny little boy," she said, and they went out

on the street, out into the crisp, cold air. Berlin lay ahead of them, and the years.

There are lots of things I could say. You know them.

She held the words to her heart. They were truer than the words in his letter, she knew. They were the words she would keep with her always.

PART FOUR

AMERICA
1974–1979

CHAPTER TWENTY-TWO
Past Forgetting

Southampton, Long Island
Summer 1974–Winter 1975

Kay was dying. The cancer had spread to her liver, the doctors told her after the surgery. Only a matter of time now. Weeks, months, half a year. By early 1975, at the latest.

But she had a story to tell and she was determined to tell it before she died. Each morning when she sat down to work at the desk in her tiny rented cottage just off the beach, she studied the silver-framed photograph of Eisenhower—Ike the soldier, taken before D-Day. The image regarded her with a commanding gaze, as if he had given her an order and was waiting impatiently for her to carry it out. *If you're going to do it, Kay,* he was saying, *goddamn it, get on with it.*

"Don't get your knickers in a twist," she said to the photo. "You're not going to like it, anyway."

She felt quite sure about that. As a general (and as a bridge player), Eisenhower had always hidden his hand. As a president, he had practiced deception on a global scale—at stratospheric heights, considering the U-2 incident. As a lover, he had never been able to put words to his feelings, especially when he felt deeply. And both of them had gone to considerable lengths to conceal their relationship. Revealing it now, after all this time, felt like stripping naked in the middle of Piccadilly Circus. But she had promised herself that her second memoir would tell the *true* story, not the story Eisenhower wanted her to tell.

She had begun writing her first memoir the year after she came to the States. *Eisenhower Was My Boss*, which was true as far as it went, told the story of their professional relationship. She had worked with a very good ghostwriter with exactly the right kind of military experience, and Colonel McAndrew had approved what they had written. Not Ike himself—Kay was sure he didn't want to know anything about the process, or about the book, either. "Deniability" was what Butch called it.

Instead, Colonel McAndrew, a plump, fiftyish bureaucrat with rimless spectacles and an utter lack of humor, had been delegated to manage her and her book. At their first meeting, the colonel had handed her a typed list of the ground rules. "If you want to write this book, you have to agree to this," he had said firmly. Rule Number One was that she could make no claim whatever to "any personal intimacy, explicit or implied."

"We don't have any problem with your telling what happened," McAndrew had told her. "Just don't tell *everything* that happened." He had smiled blandly, the light winking off his glasses. "After all, it works both ways. I'm sure you don't want to tarnish the General's reputation. Or to suggest that, in any way, you were what the newspapers might call . . ." He coughed delicately. "A loose woman."

She didn't. And she *did* want to write the book, because—not yet an American citizen—she had left the WACs and needed the money. So she had signed the document the colonel handed her, and she and her ghostwriter—Frank Kearns, a journalist she had met in London when he was part of the U.S. Army's Counterintelligence Corps—had set to work. When the manuscript was finished, Colonel McAndrew only required a dozen small changes. She and Frank had made them, the colonel approved the manuscript, and the publisher rushed the book into print in the fall of 1948, when lots of people seemed to think the General would be running for president. (That didn't happen until four years later.) *Eisenhower*

Was My Boss had stayed on the bestseller lists for months, was serialized in a magazine and newspapers, and earned enough so that she hadn't had to worry about money for a while. The hardcover edition had gone into four printings within three months and had sold over a hundred thousand copies. And then there was the paperback, and the British edition. No, money hadn't been a problem.

Ike, too, had written a book, *Crusade in Europe*, which came out the month after hers. Kay wasn't surprised to see that he had mentioned her just once. Of course—he could hardly have told the truth, could he? And then they both simply went on with their lives. She had moved to New York, worked at Bergdorf Goodman on Fifth Avenue, married, divorced, and then went back to work, this time as a fashion consultant for CBS Television.

Ike served two years as Army Chief of Staff, resigned to become (astonishingly, she thought) the president of Columbia University, then (not so surprisingly) the Supreme Commander of NATO. And then, of course, what he must have been aiming for all the time: President of the United States. He had been in his second term when Telek died, and she had written to tell him about it. He didn't answer. A president was likely too busy to remember a small black dog—and how much the little Scottie had meant to two lonely people.

After eight years in the White House, the Eisenhowers had retired to a farm at Gettysburg, where Ike raised cows and pigs and chickens. But illness caught up with him. He'd had two heart attacks and a stroke and other illnesses while he was president, and more cardiac problems and other illnesses after he retired. He had seemed to shrink a little with each bout, Kay thought, and every time she saw a newspaper photograph of him, he looked a little older.

She had cried when he died, but she'd been relieved, too. His war was over at last.

Her own war would be over soon too, the doctors said. But that wasn't the reason she had decided to write the second book—to change the story, to tell the *truth*.

Over the years, she had occasionally heard rumors about a letter to General Marshall that Ike was supposed to have written sometime after V-E Day. She'd first become aware of it in 1952, when Eisenhower was running for president. Somebody had asked her about it then, but all she could say was that she didn't know anything about a letter, and please go away and stop bothering her. The same thing happened again in 1956, when Ike was running for a second term against Adlai Stevenson. But it wasn't until after the General's death that the story made it into print.

It came from President Truman. In *Plain Speaking*, a book published in 1973, Truman had told a biographer, Merle Miller, that Ike had written to Marshall, saying that he wanted to divorce Mamie and marry Kay. Marshall had replied that if he "even came close to doing such a thing" he would see to it that the rest of his life was (in Truman's words) "a living hell."

Truman's story broke in the newspapers in late 1973, when Kay was recovering from the surgery. She was stunned, at first scarcely able to believe it, and then swept by a joy that left her giddy and breathless. Ike *had* loved her! He had wanted to spend the rest of his life with her! That he had made another choice seemed not to matter, now that so many years had passed. And Truman's report came at an important moment for her. The doctors told her she had only months to live. There was a mountain of medical bills and no way to pay them—unless she sold the one thing she had to sell: her story.

The story of her love affair with Ike. The *true* story, the one that would set the record straight. Finding a publisher wouldn't be difficult, for as soon as *Plain Speaking* hit the bookstores, she had begun getting calls. But there was still the matter of that document she had been required to sign when she was writing her first memoir. The *true* story would violate the terms of her agreement. What would happen then?

As soon as she got out of the hospital, she took the document to her lawyer. He read it carefully, frowning, then put it down and took off his glasses. "Looks to me like this document covers only the first book," he said. "I think you're in the clear for a second book." Then he had added, tapping his pencil on the desk, "However, that doesn't mean that the Eisenhower family won't object."

"What happens if they do?" she asked. "Will they sue me?"

"Forgive me for being blunt, Kay," he had said softly. "Will it matter to you?"

She had chuckled at that. In a way, her death sentence set her free. She could tell her story—she could tell the *truth*—and they couldn't hurt her. But the truth could hurt someone else.

"Can I instruct the publisher to hold the book until Mamie dies?" she asked. Mamie—whose "fragile" health Ike had fretted about during the war—was still going strong. She might live for another decade. "There are things in the story . . ."

"You can try," the lawyer said. "But it's been my experience that in a case like this, the publisher—" He broke off. "Who's your publisher?"

"Simon and Schuster."

"What's the advance? If you don't mind my asking."

"They're paying me half of twenty-five thousand when I sign the contract, and another twenty-five when I deliver the manuscript." She frowned. "Of course, the ghostwriter has to be paid out of that. But Bantam is already interested in a paperback edition, so there will be another advance."

"Who's your ghostwriter?"

"Her name is Sigrid Hedin."

"Yes. Well, back to your question about Mamie. Unless you're around to object, the publisher can do pretty much what he wants to do. The book will no doubt be a hot property, and Simon and Schuster will want to get it out quickly." He slid her a sympathetic glance. "Do you think you'll finish it before . . ."

Before you die, he had wanted to say, Kay thought. "I honestly don't know," she confessed. "I'm doing my best, but there are days when I just don't feel up to it. If I don't get it done, there's a clause in the contract that allows the publisher to finish it for me." She made a face. "Should I be worried about that?"

"Only if you think the editor will make important changes in the story." He regarded her curiously. "Do you?"

"I don't know," she said. "I suppose he might." The changes Colonel McAndrew had made in her first book simply made the General look better. But this was much different. Unless the Eisenhower family somehow managed to suppress the whole book—

"Yes, well." The lawyer shifted uncomfortably. "There will also be serial rights, dramatic rights." He looked at her. "Has anybody approached you about movie rights?"

"No." Kay was startled. A movie? Would anybody want to make a movie of her book? Wouldn't it be too—

"I'm sure that one of the studios will be interested," the lawyer said. "Have your agent refer them to me. You just concentrate on finishing that book, before . . ." His voice trailed off.

"I will," Kay said. "Thank you."

&

So that's what she had done, although it hadn't been easy. She had liked working with Sigrid, but her editor hadn't been especially pleased with their draft of the first dozen chapters and had brought in another writer, a woman named Barbara Wyden. Barbara had written several books and ghostwritten more. She seemed to know what she was doing, and the editor was comfortable with her.

Kay had tape recorded parts of the book and written out others. She wanted to make sure that the love scenes—this was a *romance*, after all—would be handled tastefully, without sensationalizing them. Writing was hard, because while she had told the story once, she hadn't told the most private and personal parts of it. Because she had never indulged in self-revelation. Because she had been silent for so long, and there were so many memories, and all of them bittersweet.

Memories of plucky little Telek—she and Ike had loved him as dearly as if he'd been their child. Of evenings at the bridge table and afternoons on horseback, of early-morning breakfasts over coffee and Mickey's scrambled eggs and bacon. Of eyes meeting in the rearview mirror, of covert smiles, of hands touching at the desk. Of their first attempt at lovemaking on the sofa at Hay's Lodge, when Ike's difficulty had been understandable, given the war's terrible pressures and his problems with Mamie. Of the other times, when they were *one and one*, as he liked to say. To tell the truth, that was a part of their relationship that gave her great pleasure: knowing that he had desired her and that she had fulfilled his desire when Mamie couldn't, or wouldn't. That she had comforted him in the worst of times and given him the strength to go on when the night seemed darkest.

That was what was important. That was what she wanted her book to show. That Ike had loved her and she had loved him and that they had found delight in one another, and comfort and release, and even joy.

There are lots of things I could say. You know them.

Yes, she knew.

℘

Kay kept her tiny apartment on Park Avenue until after Christmas. Then, as the old year ended and the new year began, she went to stay at the little vacation cottage in Southampton, where she could taste the wild salt wind that blew across the beach, reminding her of Inish Beg and Ireland and that long-ago sea voyage on the doomed *Strathallan*. She worked on her book as much as she was able, but she knew she wouldn't see the end of it. Barbara's typescript—about three quarters of the book—lay on the table next to her bed. She was pleased with what they had done, and she had given Barbara a very clear outline of the rest. But something else was troubling her.

Her editor had gotten a call from a lawyer representing John Eisenhower, whom Kay remembered as the deferential young man who had invited her to his mother's party and then taken her to New York to see *Oklahoma!* The lawyer said that the Eisenhower family had heard about the book. He wanted to get a look at it before it was published.

"I said no, of course," the editor had assured her over the telephone. "But I'd love to come out to Southampton for a visit. Are you feeling up to it?"

The January day was too blustery to go out on the deck, so they sat at a window that looked out over a tiny corner of wild beach. The editor was a handsome, dark-haired man in his early forties, urbane and smartly dressed. As it turned out, he and Kay had something in common. Over tea, he told her that his stepmother had been a driver in London during the war—and that in the blackout she had actually struck the man who became his father with Lady Mountbatten's car outside Claridge's.

Kay had to laugh at that. "The war made the world very small," she said, remembering the times she had sat at the General's dinner table with Lord Mountbatten. But she didn't laugh at the suggestion the editor had come to make.

"I've chatted with the Eisenhowers' lawyer," he said. "Of course, I haven't shared your manuscript with him. From our conversation, however, I have the idea that the family would be a great deal more comfortable if the love scenes in your book were removed—or rewritten." He cleared his throat. "I've been thinking about this, and I have a suggestion—"

"No," Kay said firmly. "They are the heart of the story. It's a *love* story, after all. And surely Americans are sophisticated enough to accept the fact that people who love one another *make* love. The General has been dead for some time, and you've promised to hold the book until Mamie is gone, which surely can't be much longer." She thought briefly of the irony: that of the three of them,

Mamie would live the longest, in spite of the "fragile" health that had kept Ike from making love to her. "You've read that part of the manuscript," she added. "You can see that the scenes aren't the least bit sensational."

"I'm sure you're right," the editor said uncomfortably. "But of course the family does have an interest in protecting its . . . reputation."

With some sympathy, Kay noted his nervousness. He was, after all, in a rather vulnerable position. "I see," she said. "Well, then, what are you suggesting?"

He leaned forward eagerly. "I was wondering if perhaps we could just leave it as you have it in that first love scene. The one at Hay's Lodge, I mean. That's the one where Ike failed. After that, we could say that he continued to . . . er, fail. He loved you dearly, but he couldn't consummate—"

"But that's not what happened," Kay protested. "In fact, Ike wanted a child. Now that I know about his letter to General Marshall, I believe it was one of the reasons he wanted us to marry. He wanted a family." The words tumbled out now, propelled by a strong conviction. "He'd lost his little boy, Icky, you see, and he thought he had missed a big part of his son John's life. He was only fifty-four. Lots of older men have children, and having a child seemed important to him. He wouldn't have wanted that if he hadn't been able to . . ."

"Please." The editor set his teacup down. "Please don't upset yourself, Kay. And don't give it another thought. It was just an idea, you know. A way for us to accommodate the family's concerns and still have the book *you* want. But obviously it's not something you—"

"It's *not*," Kay said passionately. She was breathing hard. "It's a lie."

And then she smiled a little to herself, remembering the night at Sous le Vent when Ike had said to her that if anyone asked about their relationship, they could just lie. "It's nobody's goddamned business," he had said—and here she was *refusing* to lie. It was ironic.

The editor put out his hand in a soothing gesture. "I'm sorry if I've upset you," he said. "I am prepared to stand by your book and everything that's in it. Your story is important. It needs to be told, in its entirety, of course." He smiled toothily. "Let's say no more about it, shall we?"

"Thank you." Kay leaned back in her chair.

They would say no more about it. But she could guess what was going to happen. John Eisenhower was a powerful man, and Mamie—a former First Lady—was many people's ideal of a loving, devoted wife. David Eisenhower, Ike's grandson, had married Julie Nixon, the daughter of former president Richard Nixon. These were important families, with influence. The editor and his publisher might find themselves cornered and—once she was no longer around to make a fuss about truth and lies—forced to make concessions. They might take out the love scenes altogether. Her relationship with Ike might be portrayed as intimate, perhaps even devoted, but incomplete, unconsummated. Or perhaps the book wouldn't even be published—although since it seemed poised to make a great deal of money, that didn't seem likely. They would want to publish the book. They would want it to sell a hundred thousand copies. They would want it to be made into a movie.

And they would do whatever it took to make that happen. *He's theirs, Kathleen*, her mother had said. *They've made him. They'll never let you have him.* In the end, Kay knew, her mother was right—and there wasn't a damn thing she could do about it.

"Well, then." She sat up straight and reached for the pot. "Would you like another cup of tea?"

☙

Later, after the editor had gone, Kay lay on her bed, knowing that this book, this final truth she had to offer, was out of her hands now. The ghostwriter would do what the editor told her to do. And the editor would do whatever he found necessary, depending on who leaned on him. She might as well stop worrying about it. She wouldn't be around to see how it turned out.

That morning, she had written what she thought might be the very last paragraph. She hoped they would leave it just as it was:

> Now that I am very close to the end of my life, I have a strong sense of being close to Ike again. It is almost as if he were looking over my shoulder as I write. Laughing now and then. Saying, "Christ, I'd completely forgotten about that." Or "Oh, that was a great day. Didn't we have a good time that day!" Right now, he's saying "Goddamn it, don't cry."

Kay lay back against the pillow. As she closed her eyes, she thought of the night she had stood on the deck of the dying *Strathallan* under a canopy of aloof and distant stars, with five thousand others, standing together—the moment at which one part of her life had ended and a new life began. And of the afternoon she learned that Dick was dead and that there would be no marriage, no children. And of Ike's letter, when once again, her future was an empty horizon. Of all the moments when her life had changed, and she had to go on alone.

And then she saw Telek, dear Telek, trotting toward her. He had been gone for fifteen years now, but she saw him as gay and gallant and sweet as ever, and she knew he was asking to be taken for a walk.

"Come on, then, funny little boy." She smiled and bent over to stroke his lovely black fur. "It's time. Let's go."

It was.

CHAPTER TWENTY-THREE
The Last Word

Gettysburg, Pennsylvania
August 1979

Mamie was alone now, spending much of her time in her bed-room at the Gettysburg farm that she and Ike had bought in 1950 as their "retirement home." Which of course it wasn't, not then. It was another ten years before Ike turned the Oval Office over to Jack Kennedy, that *boy*, and they left the White House.

But the farm had been worth waiting for. The century-old brick farmhouse had needed a massive renovation before Mamie would even consider living there, but it had a lovely view of the South Mountains rising to the west eight miles away, and three gorgeous ash trees in front. In the remodeling, she had insisted that the bedroom windows be lowered so she could see out from her bed: her *pink* bed—with pink sheets, pink spread, and pink uphol-stered headboard—in a room that boasted pink damask draperies, pale green walls, and mint green rugs.

Most days, Mamie loved to lie in that bed and watch the robins and squirrels in the huge ash tree outside the window. Now, though, she was watching Rosalynn Carter sitting in on one of President Carter's Cabinet meetings, taking notes. The television commentator had just said, approvingly, that Ms. Carter also advised the President on his speeches and arranged his appointments. Quoting *Time* magazine, he added that Ms. Carter was the "second most powerful person in the United States."

Testily, Mamie grabbed the remote and turned off the set. She detested the word *Ms.* A woman was either a Miss or a Mrs., nothing in-between. What's more, she herself had visited the Oval Office only four times—four!—in the entire eight years Ike had run the country. It would never have occurred to him to ask *her* to sit beside him and take notes or arrange his calendar. That was a job for a secretary, for heaven's sake, not for a wife. That's something Ann Whitman would have done.

At the thought of Ike's young, attractive personal secretary, Mamie frowned. She had tried her best to get Ann fired before the 1952 election, but Ike had found out about it and told her "nothing doing" in that flat, this-is-an-order tone. So she'd had no choice but to tolerate Ann Whitman for the next eight years, although she didn't have to be *nice* to her. Ike's staffers said she was jealous, and maybe she was, but so what? She was his wife, wasn't she? She had a right to be jealous, especially after Kay Summersby. And after Ike's brother Edgar married *his* secretary. Now, *really*.

But when Ike decided he wanted to keep Ann with him after they moved to the farm, Mamie had put her foot down—although not directly to Ike, of course. She had simply made things so unpleasant for Ann that she finally took the hint and found another employer. In Mamie's opinion, it was really too bad when women thought they had to have an outside job. The division of labor she preferred was so much better all around: the husband worked, the wife managed the home. It was very simple. "Ike runs the country," she liked to say. "I turn the pork chops."

Well, not exactly. Mamie had never learned to cook, so if they were having pork chops for dinner it was because the cook turned them or Ike turned them—he was the chef in the family. His specialties were quail hash (with birds he shot himself), beef stew, and steaks on the grill. When she was responsible for the meal, it was TV dinners in the Radarange. She'd rather spend her time playing

Scrabble, watching soap operas and *I Love Lucy*, or listening to Lawrence Welk.

Except that these days, even Lawrence Welk and *The Guiding Light* had lost their appeal, and she had watched so many reruns of *Lucy* that they weren't funny anymore. The truth was, she was bored. When she was First Lady, there was always something interesting to do. Because she spent a lot of her days in bed, people said she was . . . well, lazy. Of course she wasn't. Maybe she hadn't remodeled the White House or planted flowers along the freeways like Mrs. Johnson or attended Cabinet meetings like Mrs. Carter.

But during her eight years in the White House, she had launched charity drives, served as honorary president of the Girl Scouts, and sponsored the Easter Seal campaign. She had included Negro children in the annual Easter Egg Roll and approved of Marian Anderson singing at Ike's inaugural ceremony. She had whipped the White House staff into shape (Ike said she reminded him of General Patton) and established a chain of command in the domestic staff. She hired fifteen staff members to answer the seven hundred letters she got every month; she knew that people were thrilled to get a personal reply with her signature on it. She completed the collection of presidential china and painted so many rooms pink that some wag in the press corps renamed the White House the Pink Palace. Of course, her pink walls were nothing like the "historic restoration" Mrs. Kennedy did, which Mamie had never quite gotten over. The White House as a museum, with all that antique, Frenchified furniture? It wasn't very American, was it? You'd think a First Lady would have a little more common sense, even if she did graduate from Vassar.

But what Mamie loved most about being in the White House was that she was the *boss*. People had to do things the way she told them, or she made them do it over again. People lined up to talk to her, to see her, to shake her hand. She was in demand. She was *wanted*. People accepted her as the power behind the throne. She didn't even mind it when they said that Ike ran the country but Mamie ran Ike.

And she and Ike traveled. She had decided that her heart was strong enough to fly, after all, so while he was president, they took lots of trips. Even after Ike retired, they took trips. In the springtime, they went to Georgia, to the Augusta National Golf Club, where he liked to spend all day out on the course. In the winter, they lived at the El Dorado Country Club in Palm Desert, California, where he played golf and worked on his memoirs. Mamie did her best to keep a watchful eye over his health, but he hated it when she told him he ought to wear a hat or boots or a muffler or stop using so much salt—and especially when she told him he should cut back on the number of speeches he gave.

But she refused to feel guilty about telling Pat Nixon (behind Ike's back, of course) that she was worried about his health and that he really shouldn't campaign for Dick when he was running for president against Kennedy in 1960. Mamie knew that Ike was hurt because Dick didn't ask him and that Dick thought the President's noticeable absence from the campaign trail had cost him the election. But she didn't care that he held it against her. She'd never much liked Nixon anyway.

But all that excitement was gone now, and she had to depend on her own resources, which had never been all that dependable. These last few years . . . well, she felt pretty much the same way she'd felt during the war. Isolated. Left out. "On the shelf," she had told her sister Mike.

Or maybe "left behind" was a better term. Times had changed. People made fun of "Mamie pink," and "Mamie bangs" were definitely passé. Now, women had children *and* careers, and her definition of marriage as an arrangement where the husband ran his business and the wife ran the home seemed terribly out of date. She didn't understand why her granddaughters would want to divorce their perfectly nice husbands and start new lives, and the disapproval she didn't bother to hide strained family relationships. She tried to do what she knew Ike would want: stay optimistic. But she had always pretty much considered herself as an extension of him, and now that he was gone . . . well, there wasn't that much left of *her.*

Mamie was nearing eighty-three now. Her life was tranquil, except for a few health problems—and that old Summersby business, of course. Somehow, the stories just wouldn't go away. Every now and then, something would pop up in the newspapers, and she would get a few dozen sympathy letters from "friends." She hated those letters, for they all had to be answered, and what was she supposed to say?

The truth of the matter was . . . that she simply didn't know the truth of the matter. When Ike came back from Europe after the war, he had refused to talk about it. She asked him once or twice, but he gave her a stony look and turned away. Mamie didn't want to press the questions because she didn't want to hear the answers. As long as she didn't actually know what had happened between her husband and that woman, she could tell everyone, especially herself, that of course he had been completely faithful.

Her doubts were still there, though, just as they had been during the war, when he kept writing all those letters full of protestations of love, so utterly unlike him. So the more often he wrote things like *You are the only girl for me* and *I haven't been in love with anyone else and don't want any other wife*, the more she suspected that he was up to something.

But Mamie had always made sure that her doubts were *her* doubts. She buried them in her heart and never spoke a word about them, either to him or to anybody in the family. If the subject ever came up, she would just lift her chin and smile dismissively. "Least said, soonest mended," her mother had always said, and that was Mamie's philosophy, too. If you simply smiled and didn't talk about something bad, it would go away.

But this didn't. Over the years, the stories kept turning up, and even though Mamie didn't let on that she heard them, of course she did. For instance, back in 1947, people around Ike were worried about the book Mrs. Summersby was writing, until they got her to sign some sort of paper agreeing not to write anything that might embarrass Ike. Five years later, during the 1952 presidential campaign, she had heard Ike's staffers whispering about a letter he had written to General Marshall, saying he wanted to divorce her and marry that woman. They were concerned that if the letter surfaced during the campaign, it could keep Ike out of the White House. Mamie didn't believe there was any such letter, of course. Ike would never consider *divorce*. She just held up her head and kept smiling.

Then in 1973, Harry Truman was quoted as saying that he had actually seen the letter *and* General Marshall's angry reply, and Truman's military aide chimed in to support him. The former president might be a vulgar, hateful old man but he had a reputation for telling the unvarnished truth. Mamie finally had to accept the idea that Ike might have wanted to divorce her and marry the other woman. Smiling was difficult after that, but she did her best.

And then the unthinkable. The flurry over Truman's claim had just settled down when Kay Summersby's book, *Past Forgetting*, was published. Mamie knew that the family wanted to keep her in the dark about it, so it was never mentioned when they got together. But she read reviews with headlines like BOOK TELLS ALL ABOUT FAMOUS LOVE AFFAIR and POWERFUL GENERAL NOT SO POWERFUL WHEN THE LIGHTS WERE OUT (that one from a tabloid). And then *Parade* magazine reported that Bantam had paid $800,000 for the paperback rights.

Well! If the book was worth *that* much, Mamie thought she ought to know what was in it. So she dispatched her maid to Philadelphia to buy a copy. (Buying it in Gettysburg, of course, would have let the cat out of the bag. You couldn't do anything in that little town without having everybody know about it.) She hid the book in her undies drawer for several days until she screwed up enough courage to read it. Once she began, she wished she hadn't, for there were things in the book that sounded just like Ike and made her miss him terribly. *Past Forgetting* was obviously written by a woman who had known him inside and out. When she finished it, she pulled the pillow over her head and cried harder than she had cried when he died.

Which in a way made sense, for now she knew that the story was true. Ike *had* loved the woman. He *had* wanted to marry her. And he hadn't come home to her, Mamie, to his wife: he had come home to his duty, and his country, and the possibility that he might be president. For that, and not for *her*, he had given up the love of his life.

But she had to be brave. She got up and washed her face and put on fresh powder and her favorite pink lipstick, reminding herself that, technically speaking, there hadn't been an *affair*, not really. The book made that clear—and of course, you couldn't have an affair if you didn't have sex. Which wasn't news to her, naturally, for sex hadn't been part of their marriage, even before the war.

And in the end, she convinced herself that *she* had been the ultimate winner. She was the one who had ridden with Ike in all those ticker-tape parades. She was the one who had been elected to the White House with him, twice. She was the one with whom he had spent the rest of his life. As she had said when their new king-sized bed was installed in their pink bedroom in the White House, "Now I've got Ike right where I want him. I can reach over and pat him on his old bald head anytime I want to." And it was true. She had him *exactly* where she wanted him.

Kay Summersby, on the other hand, had gotten exactly nothing, except for that silly little dog with the ridiculous name, and whatever she was paid for her story. But she didn't live to enjoy that, either. She had died of cancer almost two years before her book was published, and it was said that her earnings went to pay her medical bills. And of course, people would eventually get tired of talking about her memoir and it would disappear from the bookstores.

But that didn't happen. The book had only been out a few months when the newspapers announced that ABC TV had paid a quarter of a million dollars for the film rights and were planning to make a six-hour miniseries. Six hours of her husband and that woman, on national television! The thought filled her with horror, and she immediately telephoned John.

"I'm sure it will be just dreadful, John," she said, in her most steely voice. "You have to put a stop to it."

John got an early look at the script. And then, as indignant as his mother, he ordered the family lawyers to sue ABC TV. The project was put on hold while the lawsuit was pending, and after almost a year, the network knuckled under. They directed the screenwriter, Melville Shavelson, to rewrite the script and take out the bad parts. Mamie shuddered to think what the movie could have looked like if she and John hadn't put their foot down. Robert Duvall and Lee Remick might have ripped their clothes off and jumped in bed together.

But they had their way. The program was aired in May, 1979, and Mamie watched the whole thing. "Of course, the story is all very silly," she said to her maid, Beatrix, who watched it with her. "There isn't a blessed thing true about it, except for the war scenes." She supposed they were true, since that part was all documentary footage provided by the army. And even though the credits said that the script was "based on" *Past Forgetting*, it wasn't anything like the book, thank heaven. Robert Duvall was properly military, Mamie thought. Lee Remick, a flirtatious little kitten of a girl, had to make do with an arm around the shoulders.

Mamie was upset about one thing, though. "Oh, how ugly they've made me look!" she exclaimed to Beatrix. "But then, they had to, I suppose," she added. "After all, I'm the villain of the piece."

She thought about that for a moment. Yes, she supposed that—if what you were after was a lovers' triangle—the wife would have to be the villain of the piece.

She frowned. Did that make Kay the heroine?

છ૭

Two months after the movie (and just four months before her death), Mamie telephoned ABC and said that she would be glad to talk to Barbara Walters, who had been pestering her for years for an interview. During the interview, which was taped at the farm, Barbara asked if her marriage to Ike had ever been in jeopardy. Pertly, Mamie replied, "All marriages are in jeopardy, of course. That's where your good sense comes in."

"Well, yes," Barbara agreed. She leaned forward, showing her teeth in a beguiling smile, and popped the sixty-four-thousand-dollar question. "But didn't you ever worry that while Ike was away at war, he might be with someone else? After all, you were apart for three whole years."

Mamie lifted her chin. "I wouldn't have stayed with him five minutes if I hadn't had the biggest respect for him," she replied. It was the last word she would say on the matter.

Barbara didn't seem to notice that she hadn't answered the question.

A BIOGRAPHICAL EPILOGUE
Kay Summersby, Missing Person

Omission is the most powerful form of lie.

George Orwell

The only thing new in the world is the history you do not know.

Harry S. Truman

I think one of the most interesting things about autobiography is what the autobiographer leaves out. . . . We look at a chair and we see the solid: We see the chair's shape in the wood. In looking at an autobiography, it's as if you're looking at the voids in the chair in order to see the form. Look at what the author is not telling you.

David McCullough

If Eisenhower's family, friends, and followers had their way, Kay Summersby would have become a missing person.[1]

We know all about Ike and Mamie. Their lives have been documented in literally hundreds of memoirs, biographies, histories, and films. But Kay's personal postwar history is much less well known and difficult to trace, perhaps because, as Ike's biographer Jean Edward Smith wryly remarks, "The burnishers of Eisenhower's image have worked overtime to eradicate her from the record."[2]

She was airbrushed out of the official photograph taken in Eisenhower's office after the signing of Germany's surrender. Harry Butcher mentions her only five times in the 876 pages of the published version of his detailed war diary, *My Three Years with Eisenhower*. Mickey McKeogh, Ike's orderly, doesn't mention her once in his personal memoir, *Sgt. Mickey and General Ike*, even though McKeogh and Kay spent a part of almost every day together from July 1942 to July 1945. And in his military memoir, *Crusade in Europe*, Eisenhower mentions her just once (page 133), as a member of his personal staff: "Kay Summersby was corresponding secretary and doubled as a driver."

It is true that Kay is mentioned frequently in almost every book about Eisenhower in World War II. But while biographers turn to her memoir, *Eisenhower Was My Boss*, as a valuable source of detailed information about the General's wartime life, they generally reject her claim in *Past Forgetting* of an intimate relationship—denials that seem to be based on little else than the intuitive conviction that Dwight David Eisenhower could not have cheated on his wife and the belief that he could have had no intention of marrying Summersby. Carlo D'Este's dismissal is typical: "It is extremely improbable that this affinity ever developed into something deeper."[3] Stephen Ambrose is willing to acknowledge a "close relationship" (whatever that means) but rejects the idea that Ike might have wanted to make it more permanent. While Kay was "the third most important woman in [Eisenhower's] life, behind only his mother and his wife," Ike "never thought of marrying [her]."[4]

Some biographers venture further. In a lengthy, four-page discussion of the relationship, Geoffrey Perret explains obligingly that "Eisenhower needed [Kay] and he indirectly admitted as much and . . . she read into his admission a passion that was not there and never would be. . . . For all that Kay Summersby wrote about love, she knew little about it, for throughout her unhappy life it eluded her."[5] Fine stuff if you're writing a novel—much less helpful in what is supposed to be a biography.

It is certainly true that, after the war, Kay Summersby became persona non grata in Eisenhower circles. But while she may have been airbrushed out of the picture, she never quite disappeared. In fact, for the rest of her life and beyond, she lingered like a threatening ghost in the margins and footnotes of the Eisenhower epic, telling first one story and then another about her three years with the Supreme Commander. And while each of her memoirs— *Eisenhower Was My Boss* (1948) and the posthumous *Past Forgetting* (1976)—tells a different and overlapping part of her story, neither tells the whole truth. Nor is it clear what the truth is, for as David Eisenhower remarks in his biography of his grandfather, the truth is "known only by them, and both are gone."

But it is possible to know some things. For example, it isn't true (as some have said) that Ike and Kay never saw or heard from one another again. Quite the contrary, in fact. There was frequent contact between them, at least by letter, until Kay's marriage in 1952, just two weeks after Dwight David Eisenhower became the thirty-fourth President of the United States.

And it's possible to know other things. What follows is an account of the arc of Kay's postwar life that I have pieced together from official documents, letters, diaries, and contemporary newspaper stories, along with my own inferences and speculations.

℘

When Eisenhower's staff was sent to Washington in November 1945, Kay was ordered to Berlin. Taking her faithful Scottie Telek with her, she worked from January to September 1946 under General Lucius Clay, the deputy governor of the U.S. Zone. (A close friend of Eisenhower's, Clay would become an adviser in his 1952 presidential campaign, help assemble his first-term cabinet, and serve in his administration.)

Kay was promoted to the rank of WAC captain in early 1946. Around that time, Ike wrote to ask her to type the official diary she had kept for him during the European campaign, and they exchanged several letters about the project.[6] In one letter (January 15, 1946), he sympathizes with Kay's desire to leave her position on General Clay's Berlin staff and offers help in finding her a job at the United Nations. In a note on the typed letter, he wrote:

> This scrawl is just to say that whatever I can do for you will be done—I don't know whether the citizenship thing [Kay was still a British citizen] will enter the picture, but all we can do is try to get you a job. I believe the organization will be stationed near N.Y. City. In any event, don't get downhearted.[7]

The letter continues the theme of "I want to help," which persists throughout their correspondence. In another letter (March 11, 1946), he says, "Our pups are doing splendidly. The one that I call 'Telek' looks exactly like his dad."[8] The puppy Telek must have been a constant reminder to him of the Scottie he and Kay had shared, and the reference to "our pups" may be a coded statement to Kay that she was remembered. In fact, the last sentence in the dictated and typed letter is even more explicit: "All of us miss you and send you our warm regard."

Kay's Berlin job—she managed the visits of military and civilian VIPs—seemed routine and she must have missed the daily excitement and sense of urgencies of the war. She had already (in October 1945) initiated citizenship proceedings; a year later, she left Telek temporarily in the care of General Clay and sailed to the States aboard the army transport ship *General SD Sturgis*. She arrived in New York on October 10, 1946, and renewed her citizenship effort in the District Court of Washington, D.C., on November 18.[9] Telek flew to California four months later, making the trip on an American Overseas Airlines plane in the personal custody of the pilot. At a layover in New York, newspaper photographers snapped his picture. There were more photographers waiting in California; wire-service photographs of Eisenhower's little dog and the attractive Kay, still in uniform, appeared in many newspapers around the country, raising the question in many minds of a possible postwar relationship.

If Kay and Ike got together when she arrived in New York or when she went to Washington to pursue her citizenship, there is no record of the meeting. This isn't surprising since, by this time, Eisenhower would have been made aware of the hazards of a continuing association with her and was being closely monitored. As biographer Michael Korda notes, from the time he returned to the States in late 1945, the General was completely "protected" and "insulated" by a staff "whose primary purpose was to make him look good."[10]

However, this is *not* to say that Kay and Ike did not manage to meet privately. In fact, after Kay's death, one of her friends told a magazine writer that the pair privately "trysted for the final time" in her New York apartment after the war, perhaps when Kay arrived from Germany.[11] Seeing her without the knowledge of his staff and/or his wife might have presented a certain challenge, but Eisenhower could no doubt have done it if he chose. It is also not a surprise that there are no meetings (other than a brief office encounter with Telek and another on the Columbia campus) described in *Past Forgetting*.

At the time of her return to the United States in 1946, Kay was still in the service. She was ordered to Hamilton Field, north of San Francisco, as inconveniently far from Washington (and the General) as possible. Her job as an assistant public relations officer was even less eventful than her assignment in Berlin—until one night in February 1947, when a man entered the women officers' quarters, picked Kay's room at random, and attempted to rape her. She screamed for help and he was apprehended almost immediately.[12] He confessed to other attempts and the matter dragged out until September, when he was found guilty and sentenced to fifteen years.

The publicity created by her attacker's arrest and trial proved difficult for Kay. She applied in May for a compassionate discharge and was separated in July 1947. In April, her mother came from

England for a visit, apparently stopping off in Washington to see Eisenhower. Replying to a letter from Kay in May of that year, he wrote, "I know that your mother's visit must be a real treat for you both."[13]

Kay had kept in touch with Harry Butcher, Ike's naval aide, after the war. Butch had divorced his wife Ruth (Mamie's wartime roommate) and married Molly, the Red Cross worker whom he met in Algiers. In the spring of 1947, Kay visited Butch and Molly at their home in Santa Barbara, where Butch had just launched Radio KIST. During the visit, she likely told Butch that she was considering writing a book about her wartime experiences. She still had in her possession the two wartime diaries that she and Eisenhower had maintained in 1944 and 1945, which Eisenhower had already suggested she might use for a book.[14] Butch, whose gossipy diary of the war was published by Simon and Schuster in 1946, may have referred her to his literary agent, George Bye. (Bye, a well-known New York agent, had a number of high-profile clients, including Eleanor Roosevelt, Charles Lindbergh, Rebecca West, and Rose Wilder Lane and Lane's mother, Laura Ingalls Wilder). Butch also wrote to Ike to let him know that Kay was considering writing a memoir. It's fair to say that this news would not have been greeted with enthusiasm by Eisenhower staffers, whose experience of Butcher's book had not been positive.[15]

Back on the East Coast in the summer of 1947, Kay took Telek to visit Eisenhower in his office in the Pentagon, the first opportunity to reunite Ike with their dog since the Scottie had arrived from Germany in March. Eisenhower, Kay says, invited her to bring Telek back to see him and—once again—offered to help her find a job.

There's something of a mystery about what happened next in Kay's life. I haven't been able to find any direct documentation, but we can reconstruct the narrative from a letter Eisenhower wrote to her and an entry in his diary. She seems to have written to Eisenhower sometime in early November from the Commodore Hotel in New York, letting him know of a change in her "wedding plans." Eisenhower replied on November 12 that he was grateful to her for informing him of the change and sent his regrets.[16] Three weeks later, he wrote in his diary (a diary he intended for later publication):

> I heard today, through a mutual friend, that my wartime secretary (rather personal aide and receptionist) is in dire straits. A clear case of a fine person going to pieces over the death of a loved one, in this instance the man she was all set to marry. I'll do what I can to help. . . . Makes one wonder whether any human ever dares become so wrapped up in another that all happiness and desire to live is determined by the actions, desires—or life—of the second. I trust she pulls herself together, but she is Irish and tragic.[17]

This cannot be, as some have suggested, a reference to the 1943 death of Kay's fiancé, Colonel Richard Arnold, and it cannot be a reference to Kay's 1952 marriage to Reginald Morgan, who was at this time still married to his second wife. Taken with the letter of November 12, it seems to suggest that Kay planned to marry in late 1947, but that the "man she was all set to marry" unfortunately died. If this is true, it would be the second such tragedy in her life. Whoever the man was and whatever happened, the details have dropped out of the records, and all we have left are hints of this tragedy—and Ike's unusual (for him) personal reflection on the high cost of emotional involvement.

In early December, living in a New York hotel and looking for options, Kay considered the possibility of reentering the service.[18] But by the end of 1947, she had taken a job with Tex McCrary, a well-known American journalist and public relations specialist.[19] McCrary, widely hailed as the creator of the talk-show format on radio and television, was organizing a worldwide news service for radio and television, with correspondents anchored at strategic spots around the globe. Kay may have met McCrary in Algiers, where he served during the war as a public relations officer for the Mediterranean Allied Air Forces. Or Eisenhower or one of his staffers (making good on the promise to help her find a job) may have recommended her.

In the early months of 1948, Kay was sharing an apartment on East Sixty-Ninth Street in New York with Anita Roberts, a former WAC who had occasionally been a fourth at Eisenhower's bridge table. At work on the wartime memoir that would be published as *Eisenhower Was My Boss*, Kay had fired her first ghostwriter and replaced him with Frank Kearns.[20] Her work on the project was interrupted in May 1948, when her sister Sheila died unexpectedly and she went to England to care for her mother, who had suffered a nervous breakdown. She wrote to Eisenhower to tell him of Sheila's death and let him know about her book.[21] The next day, he wrote sympathetically to both Kay and her mother: "It is distressing to learn of the tragedies in your family." He also expressed surprise to hear about the book (he believed that Kay had returned to military service), but complimented her on her choice of George Bye as an agent: "I feel you are possessed of a fine adviser in George Bye."[22]

The publisher (Prentice-Hall) wanted to call the book *Eisenhower's "Girl Friday"* but Eisenhower objected. In a July 1948 letter to George Bye, he said he didn't see why the book had to have his name on it and proposed the title *A WAC in SHAEF*. He also wrote to the editor at Prentice-Hall, Myron L. Boardman. To Kay, he summarized his concern and added: "You know, of course, I wish you the best of luck in this publishing venture."[23]

Kay returned from England in time to receive the British Empire Medal, awarded by the British consulate in a ceremony on board the Cunard's *Britannic*. On her return, she handed over her notes, diaries, and manuscript drafts to her new ghostwriter, Frank Kearns, an American-intelligence-officer-turned-journalist who had been based in London during the war. A skilled writer and researcher with a comprehensive understanding of Eisenhower's campaigns, Kearns was recommended to Kay and to her editor at Prentice-Hall by Edward L. Saxe, who also served in London with Eisenhower.[24] It seems likely that Kay knew both Kearns and

Saxe; she certainly knew Saxe's wife, Anthea Gordon Saxe, who had also been a civilian driver in the Mechanised Transport Corps.[25] Both of the Saxes later became her literary executors.

At the time, Kearns and his wife, a British fashion model and showgirl named Gwendoline Ethel Shoring (an expat Brit whom Kay may also have known back in London) were living in an apartment on West Eightieth Street in New York and Kearns was working as a freelance writer for national magazines. He had only one month to produce the 110,000-word manuscript, because Prentice-Hall—anxious to capitalize on the publication of Eisenhower's memoir—was rushing Kay's book into print. The October publication of *Eisenhower Was My Boss* would be just one month ahead of Doubleday's November publication of Eisenhower's memoir, *Crusade in Europe*.

Kay and Kearns were paid an advance of one thousand dollars.[26] They split the advance evenly and agreed that Kay would get 73 percent of the royalties and Kearns 27 percent. The book received strongly positive reviews from Charles Poore and David Dempsey in the *New York Times* and quickly shot up to the top of the charts. Within two months, some twenty-five thousand hardcover copies were in print. The book was serialized in *Look* magazine in October and November and excerpts appeared in over fifty newspapers. It was widely—and positively—reviewed as "the inside story of a military command from a woman's point of view." One advertisement promised, "You'll enjoy the personal, human things Captain Summersby says about her boss." Another: "Her story is a report to women—the only one of its kind to come out of World War II." The book, with side-by-side photos of Kay and Ike, was front-page news all around the country.

Kay had sent Ike (who was just beginning to settle into his presidency at Columbia University) a prepublication copy of her book, and on September 30, 1948, he replied with a dictated thank-you note. In New York, she was staying at the Hotel Winslow at Madison Avenue and Fifty-Fifth Street, but she spent the autumn and part of the spring of 1949 on the lecture circuit, speaking on college campuses and at women's clubs, libraries, and bookstores. She also appeared on radio and on the popular quiz show *Twenty Questions*. In July 1949, she flew to England, where the UK edition of the book had been published by T. Werner Laurie Ltd. She visited her mother in London; they traveled through England and Scotland and visited relatives at Inish Beg.[27]

Returning to New York on the SS *America* at the end of October 1949, Kay found an apartment at 155 East Forty-Ninth and her name began to appear in the New York gossip columns. She sent a Christmas note to Eisenhower, saying that she was working with a travel service and finding the work "very interesting."[28] Walter Winchell reported in the *New York Daily Mirror* (January 16, 1950) that she had "quietly" opened a "midtown travel agency." Dorothy Kilgallen reported in the *New York Journal American* (May 29, 1950) that her agency was located at East Forty-Second Street. In the *Los Angeles Times*, Hedda Hopper (April 7, 1950) called the venture a "lecture bureau" and mentioned that Kay was visiting Hollywood.

Whatever the project, it apparently didn't last very long, for in the fall of 1950, Kay took a job as a "vendeuse" in women's upscale retail at Bergdorf Goodman, on Fifth Avenue in Manhattan, where she worked for the next two years. She mentioned the "very good job" in a Christmas 1950 note to Ike; it, too, may have come through the Eisenhower connection, although if it did, she doesn't mention this.[29] Her letter was written just two days before Eisenhower was named Supreme Allied Commander of the North Atlantic Treaty Organization and moved with Mamie to Paris.

Kay became an American citizen in February 1951. Late in that year, she sent a holiday card to Eisenhower, with a typed note mentioning that she would be spending Christmas in Washington with Ellen Ruthman (the WAC officer who served as Ike's dietician and supervisor of his personal mess when he was at the Pentagon) and that she would be joining the WACs who had served on his staff during the war for their fifth annual get-together. She was also looking forward to seeing Butch and Molly, who were visiting in

New York. She added "Telek continues to be in wonderful shape. He looks younger than ever."[30]

Eisenhower, meanwhile, had taken a two-year leave from the Columbia University presidency so that he could serve at NATO, and he and Mamie were living in a chateau outside Paris. In early 1952, he was persuaded to run for president as a Republican when he saw a remarkable promotional film created by Tex McCrary (for whom Kay worked in 1947–1948). McCrary arranged a "We Want Ike" rally in Madison Square Garden and recorded the rally on kinescope. It was designed to convince the General that there was a massive groundswell of enthusiasm for his candidacy. It did the trick. When Eisenhower saw the kinescope, he was so moved by the demonstration that he agreed to become a candidate.[31]

Eisenhower's path to the Republican nomination was contested by Senator Robert A. Taft. Taft's campaign claimed to have a copy of the letter Ike had written to General George Marshall shortly after V-E Day, saying that he intended to divorce Mamie and marry Kay. There were even suspicions that Ike and Kay had not ended their relationship when he left Germany. Around this time, Harry Butcher wrote to warn Ike that a "group of businessmen" were attempting to raise $15,000 to tap Kay's telephone and catch calls from Eisenhower.[32] Apparently, Taft's staffers also approached Kay, attempting to get information from her. In his *Mirror* column of January 30, 1952, Walter Winchell notes that Kay "jilted Taft forces attempting to 'woo' her." Heading the column is a photograph of Kay in uniform, holding Telek, who was apparently a familiar sight in New York social circles. The caption reads, "No Soap for Taftites." There is no mention of a letter, but the newspaper audience is presumed to be able to guess that Kay has some sort of secret knowledge about Ike that—if it were revealed—would derail his candidacy.

In the summer of 1952, Kay flew to London to visit her mother. As it happened, Eisenhower and Mamie were there at the same time. In *Past Forgetting*, Kay says that she sent a note to their suite in the Dorchester Hotel, inviting them to tea with her mother. Shortly, a young major appeared at her mother's house, saying that he was there at General Eisenhower's request. Over drinks, the young man said, "Kay, it's impossible. The General is really on a tight leash. He is not his own master."

"It was [Ike's] way of letting me know," Kay writes, "that I still did mean something to him."[33] On September 24, *New York Post* columnist Earl Wilson mentions that Kay has returned from England. A month later, Wilson writes that Kay Summersby's Scottie "wears an Ike button."

Whatever the behind-the-scenes rumors and maneuvers, the issue of Eisenhower's relationship to Kay was not publicly aired in the 1952 presidential campaign. Eisenhower carried all but nine of the forty-eight states, and the Republicans, following the General's flag, took both the House and the Senate. The GOP was back in power, and Eisenhower was in command of the Oval Office.

∞

Two weeks after the election, Kay married Reginald T. H. Morgan, a partner in the New York brokerage firm of Dominick and Dominick. Kay was Morgan's third wife. His first wife had died and he was recently (June 12, 1952) divorced from his second wife. With the marriage, Kay gained four stepchildren. They said their vows in a quiet ceremony in a friend's home on East Seventy-Second Street. After a honeymoon at St. Croix in the Virgin Islands, they moved to New Canaan, Connecticut. Kay wrote to Ike to let him know of the marriage. In response, he wrote: "It was good to hear from you, particularly such happy tidings! Congratulations to the lucky groom, and to both of you my very best wishes for your continuing happiness."[34] So far as is known, it was his final letter to her.

The marriage didn't last. "It was an unfortunate experience," Kay said when the couple separated in 1957. She obtained an Alabama divorce on March 11, 1958.[35] (Morgan had other marital problems, as well. His second wife was suing him for failure to pay child support for their two children.)[36] At the time, Kay was living at 901 Lexington Avenue in New York, just three blocks from Central Park; she later moved to an apartment on Park Avenue. Through the mid-1960s, she worked as a fashion consultant for CBS Television, costuming such stars as Tallulah Bankhead, Greer Garson, and Peggy Lee. As a freelance costume designer, she worked with such shows as *Kraft Music Hall* and assisted one of Hollywood's top designers on films such as *The Group* and *The Night They Raided Minsky's*. Her last job was as a fashion consultant for *The Stepford Wives*.[37]

But while Ike might be gone from Kay's life and her marriage had proved to be a bad idea, Telek was still her constant companion—until his death in 1959, at the age of seventeen. "Such a gallant little dog. Such a faithful, loving friend," she writes in *Past Forgetting* (page 281). "From now on, there would always be something missing in my life: the spirit, the gaiety, the devotion of a small dog named Telek." The Scottie was her last link to Ike, who died ten years later, on March 28, 1969.

In 1973, Kay was diagnosed with liver cancer. The doctors gave her six months to live. At the same time, she learned that former President Harry Truman, in *Plain Speaking*, had confirmed the rumor that had been going the rounds for years. According to Truman, Ike had written "a letter to General Marshall saying that he wanted to come back to the United States and divorce Mrs. Eisenhower so that he could marry this Englishwoman."[38] Truman's statement was confirmed by his aide, Major General Harry Vaughan.

Stunned by the former president's statement, Kay says that she decided to write a second memoir that would—now that the General was dead and she was dying—tell the "truth" about the affair. She began working with a ghostwriter named Sigrid Hedin. The work was partially done when Hedin was paid and released and another ghostwriter, Barbara Wyden, took over the project. The publishing house Simon and Schuster reportedly paid Kay

$50,000—more than a quarter of a million dollars in today's money. From this amount Kay paid Hedin $8,500 and Wyden $25,000. Wyden worked from Kay's tapes and notes.[39] Kay is said to have seen about 75 percent of the manuscript before she died.[40]

Wyden came to the project with twelve years of publishing experience under her belt. She had held editorial positions at *Newsweek* magazine and worked as an editor at major newspapers in Chicago and San Francisco. She moved to the *New York Times Magazine* in 1963, then became a freelance writer in 1975. In 1980, she was described as "one of the most talented, evocative, and dependable ghosts." She went on to work with such celebrities as Dr. Joyce Brothers, Jane Fonda, and Julie Nixon Eisenhower. She may have become connected to the project through her agent, Claire Smith.

However, the posthumous book that Simon and Schuster published was not the book that the first ghostwriter, Sigrid Hedin, remembered. In a 1977 interview with investigative journalist Greg Walter, she said:

> Kay's affair with Eisenhower lasted for several years, much longer than was stated in the book . . . Eisenhower was not impotent. They actually had an affair, but they didn't really have that much time to be alone. They were living in a goldfish bowl. I think Kay probably felt she was going to marry him, you know.[41]

Hedin also claimed, in the *New York Post*, that "there was a lot in the final version of *Past Forgetting* that is not quite correct" and that she had the "real manuscript."[42]

Kay died on January 20, 1975. Her brother Seamus scattered her ashes on the family gravesite outside the parish church of Rath and the Islands, a mile and a half from her childhood home where she rode bareback and sailed down the River Ilen to the Celtic Sea.

❧

But that's not the end of the story.

Past Forgetting was published in November 1976, nearly two years after Kay's death. *New York Daily News* columnist Liz Smith, writing a few months before the publication, called it "a story that people thought would never be told about one of America's most sacred idols," and reported that the Literary Guild, a premier mail-order book club, had already bought it. Excerpts were to appear in *Ladies Home Journal.* Bantam had paid $800,000 for the paperback rights—and the book wasn't even out yet. Smith quipped, "How's that for according respectability to a kiss and tell about a married war hero with feet of clay?"[43] The Bantam paperback edition, which came out in 1977, cranked up reader expectations with a hyperbolic back-cover blurb:

> Here, at long last, is the true story of the passionate, moving secret love affair between General Dwight D. Eisenhower, Supreme Commander of the Allied Forces in Europe, and Kay Summersby, the beautiful English fashion model who became his driver in wartime London, his staff aide, by his side through every crisis and high-level meeting of the war—and the woman he loved. Written by Kay Summersby Morgan herself, *Past Forgetting* is the intimate account of a relationship that began, haltingly, in 1942, when Kay was assigned to drive the then unknown two-star general, and ended in heartbreak when Ike, victor and war hero, returned home to face a disapproving General Marshall, the adoring American public, Mrs. Eisenhower—and the possibility of becoming President of the United States.

When word got out about the book, the Eisenhowers went into action. John Eisenhower speedily arranged to have a volume of his father's wartime letters to his mother published (by Doubleday), just three months after *Past Forgetting* appeared. (His mother's letters to Ike, which may have charged the General with flirtation or even infidelity, were not available for publication and remain unavailable to this day.)

Letters to Mamie probably didn't have the effect John Eisenhower intended. Reviewers commented that Ike's letters were "defensive" and clearly written in response to rebuking letters from his wife. *The New York Times* review—which ran with photographs of Kay, Ike, and Mamie—was titled "John Eisenhower Fighting Reports His Father Had Affair during War."[44] As well, every review of Eisenhower's letters included a fairly detailed reference to *Past Forgetting*, which John Eisenhower must have wished would be ignored, or at least quickly forgotten.

It wasn't. The book did not garner strong reviews, and the question of Eisenhower's impotence seemed to dominate the conversation. In *The New York Times*, Tom Buckley was not enthusiastic, wondering why Ike, still in "the prime of his life," was so anxious to marry a woman with whom he was "sexually incompatible" and deploring Barbara Wyden's feminine "rosemary and rue" style.[45] Several reviewers found the book sensational; still others didn't find it sensational enough.

But the project had legs. In March, 1978, it was reported that ABC Television had paid $100,000 for the movie rights to the book. Veteran Hollywood screenwriter Melville Shavelson reported the price as $250,000, "nearly a record price in television for an unpublished manuscript." Shavelson should know, since he was the man who wrote, produced, and codirected (until he was fired) the six-hour made-for-television miniseries based on the book *Ike: The War Years*.

Shavelson, who devotes a full chapter to the project in his 2013 memoir, *How to Succeed in Hollywood without Really Trying: P.S. You Can't!*, made several attempts to consult with John and David Eisenhower on the project and (no surprise here) was firmly rebuffed.[46] Failing to gain the Eisenhowers' cooperation, Shavelson pursued his own investigation into the validity of Kay's claims. One of his informants was General Omar Bradley, a close friend of Eisenhower's during the war years. When Shavelson asked him about "Topic A," Bradley merely said, "I once used Ike's bathroom at his headquarters above Algiers. When I opened the medicine cabinet, I was face to face with Kay's Kotex."[47] That was enough for Shavelson; he was convinced.

Through 1977 and into early 1978, Shavelson and ABC proceeded with the script production, casting, and locations. The team had already started filming when the project was abruptly halted. The Eisenhower family had sued the network to prevent the film from being made, and ABC was forced to put it on hold while the lawsuit was pending. The Eisenhowers were especially upset about the scene in which Ike (Robert Duvall) and his commanding officer General George Marshall (Dana Andrews) discuss Ike's divorce letter. Here is how Shavelson imagined that confrontation:

INTERIOR MARSHALL'S OFFICE
—MED. CLOSE—DAY

*Gen. Marshall is on his feet confronting Ike,
who is also standing.*

MARSHALL: That was the goddamnest letter I ever read in my life, Ike! You must be out of your mind!

IKE: (quietly) I meant every word.

MARSHALL: Idiotic! Foolish! You, of all people! The Supreme Commander acting like a schoolboy who's been in the bushes with his teacher! Have you told Mamie?

IKE: Not yet.

MARSHALL: Eisenhower, mention one word of what you said to me in that letter to that wonderful woman, so help me God, I'll hound you out of the United States Army if it's the last act of my military career!

IKE: Well, goddamn it, you go ahead and try! I'm no schoolboy; I know exactly what I'm doing. I've given Kay my word, goddamn it, and my heart, not that I expect you to understand.

MARSHALL: I don't understand one damn thing you're saying. Except that you're throwing away the most promising career in American military history.

IKE: It's my life, I can throw it away if I want to.

MARSHALL: The hell you can. The hell it's your life. How many thousands of men did you order to give up theirs for their country? How many boys in the 101st Airborne came back after you shook their hands?

He takes Ike by the arm, hauls him toward the window, where the Washington Monument is visible in the distance.

MARSHALL: I want you to be the next Chief of Staff. You divorce Mamie and marry that English girl, I won't have a prayer of getting that appointment past Congress. Look out of that window. If you look real hard, that's the White House. It may look far away now, but it's getting closer all the time.

IKE: To hell with the White House. I'm no politician and I never want to be one.

MARSHALL: What are you, Eisenhower? Don't you understand your country may need you? It needs you right now. Because you stand for something. You stand for 116,000 American dead; you're the only one who has come out of this war with the respect of the mothers and fathers who gave you their sons to kill. Respect. Remember that word. It isn't yours. It was given to you by your country. By the soldiers and sailors and airmen who died for it.

He is pacing now.

MARSHALL: (cont'd) And if you want to throw it away so you can climb in the sack with some girl half your age, you go and do it, because you're going to live in history, right next to Benedict Arnold.

IKE: That's hitting below the belt.

MARSHALL: Where do you want me to hit you? How do I make you come to your senses? Your life is not your own any more. It belongs to the United States. Now, I order you to go back to Mamie and forget everything that's happened in this office and so will I.[48]

The theme of Ike's life "belonging to the United States" is threaded throughout the film, as is the theme of Kay's willing (if reluctant) renunciation of the hero. Before Ike returns to the States for his victory lap, Kay tells him, "You are free of me. I went into this with my eyes wide open, knowing I was to be swept under the rug when this moment came. I shall mind, of course, but it's been—oh, such a lovely rug."[49] Good Hollywood stuff, but in reality, of course, Kay never got a chance to surrender. When she was swept under the rug, she was given no memorable lines.

After the lawsuit was filed, Shavelson continued to work behind the scenes, revising parts of the screenplay he felt might offend John and Mamie Eisenhower, selecting shooting locations, and obtaining war footage from the army, which cooperated readily. It took a year of negotiations before the family and the network arrived at a compromise. The family dropped the suit and the network agreed to represent Mamie favorably and (most importantly) play down the Ike-Kay romance. Shortly afterward, Shavelson, who had been involved with the project from the beginning, was replaced as director by Boris Sagal.

Shavelson doesn't say whether his removal was one of the requirements the family imposed for dropping the suit. The network insisted that the Eisenhowers—and their corporate friends who threatened to pull their advertising from the network—had nothing to do with the script and personnel changes.[50] But when filming began again, the network's announcement of the project avoided any mention of romantic elements: "The story follows Eisenhower's role in the war as he rose to supreme Allied commander and five-star general," and the "romance" was reduced to a "relationship."[51] It is tempting to see the resulting diminishment of the film character of Kay as another instance of the airbrushing that began with the V-E Day photograph in 1945.

Ike: The War Years was aired in May, 1979, and earned five Emmy nominations and an Eddy (for editing). No longer the story of the Eisenhower-Summersby romance, the muscular war saga was widely praised, even in the *New York Times*, which had initially opposed the project. Some reviewers, however, were disappointed that Kay's story had been abridged and the long-whispered love affair reduced to a few meaningful glances, a kiss on the cheek, and a surreptitious cuddle. Susan Anthony, an internationally syndicated New York reviewer, observes:

> Although the question of whether Ike and Summersby actually had an affair is raised constantly in the show, no definitive answer is given. Instead, the conclusion is a resounding "maybe." While this may be comforting for Ike's family, it is irritating for viewers . . .[52]

Shavelson, an admirer of Kay Summersby and a believer in the truth of her memoir, was intent on having the last word. He novelized his screenplay under the title *Ike*; the book was published in a mass market paperback edition in America and England in 1979. In his author's afterword, he considers the question of just where, in this complex, multilayered story, the truth lies (surely one of the most interesting juxtapositions of words in the English language):

> What is truth? I do not know. . . . [But I] honestly believe that Dwight Eisenhower was human being enough to have felt what any of us might have felt, given that war and that time and that woman. By those who were there,

I have been told that he did feel, "deeply and honestly" and so did Kay Summersby.

Both Ike and Kay have now gone on. The truth, the absolute truth, if such a thing ever can exist, died with them.[53]

And that, I think, is the last true thing that anyone can say about this story.

---

[1] Because Kay's postwar life has not been systematically documented, I am referencing sources for those who would like to dig a little deeper. Casual readers can ignore the endnotes.

[2] Jean Edward Smith, *Eisenhower in War and Peace* (New York: Random House, 2012), 522.

[3] Carlo D'Este, *Eisenhower* (New York: Henry Holt, 2002), 420.

[4] Stephen E. Ambrose, *Eisenhower: Soldier and President*, 212.

[5] Geoffrey Perret, *Eisenhower* (New York: Random House, 1999), 214–217.

[6] These and other letters and notes are held in the Dwight D. Eisenhower Presidential Library. Others appear among the fifty-three Eisenhower-Summersby items offered for auction by Sotheby's in 1991 and 2008, by unnamed people who had come into possession of the material. The first set of auction items may have been offered by Edward and Anthea Saxe, Kay's literary executors; the second may have come from the estate of Barbara Wyden, the ghostwriter who worked on *Past Forgetting* and ended up with Kay's official diary (now in the Eisenhower library).

[7] Items xvi and xvii in the lot of thirty-three letters sold for $43,750 by Sotheby's in 2008. http://www.sothebys.com/en/auctions/ecatalogue/2008/fine-books-and-manuscripts-including-ameri-cana-n08501/lot.52.html (Retrieved June 29, 2016).

[8] Dwight D. Eisenhower to Captain Kay Summersby, March 11, 1946, Pre-Presidential Papers, Box 112, Summersby, Kay, Dwight D. Eisenhower Presidential Library.

[9] For this and several other pieces of factual information about Kay's life, pre- and postwar, I am indebted to Kieron Wood, author of the Summersby biography, *Ike's Irish Lover: The Echo of a Sigh* (2016), available as an ebook from Amazon Digital Services LLC.

[10] Michael Korda, *Ike: An American Hero* (New York: Harper Perennial, 2008), 609.

[11] *New York Magazine*, May 7, 1979, 69.

[12] The Associated Press story appeared on the front pages of dozens of newspapers around the country. One example: *The Daily Mail*, Hagerstown, MD, February 14, 1947, 1.

[13] Dwight D. Eisenhower to Captain Kay Summersby, May 14, 1947, Pre-Presidential Papers, Box 112, Summersby, Kay, Dwight D. Eisenhower Presidential Library.

[14] On January 15, 1946, Eisenhower wrote to Kay on his Chief of Staff letterhead: "I've asked Gen. Clay to allow you time to type your diary so that I might have a copy. I do hope you can do it so that I may have the paper in my records. [The diary she kept from June 1944 through April 1945 is now in the Dwight D. Eisenhower Library in Abilene, Kansas.] I promise I'll never publish it, if there is ever anything to make out of it, that is certainly yours. (Possibly a poor joke, but I mean to say I recognize that you have a better claim to that diary than anyone else ever had for another.)" It is likely that Eisenhower is referring to Harry C. Butcher's diary, which became *My Three Years with Eisenhower: The Personal Diary of Captain Harry C. Butcher, USNR, Naval Aide to General Eisenhower, 1942–1945* (New York: Simon and Schuster, 1946). This letter is listed as Item xiv in Sotheby's 2008 sale (see note 7 above).

[15] Korda, *Ike*, 608–609.

[16] Dwight D. Eisenhower to Kay Summersby, November 12, 1947, Pre-Presidential Papers, Box 112, Summersby, Kay, Dwight D. Eisenhower Presidential Library.

[17] Dwight D. Eisenhower, *The Eisenhower Diaries* (New York: W. W. Norton, 1981), December 2, 1947.

[18] W. Stuart Symington to D. D. Eisenhower, December 26, 1947, Pre-Presidential Papers, Box 112, Summersby, Kay, Dwight D. Eisenhower Presidential Library.

[19] "It is our understanding that . . . you have accepted a position with Tex McCreary [sic]." Lt. Col. J. H. Michaelis to Kay Summersby, December 31, 1947. Pre-Presidential Papers, Box 112, Summersby, Kay, Dwight D. Eisenhower Presidential Library. The letter was sent c/o Major Ethel Westermann, General Dispensary, The Pentagon.

[20] Kay Summersby to D. D. Eisenhower, May 31, 1948. Pre-Presidential Papers, Box 112, Summersby, Kay, Dwight D. Eisenhower Presidential Library. Summersby doesn't mention the fired ghostwriter by name, but he may have been Mel Heimer, named later by Robert Considine, "Kay Summersby: Recollections" in "On the Line" [Syndicated column], found in *Naples Daily News*, Naples, FL, February 3, 1975, 7. Heimer had just authored a book,

The Big Drag, about New York. Considine, known for his celebrity ghostwriting, claims that Summersby asked him (Considine) to ghost *Eisenhower Was My Boss*, but he had to decline.

[21] Kay Summersby to D. D. Eisenhower, May 31, 1948. Pre-Presidential Papers, Box 112, Summersby, Kay, Dwight D. Eisenhower Presidential Library.

[22] D. D. Eisenhower to Kay Summersby, June 1, 1948. Pre-Presidential Papers, Box 112, Summersby, Kay, Dwight D. Eisenhower Presidential Library.

[23] D. D. Eisenhower to Kay Summersby, July 28, 1948. Pre-Presidential Papers, Box 112, Summersby, Kay, Dwight D. Eisenhower Presidential Library.

[24] Tom Fenton, foreword to *Algerian Diary: Frank Kearns and the "Impossible Assignment" for CBS News* by Gerald Davis (Morgantown: West Virginia University Press, 2016), loc. 642. Fenton's foreword contains eight informative paragraphs about Kearns and his work on *Eisenhower Was My Boss*.

[25] Kay continued her postwar association with the Saxes. Edward, who was an executive at CBS, may have helped her find a position as a fashion consultant for the network in the 1960s.

[26] Eisenhower earned a $635,000 lump-sum payment for his book from Doubleday, the equivalent of about $6 million today. He notes in his diary (January 4, 1948) his intention to give Kay and four others $1,000 each (roughly $10,000 in today's money), in recognition of their "faithful and unselfish" service to him.

[27] Wood, *Ike's Irish Lover*, loc. 1024.

[28] Kay Summersby to D. D. Eisenhower, undated, Pre-Presidential Papers, Box 112, Summersby, Kay, Dwight D. Eisenhower Presidential Library.

[29] Kay Summersby to D. D. Eisenhower, December 17, 1950, Pre-Presidential Papers, Box 112, Summersby, Kay, Dwight D. Eisenhower Presidential Library. In his memoir, John S. Monagan quotes William L. Laurence (Pulitzer Prize–winning official journalist of the Manhattan Project): "Kay Summersby was Ike's girl . . . Bedell Smith called [me] and said 'we' have to get her a job. Bernard Gimbel got her a job, but it was not with Gimbel's but with Bergdorf Goodman. . . ." No date is given for the telephone conversation. Monagan, *A Pleasant Institution* (Lanham, MD: University Press of America, 2002), 361.

[30] Kay Summersby to D. D. Eisenhower, December 8, 1951. Pre-Presidential Papers, Box 112, Summersby, Kay, Dwight D. Eisenhower Presidential Library.

[31] For background on Tex McCrary: http://www.nytimes.com/2003/07/30/arts/tex-mccrary-dies-at-92-public-relations-man-who-helped-create-talk-show-format.html (Retrieved June 29, 2016).

[32] Dwight D. Eisenhower Library, Pre-Presidential Papers, Butcher, Harry C. Box 16, Summersby, Kay, Dwight D. Eisenhower Presidential Library.

[33] Summersby, *Past Forgetting*, 279.

[34] Item xxiii in Sotheby's 2008 sale (see note 7).

[35] *The Bridgeport Post*, Bridgeport, CT, March 23, 1958, 2.

[36] *The Bridgeport Telegram*, Bridgeport, CT, January 25, 1958.

[37] Publisher's foreword in Summersby, *Past Forgetting*, 7.

[38] Merle Miller, *Plain Speaking: An Oral Biography of Harry S. Truman* (New York: Tess Press, 1974), 339.

[39] I am grateful to Paula and Richard Woodman, Barbara Wyden's brother and sister-in-law, for sharing copies of some thirty-five pages of typed notes, a few of Kay's wartime diary entries, and what appears to be a preliminary draft outline of *Past Forgetting*.

[40] Lloyd Shearer, "Kay Summersby and Dwight Eisenhower: The True Story of Their Friendship," *Parade*, January 2, 1977.

[41] Greg Walter, "Stung by Tales of His Father's Infidelity, John Eisenhower Fights Back with Ike's Letters Home," *People*, July 11, 1977, vol. 8, no. 2. Archived: http://www.people.com/people/archive/article/0,,20068273,00.html (Retrieved June 29, 2016).

[42] Wesley O. Hagood, *Presidential Sex: From the Founding Fathers to Bill Clinton* (Secaucus, NJ: Carol Publishing Group, 1995), 134.

[43] Liz Smith, "Ike's Love Writes About It" [Syndicated column], *New York Daily News*, June 5, 1976.

[44] *New York Times*, February 12, 1978.

[45] Tom Buckley, "Past Forgetting; Kiss and Tell," *New York Times*, February 13, 1977, 80.

[46] Melville Shavelson, *How to Succeed in Hollywood without Really Trying: P.S. You Can't!* (Albany, Georgia: BearManor Media, 2007), chapter 13, "Ike: The War Years."

[47] Shavelson, *How to Succeed*, loc. 2908.

[48] Shavelson, *How to Succeed*, loc. 3187–3223.

[49] Shavelson, *How to Succeed*, loc. 3164.

[50] "New TV Twists," Richard F. Shepherd, *New York Times News Service*, April 10, 1978.

[51] "Ike's Bio Is Filmed for TV," Associated Press, March 23, 1978.

[52] "Ike's 'love affair' now a 3-part TV topic," Susan Anthony, *Sydney Morning Herald*, Sidney, Australia, May 6, 1979, 37.

[53] Shavelson, *Ike*, 301–302.

Author's Note

In wartime, truth is so precious that she should always be
attended by a bodyguard of lies.

Winston Churchill

The historian will tell you what happened. The novelist
will tell you what it felt like.

E. L. Doctorow

I first met Kate Summersby in her 1976 memoir, *Past Forgetting*,
which I read in the 1980s. The book challenged my view of
Eisenhower, the president of my childhood and young adult years.
The bald, bland, inarticulate, golf-playing president actually had a
lover? At the time, the fact that the Supreme Commander turned out
to be impotent (not just once but twice in the book) seemed to me
a marvelous example of dramatic irony. I even wondered whether
Kay was at last getting even with him, snarkily, for dumping her at
the end of the war. After all, Ike couldn't very well rise up out of
his grave and say, "It is not true! I *did* have sex with that woman!"

Then, just a few years ago, I encountered Kay again. This time,
she was played by Lee Remick in the DVD edition of the TV miniseries *Ike: The War Years*, which was widely advertised as "based on"
Past Forgetting. The film bothered me. For one thing, the book's
highly charged sex scenes had been deleted from the script, and the
film's star-crossed lovers acted like two well-mannered adolescents
conscious that Mom was looking on saying, "Now, kids, behave."

The lack of sexual tension was bad enough, but the real problem was the portrayal of Kay. Lee Remick's Kay was a charmingly kittenish version of Mary Tyler Moore, and her lines could have come straight from that comic-relief heroine of sixteen years of American sitcoms. (This may have been John Eisenhower's idea; he is quoted years later as saying that Kay had been "the Mary Tyler Moore of headquarters, perky and cute.")

But a pert, sassy, comic-relief Kay doesn't carry enough emotional weight to make us believe that Robert Duvall's heroic General Ike could have fallen for her. Even more disturbingly, Remick's Kay of the film (and of Shavelson's later spinoff book) doesn't give Ike the chance to break it off. She takes care of that herself, telling him that he owes her nothing, that she won't hold him to promises made in the heat of battle. He is the war hero, free to go into his future unfettered. "I'm a big girl, Ike," she says, yielding the field. "I know when I'm out of my class."

But wait! This isn't the Kay of *Past Forgetting*, who was inexplicably and humiliatingly dumped by the man she had loved, who went back to his wife and the Pentagon with only a brutal letter to axe their affair. Of course, an adaptation is an adaptation and Hollywood is Hollywood. (Lee Remick herself once said she wouldn't make another Hollywood movie until Hollywood started making movies for grownups.) Still, it seemed to me that something had happened during the production of this film that made it necessary to massively rewrite the love affair and completely recast the main character—to create a story that revised and trivialized and sanitized the love affair. I began to read, to ask questions, to dig into the Summersby story, which is also the story of the war in North Africa and Europe. Then I became fascinated by the way Kay's story has been told—and altered—in two memoirs, in film, in Eisenhower biographies, and more recently, in posts on the Internet.

The more I learned, the more I wanted to know, not just about Kay Summersby but about the man she had fallen in love with— Dwight Eisenhower—and the General's wife, Mamie. Who were Ike and Mamie before they became President and Mrs. Middle

America? I began to sense that the golf-playing President and the Mamie-pink First Lady with the weird bangs were two very real people who had had a very hard time of it during a very hard war, and that their marriage had been seriously jeopardized by Ike's falling deeply in love with another woman.

This novel represents my effort to learn about those real people and their real wartime love affair. Writing historical fiction, I am always mindful that I am working along a continuum that places documented fact on one end and pure invention on the other, with many points between. As I wrote this book, I was dealing with things that really happened and things that might *also* have happened—and occasionally with what happened instead.

For example, Ike and all of the characters in his wartime command are historical people. Their interactions and the settings in which they worked and fought are described as they appear in Kay's two memoirs, in Harry Butcher's minutely detailed war diary, *My Three Years with Eisenhower*, and in the references listed in the bibliography. I have fictionalized Ike's role in the Darlan affair (exactly what part he played is not known) and throughout have created an Eisenhower consistent with the picture developed in Fred I. Greenstein's masterful study of Ike's duplicities and behind-the-scenes maneuvers, *The Hidden-Hand Presidency*, a book that gives us a very clear look at a man who played his cards close to the chest. "Ike is Don Corleone, the godfather," says Daun van Ee, an editor of the Eisenhower papers, speaking about Eisenhower's behind-the-scenes destruction of the political influence of Senator Joe McCarthy. "He knows how to take somebody out without leaving any fingerprints."[1]

I have portrayed Ike's 1936 dalliance with Marian Huff (his golf and bridge partner in Manila, of whom Mamie was very jealous) as a precursor to his affair with Kay. The key events of the developing romance with Kay—Ike's gift of Telek, Ike's gift of a uniform, Ike's taking her with him to North Africa, to Egypt, and to Europe after the Normandy invasion—are documented in one or both of Kay's memoirs and in Butcher's diary. Also true: King

George's chilly snub, Winston Churchill's interest, and the desert picnic with FDR.

For Mamie's characterization, I have stayed close to the details that Susan Eisenhower gave us in her sympathetic biography of her grandmother, *Mrs. Ike: Memories and Reflections on the Life of Mamie Eisenhower*, and in several other First Lady biographies. I have somewhat fictionalized Ike's determinedly reassuring letters to her, but they are based on the real letters published in *Letters to Mamie*, which are indeed stilted, defensive, and thoroughly unconvincing. Where Kay Summersby was concerned, Ike's protestations must have caused Mamie a great many more doubts than they resolved—especially after Mamie realized that he had brought Kay to North Africa.

Also real: Mamie's 1979 interview with Barbara Walters; a copy is available at the Eisenhower Library. Mamie's comment about Ike's "old bald head" is reported by J. B. West, Chief Usher at the White House during the Eisenhowers' tenure there.[2] Her reaction to *Ike: The War Years* ("Oh, how ugly they've made me look!") was reported in the *Indiana Gazette* after her death.[3] And her well-known jealousy of Ann Whitman, Eisenhower's Oval Office secretary, is documented in *Confidential Secretary*, Robert Donovan's biography of Whitman, which also reports Mamie's efforts to get Whitman fired during the 1952 campaign. "I tried to keep out of Mrs. Eisenhower's way," Whitman said after she was finally forced to leave Ike. "It was clear that she did not want me around."[4]

Mamie's friend Ruth Butcher is real, but to serve the fiction, I have invented a number of Greek-chorus friends. They give voice to Washington and Stateside fact and opinion and allow me to get some of the goings-on in the Pentagon on the record. Cookie, Diane, and Pamela are fictional creations, and their discussion in chapter 20 of the arrival of Ike's divorce letter at the Pentagon is fictional. However, Doris Fleeson is real, and her *Evening Star* column about Kay's Washington visit—which I have quoted accurately—was published at the time Kay was there. Fleeson was a highly regarded journalist, and her column could very easily have produced the fictional result I have described in that chapter: Mamie's call to General Marshall, asking him to keep Kay in Germany, and Marshall's order to Eisenhower, directing him to return immediately to the States.

Now to the complicated matter of Eisenhower's "divorce" letter and Marshall's reply. In the fictional conversation in chapter 20, I have invented "Marv's" reported glimpse of Marshall's scolding cable to Ike. But I based this incident on a real event related by Eisenhower biographer Jean Edward Smith. Garrett Mattingly, a Pulitzer Prize–winning Columbia University history professor, served as a junior naval officer in the Washington censor's office during the war and was assigned to read outgoing cables. In the early 1950s, well before Truman placed the letters into the public record, Mattingly told Columbia colleagues that he had seen Marshall's cable to Eisenhower in Germany.[5]

In addition to Mattingly's corroboration of Truman's claim, there are other confirmations. Dr. John R. Steelman, a close Truman aide, said in a 1996 interview that he actually *accompanied* Marshall to the Oval Office to discuss Eisenhower's divorce letter with the president. (Truman's calendar contains two meetings between Marshall and Truman where this issue might have been discussed: May 16 and May 28, 1945. Steelman is not shown to be present, but since he was frequently in the Oval Office, he would not necessarily have been listed.[6]) At the meeting, Truman instructed Marshall to burn the correspondence. Steelman recalls, however, that Marshall told him that "he was going to put it in the files, because he [Marshall] didn't trust Eisenhower as much as Truman did."[7] That is, there was some doubt in Marshall's mind as to whether Ike would end his relationship with Kay. He obviously wanted the correspondence in case Ike defied him and went on with the divorce.

In 1973, after *Plain Speaking* was published, General Harry Vaughan, Truman's military aide, told an AP reporter that at Truman's order, he had retrieved the documents from the file "to keep them out of the hands of Eisenhower's political opponents" (in the 1952 run-up to the GOP nomination) and gave them to the president.[8] Jean Edward Smith surmises that Truman destroyed them and finds evidence that Eisenhower knew what he had done and was grateful.[9] Stanley Weintraub sums it up wryly: "Documents, if any, have disappeared. That itself was not unique in the self-protective bureaucracy."[10]

In any event, copies may have been made, for both the Taft primary campaign staff and the Democratic campaign staff threatened to use them in the 1952 election.[11] I haven't been able to find any evidence that the Taft campaign actually had the letters. But years later, syndicated columnist Jack Anderson wrote that the late Senator Olin Johnston (D-SC) told him that the Democrats had compiled a dossier on the Eisenhower-Summersby affair. Johnston claimed to have personally seen Marshall's correspondence "admonishing Ike to forget Miss Summersby."[12] Columnist Drew Pearson also refers to Eisenhower's divorce plans in his diary entry for December 4, 1952, when he notes a conversation with John Bennett, a Pearson staffer who reported that he had talked with Eisenhower in Paris in late 1951. Ike had wanted to know "what the effect on the public would be" if word got out about his affair with Kay. Eisenhower "seemed chiefly worried because apparently Mamie didn't know he contemplated a divorce," according to Bennett, and feared that General George Patton's letters to his wife might contain references to the affair.[13]

Some biographers have attempted to explain Truman's startling announcement in *Plain Speaking* by saying that the former president confused the divorce correspondence with another exchange of letters between Eisenhower and Marshall regarding Mamie. On June 4, 1945, nearly a month after V-E Day, Eisenhower wrote Marshall asking permission to bring Mamie to Europe. The wartime separation, he said, was causing serious personal problems for him and his wife. Four days later, Marshall sent a sympathetic refusal, saying that the request couldn't be approved when other similar requests were denied. Jean Edward Smith remarks that, in fact, this incident actually offers "tangential corroboration" of the divorce correspondence. He concludes that Eisenhower was using this letter to signal to Marshall that he had given up his plan to divorce his wife.[14] Stanley Weintraub, too, finds the letter "suspicious on its surface," especially since Mamie would have to travel by sea (she refused to fly), as well as give up her apartment and store her belongings, only a few months before Ike was due to return to the United States.[15]

My conclusion: at the time of V-E Day, Ike did intend to divorce Mamie and marry Kay. Marshall—a strong father figure, as well as Ike's boss—persuaded him otherwise. Ike signaled his altered intention with his June 4 request to bring his wife to Germany. Ike hadn't told Kay of his intention to marry her, so he didn't have to retract an offer or a promise.

But he hadn't necessarily agreed to give her up, either—he had only agreed not to marry her. I believe that, as late as November 1945, he intended to bring Kay to the States with the rest of his staff. In fact, it may have been his decision to send her to Washington in October 1945 to pursue her citizenship that set the subsequent events in motion.

With regard to Ike's impotence, as it is portrayed in the two "failure" scenes in *Past Forgetting*: as a writer of fiction, I have a wider latitude than a historian or a biographer. I feel that both Ike and Kay deserve to wrest at least a little passionate pleasure out of those dark days, so I have given them that, at times and places where I think it might have been possible. In offering this fictional satisfaction to my fictional lovers, I have trusted to my own romantic imagination and to the testimony of Sigrid Hedin, the first ghostwriter on *Past Forgetting*, who told a reporter that Kay told her the affair was consummated and that she (Sigrid) had the manuscript to prove it. (I can't help but wonder who might have bought Hedin's manuscript, how much was paid for it, and what happened to it. That's a story in itself.) I'm guessing that Hedin was removed from the project for the same reason Shavelson was removed as director of the film. Each of them had a different story to tell, and they were paid not to tell it.

To go a little further: I believe the impotence was a fabrication, either by Barbara Wyden (the second ghostwriter) or the Simon and Schuster editor—and more likely the latter. The publisher was caught in a bind. On the one hand, given the whispers and insinuations that had grown up around Ike and Kay over the years, readers were expecting a story with at least a modest dose of steamy sex. An entirely chaste memoir would have felt both disappointing and evasive—and wouldn't have done much to settle the did-they-or-didn't-they question. Further, it might have been difficult to explain to an editorial board why an editor paid today's equivalent of a quarter of a million dollars for such an unsatisfactory manuscript. On the other hand, there was the pressure from the Eisenhowers and their friends—the same kind of pressure that John Eisenhower brought to bear on ABC Television that resulted in the removal of all but a whiff of romance from *Ike: The War Years*.

Faced with this dilemma, Simon and Schuster might have considered canceling the project: the author was, after all, out of the picture. But the publisher had already invested a substantial sum in the advance. What's more, the subsidiary magazine, paperback, film, and foreign rights had already been sold, and at very nice prices indeed. *Past Forgetting* was too ripe a plum not to pick. So somebody came up with a solution that even Bill Clinton might have envied: Ike did *not* have sex with that woman because he couldn't.

In my novel, the lawyer Kay consulted is a fiction, but both the ghostwriter and the editor are real people. Barbara Wyden continued to work as a ghostwriter into the 1990s. (I was fortunate to locate and obtain copies of her notes on this project, but they tell us nothing about who might have made changes to the book.) The editor's visit to the dying Kay Summersby actually happened. Michael Korda, who was an editor at Simon and Schuster at the time, lays claim to that visit in his 2007 biography of Eisenhower, remarking that he "had the pleasure of talking briefly to Kay Summersby Morgan shortly before her death, and published her posthumous memoir."[16] In the same chapter, he relates the anecdote about his stepmother knocking down his father with Lady

Mountbatten's car, which his fictional counterpart shares with Kay. I have, however, invented that conversation and fictionalized the editor/publisher's role in the production of Summersby's memoir. I have no idea who is responsible for any deviations from the "truth" of the affair, or what those might be.

Regarding my depiction of the circumstances around the writing of Kay's first memoir, *Eisenhower Was My Boss*: Colonel McAndrews is fictional, and the nondisclosure document is pure invention. But Kay's mother would later claim to a reporter that her daughter had "General Eisenhower's approval before agreeing to write the book."[17] And after Kay's death a friend hinted that Kay had signed "some papers" that kept her from telling the whole truth about the affair.[18] It is logical to assume that she signed such an agreement, especially since some of Eisenhower's staffers were disturbed by the publication of Harry Butcher's gossipy memoir, which mixed military report and personal commentary in a way that required Ike to write apologetic letters to Churchill and Charles de Gaulle. The question of the affair aside, there would have been other very real concerns about what military secrets she might reveal. Kay, a British citizen, had been privy to some of Eisenhower's most sensitive wartime discussions and correspondence. Her book was potentially a bombshell, and Ike's staff at the Pentagon would have wanted to get out in front of the situation.

Telek and Telegraph Cottage are real, of course, and there's no reason to doubt Kay's explanation of Telek's odd name. Kay's connection with the cottage is real, as is its code name—Da-de-da, Morse for the letter K—that Butcher reports in his diary.[19]

I decided to include Kay's postwar biography as a nonfiction epilogue to the novel because her life after her three years with Eisenhower is virtually unknown, and because I thought it might answer some of the questions that the novel inevitably raises. Perhaps it can help us understand something more about why and how Kay first told one kind of truth, then another—and what happened to the "truth" after she was no longer around to defend it. The effort to erase her from the General's life and cleanse the

General of any hint of an illicit relationship with her is a part of the postwar creation of Ike the heroic figure, crafted by those who wanted to assist and ensure his ascension to the presidency.

The mature, postwar Dwight Eisenhower was fully his own man. But he was also a commodity that many people wanted to exploit and a symbol that some needed to protect. Kay Summersby was never a threat to the General; she cared too much for him to want to do him harm. But her intentions aside, she remained both a real and an imagined threat to him—even after both he and she were gone.

∞

Geraldine Brooks wrote, "The thing that most attracts me to historical fiction is taking the factual record as far as it is known, using that as scaffolding, and then letting imagination build the structure that fills in those things we can never find out for sure." There is a great deal we will never know for sure about Kay, Ike, Mamie, and the triangular relationship that existed during the darkest days of the worst war the world has ever seen. But fiction is that path that brings us to the inner life, into the heart that is hidden and ultimately unknowable behind the closed curtain of actions and events. If this fictional work leads you to want to explore the real lives of these real people further—at least as far, that is, as the histories and biographies will allow—that is my reward.

As always, I owe a great deal to the scholars whose work has helped me—a very great many, when it comes to Eisenhower and World War II. For my understanding of Eisenhower's personality and style, I am especially indebted to Fred I. Greenstein and his seminal work, *The Hidden-Hand Presidency: Eisenhower as Leader*, and to Jean Edward Smith, the only biographer who pays careful attention to the events surrounding Eisenhower's intention to divorce his wife and marry Kay Summersby. I was glad to find a recent biography of Kay Summersby by Kieron Wood, *Ike's Irish*

Lover: The Echo of a Sigh. Wood filled in many of the details of Kay's Irish heritage and prewar experience and clarified some of the murky details of her postwar life. For Mamie Eisenhower, Susan Eisenhower's *Mrs. Ike* has been most helpful. You will find a list of the other important reference works at the end of this book. I hope you will make use of it as a springboard for your own further reading and study.

I am grateful to Ben Ohmart at BearManor Media for permission to quote the lengthy scene from Melville Shavelson's memoir, *How to Succeed in Hollywood without Really Trying: P.S. You Can't!* The cover image of Eisenhower is courtesy of the Eisenhower Presidential Library, Abilene, Kansas. The image of Mamie Eisenhower is courtesy of the United States Library of Congress's Prints and Photographs Division. The image of Kay Summersby is courtesy of Wikimedia Commons.

Others have been especially helpful: Valoise Armstrong, archivist at the Eisenhower Presidential Library, who provided research assistance and copies of important documents; and Paula and Richard Woodman, who generously shared notes and papers relating to *Past Forgetting* from the estate of ghostwriter Barbara Wyden. For their careful reading of the manuscript, I thank Judy Alter, Jeanne Guy, and Susan Davenport. For their willingness to discuss various aspects of this book in detail, I owe an enormous debt of thanks to John G. Albert, William J. Albert, John E. Webber, and Kieron Wood.

Thanks are also due to my writing sisters in the WorkInProgress group of the Story Circle Network for the nurturing friendship that does so much to brighten the writing week; to Kerry Sparks of Levine Greenberg Rostan Literary Agency for her unflagging enthusiasm and belief in my work; and to my husband William J. Albert, for his steadfast love and constant support, always.

---

[1] *Prologue,* Fall 2015, "Eisenhower and McCarthy: How a President Toppled a Reckless Senator," by David A. Nichols, https://www.

archives.gov/publications/prologue/2015/fall/ike-mccarthy.pdf (retrieved June 29, 2016). Nichols portrays an Eisenhower expert in "strategic deception."

[2]   J. B. West and Mary Lynn Kotz, *Upstairs at the White House: My Life with the First Ladies* (New York: Coward, McCann & Geoghegan, 1973), 130. Among first ladies, Mamie was uniquely known for managing the White House from her bed.

[3]   "Mamie Had Been Identified by Sleek Black Limousine," July 20, 1988, 23.

[4]   Robert J. Donovan, *Confidential Secretary: Ann Whitman's 20 Years with Eisenhower and Rockefeller* (New York: E. P. Dutton, 1988), 14, 162.

[5]   Smith, *Eisenhower in War and Peace*, 441.

[6]   President's Appointment Calendar, May 15 and May 28, Truman Papers, Truman Library.

[7]   Oral history interview, Dr. John R. Steelman, with Niel M. Johnson, February 29, 1996. http://www.trumanlibrary.org/oralhist/ steelm2b.htm [122–123, 202–205, original hardcopy version of this interview], Truman Library.

[8]   The Associated Press article appeared on the front pages of many American newspapers. One example: "Ike's Divorce Letter Still Exists, Says Former HST Aide," *High Point Enterprise*, High Point, NC, November 27, 1973, 1.

[9]   Smith, *Eisenhower in War and Peace*, 364–365. Copies may have been made from the Pentagon file, since both the Taft and Democratic campaigns claimed to have them.

[10]   Stanley Weintraub, *15 Stars: Eisenhower, MacArthur, Marshall: Three Generals Who Saved the American Century* (New York: Free Press, 2007), 519.

[11]   Smith, *Eisenhower in War and Peace*, 502, 546.

[12]   Jack Anderson, "Rumors Spread in Case Involving Sen. Kennedy," Washington Merry-Go-Round [syndicated column], August 22, 1960.

[13]   Drew Pearson, *Drew Pearson Diaries: 1949–1959* (New York: Holt, Rinehart and Winston, 1974), 238.

[14]   Smith, *Eisenhower in War and Peace*, 442.

[15]   Weintraub, *15 Stars*, 519.

[16]   Korda, *Ike*, 270. The anecdote about his stepmother is on page 269.

[17]   Wood, *Ike's Irish Lover*, loc. 5012. *Chicago Tribune*, Dec. 20, 1948, 25.

[18]   "Network Shy on Girl Who Liked Ike," *New York Magazine*, May 7, 1979, 69. The friend claims that "*Past Forgetting* is not true"—that

is, that the claim of impotence is false—and goes on to say that Ike and Kay "trysted" in her (the friend's) New York apartment after the war.

[19] Butcher, *My Three Years*, entry for October 14, 1942. "Clark, Beetle, T. J., Major Lee, Mickey, and I had a so-called 'surprise' birthday party at Da-de-da." A footnote explains that Da-de-da is the "current code name for Telegraph Cottage" and a quick online check of the Morse code gives it as the letter K. Butcher deleted most of his references to Kay Summersby but allowed this coded hint to stand.

Cast of Characters

Richard Arnold: colonel in the American army and Kay's fiancé

Margaret Bourke-White: acclaimed photographer, Kay's cabin mate on the *Strathallan*

*Diane Bracken: Mamie's friend

Ruth Briggs: WAC in Eisenhower's office; Kay's roommate in North Africa, England, Europe

Harry C. Butcher (Butch): Eisenhower's naval aide, former broadcasting executive

Ruth Butcher: wife of Harry Butcher, Mamie's apartment mate

Margaret Chick: WAC in Eisenhower's office; Kay's roommate in North Africa, England, Europe

Winston Churchill: Prime Minister of Britain

Mark Wayne Clark: U.S. Army general, Eisenhower confidant

Elspeth Duncan: British stenographer on Eisenhower's staff, Kay's cabin mate on the *Strathallan*

Dwight David Eisenhower (Ike): U.S. Army General, Supreme Commander of the Allied Forces in World War II, and thirty-fourth President of the United States

John Eisenhower: son of Dwight and Mamie Eisenhower

Mamie Geneva Doud Eisenhower: wife of Dwight Eisenhower and First Lady of the United States

*Pamela Farr: Mamie's friend

SUSAN WITTIG ALBERT

Molly Ford: American Red Cross worker in Algiers, Butch's girlfriend

Bess Furman: reporter, Washington Bureau of *The New York Times*

George VI: King of England, 1936–1952

Michael Korda: Eisenhower biographer and editor of Kay's second memoir, *Past Forgetting*, at Simon and Schuster

Ernest (Tex) Lee: Eisenhower's aide-de-camp

*Clyde McAndrew: staff member in Eisenhower's office in the Pentagon

George C. Marshall: U.S. Army General and Chief of Staff, Eisenhower's boss

Evie MacCarthy-Morrogh: Kay's younger sister

Kul MacCarthy-Morrogh: Kay's mother

Mickey McKeogh: Eisenhower's orderly and personal valet

Mike Reilly: Chief of security for President Franklin D. Roosevelt

Franklin D. Roosevelt: thirty-second President of the United States

George S. Patton: U.S. Army General with various commands throughout World War II

Nana Rae: WAC in Eisenhower's office; Kay's roommate in North Africa, England, Europe

Walter Bedell (Beetle) Smith: U.S. Army General and Eisenhower's chief of staff

Sue Sarafian: WAC in Eisenhower's office; Kay's roommate in North Africa, England, Europe

*Cheryl Sullivan: Mamie's friend

Kay Summersby: General Eisenhower's driver, personal secretary, and wartime companion

Telek: black Scottie that belongs jointly to Eisenhower and Kay

Ethel Westermann: American Army nurse, Beetle Smith's girlfriend

*Cookie Wilson: Mamie's friend, wife of *General Marvin Wilson

For Further Reading

If you are interested in learning more about the background of this novel, you may enjoy these books. You will find more information about people and places on the book's website: **www.TheGeneralsWomen.com**

Ambrose, Stephen E. *Eisenhower: Soldier and President.* New York: Simon & Schuster, 1991.

———. *The Supreme Commander: The War Years of General Dwight D. Eisenhower.* New York: Doubleday, 1970.

Atkinson, Rick. *An Army at Dawn: The War in North Africa, 1942–1943.* New York: Henry Holt, 2002.

———. *The Day of Battle: The War in Sicily and Italy, 1943–1944.* New York: Henry Holt, 2007.

———. *The Guns at Last Light: The War in Western Europe, 1944–1945.* New York: Henry Holt, 2013.

Brinkley, David. *Washington Goes To War.* New York: Alfred A. Knopf, 1988.

Brown, Anthony Cave. *Bodyguard of Lies.* New York: Harper & Row, 1975.

Butcher, Harry. *My Three Years with Eisenhower: The Personal Diary of Captain Harry C. Butcher, USNR, Naval Aide to General Eisenhower, 1942–1945.* New York: Simon and Schuster, 1946.

D'Este, Carlo. *Eisenhower: A Soldier's Life.* New York: Henry Holt, 2002.

Donovan, Robert J. *Confidential Secretary: Ann Whitman's 20 Years with Eisenhower and Rockefeller.* New York: E. P. Dutton, 1988.

Eisenhower, Dwight David. *Crusade in Europe*. New York: Doubleday, 1948.

———. *Letters to Mamie*. Edited by John S. D. Eisenhower. New York: Doubleday, 1978.

———. *The Eisenhower Diaries*. Edited by Robert H. Ferrell. New York: W. W. Norton, 1981.

Eisenhower, Susan. *Mrs. Ike: Memories and Reflections on the Life of Mamie Eisenhower.* New York: Farrar, Straus and Giroux, 1996.

Hart, Scott. *Washington at War: 1941–1945.* Englewood Cliffs, NJ: Prentice Hall, 1970.

Holt, Marilyn Irvin. *Mamie Doud Eisenhower: The General's First Lady*. Lawrence: University Press of Kansas, 2007.

Korda, Michael. *Ike: An American Hero*. New York: Harper Perennial, 2008.

McKeogh, Michael, and Richard Lockridge. *Sgt. Mickey and General Ike*. New York: G. P. Putnam's Sons, 1946.

Miller, Merle. *Ike the Soldier: As They Knew Him*. New York: G. P. Putnam's Sons, 1987.

———. *Plain Speaking: An Oral Biography of Harry S. Truman*. New York: Berkley, 1974.

Morgan, Kay Summersby. *Past Forgetting: My Love Affair with Dwight D. Eisenhower*. New York: Simon and Schuster, 1976.

Murrow, Edward R. *This Is London*. Edited by Elmer Davis. New York: Schocken Books, 1941.

Perret, Geoffrey. *Eisenhower*. New York: Random House, 1999.

Shavelson, Melville, *How to Succeed in Hollywood without Really Trying: P.S. You Can't!*. Albany, Georgia: BearManor Media, 2013.

———. *Ike*. New York: Warner Books, 1978.

Smith, Jean Edward. *Eisenhower in War and Peace*. New York: Random House, 2012.

Summersby, Kay. *Eisenhower Was My Boss*. Englewood Cliffs, NJ: Prentice Hall, 1948.

Weintraub, Stanley. *15 Stars: Eisenhower, MacArthur, Marshall:*

Three Generals Who Saved the American Century. New York: Free Press, 2007.

West, J. B., and Mary Lynn Kotz. *Upstairs at the White House: My Life with the First Ladies.* New York: Coward, McCann & Geoghegan, 1973.

Wood, Kieron. *Ike's Irish Lover: The Echo of a Sigh.* Dublin: Eprint Ltd., 2016.

Discussion Questions

1. How much did you know about Ike, Mamie, and Kay before you began this book? What kind of general impressions did you have about these people? Where did those impressions come from?

2. This novel is different from other wartime romances you may have read because it is based in the actual experiences of real people. Does this affect your reading of the book? If so, how?

3. Ike is deeply involved with both Kay and Mamie. How are these two women different? What about each of them attracts and holds him?

4. War is often a catalyzing process. How does WWII affect Ike's life? Kay's? Mamie's? In what ways does the war both create and shape their relationships?

5. This novel is structured in alternating chapters, moving between Kay and Ike's wartime relationship and Mamie's life in Washington. Did you find this organization helpful in understanding the changing situation?

6. The torpedoing of the *Strathallan* is a momentous experience in Kay's life. How does this experience change her? The torpedoing of the *Strathallan* is momentous for Mamie, too, but in a different way. How does it affect her?

7. Kay's fiancé, Richard Arnold, is killed in Tunisia. What effect does his death have on Kay? On Ike? What do you think would have happened if Arnold had lived?

8. Ike gives Kay a number of gifts. What are these? How does each gift alter their relationship? After V-E Day, he offers her

a gift that she refuses. What is it? What might have happened if she had accepted it?

9. Ike's notes to Kay are very discreet. If he had been involved with her today, do you think he would have been as careful with email?

10. Albert's telling of the Darlan assassination suggests that Eisenhower knew what was to happen and conveniently absented himself from Algiers. Whether this is true may be debatable, but it does serve to characterize the General. In what way? How does this fit the characterization of Eisenhower that Albert has developed?

11. Kay's two memoirs (*Eisenhower Was My Boss* and *Past Forgetting*) were ghostwritten by different people under different circumstances. How have these two versions of the story affected our understanding of what might have happened? What do you think of Albert's idea that the second memoir was altered by the editor/publisher in order to meet the Eisenhower family's objections and at least partially redeem Ike?

12. Several historians have suggested that Kay was "airbrushed" out of Ike's wartime and postwar life—and that this is the reason there is so little evidence of their relationship. Do you agree? Do you think this kind of cover-up could happen now?

13. Ultimately, this is the story of a relationship that grew during a specific time and place—and was out of place in any other context. Have you ever been involved in a relationship like that?

14. What are your thoughts about Kay's postwar life? About Mamie's? About Ike's?

15. The fictional section of this novel (Chapters 1-23) is followed by a nonfiction "Biographical Afterword" and an "Author's Afterword" in which Albert discusses the factual postwar events and some of the real-life questions that people have raised about the Eisenhower-Summersby relationship. Did these sections help you understand more about this story? Why? Why not?

About Susan Wittig Albert

Growing up on a farm on the Illinois prairie, Susan learned that books could take her anywhere, and reading and writing became passions that have accompanied her throughout her life. She earned an undergraduate degree in English from the University of Illinois at Urbana and a PhD in medieval studies from the University of California at Berkeley, then turned to teaching. After faculty and administrative appointments at the University of Texas, Tulane University, and Texas State University, she left her academic career and began writing full time. Her bestselling fiction includes mysteries in the China Bayles series, the Darling Dahlias, the Cottage Tales of Beatrix Potter, and (under the pseudonym of Robin Paige) a series of Victorian-Edwardian mysteries with her husband, Bill Albert.

The General's Women, a novel about the World War II romantic triangle of Dwight Eisenhower, his wife Mamie, and his driver and secretary Kay Summersby, is Albert's third work of biographical-historical fiction. It follows *Loving Eleanor*, a fictional account of the friendship of Lorena Hickok and Eleanor Roosevelt, and *A Wilder Rose*, the story of Rose Wilder Lane and the writing of the Little House books. Albert is also the author of two memoirs: *An Extraordinary Year of Ordinary Days* and *Together, Alone: A Memoir of Marriage and Place.* Other nonfiction titles include *What Wildness Is This: Women Write about the Southwest* (winner of the 2009 Willa Award for Creative Nonfiction); *Writing from Life: Telling the Soul's Story*; and *Work of Her Own: A Woman's Guide to Success off the Career Track.* She is the founder of the Story Circle Network, a nonprofit organization for women writers, and a member of the Texas Institute of Letters. She and her husband Bill live on thirty-one acres in the Texas Hill Country, where she gardens, tends chickens and geese, and indulges her passions for needlework and (of course) reading.

Books by
Susan Wittig Albert

A Wilder Rose
An Extraordinary Year of Ordinary Days
Together, Alone: A Memoir of Marriage and Place
The China Bayles Mysteries
The Darling Dahlias Mysteries
The Cottage Tales of Beatrix Potter
Writing from Life: Telling the Soul's Story
Work of Her Own

With Bill Albert
The Robin Paige Victorian-Edwardian Mysteries

Edited Anthologies
What Wildness Is This: Women Write about the Southwest
With Courage and Common Sense: Memoirs from
the Older Women's Legacy Circle

Praise for Susan Wittig Albert's Fiction

For *Loving Eleanor*, the story of Eleanor Roosevelt and Lorena Hickok:

"Albert captures the turbulent thirties and forties with affecting detail, writing a novel notable not only for its emotional authenticity, but for its careful historicity. Loving Eleanor is an intelligent love story with huge historical appeal." —*Foreword Reviews*

"This warm, extensively researched novel will entrance readers and inspire them to look further into the lives of two extraordinary women." —*Kirkus Reviews* (starred review)

For A *Wilder Rose*, the story of Rose Wilder Lane, who transformed her mother, Laura Ingalls Wilder, into a literary icon:

"Albert does an excellent job of bringing historical figures to life in a credible way; her novel is well paced, its characterizations are strong, and the plot is solidly constructed. Readers begin to understand Lane's personality and mentality, as well as the things that drive her." —*Publishers Weekly* (starred review)

"A compelling depiction of one of the most significant literary collaborations of the 20th century. That the two people involved were mother and daughter adds to its complexity and human interest." —Anita Claire Fellman, author of *Little House, Long Shadow: Laura Ingalls Wilder's Impact on American Culture*

For Albert's mysteries:

"[Albert] consistently turns out some of the best-plotted mysteries on the market." —*Houston Chronicle*

"Quirky, enlightening and surprisingly profound, Albert's mysteries are an absolute delight to read." —Ransom Notes

CPSIA information can be obtained
at www.ICGtesting.com
Printed in the USA
BVOW08s2123080317
478157BV00001B/142/P